PETER LEFCOURT

SIMON & SCHUSTER

THE
WOODY

A Novel

SIMON & SCHUSTER
Rockefeller Center
1230 Avenue of the Americas
New York, NY 10020

Designed by Katy Riegel

Manufactured in the United States of America

10   9   8   7   6   5   4   3   2   1

Library of Congress Cataloging-in-Publication Data

Lefcourt, Peter.
The woody : a novel / Peter Lefcourt.
p.   cm.
I. Title.
PS3562.E3737W66   1998
813'.54—dc21   98-33816
                                                       CIP

ISBN 0-684-85393-0
    0-684-85744-8 (signed edition)

To former Senators
Gary Hart, Alan Cranston, and Bob Packwood,
whose dogs were not kidnapped.

1.

PERU

"CALL ME, Ishmael."

He folded the cell phone and flipped it onto the bed, twenty feet away from the tepid Jacuzzi in which he lay after having had what could best be described as an inconclusive sexual encounter with a lobbyist for the condom industry.

The lobbyist, Evelyn Brandwynne, exited the bathroom naked, speaking on her cell phone in a businesslike and decidedly non-postcoital tone of voice to her Washington office.

"The funding is dead. It's terminal. There's a sheet over its head. . . ."

He watched her move slowly toward the bed with a glass of yellowing white wine and a Kleenex in her hand.

"No. I don't know. . . . What time . . . ? Shit."

She sat down on the bed and, the phone still at her ear, asked the man in the Jacuzzi, "When is the last shuttle out of Logan?"

"Nine."

She squinted at the Cartier watch on the night table and said into the phone, "I may just make it."

Evelyn Brandwynne used the Kleenex immodestly, then replied to her caller's question, "Working . . ."

There was a moment's hesitation before she delivered the punch line. "In Peru." And she folded her phone and began the search for the scattered articles of clothing removed maybe forty minutes ago, when she had begun to lobby the junior senator from Vermont.

"I don't mind traveling, Senator, but this is ridiculous. It takes days to get here."

She slipped into a pair of black lace panties and rummaged through the sheets looking for her bra.

"And it's not as if it's doing me any good, is it?" she remarked, now on all fours on the bed scrounging under the pillows.

The sight of a lobbyist from the National Association of Health Prophylaxis Industries facedown on his bed in nothing but a pair of black lace panties had a small but nonetheless stirring effect on Senator Woodrow Wilson White. But by then it was too little, too late. And, besides, he wasn't going to let her bill out of committee anyway, so why put both of them through this again?

She located her bra, slipped it on, and turned back to him with a look that was not without tenderness.

"I actually like you, Woody. I'd probably be doing this even if you weren't the ranking Democrat on that goddamn subcommittee . . ."

"Medicaid and Health Care."

"It's in the public interest. Smaller families, fewer tax deductions, a lot less AFDC."

"Medicaid isn't going to fund rubbers, Evelyn."

"Why not? You get it to the Floor, and the women love you."

"The women already love me. It's the dairy farmers and the loggers who don't love me, and they're not particularly interested in having the federal government subsidize the rubber industry."

"Health Prophylaxis."

"We're trying to balance the budget."

"Nobody ever got his face on Mount Rushmore by balancing the budget."

She zipped up her skirt, slipped her sweater and suit jacket on, and went over and sat down on the edge of the Jacuzzi. For a moment, she said nothing, just sat there with a finger absently stirring the water. Then, in a softer, more compassionate voice, she said, "Look, I think I'm supposed to say something now, like, you're working too hard or it happens to everyone . . ."

"Take Eleven east to Windham, One Twenty-one to Bellows Falls, then straight down Ninety-one to Springfield and across Ninety-five. You don't hit traffic, you'll make your plane."

For a moment she held his look, searching for something appropriate to say, and, finding nothing appropriate, she got up, blew him a kiss, and walked out.

Senator Woodrow Wilson White waited for the sound of the rental car on the gravel driveway before rising from his cold Jacuzzi and slipping into a fluffy terry-cloth robe.

He padded barefoot downstairs through the drafty A-frame into the kitchen, opened the refrigerator, and found the recorked bottle of rapidly turning white wine. He would have to lay in some wine with the fire-wood. Charge it to the entertainment-and-travel allowance, though you had to be careful ever since they tightened up the rules in '91 with the congressional-allowance bill that he, like everyone else in the Congress, had had to vote for.

The A-frame was located in the village of Peru, pronounced Pee-ru, seven miles from Manchester, twenty miles from Bellows Falls. It was the only thing his first wife had left him in their divorce eleven years ago, and the one place the senator could go and be assured of privacy.

Wife number one, Sharon Rosinski, a former Miss Toledo, had been captain of the UVM women's ski team. They had bought the A-frame early in their marriage, when they were still living in Ohio, for Vermont ski vacations. Wife number two, Daphne Melancamp White, hated skiing, snow, and, for that matter, the entire state of Vermont. She had been to Peru only once, during a six-day blizzard, and vowed she'd never return. And never did.

The A-frame had helped to establish the senator's Vermont residency when he first ran for the Senate in 1986, and it was slowly falling apart. The foundation sloped four degrees toward the hillside—a problem, a structural engineer had explained, that could not be corrected without taking the house down. The window joints were warped, letting drafts of cold air in. The plumbing was rusting from long periods of disuse.

It was the bane of Woody White's Washington staff's existence because there was no easy way to get there and because the senator often didn't answer the phone when he was at the house. His Vermont staff wasn't happy about the A-frame in Peru either. It was at least a two-hour drive from Montpelier, longer from Burlington.

And there was absolutely no security at the A-frame, both staffs pointed out to him. The fact that nobody knew where it was, the senator responded, was the best security of all. Not only was Peru barely on the map, but once you got there you had to take a series of unmarked dirt roads from the center of town in order to reach the house.

It wasn't easy for a United States senator to get lost. The people of Peru, all 336 of them, by and large respected his privacy, plowed his road when it snowed, and kept the house on the fire plan for the village's volunteer Fire Department.

He thought of calling home to see if Daphne was there, but he knew she wasn't. And besides, the cell phone was upstairs, and he didn't feel like moving. He was exhausted and depressed. Maybe it happened to all men, now and then, but it hadn't happened to Woody White in a very long time.

He was counting on the lobbyist from the National Association of Health Prophylaxis Industries to be discreet. After all, if she talked, she would have to reveal the source of her information, which would be difficult without compromising her own ethics, not to mention the future prospects of the bill that was languishing in the senator's subcommittee.

As the late-winter sun began to slide behind the hill, Senator Woodrow Wilson White sat at his sloping kitchen table drinking wine that was only several days away from vinegar, thinking about having flatlined with the lobbyist and about his prospects for reelection in November and about his current wife, who might or might not be having an affair with a Finnish ice-skater, and about his first wife, who was suing him for more money, and about his daughter, who was married to an Amish blacksmith and had no telephone, and about his son, who was in the marijuana business in Miami and had serious IRS problems, and about the fact that he had to be in Rutland tomorrow for a campaign appearance at a hockey-stick factory.

He was so immersed in this dreary collection of thoughts that he didn't hear his cell phone—upstairs on the bed, half buried beneath a pillow. Even had he heard the ring, he would have been reluctant to answer it, because he knew that it would be Ishmael and that Ishmael would have a long list of things the senator needed to attend to, things that, for one reason or another, he was not attending to.

So even though he had called Ishmael and asked him to call him back, the senator probably wouldn't have answered the phone even if he'd heard it, which he hadn't.

Ishmael Leibowitz, Senator White's chief of staff, sat in his office in the suite of offices in the Dirksen Senate Office Building on Constitution Avenue and let the phone ring twenty times before putting the receiver down.

"Isn't there another number there?" Debbie Sue Allenby, the senator's chief legislative assistant, asked.

"Yes. But he doesn't give it out."

"Not even to you?"

"Not even to me."

"Does Montpelier know it?"

"Nobody knows it. His wife doesn't even know it."

Ishmael got up and started to pace around the small office, which abutted the senator's large office.

"What's he doing there?"

Ishmael gave her a look that implied that anyone who had worked for the senator for more than a few weeks should know not to ask that question.

Debbie Sue consulted her yellow legal pad.

"He's got a subcommittee meeting at four on Thursday. Plus there may be a Floor vote on the fisheries bill that morning."

"We can pair him on the fisheries vote."

"Which way?"

"It doesn't matter."

"It'll be in the *Record*."

"Debbie, Vermont is a landlocked state. They care about cows in Vermont, not about salmon quotas."

The phone rang. Ishmael grabbed it.

"Ishmael Leibowitz . . ."

There was a moment of silence, then Ishmael said, "Debbie Sue, may I have a moment, please?"

Debbie Sue nodded, making sure he knew that she knew that this was a personal call, and left the office.

Ishmael went over and closed the door, which Debbie Sue had left open on purpose. He returned to the phone and said, "Listen, I don't know about tonight. I've lost the senator."

He twisted the phone cord around his finger.

"When I find him, I'll call you. . . . Barry, it's my job, all right?"

And he hung up, irritated. Barry, who never lost *his* senator, a fifth-term nonentity from Idaho, had a hard time understanding the roller-coaster ride it was being Senator Woody White's chief of staff.

Barry called him five times a day and prattled over the phone. If he wasn't such a good source of Grade-A gossip and classified information from the Armed Services Committee, on which Senator Nonentity sat, Ishmael would have blown him off a long time ago.

But if he blew Barry off, not only would his intelligence pipeline be compromised but his status in the unofficial caucus of gay Senate aides would be in jeopardy. What if they discovered his secret and he was outed by the group, if not publicly, at least privately? He would be left to wander around making contacts with the straight Senate aides, who, by and large, didn't know what the hell was going on.

So Ishmael Leibowitz continued his subterfuge, living a lie, while trying to keep track of Senator Woodrow White. Besides being overworked and underpaid, Vermont's staff allowance being the second smallest in the Senate, Ishmael Leibowitz was, in all probability, the only closet heterosexual in Washington.

· · ·

It was already dark by the time Woody found his phone. He never used the house phone because it was not a secure line, and though it was no longer a party line, as it had been when he and Sharon first bought the house, he was never entirely convinced that people weren't listening in.

Outside of the secure line in the office, the cell phone was as secure as it got without getting the FBI involved. And you never knew about them. They had guys over there in the Hoover Building selling secrets to the tabloids. If not directly to the Ethics Committee.

These were perilous times. You didn't watch your back, you'd find yourself in that windowless room on the second floor of the Hart Senate Office Building answering questions.

Woody had already had a brush with the vice squad. In 1995 a former staffer had accused him of sexual harassment. The charge was more or less groundless—a couple of ambiguous moments in the back of a campaign bus, instigated by the woman herself.

The Ethics Committee cleared him after a first-stage investigation, preferring to concentrate on Packwood, whom they were crucifying at the time. Thank God for Packwood. He had taken the pipe for the entire Senate.

Being cleared by Ethics didn't stop his alleged harassee, however. When she was finished with Sally Jessy and Geraldo, she wrote a book called *A Fox in the Henhouse—Woody White in Washington,* which spent a week on the *Washington Post* bestseller list before sinking precipitously onto the remainder shelves.

These were among the perils of being a United States senator these days. All for $137,500, with no honoraria and a shrinking travel allowance. You couldn't even frank Christmas cards anymore.

Woody opened the flip phone and dialed his home number in Virginia. After ten rings, a melodious male voice answered, *"Pronto."*

"Hello . . ."

"Chi parla?"

"Dario, it's me."

"Chi?"

"Me. Senator White."

"Ah, buona sera, senatore. Come sta?"

Dario Farniente was an illegal immigrant from Trieste, whom he and Daphne had hired to take care of their large neo-Colonial in McLean. To compensate for his limited, if not nonexistent, English, he was a superb cook, a meticulous gardener, and extremely discreet.

He was also a neo-Fascist. In his closet were a number of black shirts and armbands that were reminiscent of the heyday of Mussolini.

His wife and he had agreed that they had to fire Dario, but neither of them was ever at the house long enough to replace him, and so Dario stayed on, cooking sumptuous meals for himself and for the dachshund, Helmut, and for God knows who else, and Woody and Daphne were reduced to communicating with him in pidgin Italian.

"*Dove* my wife?"

"*Come?*"

"My wife. *La signora?*"

"Oh! *La signora. Non c'è.*"

"*Quando* . . . uh . . . *quando ritornare?*"

"*Non l'ho vista oggi.*"

"Did you *vista* her *ieri?*"

"*Si, senatore. Ma e partita alle nove, e non lei ho parlato . . .*"

Woody hung up in the middle of his housekeeper's sentence. Feeling a little light-headed, he took a few turns around the room to clear the muck out of his brain.

He was not firing on all cylinders these days. Last week he had dozed off during the middle of a subcommittee hearing on strip mining. On Friday he had backed into Trent Lott's car in the Senate parking garage. When he got out to examine the damage and realized that nobody had seen him, he drove off. And now he was convinced that the hidden surveillance cameras had recorded the incident and that he would be hearing from Lott's lawyers any day now, if not from the guys on the second floor of the Hart Senate Office Building.

The cell buzzed. Woody flipped it open. "Yes?"

"Senator?"

"Ishmael. What's going on?"

"You asked me to call you."

"Right. Listen, call Trent Lott's office and tell them that you backed into his Ford Explorer Friday in the Senate parking garage. You left a note on his windshield, which must have gotten blown off. Then call the insurance company and report the accident."

"I wasn't in the Senate parking garage last week. Only senators are allowed to park there. I have to park in the staff parking garage."

"Well, you borrowed my car."

"Senator, may I strongly advise against filing a false accident report?"

"All right. Call him. Tell him I had to run off to Vermont and forgot to report the accident. Tell him I'm sorry. It's just a little scraped paint. He probably didn't even notice it."

"Would you like to hear your phone log?"

"Just the top ten."

"There's the Deputy Secretary of the Interior, the Minority Whip, Senator Frobisher, Beverly, Senator Kalb, someone from the GAO about your expense receipts, Lee Schumock, Irwin Posalski, Vice President Gore's office, and John Q. Adams . . ."

"Who?"

"John Q. Adams."

"Who is John Q. Adams?"

"Actually, he likes to be called John Quincy Adams. He's a maple-syrup distributor from Montpelier."

"Why doesn't he call the Montpelier office?"

"He has, apparently. But you haven't contacted him."

"Let him write a letter."

"Senator, the man donated five hundred thousand dollars to your re-election campaign."

"He did?"

"Yes."

"Isn't that illegal?"

"He ran it through a PAC called the Vermont Maple Syrup Distributors Association."

"Five hundred thousand dollars?"

"That's right. I think it would be a nice gesture to call him personally."

Woody copied the number down.

"Your Vermont people need to confirm plans with you for tomorrow."

"I'll call them. What's Beverly's husband's name again?"

"Stewart."

"Is he still in the hospital?"

"He died three months ago."

"Did I send a card?"

"Yes, Senator. And flowers."

"Good . . . look, Ishmael, I've got to go shovel some snow off the roof."

"We're going to pair you on the fisheries bill with Staubman."

"Fine. Good. I'll talk to you when I get back to Washington."

"Are you going to be at the conference committee at four tomorrow?"

"I don't know. Maybe. I've got to be in Rutland at nine . . ."

"Actually, you've got to be in *Burlington* at *ten*. Then you're having lunch with Beverly and the Montpelier staff and making a three o'clock flight into National."

"Fine. Listen, tell Trent Lott that his car was outside the yellow lines of his parking space, okay?"

Woody got off the phone and stared at the number of the maple-syrup guy who had forked over half a million.

A half a million in hard money. That was a lot of maple syrup. Woody dialed the number. A woman with a clipped Yankee accent answered the phone.

"VMSDA."

"Mr. Adams, please."

"Who would this be?"

"Senator White."

"Well, I'll be. Senator White. How're you doing?"

"Very well, thank you. I was returning Mr. Adams's phone call."

"Don't move a goddamn inch, Senator."

After a moment, a voice on the other end of the phone articulated, "John Quincy Adams here."

"Mr. Adams, it's Senator White."

"Now that's what Abigail here told me, and I'm tickled. You're not an easy man to catch up with."

"I'm terribly sorry, but we've been overwhelmed with legislation down in Washington these days. When it rains it pours."

"Don't it ever. We had two and a half inches the other day over in Barre. Practically needed a canoe to get down Main Street . . ."

"What can I do for you, Mr. Adams?"

"Well, Senator, I heard you're going to be up in Burlington tomorrow, and I was wondering if I could invite you to have a bite of lunch."

He'd have to blow off Beverly and the Vermont staff. They'd be pissed. But $500,000 . . .

"Mr. Adams, I'd be delighted."

"That's hunky dory, Senator."

"Always a pleasure to meet with a constituent."

"Bertha's on Willard at twelve?"

"I'll find it."

"Senator, can you tell me why a hummingbird hums?"

"I'm afraid I don't know, Mr. Adams."

"'Cause he don't know the words."

2

MIGHT RAIN

THE HOCKEY-STICK FACTORY was across the river in Winooski. The senator was only twenty minutes late, which wasn't bad, considering that he had hit snow flurries north of Rutland.

Beverly Levesque, the head of his state reelection committee, was waiting for him, along with a half-dozen of his other Vermont people, outside the Winooski Hockey Equipment Company.

"How are you doing, Beverly?" he said, shaking her hand.

"Fine, Senator."

"Must be difficult for you without Stephen."

"Stewart . . ."

"Of course."

He shook hands with the rest of the staff, a pink-cheeked group of healthy-looking people, who had been standing outside in the twenty-degree temperature for a half hour and looked none the worse for it.

"So what's the drill?"

"You're going to meet the owners, then tour the factory floor with them. You'll give your talk right on the floor, then we'll do photos and sign hockey sticks."

Brian Petrunich, one of his speechwriters, handed the senator a few pages.

"It's your self-reliance-and-Yankee-ingenuity speech, Senator."

As they got to the factory door, the senator asked Beverly, "How did Winooski vote in '92?"

"Fifty-six to forty-four against you."

"What does Irwin say?"

"The numbers haven't budged."

They walked into the smell of wood shavings and glue. Woody was wearing his Vermont campaign outfit—a red checkered flannel shirt and corduroy pants under a lined Eddie Bauer pea coat, and a pair of ecologically approved fleece-lined boots from the L.L. Bean catalog.

As two men in hard hats approached, Beverly whispered, "Sal Cecchi and Bob Martinson."

Woody smiled and threw out his hand, "Sal, Bob—how are you?"

"Fine, Senator. How are you?"

"Couldn't be better. Tell me . . . do you know why a hummingbird hums?"

Fifty minutes later, Woody stood in the sawdust, a hard hat over his full head of salt-and-pepper hair, and told the forty-seven employees of the Winooski Hockey Equipment Company that they represented the best that America had to offer. He told them that he, as their senator, was proud of them and that Ralph Waldo Emerson, were he still alive, would have been proud of them, and that Henry David Thoreau, were he too still alive, would have voted for NAFTA.

There was a smattering of applause. And then just as he was ready to move on to the photo op, an oatmeal-faced woman in the first row of employees said, "Senator, can I ask you a question?"

"Certainly."

Woody focused his million-dollar blue eyes right at her high, dull, inbred forehead.

"You got the zipper problem under control?"

Over his years as a politician, Woody had learned that the trick to dealing with these types of questions was to respond quickly and with complete eye contact. Like a major league third baseman, Woody could not only field the hot ones but get rid of the ball quickly.

Looking straight into the oatmeal-faced woman's widely spaced eyes, Woody smiled big and said, "You bet."

He held her look for several seconds, floating his smile across the room, as if daring her to come back at him, before letting Beverly spirit him away for the cameras.

Woody posed for pictures with Sal and Bob, examining the lathes and table saws, holding a hockey stick, having a cup of coffee with a group of employees and listening to their problems.

Outside, on their way to the cars, Beverly said, "I thought we were finished with that zipper-problem stuff."

"Beverly, as we say in Vermont, if you can't stand the heat, get out of the outhouse."

"Actually, Senator, what we say is, if you can't stand the heat, get out of the *sugar* shack. . . . I've ordered sandwiches. With all the things we need to talk about, I thought it would be best to have a working lunch."

"Beverly, I'm afraid I'm going to have to skip lunch with the group today."

"Beg your pardon?"

"I've got a pressing engagement."

She stopped walking and turned to him. "Senator, we've got a little more than seven months till the election. There are a number of major decisions that have to be made about fund-raising, staffing . . ."

"Of course. And we'll make them. Soon."

"I have people who've come up here all the way from Boston for this meeting."

"Thank them for me."

And he gave her a smile, shook her hand, and got into the rental car. Waving to his staff, he drove off, heading for the bridge to take him back across the river into Burlington.

It was a dull late-winter day, gray and cold. On the sides of the streets were piles of dirty snow that would still be there in late April. He drove slowly, badly, already regretting having blown off Beverly and her people to have lunch with some Yankee crackpot who undoubtedly wanted something from him for his five hundred grand.

But the truth was he really didn't want to have lunch with his Vermont staff right now. There were serious problems of staffing and funding for this reelection campaign, problems that he did not have solutions for.

Except the zipper problem, of course. At the moment the zipper problem was not a problem. Thanks to the flatline problem. The flatline problem made the zipper problem largely academic.

There was a urologist who had an office across the New York state line—in Troy or Schenectady, he couldn't remember which—whom he had consulted discreetly a number of years ago for a nagging case of nonspecific urethritis.

The doctor's office was maybe an hour and a half's drive from Peru. People wouldn't necessarily recognize him on the New York side.

All the way to Willard Street Woody racked his brains to remember the name of the doctor in Troy or Schenectady. He parked the car in front of Bertha's diner, took a comb out of his glove compartment, and gave his hair a touch-up.

Woody walked in the door and looked around. The place was busy with the lunchtime crowd, and nobody paid attention to the man with the bright blue eyes in the Eddie Bauer pea coat.

In the last booth, a little man wearing a cap with the earmuffs tied up above and a faded JCPenney winter coat sat alone with a newspaper. He met the senator's eyes and waved.

The man was in his late fifties, maybe early sixties, with a grizzled beard and prominent ears. He looked like he barely had $500 to his name, let alone $500,000. Woody walked over to the booth.

"Mr. Adams?"

"Yours truly. Sit down and take a load off, Senator."

Slipping into the booth, Woody took his coat off and offered his hand. "It is indeed a pleasure to meet you, Mr. Adams."

"Likewise, Senator."

John Quincy Adams handed him a menu and said, "Yankee pot roast is pretty good. So is the clam chowder. I'd stay away from the fried scallops if I were you."

Woody ordered a Spanish omelet and made some small talk about the weather. The conversation proceeded in fits and starts. He was already regretting that he'd agreed to this lunch when the man said abruptly, "You know that John Quincy Adams was really responsible for the Monroe Doctrine? Not James Monroe, who got all the credit?"

"Actually, I didn't."

"Adams was Secretary of State under Monroe. He negotiated the bejesus out of that sucker. Thanks to him we don't have the Frogs down in South America. It's bad enough we have them across the border in Quebec. Fact is John Q. was lucky to be President after Monroe. Andrew Jackson beat him in the popular vote, but it was thrown into the House of Representatives on account of it being a three-way race, and the House elected him. Then, after he serves four years in the White House, he comes back and serves seventeen more in the House. That's what I call humility."

John Quincy Adams went on about his namesake, the sixth President of the United States, and about humility, and even before the Spanish omelet arrived, Woody was planning a quick escape. Then, without the slightest introduction or even segue, the agenda was revealed.

"Senator, you aware that there's a vacancy on the U.S. Court of Appeals, Second Circuit?"

As it happened, Woody wasn't. It was one of the items on a long list that Ishmael had wanted him to attend to, but it was fairly far down on that list.

"Uh-huh," Woody replied noncommittally.

"Be nice to put a Vermonter on that court, wouldn't it?"

"Sure would."

"Got anybody in mind?"

"Well, tell you the truth, Mr. Adams, I've given that question a great deal of thought and I haven't reached a decision yet."

"Would you care for a suggestion?"

"By all means."

"Vincent Ruggiero."

"Vincent Ruggiero? I'm not familiar with the name."

"Born and bred in White River Junction. *Summa cum laude* at Middlebury. Top of his class at UVM Law School. One hell of a legal mind. And a man of great humility."

"What's Mr. Ruggiero doing now?"

"U.S. Attorney for Vermont. This would be a step up for him."

"I would say so. Well, I appreciate that suggestion, Mr. Adams. I'll look into it."

"Sure as hell make me proud. About time we had a Vermonter on that bench, don't you think?"

"Absolutely."

"Vermont's been sucking hind tit since it was admitted into the union. Three electoral votes and no judges on the Second Circuit."

"Well, I'll look into that."

"You do that, Senator. How was the Spanish omelet?"

"Good."

"Another piece of pie?"

"I'm afraid not, Mr. Adams. I've got to run."

"Might rain, huh?"

Woody looked out the window. The sun was poking its way through the cloud cover. It didn't look to him like it was going to rain. But then he remembered what "might rain" meant in Vermont, smiled, and reached for the check.

"Your money's no good in here, Senator."

"Well, I—"

"Keep it for your reelection campaign."

And then as Woody got up to leave, John Quincy Adams said, "Plenty more Spanish omelets where that came from."

It was on the plane, with the Spanish omelet churning in his stomach, that Woody remembered the name of the urologist. Dr. Haas. He was in Schenectady, on State Street. He stuck his American Express card into the slot, took the phone out of the compartment, and dialed his Washington office.

When Ishmael answered, Woody said, "Get me an office number and address for a Doctor Haas. H-A-A-S. It's in Schenectady."

"Schenectady's in New York State, Senator."

"I know that, Ishmael. And run a check on a U.S. Attorney named Vincent Ruggiero. I might be sending his name over to the White House for the vacancy on the Second Circuit."

"There's been a list on your desk of eight potential nominees, with their files, since February."

"Well, add Ruggiero's file to it, all right?"

"Okay. I spoke with Senator Lott's office. They say there's almost three thousand dollars' worth of bodywork to be done on the car."

"That's bullshit. It was just a tap."

"Not according to his chief of staff."

"What's my deductible?"

"I don't know, Senator."

"Call the insurance company and find out."

The plane hit an air bump, bringing the Spanish omelet up another inch. Woody put the phone back, leaned back in his seat, and eyed the barf bag.

He'd offer Trent Lott fifteen hundred under the table and a judgeship on the Second Circuit. See if that flew.

3.

WASTE CONTROL
AND MONTRACHET

AT SIX-THIRTY THAT EVENING, after having tossed the Spanish omelet on the plane, the senator was sitting in an overheated room in the Rayburn House Office Building trying to stay awake during a conference-committee reconciliation of a bill to increase funding for various federal waste-control projects.

His committee aide had explained that the bill was dead in the water as soon as it hit the Floor. Nevertheless, Woody listened patiently as a first-term congressman from Minnesota named Carl Kanush tried to sell him an amendment that jacked up the cost of the bill—a bill that Woody didn't support in the first place but he would vote for on the Floor precisely because it didn't stand a chance of passing and because a waste-control "yes" vote would spike his environmental score, which would make his numbers guy happy. According to Irwin Posalski, his pollster, he was dipping with the Sierra Club.

The Waste Control and Risk Assessment Subcommittee of the Environment and Public Works Committee was the type of assignment a twelve-year, second-term senator ought to have been able to avoid. But Woody had burned some bridges with the Democratic leadership, and he was still paying the price.

He had a seat on the Agriculture, Nutrition, and Forestry Committee, was the ranking Democrat on two subcommittees—Medicaid and Health Care, and African Affairs—and held seats on Waste Control and Risk Assessment, and Parks, Historic Preservation, and Recreation. But he wasn't even near any of the big ones, like Judiciary, Appropriations, or Foreign Relations.

If Senator Woodrow White wasn't in Siberia, he was definitely east of the Urals.

The bill squeaked through the conference committee, which meant that the congressman from Minnesota owed him a favor. As Woody got up to leave, the man came over to thank him.

"I appreciate your support on this, Senator."

"No problem," Woody replied. "I don't suppose you do auto-body work, do you?"

When Woody got back to his office, Ishmael was waiting with the phone log. Woody stared at it balefully. It was three pages long and growing by the minute.

"Lee Schumock? Who's he?"

"He's the writer your publisher has assigned to do the book with you. You're supposed to have dinner with him tonight."

"Tell him I've got a night session."

"You've canceled three times with him already. The Random House lawyer has sent a letter requesting a return of the advance if you don't begin work on the book forthwith."

"Forthwith?"

"That's the exact language. Mr. Schumock has reserved a table at the Summit for eight o'clock. It's on Prospect, just off Wisconsin. You can freshen up and just make it."

As Woody headed for his private bathroom, Ishmael said, "Your deductible is a thousand, Senator . . ."

Woody closed the door and approached the mirror. He looked awful. The recycled Spanish omelet had left destruction and ravage in its path.

He should have taken the $200 deductible. They were going to raise his insurance rates. Congressional immunity didn't apply to traffic accidents.

Maybe he'd call the congressman from Minnesota. Cash the marker fast before the man forgot. Find out what *his* deductible was. Maybe they could work something out.

"You're *kidding*."

"Uh-uh."

"She bought it?"

"She was an ex–cocktail waitress from Pompano Beach. What do you expect?"

Ishmael sat sipping Bardolino and half listening to Kevin Bunch, press secretary to the senator from Florida, talk about his boss's sexual exploits when he was a state representative.

"So he tells her not to worry. The Agency will take care of her if anything happens to him. But under no circumstances should she ever call them. Even if he doesn't come home at night. Meanwhile he's out there doing everything in Tallahassee with a skirt, and she never asks him why because she thinks he's an undercover *CIA agent.*"

"That's hysterical," said Jack Hernden, a legislative assistant from the House.

"Does he swing?" Barry asked.

"You kidding? If he were any farther in the closet he'd have coat hangers coming out of his ass."

They were having dinner at Hugo's, a semi-trendy Italian restaurant in Dupont Circle. Barry, Kevin, Jack, and Ishmael were joined by Denny McCardle, a White House aide who was just near enough to the action to know what was going on and just far enough away not to be suspected when there were leaks.

Denny was sleeping with Jack. Barry and Kevin had had a thing about a year ago but that was over, and now they were both unattached, though Barry had been making it pretty clear that he was interested in Ishmael.

"So," Barry said, turning to Ishmael, "you found your senator?"

"He was in Peru, not answering his phone."

"So who was he with?" Kevin persisted.

Ishmael hesitated. He wasn't sure just how much information he should throw into the stew pot.

"Are we being coy?" Jack said with a smile.

"Just some lobbyist," Ishmael said.

"Who?"

They were relentless. There was no way he was going to get out of naming names, so he named names.

"Who's *she* with?"

Ishmael tried to keep a straight face when he told them, "The National Association of Health Prophylaxis Industries."

"Rubbers?" Kevin said.

It brought down the house. They were still laughing when the cappuccinos arrived.

"So," Denny said, trying to top Ishmael, "did you hear who Hillary's new hairdresser is?"

As the conversation shifted to the relative merits of Washington's top hairdressers, Ishmael tuned out. He was feeling more and more like an undercover intelligence agent who had infiltrated a spy ring.

There was a woman he was seeing secretly, an associate deputy director in the Agriculture Department. She was five years older than he, a single mother from Indiana, with strawberry-blond hair and very fair skin. Maud, her name was. Maud Summers, a WASP so white and midwestern that Ishmael's Galician ancestors would turn over in their mass graves if they knew about her.

Ishmael was thinking about Maud, about how she looked up at him with her nearsighted brown eyes after they made love on the crisply ironed sheets of her very neat bedroom in Alexandria, when his beeper went off.

"Jesus, Ishmael, doesn't that man ever give you a moment's peace?" Barry said.

"No," Ishmael replied, getting up and heading for the phone.

When he got the senator on his cell, he was in the car on the way to the restaurant, a half hour late and lost.

"Where are you, Senator?"

"Damned if I know."

Ishmael painstakingly explained to him how to find the restaurant.

He hung up and decided to call Maud.

"You know about Hillary's new hairdresser?" he asked her.

She laughed the laugh he found so wonderfully foreign. Jews could never laugh that way. Jews laughed from the pain in their souls. WASPs laughed to cover their embarrassment at finding life funny. When Maud climaxed, she sometimes laughed. As if she were embarrassed at having come at all.

"Peggy asleep?" he asked.

That was a code phrase for them. She hesitated for a moment, then said, "Yes."

"Half hour?"

"Okay."

He had the story down before he reached the table.

"He got his zipper stuck, right?" Kevin Bunch said.

"He wants to go over his notes on the fisheries bill."

"At this hour?"

"Woody White never sleeps. Sorry, guys."

Ishmael shrugged his martyred shrug and waved good-bye. As he walked out of the restaurant, he kept his tongue pressed against the cyanide cap in his mouth. If they captured him, he'd let it slip down his throat before they made him talk.

At the Summit, Senator Woodrow White sat across the table from Lee Schumock, star biographer and his collaborator on the book he had contracted to do for Random House for a million-two, a third up front. It wasn't bad for a sitting senator. Even though they had given away the store to Dick Morris, one-point-two wasn't chopped liver.

Lee Schumock was a tall, lugubrious-looking man in his forties, who had left a tenured position at Georgetown to write important political biographies, but the research was painstaking and the money lousy, and he eventually drifted into the more lucrative and somewhat less scholarly area of hot books about controversial politicians, businessmen, and movie stars.

He had done one of the Keating Five and Jack Nicholson, so he knew where both the soft money and the pussy were buried.

The senator sipped a vodka on the rocks and sized up Schumock. The writer was wearing a cheap sports jacket and Haggar slacks. The tie looked like it had a mind of its own, hanging limply in front of him and threatening to dip into the butter dish.

"The idea, Senator, is to produce a book that tells the reader who you are. The real *you*."

"The real me?"

"That's right. We're not interested just in the facts of your life—growing up in Cleveland, your grades at law school, your first legislative victories—but in the story behind those events, how you got to be where you are today. Who *is* Woodrow White?"

Woody ordered a second vodka, even though he knew he shouldn't. If he had learned one thing as a politician, it was not to trust writers.

"For example," Lee Schumock said, "I know that you were born in Cleveland and that your family moved to Shaker Heights when you were three. I know you went to the University School, Ohio State, and Case Western Reserve Law School. What I don't know, though, is what it was like to grow up in Shaker Heights in the fifties, what it felt like being the son of a New England White on one side and an Ohio Hanna on the other side. What was the breakfast table like? What did your parents tell you about life? When was the first time you kissed a girl?"

"Cheryl Edwards. In her basement under the Ping-Pong table."

"That's exactly it. *That's* what we want."

"Look," Woody said, "as you know, I've had some problems over the last couple of years. How do I know that this book isn't just going to throw fat on the fire?"

"This is your opportunity to respond. This is your shot at telling it the way you want to tell it. Me? I'm just a facilitator for you. This is your book."

The waiter put a plate of mussels in front of Woody and some foie gras in front of Lee Schumock.

"Who's paying for this dinner?"

"Random House."

Woody felt his appetite start to return. "Bring us a bottle of something white and dry, will you?"

"Yes, Senator," the waiter said.

There was virtually no place he could go in Washington anymore without being recognized. During the Ethics Committee investigation in '95 he could barely walk out of his office without some TV reporter sticking a mike in his face for a sound byte. His picture had been on the cover of *Newsweek*. Tourists would come into the office in the hope of catching a glimpse of him.

"You know my mother's still alive?" he said, as he parted the shell of a mussel.

"She's living in California now, isn't she?"

"Palm Springs. In a condo on a golf course. Costs me forty-five hundred a month. She's eighty-nine, drives around in a motorized wheelchair, and terrorizes people in the mall when she goes shopping."

"What was your father like?"

Herbert Weit was a tight-ass workaholic. Sold carpets for a living. Never laughed. Never took a day off. Never took Woody to a ball game. Woody changed his name to White six months after his father died from colon cancer at fifty-nine.

Woody realized that Lee Schumock was going to try to get it all out of him. Sooner or later. That's why the writer had suggested this restaurant, with the foie gras to die from and the terrific wine list. They had a Montrachet here that brought tears to your eyes.

"How long do you think this book is going to take?" he asked.

"Depends on how available you and the people who know you are for me."

"I don't know. I'm on five committees and I'm up for reelection in November."

"Don't worry. I'll fit right into your schedule. I'll travel with you. I'll go to meetings with you. I'll be a fly on the wall. You won't even know I'm there."

Woody picked up his wineglass, took a sip. "What do you say we have the waiter toss this stuff, and we order a bottle of Montrachet?"

It was precisely for these types of evenings, evenings when he was out late and had drunk a little too much Montrachet, that the senator kept a *pied-à-terre* in Wesley Heights. On such evenings all he had to do was fall into a cab and manage to get his key in the door.

But for some perverse reason that particular evening, after having chased the Montrachet with a large postprandial Martel, Woody found himself in the battered Mercedes Diesel heading for McLean.

He was not drunk enough to be a complete menace behind the wheel, but he was drunk enough not to consider the possibility that he would find something he didn't want to find at home. Or, more likely, *not* find something.

As soon as he drove into the garage and saw that her car was gone, he realized what he already knew—that he should have stayed in Wesley Heights that night.

Dario, who wasn't expecting him, was curled up on the couch in the den with the dachshund. Dressed in his customary black shirt and armband, he was watching Leno on the forty-eight-inch TV and nibbling on a plate of pastries.

"*Buona sera, senatore,*" his houseman greeted him. "*Volete qualche zabaglione?*"

"*Dove . . .* my wife?"

He shrugged a particularly Italian shrug that communicated not only that he didn't know where *la signora* was but that, in a larger sense, men didn't know where women were even when they were right there.

Unfortunately, Woody *did* know where his wife was. For some time now he had known where his wife was when she wasn't where she was supposed to be.

But he said nothing to Dario and walked out of the den and toward the stairs.

"*Buona notte, senatore,*" Dario called after him, just as the laugh track exploded on Leno, as if to punctuate Woody's humiliation.

The house was decorator-furnished in knock-off Early American. Neither Daphne nor he was attached enough to the place to put much time or effort into it. They came and went according to their own erratic schedules, communicating sporadically and inaccurately through Dario, and very rarely finding themselves together under the same roof.

Daphne made the odd appearance with him at a Washington fundraiser, radiant and charming and managing to convey the impression that she was the senator's loving and devoted wife and not, in fact, the unfaithful woman, who, at the moment, was in the arms of a Finnish iceskater fourteen years younger than her and without a green card.

As Woody peeled off his clothes, bone-weary from a day that had begun at 7 A.M. in Peru, he thought about how to deal with his wife and the iceskater. What he'd like to do was walk into their love nest and shoot both of them, but he'd get forty to life and that wouldn't help him get reelected to the Senate.

He squinted at himself in the bathroom mirror. He was fifty-six years old but, at the moment, looked ten years older. It was the eyes, those steel-blue Paul Newman eyes, that redeemed the face. Without those eyes, he'd no doubt be back in Cleveland practicing real estate law, still married to Sharon, and spending his weekends on the living-room couch dozing in front of the football.

Throwing back a couple of aspirin to deal with the inevitable havoc that the Montrachet and the Martel would wreak in the morning, he staggered off to bed.

As he lay there, his head sinking heavily into the pillow, he had a final thought for the day. It was a good thought, and it helped him to drift off in a more positive frame of mind. Tomorrow morning he'd call a guy at INS who owed him a favor and find out just what you had to do to get a green-card application pulled.

4

TOPPING OFF

IN THE MORNING, Woody found Lee Schumock, carrying a bound notebook and wearing the same limp tie he had worn the night before, waiting in his office. His biographer was sitting on the edge of the senator's desk, a large mug of coffee in his hand, chatting with Ishmael.

"Good morning, Senator," he said.

Woody nodded. The man had gone fifty-fifty with him on the Montrachet and didn't look much the worse for it.

There were already several calls marked *priority* on the phone log, and it was barely ten o'clock. Beverly had called twice, the Minority Whip, whose call Woody hadn't returned yesterday, had called. Irwin Posalski had called.

As Woody sat down at his desk, the writer sat down on the leather couch in the corner of the office to become, as he said, a fly on the wall.

"Pretend I'm not even here," Lee Schumock said, and, as if to prove his point, he opened a copy of *Vermont Life* and started to read.

The bad news started with Irwin Posalski. The pollster told him that his approval rating had dipped into the high forties.

"You don't want to go below forty-five."

"Irwin, it's only March."

"You're the incumbent, Senator. You shouldn't be skewing negative this early. You could be statistically critical by July."

"Good, Irwin. I can go fishing in July."

Irwin Posalski had no measurable sense of humor, and so he simply stepped over that remark and continued. "You need to get back up there and work the college kids before they're gone for the year. That's your strength."

Then Woody got Beverly on the phone. Her sense of humor was almost as far down on the graph as Irwin Posalski's, and she, too, got right to it.

"Senator, did you have lunch with John Quincy Adams yesterday in Burlington?"

"How did you find out?"

"It's a small town. Do you know who he is?"

"The sixth President of the United States."

"Senator, please . . ."

"He's the head of the Vermont Maple Syrup Distributors Association."

"That's just a front."

"A front for what?"

"The VMSDA is a laundering operation for an extortion-and-loan-sharking organization."

"Come on. We're talking about Vermont, not Jersey City."

"You don't think we have gangsters in Vermont?"

"When they rub you out, they leave a wheel of cheddar cheese in your bed, right?"

"This is not funny, Senator."

"Beverly, he's a little guy in a JCPenney coat and a hat with earmuffs. He bought me a seven-dollar lunch."

"You don't want to be in John Quincy Adams's pocket, believe me."

Woody took a deep breath. He knew, and Beverly ought to have known, that every politician was in somebody's pocket. What was the difference if it was the Teamsters, the National Organization for Women, or the Vermont Maple Syrup Distributors Association?

"Beverly, do you know why a hummingbird hums?"

There was a long silence on the other end of the phone before Beverly responded. "Why?"

"Because he's got five hundred thousand dollars to contribute to his favorite senator's campaign."

When Ishmael put a piece of paper with the name and phone number of the Schenectady urologist on Woody's desk, the senator took it to his private bathroom, along with the cell phone, out of earshot of the fly on his wall.

When the doctor's receptionist picked up, Woody whispered, "I'd like to make an appointment with Dr. Haas."

"Are you a patient?"

"No," he replied, confident that there was no way the doctor would re-member him. It was five, maybe seven years ago that Woody had gone to see him for the nonspecific urethritis.

"Well, let's see, I have an opening the week of April thirteenth . . ."

"This is an emergency."

"What seems to be the problem, sir?"

"I'd rather not go into it over the telephone."

"Sir, if the doctor is going to see you on an emergency basis, he'll need some indication of the problem."

For a moment, he considered telling her a great deal more than she wanted to know—the slowly declining performance, what Irwin Posalski would call negative skewing, leading to the flatlining with Evelyn Brand-wynne in Peru.

"Look," he finally blurted, "I think I may have bladder cancer, okay?"

"I'm terribly sorry, sir. You understand that I was only following the doctor's instructions. When we overbook, we wind up with people having to wait inordinately long periods of time—"

"Right," he interrupted. "When can he see me?"

"I can squeeze you in at three-thirty this afternoon."

Woody looked at his watch. It was 10:45. He could catch the noon shuttle into La Guardia, then take a flight directly to Albany . . .

"I'll be there."

"Your name, sir?"

"James Monroe."

He flushed the toilet, exited the bathroom, and went to look at his ap-pointment book. Morning business on the Floor at noon. Lunch with the Minority Whip at one-thirty. The Democratic Caucus at three-thirty. Af-terward, he had been planning to run over to INS and talk to Hank Lev-enthal about pulling the ice-skater's green-card application.

It all could wait. Everything could wait. Walking quickly to Ishmael's office, he found his chief of staff on the phone. As soon as he saw the sen-ator's impatient look, Ishmael said, "Barry, let me get back to you," and hung up. "What's the problem, Senator?"

"I have to go to Peru."

"Peru? When?"

"Right now."

"You just got back."

"There's a problem with the roof. The snow's accumulated, and appar-ently it's causing a potentially difficult situation *vis-à-vis* my insurance."

"Can't you get someone up there to handle it?"

"The liability's too great. I could be sued from here to St. Johnsbury and back. I'll call you later."

As the senator headed for the door, Ishmael grabbed his appointment book and followed him into the hallway.

"Senator, what should I tell the Minority Whip?"

"Something good."

The Vermont Maple Syrup Distributors Association occupied the ground floor of a white Colonial house on Prescott Street in Montpelier, about a mile from the statehouse. There was a room in front, where Abigail Adams, the secretary, sat near a potbellied stove and answered the phone. The walls were covered with calendars showing ruddy-faced Vermonters tapping the sugar maples.

In the back of the house was a warren of small offices and a room with a large table, which was called the conference room.

That Wednesday morning, just as Senator Woodrow White's plane was banking across Flushing Bay to land at La Guardia, there was a lunch meeting taking place in the conference room of the VMSDA.

John Quincy Adams sat at the head of the table with a mug of coffee and a ham-and-cheese sandwich. To his right was his associate, Elbridge Gerry, in his plaid suspenders and shitkickers, eating a bowl of chicken noodle soup with Saltines crumbled into it. On the other side were two younger men, both on the hefty side, wearing Sears sports coats over flannel shirts. Ethan Allen and John Stark were eating tuna sandwiches on white, with chips and Diet Cokes.

"I said to Roland Boyden," Elbridge Gerry was saying, "I said to him it doesn't make a hog's ass difference to me what his problems are. I said to him that his problems weren't my problems. His problems were his problems . . ."

"Bottom line, Elbridge?" John Quincy Adams said.

"Fourteen hundred. Plus the vig."

"What do you say we have Ethan and John drop by?"

"Not a bad notion."

"Ethan, you go out there and tell Roland Boyden that we all have problems. Tell him I have problems with my septic tank. Tell him Ralph Meunier says I might have to dig up my entire yard. Now, that's a problem. Especially this time of year, with mud season on the way."

"Okay, Mr. Adams. We'll go out there right after lunch."

"Might rain, Ethan."

Ethan Allen and John Stark grabbed their sandwiches to eat in the car. After they were gone, Elbridge Gerry asked John Quincy Adams about his lunch yesterday with Senator White.

"Well, he didn't say yes and he didn't say no."

"Certainly prefer doing it this way."

"Amen."

"Sending Ethan and John up to Burlington is a high-risk proposition."

"I wouldn't send them to Burlington. I'd outsource that job."

"Tom Paine?"

John Quincy Adams looked at his right-hand man and said, "I ain't saying yes, and I ain't saying no."

"How bad's the septic tank?"

"Leaking down into the creek. If I dig up the yard, it's going to be a pool of mud big as Lake Champlain."

"You know, I was thinking about that mud. What about if Roland Boyden doesn't come up with the fourteen hundred?"

John Quincy Adams's eyes sparkled.

"You're one hell of a thinker, Elbridge."

The senator's flight from La Guardia into the Albany-Schenectady airport landed at 2:52, giving him barely enough time to make his 3:30 appointment. In the cab on the way to Schenectady, he thought about what he was going to tell the doctor.

There was no point in being coy. He'd just lay it out for him, chapter and verse, and see what the man said. If there was nothing to be done, he would drive to Peru, open a bottle of bad wine, and turn on the gas.

There were four other men in Dr. Haas's waiting room, all his age or older. The confederacy of aging men. Nobody made eye contact. Nobody wanted to admit that he was having plumbing problems.

Woody was asked to provide a specimen by a nurse sitting behind a sign that said IT IS CUSTOMARY TO PAY FOR MEDICAL SERVICES WHEN RENDERED. Then he was handed a series of forms and a clipboard and asked for his medical history and his insurance information, both of which he fabricated. It was a little after four o'clock when Dr. Haas ushered him into the consultation room. He was a slight man with thinning hair.

"Sorry about the wait, Mr. Monroe," he said.

The room was small with an examining table and one chair, which the doctor took, as he opened the file and glanced over Woody's medical questionnaire.

"My nurse said something about bladder cancer . . . ?"

"That's okay," Woody mumbled.

"I beg your pardon?"

"Well, those symptoms went away. I'm worried about something else."

The doctor looked at him peculiarly and asked, "Well, then, what *does* seem to be the problem?"

Woody had promised himself he would just get it right out when asked, but as he stood there in that chilly, antiseptic room staring at the doctor with the thinning hair, he wanted to bolt.

"Your urine is normal," Dr. Haas said, when Woody didn't say anything. "And, according to your estimation of your frequency and the strength of your stream, there doesn't appear to be a prostate problem . . ."

"I can't get it up, Doc," Woody blurted, tears coming to his eyes.

And then he was actually crying—big, wet tears were dripping down his cheeks.

"Listen, I understand that this can be an upsetting problem," Dr. Haas said in his best bedside manner voice, "but I must tell you there are a number of possible explanations, the great majority of them treatable. Tell you what—why don't you slip out of your trousers and let me examine you. Then we'll go into my office and talk."

The next fifteen minutes were not among the most pleasant fifteen minutes Woody had spent in his life, but he had been through this drill before and he knew what to expect.

When he was through, Dr. Haas washed his hands carefully and invited Woody next door to his office.

Once they were seated, the doctor folded his hands in front of him like Marcus Welby and said, "Mr. Monroe, tell me, how long has this condition been bothering you?"

Senator Woodrow White, a man who was capable of addressing the United States Senate articulately without working from notes, babbled like a teenager.

"Uh . . . well, for the last few months I was able to . . . you know, get one, but then it would sometimes just sort of disappear in the middle, you know what I mean?"

The doctor nodded sympathetically.

"The day before yesterday, it just didn't work. Zero."

"So, total erectile failure only occurred one time? The day before yesterday?"

He nodded mournfully.

"Had you anything to drink?"

"Half a glass of wine. Doc, she was a good-looking woman. We were in the Jacuzzi . . ."

They were interrupted by the phone buzzing.

"Excuse me," the doctor said, and picked up the receiver. "Yes?"

Woody could see the annoyance in the doctor's face as he listened to his receptionist, then took the call.

"Audrey, I'm with a patient . . ." There was a long pause as the doctor doodled absently on his prescription pad and listened.

"All right."

More doodling, then: "Large anchovy and sausage?"

Another minute of listening, and then he said, "Around seven. See you then. Right . . ."

And he hung up. "I'm terribly sorry, Mr. Monroe."

"Your wife?"

The doctor nodded. It was a moment of connection between them, even though *his* wife didn't call *him* in *his* office to bring *him* home an anchovy-and-sausage pizza. No, *his* wife was too busy fucking her ice-skater . . .

"Let me try to put you in a comfort zone here, Mr. Monroe. I seriously doubt that there is a fifty-six-year-old man on this earth who hasn't had trouble producing an erection at least once. There is, at your age, a completely natural reduction in the amount of testosterone that your body secretes. E.D. is not uncommon—"

"E.D.?"

"Erectile dysfunction. It's the clinical name for this condition. So, I'm going to give you a little test to take home with you. It's called the I.I.E.F., the International Index of Erectile Function. It'll take you ten minutes, and then we can evaluate your condition a little more scientifically."

"You want me to take a test?" Woody mumbled.

"Yes. The I.I.E.F. is a very useful tool. It gives us answers not just in the domain of erectile dysfunction but also in the domain of sexual desire and intercourse satisfaction. In any event, the good news is that if you *are* diagnosed with E.D., there are new oral medications coming on the market very soon. There's Viagra, there's Vasomax . . ."

"How soon?"

"As a matter of fact, the FDA is expected to clear Viagra for use in April. You're looking at a month or so."

"What if I didn't want to wait a month?"

"Mr. Monroe, are you under a lot of stress at the moment?"

"And what if it turns out that my . . . E.D. is actually due to something else? What if my testosterone level is subnormal?"

"Well, then, you could undergo a course of testosterone-replacement therapy."

"With what?"

"There are a number of products on the market these days—there's Androderm, there's Testoderm—patches you attach to your body, somewhat like nicotine patches. But instead of secreting nicotine, they secrete testosterone—about five milligrams into the bloodstream over the course of twenty-four hours . . ."

"I want some."

"Look, I think you ought to wait for Viagra . . ."

"Can you write me a prescription for Testoderm?"

Dr. Haas leaned back in his chair and ran his fingers through his sparse brown hair. It was perfectly quiet in the room. Outside the phone was ringing.

"First of all we don't even know if you're testosterone-deficient. We'd have to run some tests. And testosterone-replacement therapy doesn't always work. And it sometimes has side effects."

"Like what?"

"Like edginess and loss of appetite. And some men report having erections at inopportune times."

"I can deal with that."

"I'll want to monitor this . . ."

"No problem."

The doctor took out his prescription pad and scribbled on it. He tore off the page and handed it to Woody. "I'm giving you a thirty-day supply of Testoderm. It'll take a week or two to have any effect. We'll run the blood tests in the meanwhile."

"Thank you."

"It works best when applied to the back of your shaved scrotum."

"Really?"

"Yes. Shaving the scrotum is fairly delicate. I would suggest having your wife do it for you. You are married, right?"

"Twice," Woody replied.

There was no way he would allow either one of them anywhere near his scrotum with a razor blade.

5.

PATCHING THINGS UP

AT HALF PAST SIX that evening, Woody flew back into National, under the radar, carrying a copy of the International Index of Erectile Function questionnaire and a box of thirty Testoderm patches in his attaché case.

On the plane, he had put the questionnaire inside the cover of a position paper, "The Decline of Arable Dairy Farming Acreage in Northern Vermont," and had taken a peek.

1. Over the last month, how often were you able to get an erection during sexual activity?

   0 No sexual activity
   5 Almost always or always
   4 Most times (much more than half the time)
   3 Sometimes (about half the time)
   2 A few times (much less than half the time)
   1 Almost never or never

2. Over the last month, during sexual intercourse, how often were you able to maintain your erection after you had penetrated (entered) your partner?

   0 Did not attempt intercourse
   5 Almost always or always

4 Most times (much more than half the time)
3 Sometimes (about half the time)
2 A few times (much less than half the time)
1 Almost never or never

There were a total of fifteen such questions divided into five different domains—erectile function, orgasmic function, sexual desire, intercourse satisfaction, and overall satisfaction. You graded yourself in each area and then added it all up to get a total. If your E.Q., your Erectile Quotient, was less than a certain number, then you had E.D.

Woody started to tote up his E.Q., and then, thinking better of it, quickly returned to the decline of arable dairy-farming acreage. If there was one thing a man did not want to know—especially when he was drinking Scotch in a plastic glass at 37,000 feet—it was his E.Q.

A man could handle knowing his cholesterol level, his PSA score, his blood pressure, but his E.Q. . . . There was no way you wanted to stare that in the face. Either it worked or it didn't. You didn't need to know the numbers.

In the cab back to his office, he called Ishmael.

"The snow off the roof, Senator?"

"Yes."

"Are you coming to the office?"

"I don't know. Should I?"

"I've been telling people that you have food poisoning."

"Food poisoning?"

"Yes. Food poisoning is usually a twenty-four-hour proposition. This gives you some flexibility. Would you like the top ten?"

"Shoot."

Ishmael read off the names—the Minority Whip, whom he had stood up for lunch; Trent Lott's office; his insurance agent; several other senators with whom he was on various committees; Beverly; and Lee Schumock. Notably absent from his phone log was the name of his wife.

He dialed Daphne's office and was told by her secretary, Brandon, that she was with a client. Woody asked him to buzz her anyway. If the urologist could talk to *his* wife while Woody was sitting in his office discussing the future of his sex life, Brandon could buzz Daphne while she was advising some multinational corporate head, at $575 an hour, about the progress of his litigation.

"What is it?" she asked, irritated.

"Can you tell me why a hummingbird hums?"

"Woody, I'm in conference."

"'Cause he don't know the words."

There was a deep, audible sigh on the other end of the line before he made the suggestion.

"How about dinner at nine? At the house?"

"I don't know if I can make it."

"You do live there, Daphne. At least in theory. It would be nice if you made an appearance now and then. I'll have Dario make shrimp risotto." He clicked off before she could say no.

As he sat in the cab and watched the Capitol dome loom into view, he wondered what the hell he was going to say to his wife over Dario's shrimp risotto. There was so much to say. And so little.

All he had was circumstantial evidence. There had been a photo in a Washington magazine of Daphne and the ice-skater together in a downtown disco. That, the trip to Helsinki, and the phone-machine message that he'd picked up at the house.

Then there was the fact that he and his wife no longer slept together. Which was certainly not what they called in law school prima facie evidence. They had abandoned sex with each other years ago. Not that it had ever been great shakes in the first place.

He had married Daphne in 1987, a year after his election to the Senate. She was attractive, witty, and well connected. The Melancamps were Virginia rural gentry with less money than they pretended to have. Her growing up with the patina of wealth helped explain her cupidity.

By the beginning of Woody's second term, in 1993, theirs had become largely a marriage of convenience. Being married to a United States senator, even one from Vermont, was good for both business and cachet, and Daphne dined out on it to the tune of a partnership in Meagen, Forresy, Bryce.

For his part, he got a woman who could hold her own at a dinner party and who looked terrific in a black cocktail dress at a White House reception. In his own humble opinion, Woody had the best looker in the Senate, which counted for a lot. You didn't stop comparing dicks just because you had taken an oath to uphold the Constitution.

The timing was extremely delicate. Any open breach in their marriage now, seven months before the election, would sink him even lower than Irwin Posalski had predicted.

Therefore, even before he drove into the garage in McLean, he had resolved to finesse the situation.

The aroma of shrimp sautéing in Madeira floated through the house. Helmut, the dachshund, waddled out to greet him. Woody stared him down, and the dog retreated into the kitchen.

The housekeeper was standing at the butcher-block table slicing shrimp, expertly slitting the bellies and then laying them lovingly into the gently simmering 100 percent virgin olive oil, which Dario had had sent directly from Genoa, at $128 a pint.

"*Buona sera, senatore.*"

"Good evening, Dario. Where is Mrs. White?"

"*Alla sua camera, senatore.*"

Daphne's bedroom was actually the master bedroom, on the second floor. Woody slept in the guest wing, off the den on the ground floor.

Daphne made her appearance at twenty past nine wearing a tight-fitting knit suit without the jacket, a silk blouse, and a pair of shoes that must have cost her a billable hour or two. She had taken off her office earrings and put on a long, filigreed pair that he had bought her on a trade mission to Barcelona.

It was an odd mixture of the casual and the premeditated. She sat down at the other end of the dining-room table, which Dario had set with the good silver, forgoing the peck on the cheek she would have given him had they been in public. He poured her a glass of wine. She took a sip and said, "You look a little peaked."

"Twenty-four-hour food poisoning. A Spanish omelet yesterday in Burlington. I'm okay now."

Dario brought the prosciutto and melon on their Limoges china, a wedding present from his son, who had made a small fortune wholesaling marijuana in Florida.

They ate quickly, small-talking sporadically and listening to the sound of the silver against the exquisite faienced surface of the china. The risotto was a triumph. They had to praise it lavishly to Dario before he would go away.

"*Grazie tante.*"

He brought the *frutta* and *formaggio* and withdrew to the den to watch Jerry Springer.

Woody cut a slice of *bel paese* and said, "You're probably wondering why I've asked you here tonight."

"Woody, don't be a wiseass. I've had a hell of a day, and I'm really tired. So if you've got something you want to say to me, just say it."

"I've got a lot of things I want to say to you."

"Pick one."

He looked across the table at her. She was well worth the $575 an hour. She understood leverage. Never reveal the agenda until your opponent has revealed his.

"Okay. Here it is. As you know, I am running for reelection. I am anticipating a difficult campaign this time, for a number of reasons I won't bore you with. So, getting right to the point, what I want to know is, are you going to make it even more difficult?"

Taking a sip from the decaf espresso that Dario had left behind with the fruit and cheese, she considered her words before replying.

"Well," she said, after a moment, "if you mean am I willing to eat Rotary Club Jell-O squares on a bed of soggy white lettuce in Rutland, I suppose I can probably manage a bit of that from time to time."

She nodded, as if she herself had asked the question. Then she said, "I could be helpful to you, Woody."

"What does *that* mean?"

"Precisely what it says."

"You *could* be?"

"Yes. Or I could be unhelpful to you."

"How so?"

"You don't want to know that."

"I see. Just how helpful can you be?"

"As helpful as I was in '86 and '92."

"I thought you actually enjoyed rubbing elbows with the movers and shakers."

"Woody, I've sat next to Dick Gephardt all I need to in this life."

Woody drained his espresso and wiped his mouth with the silk napkin. Daphne was terrific at fund-raisers. She knew that the secret to pleasing men was to let them talk. The way to a man's heart, she had once confided in him, was through his ego.

"So, Daphne, am I to understand that there's a price involved for your help?"

"I wouldn't put it quite that way."

"How would you put it?"

"I wouldn't put it at all."

They held each other's look for a moment, then she said, "Woody, we're not going to say what doesn't have to be said, are we?"

She smiled at him. It was a beautiful smile, a smile that accentuated her fine bone structure and lovely skin. There was in that smile an offer of complicity. He knew there was a price and when it came, as it inevitably would, it would be the maximum that he could afford.

As it turned out, he had learned what he needed to learn without having to say what neither of them wanted said. In that sense, the dinner had been a success.

So he shook his head.

"Good," she said.

"You'll let me know, then?"

"Uh-huh."

"When?"

"Soon."

Ishmael was smack in the middle of delicate and extended foreplay with Maud when his beeper went off.

"Shit!" he moaned and gingerly unclasped her legs from around his neck.

"What an exquisite sense of timing," Maud sighed as he rummaged for his trousers on the floor.

"Where the fuck are my pants?"

"Just follow the beeping sound," she said.

He located his trousers, shut the beeper off, and went downstairs to dial the senator's cell.

"Hello?" Woody whispered into the phone.

"Yes, Senator."

"I need you to get me a breakfast tomorrow morning with Hank Leventhal at INS."

"I would have to reach him at his home, either tonight or very early tomorrow morning in order to schedule a breakfast with him, and I don't have his home number."

"Make it a lunch."

"Time and place?"

"The Monocle at one?"

"You run the risk of running into the Minority Whip there. You're supposed to have food poisoning."

"Well, pick some out-of-the-way place, then."

"What if he's not available?"

"He will be."

The senator hung up, leaving Ishmael naked and shivering in Maud's kitchen.

It was eleven-thirty at night. He'd have to get into the office early, find an appropriate restaurant, call over to INS, arrange the lunch. Why hadn't he turned the beeper off?

Upstairs, Maud had no doubt signed off for the night. The moment had been tenuous enough. Her daughter had been cranky and had refused to go to sleep. They'd had to wait till nearly eleven before getting into bed together.

He had proceeded slowly, painstakingly, and it was just at the moment when she appeared finally to have let go of her day, her cranky daughter, her problems at work, just at the moment when the yellow flag was down at last and the track was clear, that the fucking beeper went off.

He went back upstairs and got into bed beside her.

"I'm sorry," he whispered and slipped one hand around a breast.

She removed his hand from her breast.

"You want me to go?"

"You were never here," she replied and pulled the covers tightly around her.

The restaurant was on K Street, off New York Avenue. It was one of those touristy places that featured Dolly Madison apple cobblers and waitresses in eighteenth-century roadhouse-wench dresses. Nobody who was anybody ever went there, which was why Ishmael had chosen it for Woody's discreet lunch with the guy from the INS.

The senator sat in a booth in the rear, across from Hank Leventhal, a Vermonter whom he had helped get transferred from the Burlington INS office to the main office in Washington. As favors went, it was a pretty decent one—a real career opportunity for Leventhal, as well as a substantial pay raise.

So when their Thomas Jefferson prime ribs arrived, Woody began by focusing on the positive.

"So, how's life, Hank?"

"Couldn't be better, Senator."

"You're pulling down, what, a hundred-five, a hundred-ten?"

"One-thirteen-five, plus the IRA."

"Jesus, the poor taxpayers. Medical plan, low-rate mortgage, the whole entitlement package. Where's the house?"

"Silver Spring."

"I love Silver Spring. Kids in school?"

"Silver Spring Academy."

"That must cost you an arm and a leg."

"Twelve a piece. And that's without the bus."

"Well, I got to hand it to you, Hank. You've come a long way. Shit, I can remember when you were freezing your nuts off in Burlington, running Canucks back across the border. Now here you are, an office in the Chester A. Arthur Building, attaching people's bank accounts."

Woody waited for all that to percolate into the soil that he had just prepped with his hoe. Then, as the Dolly Madison apple cobblers arrived, he laid it out.

"Suppose I asked you for a little help on something, Hank?"

"You name it, Senator."

"I'd like you to look into a green-card application for me."

"Well, sure, but . . . I'm in asset forfeiture. You'd do better with someone in adjudications and naturalizations."

"You're in the same building with them, aren't you? You make a call. How hard is that?"

Their wench came over to refill the coffee cups. Leventhal waited for her to withdraw before leaning toward Woody and saying, "Where is this person from?"

"Finland."

"Finland?"

"That's right. Helsinki."

"You know, we don't have a whole lot of employment-visa requests from Finland. They've got close to full employment over there." Hank Leventhal looked around carefully, lowered his voice, and asked, "Is there any particular reason you want me to look into this?"

Woody leaned forward and said, in the confidential tone he often used in questioning witnesses in front of his subcommittee, "If I told you, then you'd know more than you needed to know. Your deniability would be compromised."

"Uh-huh . . . Well, the only reason is . . . the guy in A and N is probably going to ask me why."

"Just say it's a request from the Senate Immigration Subcommittee."

"I didn't know you were on that committee."

"I'm not. Hank, this is strictly need-to-know stuff, you understand what I'm saying?"

Hank Leventhal nodded and returned to his apple cobbler.

"And, believe me, you don't want to know," Woody continued.

"Uh-huh."

"You know what would have happened if John Poindexter had told Ronald Reagan where those funds for the Contras were coming from? We'd have had George Bush two years earlier."

"You think so?"

"You kidding? They'd have reconvened the Ervin committee, and the next thing you knew, Ronnie would have been in the helicopter with Nancy waving good-bye from the South Lawn. You see, there would've been no deniability. That's what saved Reagan, Hank. Deniability."

Woody handed Hank Leventhal the piece of paper with his wife's lover's name on it.

"Just see what you can find out about the immigration status, all right?"

"All right."

Leventhal put the piece of paper in his pocket without looking at it.

"Uh . . . what does . . . he do for a living?"

"It's a she. And she's an ice-skater."

"N.A.H.P.I."

"Evelyn Brandwynne, please."

"May I tell her who's calling?"

"Senator White."

"Just a moment please, Senator."

Woody sat alone in his office, on the red phone, having sent Lee Schu-mock off to lunch with Ishmael. As he waited for her to pick up, he glanced at the TV monitor broadcasting Floor debate. The alarm buzzer was at nine minutes to a vote. He tacked on another five minutes for the time it would take before his name was called, the forty-eighth on the al-phabetized list of senators. Fourteen minutes and counting. It was going to be tight.

"Hi there," she said, picking up.

"How are you, Evelyn?"

"*You* tell *me*, Senator."

"Your bill's alive."

"Well, then, so am I."

"You free tonight?"

"I could be."

"Evelyn, I need a favor from you."

"Shoot."

"I can't tell you over the phone."

"All right. Where and when?"

"My apartment at ten."

A moment of silence, then, "Sounds like I'm going to be doing some se-rious lobbying."

"You have no idea how serious."

He hung up and hurried out of his office, getting to the cloakroom with two minutes to spare. The Minority Whip looked up from his vote tally-ing and said, "How's the stomach?"

"Better."

"What got you?"

"Spanish omelet."

And Woody pushed the door into the chamber. They were up to the S's.

"Mr. Sarbanes, Mr. Shelby, Mr. Smith, Ms. Snowe . . ."

As Woody walked down the aisle, he saw Trent Lott watching the tally. He should have asked the Minority Whip if they needed his vote. If they didn't, Woody could have cut a deal with the Majority Leader—his vote for fifteen hundred in cash, down and dirty and nonreportable.

"Mr. Specter, Mr. Stevens, Mr. Thomas, Mr. Thompson . . ."

He had almost reached the well when he suddenly couldn't remember which way he was voting or, for that matter, what the bill was he was voting on. It was happening more and more frequently of late, these bouts of short-term-memory loss.

He sat down at a desk, closed his eyes, and tried to concentrate.

"Mr. Tremaine, Mr. Wallingford, Mr. Whetstone . . ."

All he could think of was his appointment with Evelyn Brandwynne that evening and the amount of trust he was putting into her hands.

"Mr. White, Mr. Young, Mr. Zabriskie . . ."

At the sound of his name, it came back to him. They were voting on an appropriations bill out of the Environment and Public Works Committee to establish a federally protected wetlands in Maryland. Your basic ecologists-versus-local-business-interests vote. He didn't owe Sarbanes or Mikulski anything at the moment. Your basic no-brainer.

Woody opened his eyes and stuck his thumb up.

"So how much should I take off?" she asked.

"Everything," he replied.

"Everything?"

"Uh-huh."

"I think I ought to use very little, don't you?"

"I don't know. How's your eyesight?"

"I've got my reading glasses on."

"That's comforting."

"Okay. Ready?"

He nodded and closed his eyes.

"You're not going to watch?"

"Nope."

She took some warm water from a basin beside the bed and applied it. Then she shook the shaving-cream can.

Gently, she spread the shaving cream over the surface area, as described in the instructions on the package. As she did this, he let his mind wander, but the more it wandered, the more it came back to the situation at hand, which was developing in an unforeseen direction.

"Uh, Woody . . . ," she said.

"What?"

"Something's happening."

"Yeah, I know."

"Should I continue?"

"Yes."

"With the procedure, or with—"

"What do you mean?"

"Maybe we ought to forget about the procedure, I mean, given what's happening."

"It's probably just temporary."

"I don't know. It looks pretty . . . permanent to me."

"Oh . . ."

"What if we tried it out?"

"Tried it out?"

"Took it out for a spin."

"Hmm . . ."

"It'd be a shame to let it go to waste, don't you think?"

"Uh-huh . . ."

He kept his eyes closed and listened to the sound of zippers and snaps.

"You want to take the cream off?" he asked, his eyes still closed.

"Let's leave it on," she said in a breathy whisper, as she straddled him and very slowly, very delicately, took a seat.

6

AFRICAN AFFAIRS

THE AFRICAN AFFAIRS SUBCOMMITTEE of the Senate Foreign Relations Committee met on Friday afternoons in a small, overheated committee room on the third floor of the Dirksen Building. Though still a backwater committee, it was a little less backwater than Waste Control and Risk Assessment, and, as the ranking Democrat, Woody wielded a certain amount of power in the room.

In '95, during the heat of his ethics problems, Woody had headed a congressional delegation that toured West Africa to evaluate foreign-aid needs in the region. They visited ten countries in ten days, ate a lot of exotic food, took photos of themselves at nascent public-works projects, danced the high life, and returned with a majority recommendation that aid to the region be cut.

The West Africans didn't have a lot of clout on the Hill and were thrown to the budget dogs. Woody had put up a fight against the cuts, but the committee voted straight down the middle of the aisle, and the cuts were brought to the Floor, where they sailed through on a rider to a transportation bill.

As a result, Senator Woodrow White emerged as a champion of West African economic aid. Parcels arrived in his office containing colorful cloth robes, indigenous folk sculpture, musical instruments made from the skin of obscure animals, an ossified wild boar's penis.

On this Friday, the day after his successful late meeting with the lobbyist from the National Association of Health Prophylaxis Industries, Senator Woodrow White was feeling particularly feisty, and so when the chair-woman suggested that they table an aid-appropriation bill for the tiny West African country of Togo, effectively killing it, Woody protested.

"Madam Chairperson," he began, "the Republic of Togo has always been a friend of this country. There is a history of cooperation and under-standing between Washington and Lomé dating back to the first Peace Corps volunteers sent over there in 1962. Of course, you may be too young to remember this, but when John F. Kennedy said, 'Ask not what your country can do for you, ask what you can do for your country,' thou-sands of Americans flocked abroad to countries, such as Togo, to begin forging a tradition of aid and cooperation that has stood us well through the years. . . ."

Laptops began to click in the back of the committee room, where sev-eral observers in native dress were sitting.

"As you know, Madam Chairperson," he continued, referring to the notes prepared for him by a legislative aide, "Togo is not a wealthy coun-try. Its per-capita GDP is nine hundred dollars. Average life expectancy is fifty-six years. There is one physician for every thirteen thousand people in Togo. Do you know what that ratio is in this country, Madam Chair-person?"

The laptops started clicking more furiously as he answered his own question, "One for every four hundred . . . Infant mortality? In Togo we're looking at eighty-two deaths for every thousand live births. What do you suppose we're looking at here?"

"I appreciate the senator from Vermont's concern for the Togolese peo-ple," the chairwoman responded, "but we are debating the merits of legis-lation to allocate forty million dollars for phosphate mining in Togo. And I, frankly, don't see the relevance of infant mortality to phosphate min-ing."

"Allow me to elucidate the issue for the senator from Maine. Every sin-gle kilogram of phosphate that is successfully mined, Madam Chair-person, will contribute to the improvement of economic conditions in Togo, which in turn will provide better nutrition, better prenatal care, bet-ter medical facilities . . ."

By the time Woody was finished, he had mopped the floor with her. If only the Togolese could vote in the Vermont senatorial election. In the end, however, he got only one of the two Republican committee votes he needed to kill the motion, and the bill was tabled.

On his way out, the chairperson stopped him and said, "You know, Senator, I was in high school when Kennedy made that speech."

"That so?"

"I wanted to join the Peace Corps. But I was too young."

"I'm sure the Togolese people would appreciate the sentiment," he said, then added, "Might rain," before walking out the door.

He'd send the next ossified wild boar's penis he received to the senator from Maine's office. He'd get it laminated and engraved. FROM THE PEOPLE OF TOGO.

The taste of blood still in his mouth, Woody poured himself a Chivas, swiveled in his chair, and looked out at the flow of early rush-hour traffic along Constitution Avenue. In two weeks the cherry blossoms would be in full bloom, and Washington would be invaded by high school students. Woody would have to get his ass up to Vermont, where it wouldn't really be spring for at least another month, and get himself reelected.

The Republicans were running a woman against him—a former state's attorney from Burlington named Rebecca Gatney, who was going to go after him on everything from the zipper problem to his absentee voting record.

Running a woman against him was a clear attempt to co-opt his power base. According to Irwin Posalski, it was the women and the students that got him elected in '86 and reelected in '92.

In order to counterattack quickly and forcefully against Rebecca Gatney, Woody needed to build up the campaign war chest. He needed an infusion of serious cash to finance TV ads. Otherwise, it was going to be a lot of Jell-O squares in Rutland.

It was time to go to work. And, for the first time in a while, Woody felt up to it. His Erectile Quotient had climbed into the "moderate to high" range.

His successful lobbying session with Evelyn Brandwynne last night had imbued him with optimism. It was amazing what a "moderate to high" E.Q. could do for a man's self-esteem. A few more successful outings, and he could move up to "high to very high." And there was no stopping a man walking around with a "high to very high" E.Q.

He had woken up that morning feeling like a rooster on his way to the henhouse. Over breakfast, he gave his biographer an hour of inspiring material about his youth. Then he went onto the Floor for morning business and, during special orders, got a good twelve minutes of C-SPAN coverage on a bill promoting clean drinking water.

Lunch with the Minority Whip was reassuring. He was pledged party support and as much soft money as they could slip his way. Then the subcommittee meeting and his rhetorical victory over the chairwoman.

Woody swiveled back and opened the files of prospective nominees for the seat on the Second Circuit. He leafed through them, skim-reading the

résumés and letters of reference. They were all more or less equally qualified. Except for Vincent Ruggiero. Vincent Ruggiero was more equally
qualified.

Woody's first call was to the White House. Invoking senatorial courtesy,
he pitched Vincent Ruggiero to the President's chief aide for judicial appointments and was assured prompt action if everything checked out.

Then he dialed Montpelier.

"VMSDA."

"Yes, this is Senator White. Is Mr. Adams available?"

"You betcha, Senator," Abigail Adams replied.

It was only a matter of seconds before the inflectionless voice of John
Quincy Adams came over the phone. "Senator, how are you doing?"

"Very well, Mr. Adams. And how are you, sir?"

"Well, except for a little backup problem with the septic tank, I can't
complain."

"I know how you feel. I had a tank back up on me a couple of years
ago. You don't want to be downwind of a backed-up septic tank, do you?"

"No, sir."

"Mr. Adams, let me tell you why I'm calling . . ."

The steam room in the Senate Health Facility, as it was now officially
called instead of the more familiar Senate Gym, was the type of place
where you could lose a pound or two of excess water weight while you
were trawling for support on a piece of legislation. In the midst of the wet
steam, partisan politics were replaced by a sort of bonhomie that was fos-
tered, perhaps, by the humbling sight of the naked middle-aged male body
devoid of any type of sartorial or cosmetic embellishment. It was difficult
to posture with your belly hanging out.

What you saw was what you got.

Woody sat up on the top tier that Friday evening after having done his
pro forma twenty-minutes on an Exercycle. Sitting naked on a towel, feeling the perspiration trickling down his chest, he half-listened to the desultory conversation of three older senators on the other side of the steam
room.

"They're going to have to carry Strom out on his sword. Shit, he's old
enough to be my father, and I'm seventy-six."

The voice was high-pitched and southern, and Woody knew who it belonged to. One of the things he liked about the steam room was the ersatz
anonymity caused by the steam. You could recognize a voice but you
couldn't see a face unless you were sitting right beside the person.

"You stick around here longer than Strom, they'll have to plant you in the lobby."

"Byrd's been here since '59."

"What about Teddy?"

"Teddy came in '62."

"Teddy almost didn't make it back in '94."

"The old zipper problem."

"Yeah. Well, at least he's still here. He didn't have to fall on his sword like Packwood."

"Packwood didn't have a zipper problem. Packwood had a public-relations problem."

"Packwood had a Boxer problem."

"She went after him the way Nixon went after Alger Hiss. She hung poor Bob's balls up on the wall of the Women's Caucus Room."

"Right next to Wilbur's."

"Let that be a lesson to all of us."

"Yes, sir. You got to watch your ass these days."

"My ass is too old to have to watch anymore."

A round of soft, self-pitying laughter. Then, a series of sighs.

"Tell you what I think. I think it won't be long before they start giving us spot checks. You know, the way they do with ballplayers, swooping down on them and telling them to go pee in a bottle."

"You really think they're going to give United States senators random drug tests?"

"Not drug tests. Ethics tests. They're going to hook us up to polygraphs and ask us if we ever got a woodie when the secretary bent over the desk or made a phone call to try to get a lobbyist's kid into Yale."

"You think it'll come to that?"

"Yes, sir, I do."

Woody wondered if they knew he was up there. Was this conversation for his benefit? They were all three of them Republicans. His seat was hanging like a ripe piece of fruit about to drop off into the Republican bushel.

After the next exchange, however, he was convinced that either they didn't know he was there or they didn't give a shit.

"'Course, Woody White's about to get *his* ass handed to him."

"Think so?"

"Uh-huh. I hear the Democrats have already conceded the seat."

There was a moment of silence. Woody listened to the sweat drip. Then he heard the senator from North Carolina say, "You ask me, it's no great loss."

7

QUID PRO QUO

"WHAT?"

"It arrived Friday."

"I'm already paying her twenty-three hundred and fifty bucks a month. How much more does she want?"

"She's leaving that for the court to determine."

Woody glared across the exquisite burl-wood desk of his lawyer, Phil Yalowitz, a short, dapper man about his own age who had handled his divorce from number one in 1987.

"She's claiming change of circumstances."

"What change of circumstances? If anything, I'm broker now than I've ever been."

"Her attorney mentioned your book deal."

"C'mon, Phil. I only got a third up front, and after taxes and commissions, it's gone."

"Unfortunately, these determinations are based on gross income. If you remember, we have to send a copy of your federal tax return to her every year."

"So I just have to give her the money?"

"No. We can contest it . . ."

"But?"

"Before we get into that, there's another matter I have to bring up."

"Oh, boy . . ."

"You want some more coffee?"

"No."

"We have decaf."

"Just lay it out for me, Phil, will you?"

The lawyer folded his exquisitely manicured hands in front of him and exhaled. Deeply.

"The day after I received the Order to Show Cause from Sharon's attorney, I received a call from an attorney at Hotchkiss Behrend on behalf of your present wife. Hotchkiss Behrend, as you know, is also a firm that specializes in family law."

Woody felt his blood sugar dip about fifty feet. He rubbed his eyes wearily, even though it was only a little after ten in the morning, and asked, "Is she filing?"

"Frankly, I'm not sure what she's doing."

"What do you mean?"

"The lawyer said to me that he would like an itemized list of assets, both community and preexisting. When I asked him why, he said I should ask you."

"An itemized list of assets?"

"Yes."

"Why would she want that?"

Phil Yalowitz unfolded his hands and looked across the desk at Woody, as if to say, *You* tell *me*.

Woody got up from the expensive leather chair that he had helped pay for with the 1987 bloodletting and paced a few times across the even more expensive Berber carpet.

"Okay," he said after a moment, turning to face his lawyer, "the marriage is a little shaky. But it's been this way for years. And I was under the impression that she was satisfied with the status quo. This . . . I mean, couldn't this be construed as some sort of extortion?"

"Not without a quid pro quo."

"You need a quid pro quo?"

"To establish extortion, we would have to document what she was extorting you *about*."

"I'm running for reelection. She's threatening not to help me. Isn't that extortion?"

"There is no marital obligation, either explicit or implicit, to help a spouse get reelected to public office."

There was a long silence as Woody tried to get a grip on his emotions. Then his lawyer stole a quick glance at his watch and asked, "How would you like me to respond?"

"Fuck her."

"All right. I'll inform the lawyer that we see no reason to comply with this request absent a court order. Now, about Sharon . . ."

"Fuck her too."

He had Hank Leventhal beeped out of a staff meeting. When the asset-forfeiture associate director got on the phone, Woody explained that there were now more pressing reasons to accelerate the investigation of the immigration status of the Finnish ice-skater.

"I'm doing what I can on that, Senator."

"I appreciate that, but there's been a reprioritizing on the committee."

Woody glanced at his taxi driver to make sure he was listening to the radio.

"Hank," he said in a tone just above a whisper, "tell me something. Under what circumstances can you have someone deported?"

"Deported?"

"Yes."

"Well . . . I mean, there's criminal activity, there's subversion, there's violation of status. . . . Senator, are you trying to get this person deported?"

"Hank, let's not forget about your deniability."

"Uh-huh."

"Get back to me on this as soon as possible, okay?"

"Uh-huh."

Flipping the phone closed, Woody leaned back in his seat. He'd had the driver take him to the Capitol by a circuitous route, which was designed to keep him out of the building for a quorum call on a bill the Minority Whip was trying to delay. The Minority Whip had asked him to take one for the party by being absent in case the Republicans sent the sergeant at arms to his office to force him to appear for the quorum call.

Woody needed to stay on the good side of the Minority Whip. He had missed the last two party caucuses, and he was going to have to miss tomorrow's caucus as well. Beverly had told him, more or less point-blank, that if he didn't show up in Montpelier for a campaign strategy meeting, she was quitting.

So tomorrow he'd head up to Vermont, leaving Phil Yalowitz in Washington to do battle with numbers one and two, who had combined forces in a pincer attack on him. It was like the Hitler-Stalin pact of 1939. And he was Poland.

Sharon was just lazy and greedy. But Daphne was beyond that. Daphne was malevolent.

The fucking nerve of her to have a lawyer call to threaten him. It was developing into something beyond mere pre-divorce positioning. The years of what he thought was benign indifference on both their parts had festered, producing an animosity that threatened to erupt into open warfare. The one thing he couldn't afford right now was open warfare. And she knew it.

Lowering the radio, the driver looked back in the rearview mirror and asked, "Senator, you sure you don't want me to make time?"

"That's all right—I'm in no rush," he said, squinting at Thelonius Paxton's cab license.

"Are you married, Thelonius?"

"Yes, sir. Twenty-six years."

"You get any time off for good behavior?"

The cabbie laughed a big, throaty laugh and said, "No, sir. I'm doing hard time."

Thelonius Paxton laughed the tribal laugh. It was a guy joke, and the senator knew just when to trot it out.

Too bad the man didn't live in Vermont.

Woody checked his watch. The quorum call was scheduled for eleven. It was ten past. He flipped the phone and dialed Ishmael.

"Coast clear?"

"Ten-four, Senator."

"Be right in."

Woody put the cell in his pocket, and said, "You know something, Thelonius—maybe we ought to step on it after all."

He sat back in the taxi, closed his eyes, and thought about Evelyn Brandwynne and whether or not he wanted to take it back out for a test drive before he left for Vermont. It was risky. He could crash and burn and wind up back down in the "moderate to low" range.

A man's E.Q. was basically like a pitcher's Earned Run Average. It rose or fell with each appearance on the mound. How many times did you have to try it out before it became statistically significant? He could call Irwin Posalski and ask him. . . .

"Listen, Irwin, here's the raw data . . ."

Fuck it! He'd go back out on the mound and take his chances. He would just have to keep the ball low and hit the corners. As long as he stayed above "moderate," he was in the ballpark.

Roland Boyden was laying some boards over the expanding pool of brown muck in his front yard in West Plummersville, Vermont, fifteen miles of bad roads east of Montpelier, when a mud-splattered Buick Riviera pulled through the gate. Ethan Allen and John Stark got out of the Riviera, doing their best not to get their new boots too dirty.

"Coffeepot on?" John Stark asked.

"Not so as you'd know it," Roland Boyden replied.

"You mean to tell me that Ethan and I drove all the way out here to see you and we're not getting so much as a cup of coffee?"

Roland Boyden stared hard at them.

"Might rain," Ethan Allen said.

"I suppose I could put some on."

They walked over the boards and into Roland Boyden's kitchen, a dim room with a fire going in the stove, and sat down on the two rickety chairs at the oilcloth-covered table.

"Got any cookies to go with the coffee, Roland?" John Stark asked.

"About fourteen hundred of them?" Ethan Allen put in.

"Plus the icing," John Stark added.

"I was counting on a check coming in the mail . . ."

"We all got problems, Roland. Mr. Q.'s got a backed-up septic tank. Ralph Meunier told him they might have to dig up the entire yard."

"That a fact?"

"Afraid so. The thing about digging up the yard, Roland, is you got one big damn mess of mud lying there for weeks mixing with the chemicals and God knows what else out of the septic tank. You understand what I'm saying?"

Roland Boyden nodded.

"We're going to have to look at finding something to mop up the mess in Mr. Q.'s yard. Now we could use boards like you're using, or we could get a backhoe in there and shovel it away—"

"Or we could use you," John Stark broke in.

"Yes, sir. You'd be surprised how much of that stuff a human body could absorb. Am I right, John?"

"You bet, Ethan. I once had a dog got stuck in the yard during mud season. Hell, we didn't see him again till August."

"So are we making our point here, Roland?"

"I believe you are."

"Good. Because Mr. Q. is having Ralph Meunier start digging out the yard on Thursday. I figure a day or two after that, he should be swimming in shit."

"Saturday?"

"Saturday's the big day, Roland."

· · ·

The test drive was not a success. Woody came out of the box with his tires smoking but was lagging by the first turn and flat on the backstretch. He was dead by the clubhouse turn.

This time Evelyn Brandwynne had the wisdom to say nothing. They were in the bedroom of her tastefully furnished apartment in Georgetown. The clock at nearby Holy Trinity tolled eleven times, as if to rub it in.

She got out of bed and poured them both a glass of 1971 Chateau Petrus, which they had opened about an hour ago, when things were looking optimistic. Handing him the wine, she got back into bed beside him and grabbed the TV remote. It was either that or talking, and talking was perilous at the moment.

So they lay there side by side like an old married couple, backs against the headboard, watching the eleven o'clock news in silence.

There was a story about a battle in the Senate over a tariff provision of a trade bill. Sam Donaldson was interviewing the Majority Leader in his office on the Senate side of the Capitol.

"So, Senator, how do you think this is going to turn out?"

Trent Lott looked right past him at the camera and, therefore, right at Woody, who was lying amid the wreckage sipping Chateau Petrus with the lobbyist from the National Association of Health Prophylaxis Industries.

"Tell you the truth, Sam, it's going to be very close. Some of my colleagues on the other side of the aisle are putting their own interests ahead of the country's."

That afternoon the Majority Leader's office had called Woody's office and told Ishmael that the adjustor had increased the damage estimate to $5,500. Something about invisible frame damage that had not been apparent on first examination.

"Anybody in particular?" Sam Donaldson pressed.

"Well, I'd rather not get into name-calling here, Sam, but I think that if the bill goes down to defeat, the American people will know where to point the finger."

Woody clicked the remote, switching to coverage of a U.S. Attorney being interviewed in Burlington. The graphic read VINCENT RUGGIERO, U.S. ATTORNEY FOR VERMONT.

The reporter asked him if it was true that he was up for a federal judgeship. Ruggiero neatly sidestepped the question.

"At the moment my job is heading up the Organized Crime Task Force that has been working here in Vermont to prosecute criminals under the RICO statutes in place . . ."

Woody woke up suddenly from his depressive stupor and listened to the man he had just pitched the White House for the vacant seat on the Second Circuit speak about his pursuit of organized crime in Vermont. Then he remembered Beverly's warning about John Quincy Adams. Then he did the math.

He turned to Evelyn Brandwynne.

"Remember when Al D'Amato tried to get Reagan to offer Rudy Giuliani the directorship of the FBI?"

"Frankly, no."

"Then he tried to get him to run against Moynihan for the Senate in '88. You know why?"

"I haven't the foggiest."

"Because Giuliani was U.S. Attorney for the Southern District of New York and was investigating the Wedtech scandal."

Evelyn Brandwynne was still waiting for the punch line.

"D'Amato was up to his eyeballs in Wedtech."

"So . . . ?"

"What do you do when somebody's making your life miserable?"

"What?"

"Get him a better job."

8

THE VALISE-DENIAL STRATEGY

THEY WERE SITTING AROUND a conference table at the junior senator from Vermont's regional office on St. Paul Street in Burlington. Besides Beverly Levesque and Irwin Posalski, there were his other key Vermont people—his money man, Dickie Thong; his press secretary, Janine Caravaggio; his speechwriters, Brian Petrunich and Linda Mae Berken; and his pundit, Rav Monsjar.

Irwin started off the meeting by running the latest numbers.

"We're seeing a drop of three to five points in general satisfaction and five to seven on the character issues."

"Is this the zipper problem again?" Janine Caravaggio sighed. "I thought people were tired of that."

"Not Rebecca Gatney," Beverly said. "She's just getting warmed up. She had a press conference in Montpelier on Friday where she said that the senator was a disgrace to Vermonters."

She turned to Woody and said, "Sorry, Senator, but I thought it would be preferable to lay it all out on the table."

Woody smiled indulgently and nodded.

Brian Petrunich, a graduate of Princeton and the author of several books on political theory, asked, "What do we have on her?"

"Brian, we're not going to stoop to slinging mud back."

"Why not? It's mud season."

Ordinarily this remark would have gotten a laugh, but not on this gray early-mud-season Tuesday afternoon. There was a heaviness in the room, a feeling that in the face of the numbers, they were in for a steep uphill battle.

To make matters worse, Dickie Thong told them that the larder was nearly empty. They had spent most of what had been raised over the winter in early mailings, and there was very little left, certainly not enough for large-scale media ads.

"We need to start hitting the Rotary Club dinner circuit."

"Yes, but we need a message. We need to take the offensive here and tell the voters why they should send the senator back to Washington for another six years."

Rav Monsjar, a thin, ascetic man with a rumpled hippie look, sat quietly eating a bran muffin and listening to the debate. Rav Monsjar had spent those halcyon years of the sixties in various alternative living arrangements in Vermont. In 1972 he had published a book called *Composting Your Life,* which had wound up a cult classic and had enabled him to become a minor celebrity before drifting into the world of liberal political consultancy during the Reagan years. He lived on an old farm outside of Brattleboro and communicated mostly by e-mail, when he communiated at all.

When he finally spoke, a respectful hush came over the room. "You know what I'm hearing?" he said in his quiet, oracular voice. "I'm hearing the sound of numbers. They're marching around this room like a hoard of army ants eating everything in their sight. Irwin says the graphs are skewing this way or that way. Dickie says we're broke. Numbers. The thing about numbers is they're a zero-sum game. You can twist them any way you want and back again. If we respond to the numbers, then we become numbers ourselves."

"So what do you recommend?" Beverly asked.

"Consolidation."

"Excuse me?"

"Absorb the blows, neutralize them, consolidate them. Newton's First Law: A body at rest remains at rest unless acted upon by an external force."

The room was dead quiet as everyone looked at one another, wondering if Rav Monsjar had become completely unscrewed. It was well known that he had taken a lot of LSD in the sixties, and there was some doubt about the state of his brain cells.

"You see," Rav Monsjar said, "if we go out to meet her on her turf—that is, on *her* issues—we lose the value of the defense. We lose the fort."

"Are you suggesting that we simply ignore her?"

"No. We envelop her. And by enveloping her, we dispose of her. But we don't go out there and start yelling about the character issue, because there *is* no character issue. The character issue is her little valise that she drags around the state with her and opens up like someone selling patent medicine at the fair. But if you don't look in the valise, then you can't buy the medicine, right?"

"I don't get it," Brian Petrunich said. "We do *nothing*?"

"We just don't look in the valise, Brian. It's that simple."

"But if . . . if everyone else looks in it . . ."

"Brian, you don't get it. There *is* no valise."

The valise-denial strategy, or VDS, as it was referred to by the staff, was inaugurated the next day at the Rock of Ages Tourist Center in Graniteville. The senator stood out in the quarry and delivered an impromptu speech for a collection of Vermonters and tourists who were visiting the museum.

"We're as tough as granite and just as solid. We don't give in when we know we're right. And we don't drop the ball on the five-yard line," he perorated, freely mixing his metaphors.

After the smattering of polite applause, a young woman wearing a pin that had a picture of Woody with a line through it, shouted, "Rebecca Gatney says you're a disgrace to Vermont."

Woody took the remark on a clean hop and fired it right back. "You want to talk about a disgrace, young woman? Let me tell you what's a disgrace. A woman up in Burlington—a woman who as far as I know has never been to Washington—sitting around and tossing cow chips at someone who for the last twelve years has devoted every waking hour to the welfare of this state. I want to know where Rebecca Gatney was when seventy-two million dollars of federal highway funds were allocated to the widening of Route Ninety-one from White River Junction to St. Johnsbury. I want to know where Rebecca Gatney was when the Connecticut River Clean Water Act was passed. I want to know where Rebecca Gatney was when price supports for dairy farmers were included in the farm bill. I'll tell you where she was. She was sitting up in Burlington tossing cow chips. Now *that's* a disgrace."

It had been a while since he had thrown a punch at an opponent, and it felt good. He looked out at the crowd of people in the quarry and saw that he had won the round decisively. There was no point in overkill. He just had to retreat to his corner and wait for the mandatory eight-count.

"So," he concluded, "if she wants to come down here to the quarry and talk, I'll be here. We'll go back and forth right in front of you, and we'll see who's the disgrace to Vermont. And who's tossing the cow chips."

In the bus on the way down to Middlebury, where the senator was going to address the faculty and students of Middlebury College, Beverly said, "You were in midseason form, Senator."

"Shooting fish in the barrel, Beverly."

"In Vermont we don't say 'shooting fish in a barrel.' We say 'shooting deer at the salt lick.'"

"I'll remember that."

"You don't put freshwater fish in a barrel. You put them in a basket."

"Right."

"In Maine, or Massachusetts, you'd say fish in the barrel because they have seacoasts . . ."

There was no conceding a point to Beverly. She would hammer you over the head with it.

Woody wasn't thinking about the appropriateness of shooting fish in barrels in Vermont. He was thinking about Vincent Ruggiero. He had been thinking a lot about the U.S. Attorney ever since he saw him on TV at Evelyn Brandwynne's apartment.

On the plane up to Vermont, Woody had reached the conclusion that if John Quincy Adams was, in fact, doing an Al D'Amato with the Vincent Ruggiero nomination, there was no way to prove it—just as there had been no way of proving Al D'Amato's own Al D'Amato. And even if it were to be proved, there would have to be a known connection with Woody, or, as Phil Yalowitz would put it, a quid pro quo.

So Woody hadn't discussed with Beverly his conversation with John Quincy Adams or his phone call to the White House recommending the prosecutor for the vacant seat on the Second Circuit. He saw no point in giving people information they had no need to have.

Following Woody's speech at Middlebury, he went up to Vergennes for a potluck church supper.

After dinner he was speaking at the rostrum, trying his best not to belch up the succotash, when he noticed the little man in the earmuffs standing at the back of the hall beside a couple of large men in Sears overcoats.

When Woody was finished with his speech, John Quincy Adams gave him the thumbs-up sign. Woody did not reciprocate, but on his way out of the hall, the little man in the earmuffs came up beside him and said, "Way to go, Senator."

"Thank you. Septic tank still backed up?"

"Worse than my grandfather's bowels."

"Sorry to hear that."

"How's it going down in Washington, Senator?"

Woody looked around. Beverly had noticed him talking to John Quincy Adams and was approaching on the double.

"No problem. Like shooting a deer at the salt lick," he said quickly.

When Beverly reached them, John Quincy Adams looked at her and said, "How you doing, Miss Levesque?"

"Fine," she responded icily. She turned to Woody and said, "Senator, there's a reporter from the *Free Press* waiting for you in the van."

He nodded at her and then shook John Quincy Adams's hand.

"Nice to see you again, Mr. Adams."

"Likewise, Senator."

On the way to the van, Beverly said, "You shouldn't be seen with that man."

"We were just talking about his septic tank."

"Senator, that man could be up in front of a grand jury by this summer."

"Uh-huh . . ."

"I'm sorry. The senator will get on that as soon as he returns from Vermont."

"And when might *that* be?"

The voice was snide and southern, undoubtedly Ole Miss and Duke Law School. Ishmael was tempted to tell the man he hadn't the slightest idea—he hadn't, in fact, the slightest idea—but he knew he had to say something, so he told Trent Lott's chief of staff that it would be next week.

"The Majority Leader can't proceed with the repairs until the adjustor sees it."

"Well, it is drivable, isn't it?"

"Yes, it is drivable. But I don't think it behooves the Majority Leader of the United States Senate to be driving around Washington in a car with a damaged front end, do you?"

"Can't he rent something meanwhile?"

"His insurance policy provides rental-car coverage only after the adjustor has certified the damages and an accident report is filed."

"They'd reimburse him retroactively, I'm sure . . ."

Ishmael wondered how long it would take this effete schmuck to take off the gloves.

"Next week?" the chief of staff said, retreating into his southern passive-aggressiveness.

"At the earliest," Ishmael said.

"We'll . . . await your call, then."

"Good," Ishmael said and hung up.

He leaned back in his chair and smiled. At times like this, Ishmael realized just how much he had learned from Senator Woodrow White. He could antagonize with subtext, engage in conflict without taking the weapon out of the pocket. He had watched the senator reduce an opponent on the Floor to overaggressive counterattack by simply needling him to death.

When the phone rang again, however, it was Barry, and Barry didn't respond very well to subtext.

"You have any plans tonight?" Barry asked him.

"I don't know . . ."

"I thought that since your senator was in Vermont, you might actually have the night off."

"I have a lot of paperwork."

"Assign it to one of the junior staffers. Come on. What do you say we pick up a couple of salade niçoises from Regio, a baguette, and a bottle of Saumur from Henri Paul's, and rent *Beaches*?"

"*Beaches*?"

"You've *never* seen *Beaches*?"

"I don't think so."

"I can't believe you've never seen *Beaches*."

There was no way Ishmael was going to have a bottle of Saumur tête-à-tête with Barry at his apartment, but he couldn't think of any decent excuse at the moment. Fortunately, he was interrupted by a call from the senator.

"It's the senator calling from Vermont—got to run," Ishmael said and took the senator's call.

"Is Hank Leventhal from INS on the phone log?"

"Sorry, Senator, he hasn't called."

"Shit. How about Phil Yalowitz?"

"I'm afraid not."

Ishmael could tell from the senator's tone of voice that this was not the moment to get into the Trent Lott bodywork conversation. So he thought he'd say something light and amusing.

"You know what did arrive today, Senator?"

"What?"

"Two gallons of Vermont maple syrup."

"Where's it from?"

"The Vermont Maple Syrup Distributors Association in Montpelier."

There was a pause, then: "Listen: Ishmael, take it out the rear door and put it in the trunk of your car. Then dump it into the Potomac."

"You want me to dump the maple syrup into the Potomac?"

"Yes."

"You're allowed to keep nonmonetary gifts with a value of under a hundred dollars."

"Dump it."

"I could run it by the Ethics Committee . . ."

"Ishmael, dump it."

Ishmael put the receiver down and took a deep breath. But something occurred to him and he exhaled quickly. There was a bright side to having to drop two gallons of maple syrup into the Potomac. He couldn't watch *Beaches* with Barry. He had work to do.

9

BREAKING THE TAPE

IT HAD TO BE at least 102 degrees on the sunporch of Adele Hanna Weit's un-air-conditioned condominium, which backed onto the sixteenth hole of the Agua Caliente golf course in Palm Springs. Through the thermal glass, Lee Schumock could see the foursomes come and go, three-putting the tricky sloped green, as he listened to Senator Woodrow White's eighty-nine-year-old mother talk about the family's early years on the west side of Cleveland.

She sat in her motorized wheelchair, sipping vodka and prune juice, smoking Virginia Slims, and telling her son's biographer what it was like in the wood-frame house on De Kalb Street in Cleveland after her father disowned her for marrying a penniless carpet dealer from Hartford.

"We didn't have a goddamn pot to piss in. Herbert had just opened the store downtown on Euclid, and we were living on bank loans. Of course, my family could have bailed us out without blinking an eye, but my father said that if I married that Unitarian idiot, he wouldn't even show up at the wedding. Did you know that Mark Hanna was my great-uncle?"

"No, I didn't," Lee Schumock replied, even though he did.

"That's why Herbert named Woody after Woodrow Wilson. To piss off the Hannas. My great-uncle put William McKinley in the goddamn White House. Wasn't for Mark Hanna, we would've had William Jennings Bryan and the goddamn silver standard in 1896."

"So what type of kid was Woody?"

"A pain in the ass."

"Really? How so?"

"He was thinking all the time. He'd just lie in the goddamn crib and think. And the thing was, you didn't know what the hell he was thinking about."

Perspiration was trickling down from Lee Schumock's armpits. Adele Hanna Weit stared off through the window at the sixteenth hole, sucked on her prune juice and vodka, lit yet another Virginia Slim, and said nothing.

"How did he do in school?" the writer asked finally, trying to reprime the pump.

"Who remembers? He graduated goddamn law school, so I suppose he pulled it off, didn't he? He pulled everything off. Jesus, you should have seen his goddamn bedsheets when he was twelve . . ."

Before she told him, Lee Schumock quickly asked, "Was he popular in high school?"

"Woody was always popular. He could bullshit anybody. You got to watch your wallet when you talk to Woody. Did you know he owes me eighty-one hundred dollars?"

"No, I didn't know."

"Goddamn central air-conditioning went out. I had Woody take bids. Over the goddamn phone from goddamn Washington, of course. You'd think maybe he could come out here and help me out. I'm goddamn ninety-seven years old—"

"I thought you were only eighty-nine, Mrs. Weit."

"I told you, he bullshits everybody."

"What happened with the air-conditioning?"

"What air-conditioning? You see any air-conditioning around here?"

"So . . . did he have a lot of girlfriends in high school?"

"You kidding? Did I tell you about the bedsheets?"

"Uh . . . yes, you did . . . So when did the family move to Shaker Heights?"

"When Herbert started selling some goddamn carpets. We had wall-to-wall deep pile in Shaker Heights. You could walk barefoot on that goddamn carpet."

"And Woody went to the University School?"

"Who remembers?"

"They have him enrolled there in the ninth grade in 1956."

"They almost didn't take him because he was named Woodrow Wilson White. The Hannas endow the whole goddamn school."

"What about Ohio State?"

"What?"

"Ohio State, in Columbus. He went there from, 1960 to 1964."

"He brought his goddamn laundry home. You'd think he could afford to go to the goddamn Laundromat, but he comes home with a goddamn bag of laundry you could choke a cockroach with. And you don't want to know about the condition of his goddamn bedsheets . . ."

While Lee Schumock was debriefing Adele Hanna Weit in her condo in California, the senator was in his suite in the Capitol Plaza Hotel on State Street in Montpelier, eating lunch and debriefing Hank Leventhal in Washington.

"What the hell does that mean, Hank?"

"It means that she came here on a special ninety-day sports visa to work in the Ice Capades. When that ran out, she applied for a change of status. From a sports visa to a student visa. If you're enrolled in an accredited college or university, you can stay in the country with what we call an S-status visa."

"So she's enrolled in college?"

"According to her application for change of status, she intends to take a degree in women's studies at Georgetown."

"Intends?"

"Yes."

"Well, is she?"

"According to her application."

"Don't you guys check up on this?"

"We're supposed to, but between you and me, Senator, if we have an ice-skater from Finland who probably isn't going to wind up in jail or on the welfare rolls, then we don't always check."

Woody took a bite of his room-service club sandwich and asked, "Hank, let me ask you something. What would happen if it turned out that either she had never applied to Georgetown or she was no longer attending?"

"If she failed to report that to us, it would constitute a violation of status."

"What happens to status violators?"

"We give them ninety days to rectify the situation before instituting deportation procedures. They can appeal, but I suppose if we establish intention to defraud, we could deny the appeal."

"Wouldn't failure to report constitute, *ipso facto,* intention to defraud?"

There was some hesitation on the line. "Senator, I'm really not very comfortable with this matter."

"Hank, I'm sorry to hear that. But if I were you, I'd stretch my comfort zone just a little bit, say, as far as from I Street to Silver Spring."

Woody heard a deep sigh. "All right."

"Don't worry. Ollie North came out smelling sweet. He almost got elected to the Senate, didn't he?"

After his phone conversation with Hank Leventhal, Woody went on to an afternoon of rallies in Rutland and Manchester and a dinner of ski-resort owners in Wilmington, at which he spoke about his commitment to federal tax credits for the tourist industry. At nine the next morning, the senator woke up in the Wilmington Inn thinking about his E.Q. After the recent flatlining with Evelyn in Washington, he was down the graph again.

As it happened, Wilmington was only about fifty miles from Schenectady.

He ordered a stack of Molly Stark pancakes, picked up the phone, and dialed the urologist's office.

"Dr. Haas's office."

"Good morning. This is James Monroe. I'm calling to confirm my three-thirty."

"Excuse me?"

"I have a three-thirty with Dr. Haas this afternoon."

"I don't seem to have you listed today."

"I have the appointment card right here—three-thirty, Friday, March twenty-seventh."

"Are you absolutely sure?"

"Absolutely."

"We're really stacked up today—"

"See you at three-thirty."

Beverly would be trickier. He checked his schedule—a photo op at the Molly Stark Trail at eleven, a tour of a paper-products factory in Brattleboro, then a trip back up the mountain to Marlboro College, where he was due to address the student-faculty town meeting.

He could do Molly Stark and the paper factory, then grab a car in Brattleboro and be in Schenectady by three-thirty. The only thing he'd have to blow off was Marlboro College. Two hundred twenty-five students and forty teachers. Rebecca Gatney could have their votes.

In the men's room of the paper factory in Brattleboro, Woody asked Brian Petrunich for the keys to his rental car.

"I've got to run to Peru. See about my compost heap."

"What about Marlboro?"

"We'll reschedule."

"Does Beverly know?"

"You'll tell her."

At three-thirty the senator was sitting in Dr. Haas's waiting room, among the stacked-up middle-aged men, avoiding eye contact and reading a pamphlet entitled *Warning Signs of Prostate Cancer*.

By the time he was ushered in to see the doctor, Woody was convinced he had most of the symptoms.

"You know, Doc, maybe I should have a PSA."

Glancing at Woody's chart, he said, "We gave you one . . . nine days ago."

"You can't be too sure."

"Mr. Monroe, what's the problem today?"

Woody took a moment to collect himself. He really disliked having to confess these problems to the little man with the thinning hair. But he was due back in Manchester for a VFW dinner at seven-thirty, so he told the doctor about his two very different experiences with Evelyn Brandwynne. "I guess you'd have to say that it was inconclusive."

The intercom buzzed. The doctor picked up. "Yes?"

His features screwed up tightly, and he exhaled a sigh of displeasure. "Put her through . . . Audrey, I'm with a patient . . ."

Didn't this man's wife ever leave him alone?

"Lemon chicken, steamed dumplings, Szechuan noodles. Right? Seven . . . seven-thirty . . . Extra soy sauce . . ."

He hung up and apologized. Then, glancing at Woody's file, Dr. Haas said, "Your blood test came back at three hundred nanograms per deciliter, which puts you right smack on the borderline between normal and deficient. But with the Testoderm, you should be above three hundred by now . . ."

"I haven't used the patch yet."

"You haven't? How come?"

"My wife had to go to Utica, and my hands shake when I thread a needle. That's why I'm here. I want you to shave me so I can put the patch on."

"Are you sure you don't want to wait for Viagra? The FDA approved it today. It'll be available in a week or so."

"If the patch doesn't work, I'll try it. But in the meantime, could you please patch me up?"

Ernest Haas looked at the junior senator from Vermont, who was masquerading as the fifth President of the United States, and chewed his lower lip. Then he sighed and said, "All right. I'll have my procedures nurse do it."

"I'd rather you do it."

"Mr. Monroe, first of all, my nurse has shaved a lot more scrotums than I have. We do it routinely when we do office vasectomies. And second of all, I have a half-dozen patients waiting to see me, and I'm already running behind."

Ten minutes later, Woody found himself lying with his underwear off on an examining table, as Esmeralda Perkins, the urologist's procedures nurse, slipped on a pair of rubber gloves, taped his penis to his thigh, and then began to apply rubbing alcohol to his scrotum.

"This may tingle just a bit."

Esmeralda Perkins was young and black and better-looking than a urologist's procedures nurse ought to have been. And even though she did her best to handle him in a clinical fashion, it wasn't long before Woody, as he had done the first time with Evelyn Brandwynne, began to move back up the graph.

"I'm sorry," he stammered.

"No problem, Mr. Monroe. Happens all the time. Actually, it makes the job easier. Tumescence dilates the blood vessels and tightens the scrotum, which gives you a better surface."

Woody closed his eyes tightly and tried to think about his blood vessels. But it didn't do the trick. Slowly, inexorably, the tape began to separate from his thigh.

"Of course, occasionally it does cause problems with the pre-procedure precautions," Esmeralda Perkins said, as she cut a new piece of tape and strapped him firmly back down.

As he drove east back across the Vermont border, he called Evelyn Brandwynne on the cell phone. When she picked up he asked her, "What are you doing tomorrow night?"

"I don't know."

"I'll be back from Vermont."

"Maybe we should postpone that meeting, Senator."

"Evelyn, I'm onto something."

"Really?"

"I think so. Can you pick up a bottle of medicinal alcohol?"

"Medicinal alcohol?"

"Right."

"Any particular year?"

"It doesn't matter."

"Should I let it breathe?"

He flipped the phone closed, and, as he drove past the sign that said WELCOME TO VERMONT—THE GREEN MOUNTAIN STATE, he started to hum softly to himself.

10.

PAVLOV'S DOGS

ISHMAEL LEIBOWITZ was on the phone with the senator's insurance company, Barry holding on one line and a committee aide on another, when one of the interns from the front office told him that there was a UPS guy rolling in an enormous wooden statue on a hand truck.

Since he didn't want to speak to any of the three people he was currently speaking to, Ishmael handed the phone to the intern, asked her to tell all three of them he had been called away on pressing business, and walked down the narrow corridor to the front office.

He opened the door and saw an eight-foot wooden statue with garish faces painted on it. It was big. It was ugly. He had no idea what it was.

Taped to the base of the statue was a small envelope. Ishmael opened it and read, TO SENATOR WOODROW WHITE FROM THE PEOPLE OF THE RE-PUBLIC OF TOGO.

"What are we going to do with it?" Debbie Sue Allenby asked.

"Keep it in the office, I guess."

"It's not very Vermont, is it?"

"I don't know, Debbie, I can see this outside the I.G.A. in East Dummerston, can't you?"

"No."

Debbie Sue had about as much sense of humor as Arlen Specter.

"If it's from the Togolese government, don't we have to return it?" she asked.

"It's from the people, not the government. Besides, if it doesn't have a monetary value of more than a hundred dollars and we keep it in the office, it'd probably clear Ethics."

Ishmael got the interns to move it into the corner, beside the Currier and Ives Vermont snowscapes, and was standing there admiring the new piece of office decor when he was told that the senator was on the phone from Manchester.

Back inside his office, Ishmael picked up the phone. "Yes, Senator . . ."

"Call Georgetown. And find out if there's a Finnish ice-skater named Sonja Aura enrolled in their women's studies program."

"Spelling?"

"S-O-N-J-A A-U-R-A."

Ishmael grabbed a yellow pad and wrote, *Georgetown, Finnish ice-skater, Sonja Aura, women's studies.*

"Anything else?"

"Yes. I'm coming into National at four tomorrow afternoon. Get me a quiet table at Leonardo's for eight and send someone over to the drugstore for a roll of surgical tape."

"Any particular type of surgical tape?"

"The strongest possible."

"Got it," he said, and wrote *surgical tape, strong* on the yellow pad beside *Georgetown, Finnish ice-skater, Sonja Aura,* and *women's studies.*

It was late, after ten, when the phone rang in Woody's room at the Ramada Inn in Manchester. The senator had been nodding out over a markup of a conference-committee bill and was barely awake.

"Yes?" he said in a hoarse, sleepy voice.

"Hope I didn't wake you, Senator."

"Mr. Adams?"

"At your service."

"How did you find me?"

"Senator, that was about as hard as sliding your dick into a greased heifer. Anyway, I just wanted to inquire about our little business down in Washington."

"Oh . . . that. Well, that's in the Judiciary Committee now. You see, they exercise the right of advise and consent on the President's appointments to the federal bench."

"Separation of powers."

"Right."

"Alexander Hamilton was against advise and consent. He wanted to centralize the government. Wasn't for Tom Jefferson, you'd be sitting with your thumb up your ass while the President stacks the bench with his pals."

"I'm not on the Judiciary Committee."

"I know that, Senator. You already did me a great service calling over to the White House. Did you get the maple syrup?"

"As a matter of fact, I did. You know, Mr. Adams, we're not supposed to accept personal gifts."

"Don't worry. You can give a pancake breakfast fund-raiser. It'll come in handy. I was wondering if I ought to send some syrup down to Orrin Hatch."

"Probably not a good idea."

"What about Joe Biden? Or Ted Kennedy?"

"They're not allowed to accept personal gifts either."

"Their loss."

"Well, I appreciate the call . . ."

"My pleasure. You just keep on doing your job representing your constituents down there in Washington. And we'll keep sending you on down there."

"Thanks for the support."

"Senator, you ain't seen nothing yet," he said and hung up.

Woody lay back on the bed and tried to find the energy to get out of his clothes and crawl under the covers. It had been a draining day, starting with the Molly Stark Trail and progressing to the paper factory in Brattleboro, the hard-on in Schenectady, and the Jell-O squares in Manchester.

He thought about the Finnish ice-skater, John Quincy Adams, the Judiciary Committee, Trent Lott's front end, and, finally, about Evelyn and the medicinal alcohol, and as he did, he drifted off to sleep on a wave of fragile optimism.

At the morning staff breakfast in the All-Purpose Room of the Manchester Ramada Inn, Dickie Thong announced that their Vermont fund-raising was running at barely 70 percent of what it had been at the same time in 1992. And, if they didn't kickstart the money soon, he said, they'd be sucking fumes by August.

"I don't understand," Janine Caravaggio said. "The economy's good, people have money to spend . . ."

"Well, they're not spending it on this campaign."

"I'm telling you, we have to go on the offensive," Brian Petrunich argued. "We have to go after her."

"How can we go after her? She's a Girl Scout."

"There's a second mortgage on her ski condo at Stratton. That's a little fast and loose for Vermont."

"Brian," Beverly said, "I thought we had decided that we were not going to campaign negatively."

"Why? She's going around popping off about the senator's zipper problem."

"What else do you have, Brian?" Dickie Thong asked.

"I found out she's seeing a dermatologist. She could have skin lesions from tertiary syphilis. What if we offered to make the senator's medical records public if she does the same?"

"Is that it?"

"Well, her daughter was kicked off the Winooski High cheerleader squad for smoking."

"Smoking what?"

"Cigarettes, unfortunately."

"Can we get real here? Please." Beverly turned to Woody and asked, "Senator, do you want to go after Rebecca Gatney?"

The truth was he wanted to shoot Rebecca Gatney. Then drop her body into Lake Champlain attached to a cement block. Along with the bodies of numbers one and two, his Italian housekeeper, and Trent Lott.

But he didn't share these thoughts with his staff. He remembered Rav's words: "There *is* no valise." When he spoke, it was with sincerity and purpose.

"Rebecca Gatney is a woman of limited imagination and no sense of humor," he said. "She would get nothing done in Washington because she doesn't know how to pull her punches or how to deal. She would come marching in with a laundry list of flashy legislation that would never get anywhere near the Floor. She would be on C-SPAN endlessly, saying the right things, and boring people to death. And four years later, you'd never know she was even there."

Then, by way of conclusion, he said, "Whatever else you can say about Woody White, you know he's there."

For a long time, nobody spoke. They were not accustomed to *ex cathedra* pronouncements from their senator. It took them by surprise.

Everyone but the pundit. Once again, it was Rav Monsjar who was able to encapsulate these thoughts into a campaign slogan.

"He's there," Rav Monsjar said.

"What?"

"Woody White—he's there."

"Isn't it a little . . . understated?" Beverly asked.

"That's the beauty of it. Don't you see what it doesn't say? What it doesn't say, and therefore says even better than if it did say it, is that she *isn't*."

"She isn't?"

"She isn't *there*."

Woody smiled. He loved Rav Monsjar. He was worth every penny of the exorbitant salary he paid him.

"I like it," he said. "Let's run with it."

WOODY WHITE—HE'S THERE would become the official slogan of the senator's reelection campaign. It would be printed on mailings, on signs, on buttons. Campaign workers would answer the phone, "Woody White—he's there. How may I direct your call?"

The corollary to *he's there—she's not there*—would become the war cry of his campaign workers. At rallies around the state, someone would shout, "Where's Becky?" And the crowd would shout back, "She's not there." Then, "Where's Woody?" And the even louder response, "He's there."

But before the rallies and before mailboxes were stuffed with flyers and front lawns were blanketed with signs telling everyone just where their senator was, there remained a long, wet mud season to get through and a lot of dollars to raise in order to print that slogan on all those signs on all those back roads in Vermont.

As it happened, one of the White campaign's major contributors was having a small accounts-receivable problem himself.

So on that same Saturday morning in early mud season, while Woody met with his staff, Roland Boyden found himself taking a ride in Ethan Allen's Buick Riviera down a long dirt road that was slowly melting into a fragrant mixture of mud and slush.

He sat in the backseat, tight-lipped, staring blankly out the window, wondering what they were going to do to him. There were rumors about what happened when you stiffed John Quincy Adams. There was a guy from Barre nobody ever saw again after he took a trip out to see the septic tank.

Eight miles east of Montpelier, Ethan Allen pulled the Riviera onto a smaller dirt road that led to a sprawling farmhouse, and then through a peeling white gate and into a yard full of old car and tractor carcasses and a couple of dozen tires.

There was a wisp of smoke coming from the chimney and a thin, mean-looking Doberman patrolling the grounds.

As they got out of the car, the Doberman approached, baring his teeth, until Ethan Allen said, "Back off, Aaron Burr," and the dog slinked off to play in the mud piles.

"Mr. Q. named him after the son of a bitch who did Hamilton," John Stark said to Roland Boyden.

"Burr was pissed at Hamilton because the guy wouldn't support him for governor of New York. So he popped him."

"*Adiós,* Hamilton," Ethan Allen said.

They entered the house and found John Quincy Adams and Elbridge Gerry playing checkers in front of the potbellied stove.

Ethan Allen pulled up a chair for Roland Boyden and lowered him into it.

"Cup of coffee, Roland?"

"No thanks."

John Quincy Adams hooked his thumbs underneath his suspenders and slowly shook his head.

"What do you suppose we ought to do about this situation, Roland?"

"I told them that I was getting a check any day."

"Roland, you been getting a check any day for a couple of weeks now."

"There's something wrong with the mail."

"I'm not having any trouble with my mail, am I, Elbridge?"

"Nope. Your *Vermont Life* came right on time today, like it always does."

"What about my JCPenney catalog?"

"Yesterday, right on time."

"Vermont Power and Light bill?"

"Wednesday, like always."

"So, you see, Roland, there ain't nothing wrong with the mail, is there?"

John Quincy Adams got up and walked over to the kitchen window. He looked out at the fields in back of the house—a couple of acres of scrub pine and wildflowers, now a sea of mud that had been churned up by Ralph Meunier's backhoe. The septic-tank-repair specialist was gone till Monday. He was waiting on a part.

"Tell you what, Roland," John Quincy Adams said. "I'm going to have Ethan and John take you out back and show you the septic tank."

Roland Boyden started to shake as Ethan Allen and John Stark took him by the arms and stood him up.

"Roland, my best advice to you in this situation is to breathe through your nose."

They dragged Roland Boyden out back as John Quincy Adams went to pour another cup of coffee. By the time he returned to the window, Roland Boyden was chained by his arms to the tractor. Ethan Allen climbed up onto the tractor seat and started it up.

Elbridge Gerry walked over and stood beside John Quincy Adams, and the two men watched silently as Roland Boyden took a couple of turns around the yard.

"Beats the hell out of a rototiller, don't it, Elbridge?"

Later that night, in Washington, Woody White and Evelyn Brandwynne were in bed in her Georgetown apartment. This time, however, they were not watching TV. Far from it. They had been carnally engaged for the better part of an hour after some very successful preoperative foreplay involving medicinal alcohol and surgical tape.

They lay there together in the quiet afterglow of their lovemaking. There was a small, stupid grin on Woody's face, as if he had accidentally eaten an entire box of Mallomars and lived to tell the tale.

It was Evelyn who finally broke the silence. "Well," she said, "I guess you'd have to call this Pavlovian."

"I guess so."

"Do you know that after Pavlov did the experiment with the dogs, the lightbulb, and the dog food, he tried shaving just before he made love to his wife? Then when he stopped making love to her and just shaved, she lubricated anyway."

"Uh-huh."

"Conditioned reflex."

"Right."

"If making love is the dog food, and shaving is the lightbulb, I must be the dog."

"No," Woody said, "I'm the dog."

"Who am I?"

"You're the dog food."

"That's very romantic, Woody."

He just smiled. Twenty minutes later he suggested that she tape him up once more.

"You sure you want to try it again?"

"In the interest of science."

She slowly opened the bottle of alcohol and reached for the tape. But this time he just had to smell the alcohol before taping him down became not only difficult but gratuitous.

"Woody, you're salivating."

"Uh-huh."

"Boy, are you ever."

"Evelyn?"

"What?"

"Shut up." And as he climbed on top of her, he closed his eyes and silently thanked Ivan Pavlov.

11.

SENATORIAL COURTESY

ON THE FOLLOWING rainy Monday morning, Ishmael found himself having a cranberry-bran muffin and double latte with Barry and Kevin at the Chickadee coffee shop on Eighteenth and S.

It was during this breakfast that he learned a useful piece of information. It was precisely this type of intelligence that kept him a member in more or less good standing of this particular coterie of Senate aides.

Barry was talking about some dead-end committee legislation that his senator was pushing, insisting that he, Barry, work the committee aides in spite of the fact that the legislation, according to his, Barry's, sources, was stuck in the committee with no chance of getting out.

"You couldn't get this bill out of that committee with a laxative," he said.

"You know what I heard?" Kevin said, taking a sip of his double decaf mochacino. "I heard a certain senator got his front end dented by another senator in the Senate parking garage, and the first senator is so pissed off that the second senator is dragging his ass getting the insurance forms filled out that the first senator is dragging *his* ass over a nomination in Judiciary that was supported by the second senator."

"Who?" Barry asked.

"I don't know."

"Kevin . . ."

"I swear I don't know. Denny told me this on the phone last night, and he said he didn't know either."

"Who did Denny hear it from?"

"Grassley's aide on Judiciary."

"Well, was it Grassley?"

"No, it's not Grassley. It's someone else."

"You have any idea who it is, Ishmael?"

Ishmael shook his head and took a big bite of his muffin in an attempt to keep his face neutral.

"Well, let's see," said Barry. "Who's on Judiciary? Hatch is chairman. Biden is ranking minority. Then you got Strom, you got Specter, you got Teddy, you got Grassley, you got Feingold, Kohl . . . who else?"

"Leahy, DeWine, Feinstein . . ."

"I bet it's Dianne. Hatch doesn't like her. There must be an opening on the circuit court. What's California?"

"The Ninth," Ishmael said, in an effort to encourage the speculation regarding Feinstein.

"Is there an opening on the Ninth?"

"I heard there was," Ishmael said.

"Feinstein backs into Hatch's car, and now Hatch is holding up a judgeship in Judiciary. Don't you love it?"

By lunch the rumor had worked its way up the Hill and into the steam room of the Senate Health Facility, where two senators, from opposite sides of the aisle, as it turns out, were discussing it.

"I happen to know that it's not Grassley," said the senator from Pennsylvania.

"Who do you think it is?"

"Dianne's denying it."

"What about Barbara?"

"Which Barbara?"

"The one with the big mouth."

"She's not on Judiciary."

"You don't have to be on Judiciary to support a judgeship."

"She's not a big fan of Orrin's either."

"Well, tell you what I think. I think it's a crock of shit. With all the problems we have in this country, we've got a couple of senators fighting over a dented fender."

"Apparently, it wasn't just the fender. There's frame damage too."

The senator from Massachusetts got up, pulling his towels around his large frame.

"Whatever happened to fucking senatorial courtesy, that's what I want to know," he said, and left the steam room.

. . .

It was Ishmael's experience that when he had information that he needed from the senator as well as information to convey to him, the order in which he took up these matters was crucial. At present he needed to find out how the senator wanted him to proceed with negotiations over the bodywork with the Majority Leader's chief of staff, and he also needed to tell him that he had found out that there was no Finnish ice-skater by the name of Sonja Aura, or by any other name, enrolled in women's studies, or in any other program, at Georgetown, or at any other capital-area institution of higher learning.

Ishmael led with the bodywork.

"The insurance company's position is that if the accident was your fault, there would be an adjustment in your premium. It usually runs from thirty-five to fifty percent."

"What? I have a clean record."

"Apparently, it's not quite as clean as you thought, Senator. There was an illegal U-turn in September. And a speeding ticket on the Rock Creek Parkway a year ago."

"He was improperly parked."

"He's not admitting to that."

"Discrepancy of fact. We could ask for a jury. I like my chances in front of a jury."

"I don't think you'd get a jury on a traffic accident, Senator."

Woody leaned back in his chair. "All right. Go to seventeen-fifty under the table and my body shop. See if it flies. What else?"

"I did a check on the Finnish ice-skater, and, according to the registrar's office at Georgetown, there's nobody enrolled there by that name."

Woody's eyes lit up. "Really?"

"I took the liberty of checking with GWU, Howard, University of Maryland, and with a half-dozen other places in commuting distance from the District."

"That's . . . that's very interesting, Ishmael."

"I'm glad, Senator."

"Get me Hank Leventhal at INS and then Phil Yalowitz at Schonblum Yalowitz."

Ishmael returned to his office and dialed INS. He buzzed the senator and told him that Hank Leventhal was on the line. Then, for the senator's own protection, he rationalized, Ishmael listened in on the conversation.

"Hank, she's not enrolled in school."

"Excuse me, Senator?"

"Sonja Aura, the Finnish ice-skater, remember?"

"Uh-huh."

"You know what I want you to do?"

"What?"

"Don't do anything."

"Uh-huh."

"For the moment."

"Uh-huh."

"But get the forms ready. I may want to move quickly on this, okay?"

"Uh-huh."

"I'll keep you posted, Hank."

"Uh-huh."

The conversation with the lawyer was even less enlightening to Ishmael.

"Phil, she violated her status."

"I beg your pardon?"

"Sonja Aura's not enrolled in school. It's fraud, Phil. We can get her sent back to Helsinki."

"I'm not following you, Senator."

"I want you to reply to her lawyer."

"Which lawyer would that be?"

"Number two's, my present wife's. Tell her lawyer what she can do with the list of assets. And then, after you say that, you add that we may be getting back in touch with a list of assets of our own. But don't get specific. You talk about assets as if you were replying to their demand for assets. Say something like, Your assets are tied up in Helsinki."

There was a moment of silence on the line, before the lawyer said, "Senator, I'm not very comfortable with this type of negotiation."

"Phil, I furnished half your goddamn office. So get comfortable with it."

Ishmael hung up a split second after the senator did. As he was trying to digest the information he had learned from the two phone calls, his phone rang.

"Guess what? There's no opening on the Ninth Circuit," Barry told him. "There's an opening on the Second. Woody got anybody up?"

"Not that I know of," he lied.

"Maybe it's Leahy. What do you think?"

"Could be."

"I love it. Leahy backs into Hatch. Hatch fucks Leahy on a judgeship. I got to tell Kevin about this. He'll love it."

Ishmael hung up and decided not to think about that either. Instead he dialed the Majority Leader's chief of staff and told him that they could close at seventeen-fifty under the table and the body shop in Anacostia.

Washington rumors are like brushfires: It takes an errant spark to set them off but a couple of hundred firemen with fire-retardant helicopters to put them out. In this case, both Patrick Leahy's and Orrin Hatch's staffs had to spend time over the next few days denying they were involved in a car-accident-payoff-for-judgeship quid pro quo.

Eventually, someone going through the Senate parking garage came across the Majority Leader's Ford Explorer with the ugly crater in its front end. And Trent Lott's chief of staff found himself denying that there was any deal with Pat Leahy or with any other senator over car repairs.

Furious, the young gentleman from Ole Miss, via Duke Law School, got Ishmael on the phone.

"Mr. Leibowitz, this situation has gotten completely out of hand."

"Sorry, but we have no control over rumors."

"If we don't settle this expeditiously, I'm afraid we'll have to publicly complain."

"That's a split infinitive."

"I beg your pardon?"

"'To publicly complain' is a split infinitive."

"Perhaps you have time to engage in puerile games and little witticisms, Mr. Leibowitz, but in this office we are engaged in the business of the United States Senate."

"So what does that make us—chopped liver?"

Ishmael hung up and walked into the outer office, where a group of Vermont dairy farmers had been waiting for over an hour to see the senator. The farmers sat uncomfortably beside the Togolese fertility fetish in their Kmart sports jackets.

Around them, interns answered the phone with "Senator White's office—he's there."

Woody overheard one of the farmers say, "If he's not here, why are they saying he's here?"

"They're not saying he's here. They're saying he's *there* . . ."

Ishmael introduced himself to the farmers and apologized for making them wait.

"The senator was called to the Floor for a roll-call vote. He should be back momentarily."

The farmers nodded, looked at their Casio watches and said, "Might rain."

Ishmael left the office and headed for the subway to see if he could get the senator off the Floor to come back and greet the farmers before it rained. He ran into Jack Hernden in the basement of Dirksen.

"Going to the Floor?"

"Uh-huh. I've got an office full of pissed-off dairy farmers."

They rode for a moment, and then Jack lowered his voice and said, "I don't think it was Hatch and Leahy. I think it was Teddy and Thompson."

"You think so?"

"Yeah. Teddy and Thompson are probably the front-runners for the White House in 2000, right?"

"Right."

"So Teddy wants to send Fred a message, right?"

"Right."

"So he backs right into him."

Jack wore the febrile expression of a conspiracy theorist who has finally hit on the smoking gun.

"I think you're onto something, Jack."

12

MORE QUID

"Dad wasn't around a whole lot when I was growing up. He was in Columbus in the state legislature when Maddie and I were young. He'd come home to Shaker Heights on weekends and sleep, you know what I mean? We had to tiptoe around the house all weekend because he was crashed out on the living-room couch."

"Did he play ball with you or take you fishing?" Lee Schumock asked Bobby White, Senator Woodrow White's thirty-one-year-old son, as they sat on the deck of his IRS-liened boat in Miami's Inland Waterway.

"Dad didn't go in for that type of shit. Dad liked to talk. When you spent time with him, you talked."

"What did you talk about?"

"Him."

"So he wasn't a very attentive father?"

"He had his moments. You just had to weed through it all to get to the good stuff. I remember during Watergate . . . I was just a little kid but I sat around with him and watched the hearings on TV. I used to love to listen to him needle Nixon and the Germans—he used to call Ehrlichman and Haldeman the Germans. And he called Dean Rudolf Hess. He said that Dean's testimony in front of the Ervin Committee was like Hess's testimony at Nuremberg. They were both rats leaving sinking ships."

"How did you feel when he ran for the Senate?"

"It was cool having a famous father. I used to watch him on TV.

Mom would throw things at the screen. She was really pissed off at him, man."

"The divorce must have been painful for you?"

"Tell you the truth, it was no big thing. I was twenty. I was into smoking dope and getting laid."

"How'd your father feel about that?"

"He didn't like the dope stuff. Different generation. But he couldn't very well lecture me about pussy, could he?"

There was an audible click on the small tape recorder to indicate that the tape had run out. As Lee Schumock changed the tape, Bobby White took a deep pull from the tightly rolled joint, leaned back in his deck chair, and held the smoke deeply in his lungs. Then he exhaled and said, "When I was in college, I used to get toked up and watch C-SPAN. Once I was with some babe, and we were goofing on the TV, channel-surfing, and suddenly there's Woody looking out at me. I mean, it's weird, you know. I'm like about to slip it to this chick, and there's my old man talking about some appropriation for some fucking bill, and I look at him and start to laugh. And I can't stop laughing because it's the same shit he used to lay on me when he lectured me about school and grades and that shit. Weird, huh?"

Lee Schumock nodded and asked, "What do you think his chances of reelection are?"

"Fuck do I know. But he better win because if he doesn't, I don't know what the hell he's going to do."

"He can always practice law."

Bobby White delivered a full-bellied laugh, took another hit off the joint, and said, "Woody practices law like Rudolf Hess flies airplanes. You know what I mean?"

Bobby White got up, walked over to the side of the boat, and sent a large gob of phlegm overboard.

When he turned around, he said, "Listen, man, I got to go take a nap."

"*Pronto?*"

"Dario, where is my wife?"

"*Come sta, senatore?*"

"I'm fine, Dario. Where is my wife?"

"*Chi?*"

"My *moglie?*"

"*Alla suo ufficio.*"

"Office?"

"Sì. Ritornerà a casa questa notte?"

"Why do you ask, Dario?"

"Voglio andare al cinema."

"You're fired, Dario."

"Che dice, senatore?"

Woody flipped the cell closed and climbed onto the stationary bicycle in the Senate Health Facility, where he was engaged in one of his sporadic bouts of physical damage control. There were a couple of pounds he wouldn't mind shedding now that his E.Q. was back into the "moderate to high" range. Thanks to Evelyn Brandwynne. The medicinal alcohol. The razor. And Ivan Pavlov.

There had been no response yet from Daphne's lawyers to Phil Yalowitz's counteroffer. Woody decided it was time to see just how much quid the quo was going to fetch. There was a cocktail reception at the White House tomorrow night. The President was going to try to rally support on a trade bill that was languishing in the Senate.

He dialed Daphne's office, and, when Brandon told him that she was in a deposition, he told the secretary that there was a household emergency.

"What's wrong?" she asked, picking up.

"I just fired Dario."

"What? Why?"

"It was either that or learn Italian, and I don't have the time."

"Look, I'm in a deposition—"

"Tomorrow night. Cocktail dress. I'll pick you up at the office at seven P.M."

"Where is it?"

"The big white house at the foot of the hill."

"I'm supposed to have dinner—"

"Daphne, you know how much the President likes you in a cocktail dress."

A long pause. Then: "All right."

He closed the phone, stuck it in the canvas flap on the side of the exercise bike, torqued the gradient up a couple of degrees, and started pedaling.

Dick Gephardt sat down on the bicycle next to him with a copy of the *Record*.

"Hey, Dick," he said, "why aren't you using the facility over on the House side?"

"Too many Republicans over there. They hog the bicycles."

"You going to the White House reception?"

"Sure am. How about you?"

"Wouldn't miss it."

"Bringing the wife?"

"You bet, Dick."

"Great."

He watched her move gracefully through the revolving door of the glass-and-chrome office building that housed Meagen, Forresy, Bryce and a number of other high-end law firms, and realized that, in spite of everything, she could still take his breath away.

She looked even better than she usually did when she dressed for the White House. He got out and opened the car door for her, admiring the beautifully cut black leather coat and the three-inch Italian heels that looked good enough to drink Champagne out of.

"We'll come back here afterward to get my car," she announced as soon as she got in.

"Staying in town tonight?"

"Yes. I have an early meeting."

"You've been having quite a lot of early meetings lately."

She didn't touch it. She just left it there on the seat between them like a time bomb and looked absently out the window.

They rode up Pennsylvania Avenue in silence and pulled up to the east gate of the White House at 6:50. The protocol officer checked them off the list and nodded to the guard, who raised the barrier to admit them.

A trio played cocktail-lounge Mose Allison softly as they entered the Blue Room and blended into the sea of senators and representatives with their wives and husbands.

It didn't take Daphne long to be encircled. Woody helped himself to a glass of Champagne and marveled at the ease with which she magnetized men. Maybe it was this very ease that drove her into the arms of her ice-skater . . .

"How are you, Woody?"

Woody turned and saw a broad-shouldered man in a suit a half-size too small for him.

"Fine, Al. How are you?"

"Not bad. I'm telling you, that wife of yours can really dress."

"Well, you wouldn't want to pay the bills."

"Couldn't be worse than Tipper, believe me. I thought when we got over here, the clothing allowance would make a difference. But, tell you the truth, we were doing better in the Senate. So, Woody, do we have your vote on SB 235?"

"I haven't even finished my first drink."

"It's a big room to work."

"You can always go upstairs and work the phones, Al."

"That's not funny," the Vice President said and walked away to lobby Daschle.

Pat Leahy wandered over.

"Woody."

"Pat."

"Woody, I hope you don't mind me asking, but did you back into Orrin Hatch's car in the parking garage?"

"No. Why would I do that?"

"There's a vacancy on the Second Circuit, and Hatch is holding up a nominee from Vermont that Justice sent over. It's not my nominee. Is he yours?"

"I'm afraid not, Pat."

"That's peculiar. Who do you suppose did send it over?"

"Maybe Teddy."

"Teddy?"

"Maybe it's some sort of pan–New England thing."

"You think so?"

"You never know."

"I'm going to ask him."

"Is Teddy here tonight? I haven't seen him."

"He's over with Dick Gephardt. Hitting on your wife."

There was a sudden hush as the President entered the room. Bush would have had the band break into "Hail to the Chief." But not this President. The band played "Parchman Farm."

Woody watched him work the room. The man had the fastest handshake in the West. It would be out of the holster and into your pocket before you could react. He could squeeze your nuts tighter than Tip O'Neill and without inflicting any permanent damage.

"Woody, good to see you."

"Good to see you, Mr. President."

"You know who I just got a letter from? The President of Togo. He said you're their best friend in the whole damn United States Senate."

"That's nice, but I couldn't get the phosphate-aid bill past Madam Chairperson."

"You want me to give her a call?"

"I'd appreciate that."

"I'm three votes short on SB 235."

"I'm hearing you loud and clear, Mr. President."

The President gave him one of his big horsey smiles and another handshake before moving on to join Teddy and Dick Gephardt in hitting on Woody's future ex-wife.

. . .

In the car on the way back to Daphne's office, Woody said, "Looked to me like you had the President twisted around your little finger. You also had Dick Gephardt. You know, I could trade you to Gephardt for three judge-ships and a committee chairmanship. . . . So did Tipper ask you where you bought your clothes?"

She shook her head.

"Al's in big trouble. He better start working the phones again."

Woody's attempts at levity weren't playing. He gave up, and they drove in silence, both of them staring vacantly in front of them at the hypnotic whir of the windshield wipers.

They pulled up in front of her office building. As Daphne started to get out of the car, Woody grabbed her arm impulsively. "You know, Daphne," he said. "If we got rid of the lawyers and cut the deal ourselves, we'd both come out a lot better."

She smiled, but it wasn't a friendly smile. It was the smile of a boa con-strictor about to wrap herself around a man's torso. But she said nothing, just sat there waiting for him to let her out of the car.

"Look," he said, "I've got to level with you. I can't figure out what the hell you want."

She looked him right in the eyes. It was the same look that had nailed Teddy, Gephardt, and the President.

"I want everything, Woody."

He released her arm. "What does that mean?"

"You don't know what *everything* means?"

"There's everything, and there's *everything* . . ."

"That's right."

"How do we decide what *everything* is?"

"That's why lawyers were invented, Woody. They know the difference between everything and *everything*. Good night."

And she smiled once more and got out of the car.

13

JEAN-LOUIS TRINTIGNANT

THERE WERE TWO VOTES in the Senate over the next month that would lead to sizable contributions to Senator Woodrow Wilson White's reelection-campaign fund. On the surface, these votes appeared to be no more than business as usual. At the time, these apparently unrelated votes were merely two votes that took place in two committee rooms, along with all the other votes that took place in all the other committee rooms in the Senate.

The first vote was the confirmation of the Justice Department's nominee, Vincent Ruggiero, to fill the vacancy on the bench of the Second Circuit Court of Appeals. After weeks of preventing the nomination from coming to a vote, the chairman of the Senate Judiciary Committee, claiming to be tired of the scurrilous rumors about under-the-table car-accident payoffs, allowed the vote to proceed and the nomination to be approved.

The second vote followed an unexpected reversal of position on the part of the chairperson of the African Affairs Subcommittee of the Senate Foreign Affairs Committee regarding a $40 million foreign-aid allocation to the Republic of Togo to stimulate its phosphate industry. After she allowed the bill to be reported out of committee and attached to a continuing resolution, it sailed through the Senate on a voice vote.

A week after the Ruggiero nomination cleared Judiciary, Woody got a call from John Quincy Adams.

"I just heard the good news, Senator."

"What good news is that, Mr. Adams?"

"The Second Circuit. Nice to have a Vermonter on that court, isn't it?"

"I appreciate your bringing Mr. Ruggiero's name to my attention . . ."

"Don't mention it, Senator. And I'll tell you what we'd like to do to express our appreciation up here. The VMSDA would like to throw you a little fund-raiser."

"Well, I certainly appreciate the offer, but I'd have to confer with my staff on that."

"Senator, when you have a cow that gives you a shitload of milk, you sure as hell don't throw it down the well, now, do you?"

"Now, I don't suppose you do."

"We'll have a little pancake breakfast out at my place. Pass the hat around. As soon as the mud's all gone and the septic tank's fixed, we can put this thing together. Fact, we could do it on the Fourth of July. Makes a nice statement, don't you think? Let me know as soon as you can, Senator. You don't want that milk to go sour, now, do you?"

A few days later, there was more encouraging news on the fund-raising front. Dickie Thong called from Montpelier to tell Woody about a contribution that had just come into the office from an organization called NAPTOTS.

"What the hell is NAPTOTS?"

"The letterhead says it's the National Association for the Prevention and Treatment of Tourette Syndrome."

"Never heard of them."

"They have offices in Washington, on Seventh Street."

"Isn't Tourette syndrome the thing where people uncontrollably shout out dirty words?"

"I believe so."

"Wasn't there a ballplayer on the Phillies . . . ?"

"There may have been. The thing is, they're registered as a PAC but no one has heard of them."

"How much is the contribution, Dickie?"

"Four hundred thousand dollars. Doesn't it seem odd, Senator, that you should be receiving that large a contribution from an organization you're not familiar with?"

"As long as it's a worthy cause, I don't see what the problem is."

"The problem is that a large contribution from an unknown organization can be questioned. And given Rebecca Gatney's attack on your ethics, I thought we ought to steer clear of anything like this."

Woody leaned back in his chair and sighed. It was getting to the point where you couldn't take money from anybody anymore. Pretty soon they'd all be reduced to standing on soapboxes with megaphones.

"I think we should at least look into the organization," Dickie Thong said.

"Sure. But first cash the check."

Throwing caution to the wind, Ishmael took Maud to see *My Night at Maud's* at a revival house in Dupont Circle after having told Barry that he couldn't go see *H.M.S. Pinafore* with him at the National Theatre because he had to work late.

Ishmael sat in the dark movie house, watching Maud watch Jean-Louis Trintignant and slowly melt from the actor's boyish charm.

After the lights came up, she stood on wobbly knees, swaying gently. Ishmael suggested they skip the post-film cappuccino and drive back to Alexandria for a nightcap.

She nodded quickly. As they walked out of the theater, Ishmael could feel the heat emanating from her. The spring air was redolent of dead cherry blossoms. Ishmael had high hopes for the remainder of the evening.

But just as they prepared to dash across New Hampshire Avenue to the car, Ishmael heard a familiar voice calling his name. He turned abruptly and found himself face-to-face with Kevin Bunch.

Ishmael quickly removed his arm from around Maud's waist, but it was too late. He'd been nailed. In an effort to mitigate the damage, he blurted out, "Kevin Bunch, Maud Summers, a . . . an attorney for the . . . senator."

Maud flinched. He could feel her stiffen, the heat moving from her middle to the back of her neck.

"You guys want to grab a cup of coffee?"

"Love to, Kevin, but Maud has an early meeting," he said, looking desperately for a break in the traffic so that they could make their getaway across New Hampshire Avenue.

"So, you keeping the senator out of trouble?" Kevin asked Maud.

Maud looked at Ishmael, who picked the ball up from the ground and ran with it.

"She won't tell you a thing, Kevin. She's awfully discreet."

"I guess you've got to be when you work for Woody White. Didn't you just love Trintignant?"

Ishmael saw an opening in the flow of cars, and, grabbing Maud awkwardly by the elbow, he said, "See you, Kevin," and pushed her into the street, nearly knocking her over.

He could tell by the way she got in the car that he was looking at a quick round trip to Alexandria and back. All the Jean-Louis Trintignant lubrication would be for naught.

"The reason I said that," he explained, "was that I begged off a foreign-policy talk that a mutual friend's senator was giving, and I . . . wanted it to seem as if we were working. You and I."

"I don't like lying, Ishmael."

This particular lie was going to cost him dearly. Not only was he going to be shut out tonight, but he was now standing with one foot sticking out of the closet. If Kevin Bunch chose to tell Barry, Barry could eighty-six him from the group. Or worse. He could proclaim a *fatwah* against him, leaving him without the type of intelligence he needed to help Woody White navigate through the perilous waters of senatorial politics.

"You want to put the heater on? I'm cold," Maud said, turning away and staring out the window.

Evelyn Brandwynne stepped out of her skirt and unbuttoned her blouse, hung them up carefully, slipped out of her underwear, and then stood and admired her forty-five-year-old body in the full-length mirror of her walk-in closet. Not bad. Not bad at all. There was a minimal amount of age-appropriate sag but not one stitch mark in her. Maybe when she was fifty she'd get a couple of nips and tucks, but for the moment, she was doing just fine, thank you.

She took the nurse's uniform down from the hanger and pressed the starched whiteness against her skin, feeling her nipples harden and that tiny glowing ember from her middle spreading to her arms and legs.

She slipped into the uniform, starched to within an inch of its life, and smoothed it out against her body. The thermostat clicked back on. Along with the glow came a very slight weakness in her knees.

She slipped her white nurse's shoes on, teetered a little bit, and walked into the adjoining bathroom.

Inside the blue-and-cream Provençal-tile bathroom was a steam shower, a Jacuzzi tub, and, though she lived alone, a marble double sink. The drawers beside the sink were filled with condom samples. She had dozens of different types of prophylactic products, lagniappes from her clients, given to her with cute little notes, which she collected.

Along with the nurse's uniform, she had bought, at Crabtree & Evelyn, an ebony-handled English razor, and a shaving brush and bowl. She kept them displayed on the sink to remind her of the magic that life sometimes serendipitously presented.

She had discussed this magic with her therapist, a slinky French neo-Jungian named Nathalie Portmanteau, who told her that it wasn't the uniform so much as the starch. She had pooh-poohed the Pavlovian interpretation, even when Evelyn told her that all she had to do now was put on the uniform to become aroused.

"Don't you see—it's the starch against the body," Nathalie Portmanteau had explained. "Do you remember the feel of those starched overalls? You are eleven years old again, aren't you, and it is summer and you are putting on a pair of *salopettes* after going bathing. And you are feeling the starch against your nipples, which are just beginning to bud. This experience you are having is not Pavlovian. It's Proustian. Don't you see, the starch in the nurse's uniform is the madeleine?"

In the drawer below the condom samples, there was a large roll of surgical tape, manicuring scissors, and a bottle of medicinal alcohol. Evelyn put the tape, the scissors, the alcohol, the shaving cup, the razor, and the brush on a little tray, then filled a small bowl with warm water, and turned off the bathroom light.

Through the door she could see the senator lying on the bed in his boxer shorts, reading a copy of *Health Prophylaxis Report*.

Setting the tray on the bedside table, she turned down the reading lamp, and sat beside him on the bed.

"Ready for your procedure?"

"Yes, ma'am . . ."

"We'll just put this magazine down for a moment, all right?"

He nodded, as she took the magazine from him.

"Let's just slip out of those shorts, shall we?"

"All right . . ."

He lifted his backside and let her slip the boxer shorts down his legs and over his feet.

"Attaboy."

As she took the tape and cut a large strip, she saw that the fragrance of the madeleine had drifted up to the senator's nostrils. It looked as if they wouldn't be needing the tape tonight. In fact, it looked as if they might soon be able to dispense with the razor and the shaving bowl. As well as the surgical alcohol. Maybe all they needed was the nurse's uniform. Maybe just the *idea* of the nurse's uniform.

"Well, Mr. Monroe, it looks like we might be having a little problem with the procedure today," she said, sliding the uniform up over her thighs and lowering herself slowly down on top of him, opening like a warm madeleine to the butter knife.

Woody was on the secure line to Phil Yalowitz. The fly on the wall was en route to East Gethsemane, Ohio, to talk to the senator's daughter. Ishmael was in his office doing damage control on various fronts. It was raining on the decomposed cherry blossoms that littered the sidewalks.

"Is this number one or number two, Phil?"

It was number one, and she wanted a copy of the publishing contract.

"Fuck it. You might as well photocopy it and send it to number two while you're at it."

Number two, Phil Yalowitz told him, wanted a statement of all income, if any, he had inherited from his mother's estate.

"My mother is still alive, for chrissakes."

Phil Yalowitz took a minute to explain estate-planning strategies involving tax-free gifts that could be made before death that would minimize inheritance taxes.

"Phil, even if my mother were dead—and, believe me, she wouldn't give me the satisfaction—she doesn't have a nickel."

Phil Yalowitz discussed the difficulty of convincing an opposing attorney of the likelihood of someone whose maiden name was Hanna not having a nickel.

"They cut her off. She married a Democrat. They didn't even buy a fucking carpet from my father's business."

In family law, Phil Yalowitz explained, it was often the perception of wealth, more so than the actual wealth, that affected the court's decision.

"So you're telling me that even though my mother doesn't have any money, even though I am, in fact, actually supporting her, this is going to cost me."

Sometimes, Phil Yalowitz reflected, it is better to succumb to the basic injustices inherent in divorce litigation and concentrate on minimizing exposure.

"Just put on a helmet and duck, is that it?"

That wasn't a bad strategy, Phil Yalowitz concurred, when you were dealing with what was referred to in the business as a kamikaze. In this case, Phil Yalowitz elaborated, the senator was dealing with two kamikazes. Each of whom had retained a barracuda to litigate. When barracudas represented kamikazes, you needed to react defensively in order to limit exposure.

The senator swiveled his chair around and looked out on the rain falling on Constitution Avenue. He began to feel the bile rise in his throat.

"Tell you what, Phil. I'll keep my helmet on, but I intend to lob a few shells into her position. Just to soften her up a little. Then we'll see if the kamikazes call off the barracudas."

Phil Yalowitz responded that kamikazes had no interest in self-protection and that barracudas had no interest outside of billing hours.

"Humor me, Phil."

He hung up with his lawyer and called Hank Leventhal at INS.

"Hank," he said, when the asset-forfeiture associate director picked up, "let's fire away."

"I beg your pardon?"

"A couple of ninety-millimeter shells right into her bunker."

"Senator, I'm not following you."

"I want you to send a deportation notice to Sonja Aura."

"On what basis?"

"Violation of status."

"Are you absolutely sure that she's not in school?"

"Not in the District. And she lives here."

A long pause, then: "All right. You want me to copy you on the paperwork?"

"Absolutely not."

"I just thought that if we established a paper trail—"

"Just say you got an anonymous phone call."

"We're not supposed to follow up on anonymous tips."

"Hank, she's a flagrant status violator."

"All right. I'll get it in the mail this week."

"Don't mail it, Hank. Send it FedEx."

"We don't send deportation notices FedEx. We send them registered mail."

"Fine. Send it registered mail. But send it today."

"You are asking me to send the deportation notice, is that it?"

"That's what I just said."

"Okay, Senator. I'll take care of it."

"Attaboy."

That afternoon Woody was sitting in the Senate barbershop waiting his turn to avail himself of one of the few remaining perks in the business. Al D'Amato was in the chair, getting what was left up top redistributed.

The short, balding Republican looked down at Woody from his chair and flashed an acrid smile.

"Woody, why the hell don't you just give Trent his money?" the junior senator from New York said loudly enough for everyone in the barbershop to hear.

Woody waited a moment, just long enough to make sure that everyone who was still listening was still listening, and replied, "Sure, Al. Just as soon as you pay back all the money you pilfered from the Nassau County Treasury to give to your relatives."

That quieted the room. All you could hear was the sound of the blood rising in Al D'Amato's neck.

Woody turned a page in his *People* magazine and found himself looking at the face of another short, balding man he knew, but this man was twenty-some-odd years younger than Al D'Amato. And he was dead.

According to *People,* "Schenectady urologist Dr. Ernest Haas, 39, was killed, on March 27, as the result of a bizarre sexual encounter with his wife, Audrey, 38."

The article described how Dr. Haas, dressed in women's clothes, had handcuffed his wife to the handle of their kitchen stove and made love to her, expiring in the act as a result of his wife's allegedly cutting off his penis with a Sunbeam electric carving utensil.

Jesus. Who would have thought that this mild-mannered little man—this man who wrote his Testoderm prescription and whose nurse was indirectly responsible for the rebirth of Woody's sex life—indulged in this type of kinky shit?

Well, at least the man didn't have to worry about his E.Q. anymore.

Heart beating, Woody scoured the article for details. It wasn't until he was sure that there was no mention of a patient named James Monroe that he was able to breathe easier.

Still, you couldn't be too careful. He would have Ishmael remove the doctor's Rolodex card and shred it.

14.

PHOSPHATES
FOR HOCKEY STICKS

ON A WARM DAY in early June, Dickie Thong called Ishmael from Montpelier and asked him to check out an organization called the National Association for the Prevention and Treatment of Tourette Syndrome.

"They sent us four hundred thousand dollars, and we don't know anything about them. I spoke to the senator about it, and he agreed that we had to check them out."

"Are they a registered PAC?"

"Yes, but I'd still like you to go down there and have a look around."

"Dickie, don't you think I have anything better to do than to look a gift horse in the mouth?"

"It's a big contribution, and it could be questioned."

So Ishmael found himself in a cab on his way to Seventh Street.

NAPTOTS was located in a small, faded brick building on Seventh, between R and S. Listed on the lobby board were a detective agency, an acupuncturist, a *se habla español* income-tax service, a travel agency, something called Atlas Out-Call, and NAPTOTS.

He walked up to the third floor, passing an overdressed woman in very high heels trailing in her wake the type of perfume that was sold by the pint.

NAPTOTS was lettered in plastic on the wooden door to Suite 3A. He knocked and waited for a response. Then he knocked again and tried the door. It felt to Ishmael as if he could bust the lock with his shoulder.

On his way back down, he passed a man in colorful African native dress. They had to turn themselves sideways to get by each other in the narrow stairwell. Ishmael had reached the second-floor landing when he looked back up and noticed the man in African dress taking out a key and unlocking the door to NAPTOTS.

Standing there on the second-floor landing of a building that did not appear to be a building that would house an organization with $400,000 lying around to donate to the reelection campaign of a senator from Vermont, Ishmael reviewed his options.

The simplest thing would be to leave, call Dickie Thong, tell him it all checked out, and spend the $400,000 on much-needed television advertising.

But the simplest thing wasn't necessarily the strategic thing. So Ishmael went back upstairs and knocked on the door to Suite 3A.

The man in colorful African dress answered the door. He looked at Ishmael and said, "Good day."

"Hi . . . I'm from Senator White's office . . ."

"Do come in, sir. What a pleasure."

He ushered Ishmael into a small, freshly painted room that had a desk, some file cabinets, some old furniture, and a WIPE OUT TS poster on the wall. The office smelled of cooked vegetables and cat litter. A fat gray cat was asleep on the radiator.

"Kodjo Kponvi, at your service."

"Ishmael Leibowitz."

They shook hands.

"*Enchanté,* Mr. Leibowitz. Please. Sit down. May I offer you some Darjeeling tea?"

"No thank you," Ishmael replied, sinking into the smooth leather chair that faced a desk that had nothing but a telephone and a few file folders on it.

"And how is our dear senator?"

"He's very well."

"Splendid."

"He asked me to come down to thank you personally for your generous contribution."

"Oh, that. It was nothing. *Le moindre des choses.*"

"How long have you been in existence?"

"Seventeen years. We started in a little storefront down the block, and look at us now."

Ishmael didn't see a trace of irony in the man's face.

"So . . . you're making progress in . . . wiping out TS."

"Most definitely, my good friend. Most definitely."

Kodjo Kponvi went into one of the file cabinets and came back with a brochure entitled *We Can Lick TS*. It looked like it had been run off at Kinko's.

"Did you know that once every seven and a half hours someone in this country is stricken with TS?"

"I didn't know that."

"It's a dreadful disease. But we are making progress, *n'est-ce pas?*" He smiled.

Ishmael smiled back. The phone rang. Kodjo Kponvi picked up. "NAPTOTS, how may I direct your call?"

Kodjo Kponvi's face creased, revealing the tribal markings on his forehead, and he began to speak on the phone in rapid-fire French.

Meanwhile Ishmael took a closer look around the office. There was a hibachi next to the window. A bag of charcoal. A cat-litter box. A bookshelf that was mostly empty except for some old *National Geographic*s.

He leafed through the brochure—a collection of statistics about the ravages of Tourette syndrome written in a somewhat stilted English—until Kodjo Kponvi got off the phone.

"Terribly sorry," he apologized.

"No problem. So, you are making progress in eradicating TS?"

"By bounds and leaps. Bounds and leaps."

"That's terrific . . ."

"Splendid."

They smiled at each other for a few more awkward moments. Then Ishmael got up and said, "Well, I'm sure you're a busy man. I'll be on my way."

"By all means. Please do not miss telling the senator how much we are fond of him."

"I will. I mean, I won't. Miss. Telling him."

"Splendid."

They shook hands again, and Kodjo Kponvi showed him to the door.

On the way down Ishmael could still smell the out-call woman's perfume in the air. It mingled with the odor of cat litter and charcoal-broiled vegetables.

He slipped the brochure into his pocket and chuckled to himself. It was brilliant. Though the scale wasn't nearly as big, the ingenuity of the scam was right up there with Iran/Contra.

What he didn't know, however, was whether the senator was Poindexter or Reagan.

Ishmael chose a working lunch that Friday to have the NAPTOTS discussion with the senator. They were alone in the office, eating take-out sandwiches and going over the phone log, when Ishmael brought up Dickie Thong's call and the trip down to Seventh Street.

"A cat and a hibachi?"

"Yes. And this brochure."

He handed Woody the *We Can Lick TS* brochure. The senator glanced quickly through it, then put it down and said, "Every seven and a half hours?"

"Apparently."

"I've never met anybody with the condition, have you?"

Ishmael shook his head.

"There was that ballplayer on the Phillies . . . what was his name?"

"I don't know, Senator."

Woody crumpled up the sandwich paper and tossed it into the wastepaper basket. He ran the tip of his tongue against his teeth, grimaced, and said, "Let's go directly to the worst-case scenario. Run it down for me."

"All right. Either Rebecca Gatney or the Ethics Committee decides to check out the contribution. They go down to Seventh Street and meet Mr. Kponvi. They see the cat and the hibachi and the Kinko's brochure. They investigate and find out that Kodjo Kponvi is not a fund-raiser for Tourette syndrome but, in reality, an African national, say, from the Republic of Togo, who is using the disease as a front to channel money to congressmen in exchange for votes on issues that affect them."

Woody nodded and smiled. "One thing about you, Ishmael. You're always refreshingly candid."

"Thank you, Senator."

"That's why you'd never make it as a politician. You couldn't bullshit your way out of a paper bag."

Ishmael nodded, choosing to interpret the remark as a compliment. Woody leaned back in his chair and slipped into philosophical mode.

"Okay," he postulated, "since we're talking ethics, let's look at this from an ethical point of view. On one side we have four hundred thousand dollars from the Republic of Togo. A small investment for them, one percent of the forty million they're getting in return. So the people of Togo aren't being hurt—am I right?"

"Yes."

"Now, on the other side we have the American taxpayer, or, more precisely, the Vermont taxpayer. He sends me to Washington to look out for his interests. In addition to all the pork I'm able to throw his way, I take a global point of view. This is, after all, a global economy. And, like it or not, Vermont is part of the global economy, right?"

"Right."

"I select a country like Togo—per-capita GDP nine hundred dollars, average life expectancy fifty-six years—and decide to help them develop their phosphate industry. What happens? The Togolese, with money in their pockets, become a fresh market for American goods. They develop a middle class. They start buying cheddar cheese, maple syrup, hockey sticks—"

"Hockey sticks?"

"They've got hockey teams in Fort Lauderdale and Tampa Bay, don't they? Why not Togo?"

"All right," Ishmael countered, taking up his customary part in the Socratic dialogue, "let's say that the Togolese take up hockey and that money comes back to Vermont in the form of increased hockey-stick orders. Nevertheless it is still illegal for foreign governments to contribute directly to political candidates. I mean, what about all the grief the President got about the Taiwanese money?"

"The President fucked up. He gave those coffees. There was a quid pro quo."

"Wouldn't your vote on the African Affairs Subcommittee be considered the quid pro quo?"

"No, because it wasn't until the chairperson let the vote come up that it got out of committee. And it wasn't my vote that got it reported out. It was the President calling her up and twisting her arm. So, you see, there was no quo. There was just a quid."

Then the senator quickly switched contexts, moving from ethics to pragmatism. "Who knows about the contribution?"

"Well, let's see, there's Dickie. And Beverly."

"What about the list of contributors?"

"It's public information. Anyone can see it."

"So we have to figure that Rebecca Gatney's people are going to see it, right?"

"Right."

"And they may eventually go down to Seventh Street and see the hibachi and the cat, right?"

"Right."

"And then they're going to look for any legislation I may have sponsored promoting federal funds for Tourette syndrome to justify the PAC support for my campaign, right?"

"That's what I would do if I were them."

The senator got up and took a tour around the office, his arms behind him. Ishmael watched him wrestling with the problem, deep in thought.

When he was finished wrestling, he sat down on the edge of his desk, faced his chief of staff, and smiled.

Ishmael smiled back. Though he didn't know why.

"Here's what we're going to do, Ishmael. Get my Medicaid and Health Care staffer to gather all the material he can get on Tourette syndrome. Then alert Debbie Sue."

He smiled again, nodded to himself.

"First we do the research. Then we write the bill. Then we get a co-sponsor. Maybe Teddy. The White-Kennedy Bill. Sound good?"

"Uh-huh . . ."

As he dialed his home number, Woody hoped that Dario hadn't taken his firing literally. He had a small task for the housekeeper to perform, which would save the senator a drive out to McLean.

He was relieved to hear the familiar voice on the other end of the line.

"*Pronto.*"

"*Pronto,* Dario."

"*È lei, senatore?*"

"Yes, Dario, it's me. Now listen—go to my wife's bedroom and pick up the extension in there, *capito?*"

"*La camera della signora?*"

"Right."

"*Subito, senatore.*"

As he waited for Dario to go to Daphne's bedroom and pick up the phone, he glanced down at the message he was going to fax her. It was terse and to the point.

One of the several things that had driven Woody out of his wife's bedroom years ago was the fax machine she kept by the bedside for late-night documents from her office. He'd be just about to nod off and suddenly the machine would start spewing affidavits and depositions into the night.

Dario picked up the bedroom extension.

"*Eccomi, senatore.*"

"Dario, do you see the fax machine on the bedside table?"

"*Sì.*"

"What is the number?"

"*Non lo so.*"

"Dario, look in the display window. There should be a phone number."

"*Non vedo niente . . .*"

"There is no number?"

"*C'è l'hora et il giorno. È tutto.*"

Woody thought for a moment, then said, "Dario, is there any paper by the machine?"

"*Carta? Sì.*"

"Take a sheet of paper and feed it into the machine."

"Feed? *Che cosa* feed?"

"Feed . . . *mangiare* . . ."

"*Mangiare? Non mangia un fax, senatore.*"

"Just put the fucking piece of paper in the fucking machine, Dario."

"*Certo.*"

"Now I'm going to give you a number. You press the numbers on the keypad and then press the button that says 'send.' *Capito?*"

"*I numeri, sì* . . ."

"Two-oh-two . . . seven-three-four . . ."

"*Come?*"

"*Due-zero-due . . . sette-tre-quattro* . . ."

When Woody received the fax, he read the return number on the top margin. Then he put his fax in the machine and pressed *send*.

Whenever Daphne came home she would find a fax waiting for her in her bedroom. It was brief and to the point.

BACK OFF OR BACK TO HELSINKI.

15.

THE WHITE-KANUSH BILL

SENATOR WOODROW WILSON WHITE'S authorized biographer, Lee Schumock, flew to Cleveland and drove a hundred miles in the rented Taurus with the air conditioner on high to East Gethsemane, a hamlet on the Ohio-Pennsylvania border about an hour south of Youngstown. East Gethsemane turned out to be a filling station, a general store, and a phone booth.

The phone booth wasn't of use to him, since Maddie White, the senator's daughter, didn't have a phone. She had renounced such conveniences when she had married an Amish blacksmith and gone to live among the dour Luddites of eastern Ohio. Her brother the dope dealer had given Lee Schumock a rural delivery mailbox for an address. Instead of waiting for an exchange of letters, the writer had decided to fly out and drop in.

Dropping in, however, turned out to be more problematic than he had anticipated. The box with the correct number was one of dozens of hand-made wooden mailboxes at the end of a dirt road off a two-lane blacktop that led to dozens of fairly identical-looking small farms, none of which had names on them, and all of which seemed to have unfriendly dogs roaming around unleashed.

Lee Schumock waited for a horse and buggy to come clopping up the road and asked the bearded man at the reins if he knew where Maddie White lived. The man shook his head. Two more buggies came by, and they, too, were unable to tell him where the senator's daughter lived.

Lee Schumock drove back into town and called Bobby White from the phone booth.

"Hey, man, what's going on?"

"I'm in East Gethsemane trying to find your sister. I ask people if they know where Maddie White lives and they just shake their heads."

"Oh, wow, man, I forgot to tell you. When she went to live with the Amish, she changed her name to Ruth."

"Ruth what?"

"Just plain Ruth. You know that whither-thou-goest shit in the Bible? Ruth goes down to Moab, marries a guy named Boaz, and they get it on . . . ?"

Lee Schumock went back out to the mailboxes and waited. It was ninety-one degrees and humid. It was over an hour before another horse and buggy came clopping down the road.

"Excuse me—would you happen to know where Boaz and Ruth live?"

"Boaz the blacksmith?"

"Yes, I think so . . ."

"Mile and a half down the road, right side with a red barn missing a couple of windows."

The farm with the red barn missing a couple of windows was, thankfully, the only farm for miles around without a dog patrolling the perimeter. He walked across a yard full of chickens to the door and knocked. No answer. He knocked again. When there was still no answer, he tried the door, which opened with a loud squeak.

A large German shepherd with the biggest teeth that Lee Schumock had ever seen chased the writer back to his car, where he sat with the doors and windows closed as the dog circled the car barking viciously.

The dog's barking eventually attracted a heavy man in a leather apron with a long gray-flecked beard.

Lee Schumock rolled down his window and said, "I'm trying to find Ruth."

The writer handed the blacksmith a printed card that read: LEE SCHUMOCK, PH.D.—BIOGRAPHICAL RESEARCH AND EDITORIAL SERVICES. BY APPOINTMENT.

"You see, I'm writing a book about Senator White. And I believe that Ruth is his daughter. She used to be called Maddie White. So I wanted to talk to her."

The man handed him back the card, turned around, and went back across the yard and into the house, closing the door behind him.

Rivulets of sweat rolled down Lee Schumock's face. He started the engine to run the air conditioner. The needle had just lurched another fraction of an inch toward the red zone when the door to the house opened and a young woman in a long skirt, shawl, and bonnet emerged, four dour children hanging on to her dress. She stared across the yard at him, frowned, then detached herself from the children and came over to the car.

"I apologize for Boaz's reception," she said, getting into the car. "He doesn't like my father. My name is Ruth. How may I be of help to you?"

"I'm writing a book about your father," he said. "Your brother gave me your address."

"And how is my brother, the sinner?"

"Fine."

"You'll tell him I pray for him when you see him?"

"Of course. Perhaps we can go someplace and talk."

"I don't travel in automobiles."

"Could we . . . is there anyplace . . . here?"

"We may speak right here."

"Do you mind if I tape this?"

"Yes."

"Is it against your religion?"

"Ask what you want to know."

"Could you tell me what it was like growing up with him?"

She smiled. He imagined that she must have been pretty at one point, but the years of drudgery without conveniences or cosmetics had apparently taken their toll.

"My father is a lost soul. He wanders around looking for purpose and finds none."

"Were you close to him when you were young?"

"We rarely saw him. He came and went. He was an important man."

"You must have some memories of him."

She thought for a moment, her brow curling in the effort.

"When I think of my father I think of a man arguing with the devil."

He waited for elaboration. It took a minute.

"I sometimes think that my father will not go to hell because he'll talk his way out of it."

"Do you think he should go to hell?"

More silence. Then she shook her head and said, "He kissed me on the forehead every night when I went to sleep. He would come in, whatever time it was, and kiss me on the forehead. Most of the time I was already asleep, but I knew he had been there. It made me feel protected. For that reason alone he should not go to hell."

"What about heaven?"

She laughed. It was a surprisingly girlish, almost coquettish laugh.

"Heaven is not big enough for my father. He would be bored in ten minutes."

"When was the last time you saw your father?"

"In 1994. We sat in his car, much as you and I are right now, and he told me all about his life in Washington. Then he kissed me on the forehead and left. He had an appointment in Cleveland."

"Do you want to see him?"

"It is enough that he comes here every four or five years and kisses me on the forehead."

The needle was entering the red zone. It was time to wrap this up.

"So . . . you're happy here, on the farm?"

"I have come here to live with Boaz."

"'Whither thou goest'?"

"'And she lay at his feet until the morning.'"

"Uh-huh . . . any message for your father?"

"Tell him to read Ruth 4:14."

"Want to paraphrase it?"

"'Blessed be the Lord, which hath not left thee this day without a kinsman, that his name may be famous in Israel.'"

"I'll let him know."

Representative Carl Kanush, of Koochiching, in Minnesota's Eighth Congressional District, said that he would be only too happy to have lunch with Senator Woodrow White. As recently as last March, in a conference committee, the senator had supported the first-term congressman's amendment to increase funding for a federal waste-control facility.

Although the bill died a quick death on the Floor, it had gotten Carl Kanush's name into the *Record,* which would look good in his mailings back home. So, as far as the senator was concerned, Carl Kanush owed him one.

Woody chose the same tourist restaurant on K Street he had chosen for his lunch with Hank Leventhal, and for the same reason.

"The Thomas Jefferson prime rib is very good here," he said as they glanced at their menus.

"Sounds good to me," Carl Kanush replied.

"And make sure to leave room for the Dolly Madison apple cobbler."

"You got it, Senator."

"Call me Woody."

They talked hunting—which Woody abhorred but could talk about convincingly enough to satisfy those of his constituents who liked to tramp around in the woods shooting animals—until the prime rib arrived.

"Carl, I've been admiring your work on the conference committee."

"Well, thanks, Woody."

"Next time, we'll have the votes."

"You bet."

"Tell you what I've been thinking about, Carl. I've been thinking about Tourette syndrome."

"Beg pardon?"

"TS. It claims a new victim in this country every seven and a half hours."

"I'm not familiar with it, I'm afraid."

"It's a neurological disorder. Causes involuntary muscle spasms and vocal outbursts—everything from echolalia to palilalia to, tragically, coprolalia."

"Coprolalia?"

"You ever run into someone who's shouting dirty words at you without any apparent reason?"

"Can't say that I have."

"It's sad, Carl, very sad. Because they can't help it. It's a form of OCD. Obsessive-compulsive disorder. People can't stop doing things like washing their hands and counting to ten. Affects one in every hundred males and one in every three hundred females in this country alone. You know that?"

Carl Kanush shook his head.

"There's a goddamn epidemic going on, Carl. And we're unprepared to deal with it. There are organizations trying to help victims, but they need help. And they need it right away. So instead of dicking around in committee for months, I figure that if I could get a companion bill going in the House, it'd save a lot of time when we got to conference committee. So imagine how pleased I was when I checked the roster of the Health Subcommittee on Ways and Means, and there's my friend Carl Kanush from Minnesota."

"Well, I'm honored, Woody . . . I really am."

"This is going to be ground-breaking legislation."

"I would need, of course, to have my staff do the research . . ."

"I've got reams of it. I'll send it over to you this afternoon."

"Sure."

"The White-Kanush Bill. Sound good to you?"

"Very good."

Woody raised his wineglass. Carl Kanush raised his iced tea glass. They clinked.

"We'll be right up there with Taft-Hartley," Woody said as the Dolly Madison apple cobblers arrived.

"I don't get it. He has bad bone structure. His cheekbones actually sag. Have you noticed?"

"Yeah."

"He needed work even back then."

Ishmael was in his office discussing Jean-Louis Trintignant's bone structure on the phone with Barry when an intern buzzed to ask if the senator wanted to take a call from Phil Yalowitz. Ishmael told Barry he'd call him back and put Phil Yalowitz through to the senator, keeping the line open so he could listen in.

"Who is it this time, Phil, one or two?"

"Neither of them. You're being sued by Trent Lott."

"What?"

"Fifty-five hundred dollars plus legal fees for damage to his car. Did you back into his car in the Senate parking garage on . . . March thirteenth?"

"Yes, but he was parked badly. His car was sticking over the yellow line. Threw off my judgment."

"Why didn't you have your insurance company deal with it?"

"They'll raise my rates. I offered him a decent settlement. He's just pissed off over the transportation bill."

"How would you like me to reply to the suit?"

"Offer him two grand, plus a body shop selected by a neutral party."

"Excuse me?"

"If he takes it to his body shop, it's going to cost me fifty-five hundred. I've got a thousand-dollar deductible. So I pay a grand and my rates go up at least a grand, a grand and a half, a year. We do it under the table, nobody's rates go up, he doesn't have to report the income, and it only cost me maybe three, out the door."

"Two thousand dollars cash and a . . . neutral body shop?"

"Uh-huh."

"What exactly is a *neutral* body shop?"

"A body shop chosen at random from the Yellow Pages by a disinterested party agreeable to both of us."

"You would like me to call the attorney for the Majority Leader of the United States Senate and suggest that we agree on someone to pick a body shop at random from the Yellow Pages?"

"Yes. Otherwise, we go to court and I testify about how irresponsibly he was parked."

"Senator, should this ever get anywhere near a court, and I sincerely doubt it would, it will be thrown out on summary judgment, and you'll be looking at court costs on top of legal costs far exceeding the amount claimed."

"Just run it up the aisle, Phil. See if we get a quorum."

16.

MORE DAMAGE CONTROL

IN THE SENATOR'S PRIVATE OFFICE, inside a locked antique cabinet behind the Vermont Shaker rocking chair, was a fax machine that was used for last-minute markups to pending legislation and sensitive party caucus business. The senator, Ishmael, and Debbie Sue Allenby were the only ones with keys to the cabinet.

In her capacity as chief legislative assistant to Senator White, Debbie Sue Allenby checked the machine first thing every morning on her arrival in the office. More often than not, the machine was empty, and she re-locked the cabinet, rechecking it at two in the afternoon, and then again just before she left for the day.

On the morning of June 18, Debbie Sue Allenby found a short and very disturbing fax. There was no cover sheet. It was one sentence. CALL OFF INS OR YOU'RE DEAD.

Though it was not that unusual for a senator to get a death threat, Senator White had never received one in his twelve years in the Senate. What was even more curious was that whoever sent it had access to the private fax number. She searched for a return transmittal number on the top of the fax and found none.

Though she had made it a practice never to disturb the senator at home, she decided she'd better contact him and find out if he wanted her to report this to the Capitol Police.

She dialed the McLean number and waited for ten rings before a sleepy voice answered.

"Pronto?"

"Excuse me—is this Senator White's residence?"

"Non c'è."

Debbie Sue Allenby didn't speak Spanish, so she hung up and redialed the number. The voice sounded even more annoyed than it had before.

"Pronto!"

She hung up and dialed Ishmael at home.

"Hi. Call me Ishmael. Leave a message at the beep."

If Ishmael had been home, he would have told her not to do anything at all about the fax. But Ishmael was in Alexandria, waiting for Maud to pack her daughter off to school to see if he could negotiate a pre-breakfast quickie.

Debbie Sue Allenby reread the fax. The senator did not have a seat on the Immigration Subcommittee of the Judiciary Committee. What business would he possibly have with the INS?

So Debbie Sue Allenby decided it was better to be safe than sorry. She would call the Capitol Police. Let them deal with it.

Ishmael found Sergeant Harvey Grimes of the Capitol Police in the senator's office when he got in from Alexandria at nine-thirty, having been denied a quickie by Maud, who was still pissed off about the Dupont Circle movie incident and hadn't permitted anything beyond heavy petting since.

As soon as the policeman showed him the fax, Ishmael went into damage-control mode.

"Oh *that*," he said. "That's a joke."

"How's that?"

"It's an old college friend of the senator. They send each other gag faxes all the time. You know, old jokes from their college days."

"What's the name of this old friend?"

"Ken. Ken . . . Mason. Case Western Reserve Law School. Class of '67."

Grimes took out his notebook.

"You happen to have an address and phone number for Mr. Mason?"

"Yes. No. . . . Look, Sergeant, believe me, this is nothing."

"It's our job to investigate death threats that occur on the grounds of the Capitol, Mr. Leibman."

"It's Leibowitz."

"I don't know if you are aware of this, but transmitting a fax without a return number is a violation of FCC statutes."

"Actually, I wasn't aware of that."

"You got a fax number for this Mr. Mason?"

"I'll check the Rolodex."

Ishmael went into his office, closed the door, and dialed the senator's cell phone.

Woody had been luckier than his chief of staff the previous night. He kept a spare starched nurse's uniform in the closet of the *pied-à-terre* in Wesley Heights, and he and Evelyn Brandwynne had been at it till after midnight.

At nine-thirty that morning the senator was sitting with the lobbyist from the National Association of Health Prophylaxis Industries over a leisurely breakfast when he got the call from Ishmael explaining the problem with the fax and the Capitol Police.

"Shit. Who gave them the fax?"

"Debbie Sue. She thought it was a death threat."

"What did you say the guy's name was?"

"Ken Mason. Case Western Reserve Law School. Class of 1967."

"Tell him you had a new secretary update your Rolodex and she accidentally threw out his phone number."

"What about the INS?"

"Tell him . . . it's an abbreviation for insurance, and it's this running gag about a football bet we made."

"It's baseball season."

"Say it's a running gag about . . . insulin."

"I think we're better off with just the new secretary and the Rolodex."

"All right. Run with it."

As Woody clicked off the phone, Evelyn Brandwynne looked up from the newspaper.

"I don't want to know about this, do I?"

"No, you don't, Evelyn."

"Good."

Rumors of the death threat to Senator Woodrow White landed in the steam room of the Senate Health Facility before lunch.

"You don't think Trent would have threatened him over a fender bender, do you?"

"Maybe. Herb's aide thinks that Woody may be trying to get Trent's illegal housekeeper deported."

"Trent's got an illegal housekeeper?"

"Everybody has an illegal housekeeper."

"It was an inside job. It came over his security fax."

"That'd give us only ninety-nine suspects in the Senate alone, not to mention the House."

"Could be the zipper problem again."

"Think so?"

"Some woman he hit on trying to extort money."

"I heard he was screwing some lobbyist."

"A lobbyist? Who with?"

"Hank's girl thought it was the NRA."

"The NRA? That ought to play in Vermont."

"Woody on Wildlife and Conservation?"

"I don't know."

The sound of dripping sweat hitting the tiles punctuated a long silence.

"Anyway, a death threat can't hurt his poll numbers, that's for sure."

"No, sir."

Barry, Kevin, Jack, and Denny were all over Ishmael on the death-threat rumors. Convinced that Woody White's chief of staff knew more than he was letting on about the fax and the INS connection, they badgered him relentlessly.

Kevin's senator happened to be the chairman of the Immigration Sub-committee, and so the aide, feeling he had a vested interest in finding out what type of deal Woody White had going with the INS, was particularly relentless.

In addition to his professional interest, Kevin had leverage. Though as far as Ishmael could tell, Kevin hadn't mentioned anything to Barry, Jack, or Denny about the post–*My Night at Maud's* arm-around-the-woman's-waist episode, there was always the threat that he would.

Whatever Kevin's interpretation of the incident outside the movie the-ater, he didn't seem to see it as a deterrent to his own advances. There had been an invitation to a tête-à-tête dinner at Kevin's duplex on Hill-yer Place, followed by a video of *The Conformist,* to which Ishmael had pleaded overwork, and another invitation for Ishmael to take advantage of a complimentary guest pass to Kevin's health club, to which Ishmael had pleaded knee problems.

So Ishmael found himself fending off Kevin's interest not only in the fax but in him as well.

Ishmael already had enough on his plate these days. Besides the ongo-ing Trent Lott car-accident negotiations, he had to ride herd on a staff-wide effort to gather information for the bill on Tourette syndrome that the senator wanted to slam-dunk through the Medicaid and Health Care Subcommittee.

The legislative aide to Congressman Carl Kanush, an earnest young man with a bad stutter named Owen Lundkeim, called him three times a day to discuss the bill.

"W . . . w . . . w . . . w . . . what about the A . . . A . . . A . . . American A . . . s . . . s . . . sociation of U . . . U . . . U . . . University A . . . A . . . A . . . Affiliated P . . . P . . . P . . . Programs and P . . . P . . . P . . . Persons with D . . . D . . . D . . . Developmental D . . . D . . . D . . . D . . . D . . . Disabilities?"

"Can I get back to you on that?"

"S . . . s . . . s . . . ure. W . . . w . . . w . . . what about the O . . . O . . . O . . . C . . . C . . . C . . . F . . . F . . . F . . . F?"

"The what?"

"The O . . . O . . . O . . . Obsessive C . . . C . . . C . . . Compulsive F . . . F . . . F . . . F . . . F . . . F . . . F . . . Foundation."

And so it went. Hours on the phone learning a great deal more about Tourette syndrome than Ishmael wanted or needed to know. Hours on the phone with Kevin, Barry, Jack, and Denny debunking rumors about the senator's INS connection. Ducking calls from Trent Lott's chief of staff. Holding Debbie Sue Allenby's hand when she began to obsess about the Tourette-syndrome bill.

And now he had to deal with Sergeant Harvey Grimes, who was doggedly investigating the threatening fax. Ishmael knew just enough about the INS and about a deportation threat to know that he didn't want to know anything more.

The senator had told the head of the Capitol Police that Ken Mason had died last month in a fourteen-car collision in Cleveland and that he did not believe that the fax had any connection with the Immigration and Naturalization Service. He was not on the Immigration Subcommittee and had no business with the INS. Frankly, Woody told Sergeant Grimes, he had no idea what the initials *INS* meant on the fax. And since there was no cover letter, wouldn't it be plausible that whoever sent the fax was meaning to send it to someone else and simply misdialed?

So, in addition to checking phone-company records for the transmitting fax number, the FBI undertook a computer-generated random analysis of all fax numbers at the INS headquarters in the Chester A. Arthur Building, looking for numbers with one or two digits in common with the senator's office fax number.

The computer scan of the Chester A. Arthur Building amused just about everyone working there except the asset-forfeiture associate director, who called Woody from a phone booth on I Street.

"What the hell's going on, Senator?"

"Nothing, Hank. Relax."

"The FBI's checking fax numbers."

"Did you send the fax?"

"No . . ."

"Then you've got nothing to worry about."

"Who the hell *did* send it?"

"Hank, remember our talk about deniability?"

"Uh-huh."

"No way this gets back to you."

"Uh-huh."

"So where are we on the Finnish ice-skater?"

"I've got to run. Meeting."

Hank Leventhal hung up, looked carefully around him, then walked around the block twice before reentering the building.

Hank Leventhal wasn't the only one made nervous by the reference to the INS on the fax. Dario Farniente, the Whites' illegal Italian house-keeper, was extremely upset when he heard the story on the news.

One word he understood perfectly well in English was *INS,* but with his erratic command of the language, he thought that his boss had gone to the INS to get him deported instead of having him fired.

Stronzo!

He wasn't going to take that lying down. He would make sure that the *senatore* knew that if anything happened to him, he would take Helmut the dachshund down with him.

Dario had a cousin in Houston. Also illegal, but in the process of get-ting his papers. Dario would grab Helmut and go to Houston. If the *sena-tore* wanted his dachshund back alive, he'd better drop the deportation business. *Rapidamente.*

John Quincy Adams and Elbridge Gerry had turned in early. They went upstairs with cups of Ovaltine, slipped into their nightshirts, got under the handwoven quilts of their twin beds in the big bedroom of the house out-side Montpelier, and watched the ten o'clock news on the thirteen-inch-black-and-white TV perched on the solid oak dresser.

The story of the death threat against the senator played just before the farm report. Over file footage of Woody White confronting reporters dur-ing his zipper-problem days, the local anchor, Doug DeBoeuf, told the viewers that their controversial senator was in the news again.

"Though no one has come forward to claim responsibility for the fax," Doug DeBoeuf said, "there is speculation that environmental or feminist radicals may have been involved. Since sending a fax without a return number is a federal offense, the FBI crime lab in Bethesda, Maryland, is in-vestigating."

Then there was a standup with Rebecca Gatney outside her suburban home in Burlington.

"I am not claiming that this threat is a direct result of Woody White's well-documented character problems," she told the reporter, "but I wouldn't rule it out. If you play in the mud, you're going to get your clothes dirty."

Following file footage of Rebecca Gatney playing in the snow with her collie, Doug DeBoeuf wrapped it up by saying, "It looks like the Senate race is heating up."

John Quincy Adams zapped the TV with the remote and sipped his Ovaltine.

"Tell you what I think, Elbridge."

"What's that?"

"I think that woman could use a turn around the yard."

"Amen."

"'Course the mud's gone."

"There's the south meadow. We could hook her up to the tractor and run her through the cow chips."

"Probably wouldn't shut her up."

"Probably wouldn't."

John Quincy Adams turned off the bedside lamp.

"Good night, Elbridge."

"Night, John."

17

THE EMPTY-DOG-DISH STRATEGY

Just before noon the next day, a Senate page approached Woody during morning business and told him there was an FBI agent waiting for him outside the cloakroom.

Special Agent Gary Sonnenfeld, of the FBI's Domestic Terrorism Division, asked Woody if there was someplace they could talk privately.

"What about?"

"I'd rather not go into it here, Senator."

Woody led him to his cubbyhole office off the Floor and closed the door. The office, designed to spare the senator a trip all the way back to Dirksen when there was a series of roll-call votes, was small and cluttered, with a count-down clock and alarm buzzer to indicate the number of minutes to the next vote. It had belonged to Alan Simpson, who had retired and returned to Wyoming. If you breathed deeply enough, you could still smell the horseshit.

At the moment, the desk was covered with Tourette-syndrome literature so that the senator could read up on the disease while waiting for a vote. He cleared away some space, sat on the desk, and offered Gary Sonnenfeld a seat.

"What can I do for you, Agent Sonnenfeld?"

"Senator, do you have a fax machine at your house in McLean?"

Woody had trained himself never to answer a question until he knew where it was leading. So he hit the ball back over the net.

"Why?"

"According to phone records, the threatening fax was sent from your house in McLean."

"Really?"

"The number is registered to you."

"No kidding."

"Senator, is there anybody who has access to that machine besides you and your wife?"

It took only a moment for the clouds to clear away and the sun to shine through. In one beautifully illuminating blast of light, the elegant solution presented itself. He could solve two problems at once.

"Let's see, there's our housekeeper . . ."

Agent Sonnenfeld took out his notebook and his government-issue ballpoint.

"His name is Dario Farniente. He's from Trieste."

"I'm sorry to have to ask you this, Senator, but is he in the country legally?"

"Well, he represented himself as having a green card when we hired him. But, you know, my wife and I have been having our suspicions lately. Whenever we ask to see it, he tells us it's somewhere in his room. The truth is Daphne and I have been thinking of letting him go."

"Is Mr. Farniente aware of this?"

"I've spoken to him about it on several occasions, explaining that he was putting not only himself in jeopardy but Daphne and me as well. We are aware, of course, that it is the employer's responsibility to check these things out, but what with my Senate business—I'm on five committees—and pending legislation on a new bill I'm sponsoring in Medicaid and Health Care . . . I don't know if you are aware, Agent Sonnenfeld, of the ravages that undiagnosed Tourette syndrome is causing in this country . . ."

When Dario Farniente saw the dark-gray Plymouth pull up in the driveway and two men in unfashionable suits get out, his worst fears were confirmed.

He quickly closed the blinds and grabbed Helmut from the couch. He ran into the kitchen, opened the refrigerator, and began stuffing *cannolis* into Helmut's mouth to distract the dachshund from the sound of the doorbell.

When the doorbell stopped, he put a dozen slices of prosciutto in Helmut's dish and ventured carefully up the stairs.

From the vantage point of the *signora*'s bedroom, he carefully parted the curtains and looked out. The dark-gray Plymouth was still parked in the driveway. Dario Farniente knew from *The People's Court* that the police couldn't enter a house without a warrant. He also knew that the back door off the kitchen led to a small wooded area, on the other side of which was a street that was about a quarter of a mile from a shopping center.

He went back down to his room and filled a small suitcase with clothes, collected his cookbooks, his jewelry, and his first edition of Gabriele D'Annunzio's classic novel *Notturno*.

Then he took the accumulated savings from his monthly salary, helped himself to the $400 left in the grocery fund for June, and ripped the taxi-cab listings out of the Yellow Pages.

By the time the FBI crime lab in Bethesda reported that the fax paper used in the death threat to Senator White was not the type allocated by the Government Printing Office to members of Congress or to INS employees, Special Agent Gary Sonnenfeld had already discovered that the senator's housekeeper, Dario Farniente, had not only sent the fax but had also absconded with the grocery fund and the family dachshund.

Accordingly, the story transformed itself from a death-threat story to an illegal-housekeeper story to a kidnapped-dog story. Rebecca Gatney's people immediately started firing off rounds.

"This is just another disgrace for the people of Vermont," she pronounced during a campaign appearance in Putney. "What about all the honest people in our state, people who are upstanding enough to pay Social Security taxes and Medicare for *their* household help?"

Woody's people went into emergency session. With the senator and Ishmael on the speakerphone from Washington, and Rav Monsjar on the phone from Brattleboro, the Montpelier staff batted around damage-control procedures for handling the issue of the undeclared Social Security and Medicare taxes for Dario Farniente.

It was decided that the best alternative was to plead the senator's preoccupation with pending business in front of his committees, spinning it into a positive message about all the work the senator was doing. He would make restitution, with penalties, of any unpaid Social Security and Medicare taxes.

But it was Rav Monsjar, as usual, who saw the pearl in the oyster.

"Fuck the taxes," he said. "It's the empty dog dish."

When no one picked up on that immediately, he expanded on it. "Don't you see—the man comes home to an empty dog dish? You've got Rebecca Gatney screaming about Social Security taxes while Woody White is deprived of the love of his dog. The taxes are the suitcase. We just don't open it. We leave it there and talk about the dog dish."

So a variation of the valise-denial strategy was put into motion. The unpaid Social Security taxes went up against the empty dog dish. Any opprobrium that the senator may have gotten for not checking out his housekeeper's immigration status and paying him off the books was quickly neutralized by the image of the empty dog dish.

Woody made a public appeal to Dario Farniente to return Helmut. Standing in the living room in McLean in front of the hearth with a framed picture of Helmut, he held the empty dog dish up to the TV camera and offered a reward for information leading to the location of the family's beloved dog.

The voters of Vermont, even those without dogs, were unable to look at a man holding an empty dog dish without sympathy. Irwin Posalski did an overnight poll and reported that the kidnapped dog was worth 2.3 points.

Nevertheless, Woody had to put up with a certain amount of cloakroom humor on the whole matter of the death threat and the kidnapped dog. The Minority Whip asked him if he thought this was connected to the bad Spanish omelet in March. Jesse told him that it went with the territory.

"That's the price you pay for doing the people's business, Senator. Always going to be some crackpot doesn't like what you're doing, takes a double-gauge off the back of the truck and squeezes off a few rounds, or steals your dog. I'd be careful, I were you."

Woody thanked him for his concern.

When Beverly Levesque found out about the July Fourth pancake-breakfast fund-raiser at John Quincy Adams's place in Montpelier, she called the senator's office and had Ishmael page him in the Senate Health Facility.

Dripping sweat, Woody listened on the cell to the head of his state re-election committee explain the political liabilities that would stem from accepting help from the head of the Vermont Maple Syrup Distributors Association.

"If you think not paying your housekeeper's Social Security taxes is grist for the mill, wait till Rebecca Gatney gets her hands on this."

"Mr. Adams is the head of a legitimate political-action group."

"The VMSDA is just a front. I told you that."

"Has he been indicted?"

"The only reason he hasn't been is that Vincent Ruggiero is no longer a U.S. Attorney."

"Beverly, if I took money from Ethan Allen himself, Rebecca Gatney would come after me."

"All right, look. Make sure Dickie reports the money. And, for godsakes, don't do the man any favors."

"Why would I do him a favor?"

"I don't know. But whatever he asks you to do, don't do it."

"All we're going to do is eat some pancakes and put some checks in our pockets."

"Do you want us to book you at the Capitol Plaza?"

"Yes."

"For you alone, or will your wife be joining you?"

"I don't know yet."

"Senator, it would be nice if you could get her to make some local appearances with you."

He clicked off the phone and started to pedal faster, his mind spinning with the exercise bike.

This wasn't a cocktail party at the White House with the President and Dick Gephardt fawning over her. This was pancakes and maple syrup at the home of a man with a backed-up septic tank. This was really a quo.

He would have to put another quid on the table. A moratorium from Hank Leventhal's storm troopers might sweeten the deal. A short trip to Vermont ought to be worth a thirty-day reprieve.

He'd fax her in McLean, lay out the deal for her. Thirty days for a pancake fund-raiser.

The truth was that Daphne Melancamp White had never intended the death threat to be more than a negotiating ploy—an offer to solicit a counteroffer. And so she was appalled by all the attention it had gotten.

Thank God for the housekeeper.

Though her fax may have been a negotiating ploy, it was not sent without passion. Woody's blackmailing her over her lover's immigration status had infuriated her. Sonja was so upset that her ulcer had flared up and she was reduced to eating white-meat chicken and cottage cheese.

Daphne had consulted an immigration lawyer, who told her that if the INS had documented proof of Sonja's failure to be enrolled in an educational institution during the period in which she had reported to them she was, their legal position was shaky.

The lawyer, a cheerful man named Ira Bink, worked out of a shabby office in Lincoln Park with dreadful wallpaper and a waiting room full of undocumented Central Americans. He told Daphne that getting Sonja into some educational program as soon as possible would help. And so Daphne had to call around town to see if someone would enroll a Finnish ice-skater with only a secondary-school education.

Sonja herself didn't lift a finger. The willowy, blond ice-skater had taken to her bed in the apartment that Daphne paid for near the National Cathedral and played Camille, eating her cottage cheese and watching daytime soap operas while Daphne spent hours on the phone talking to registrars at various educational institutions about the possibility of enrolling Sonja in some sort of course of study that would satisfy INS regulations.

The Immigration and Naturalization Service, Ira Bink explained to her, required that the course of study be for a degree in some area that would eventually lead to gainful employment. "You can't do yoga or interpretive dance," he said, "though in her case, if you could find an ice-skating course, that would probably fly."

Sonja herself showed very little interest in anything that required any work on her part. She enjoyed spending her days watching TV, playing tennis at Daphne's tennis club, and lounging in the sauna at Daphne's exclusive women's health club in Georgetown. Studying European history or sociology didn't interest her very much.

"I don't like books," she declared.

"They have courses on cassette these days."

"Perhaps I must go back to Helsinki," she announced. "There I am an artist. Here I am a nothing."

It was emotional blackmail. Sonja must have known that Daphne couldn't leave Washington, D.C. Not yet, at least. At some point, when she got her hands on some of the Hanna millions that Adele Hanna Weit was sitting on out in Palm Springs, she and Sonja could go live together on Mykonos. They could walk hand in hand on the beach. Sonja could water-ski naked for her. At night she would whisper dirty words in Finnish in her ear . . . But not yet.

For the time being, Daphne Melancamp White was engaged in a nasty little war of attrition with her future ex-husband. The deportation business had hit her in a vulnerable spot. They were each pointing a gun at the other's head, but her head was a little closer to her heart than his was.

So when Woody's next fax arrived at McLean, she was ready to deal. It was a little longer than the last one, but just as candid.

SHORT CAMPAIGN SWING TO MONTPELIER JULY 4TH WEEKEND FOR THIRTY DAYS' REPRIEVE ON DEPORTATION? PHONE DON'T FAX REPLY. ALL MY LOVE, WWW.

18

THE BATTLE OF BENNINGTON

DAPHNE MADE SURE HER PLANE got into Burlington after dark. She wasn't going to give Woody anything more than the letter of the deal in exchange for the thirty days. In her reply to his fax, she had negotiated deal points as if she were closing a corporate merger. Twenty-four hours, in and out, no cow-chip-tossing contests, twin beds.

Beverly had hoped for at least a photo op with the senator and his wife on the steps of the state Capitol, but by the time Daphne's car pulled up in front of the Capitol Plaza Hotel in Montpelier on July 3, the light was completely gone, and the photographer had to settle for a peck on the cheek under the awning of the hotel.

A late supper with the staff in the hotel restaurant was full of awkward pauses and forced gaiety. Daphne smiled her $575-an-hour smile, expressed the appropriate amount of concern for the missing dachshund, and had a piece of strawberry shortcake. But at the first yawn, she pleaded fatigue from the journey and excused herself.

When Daphne was gone, Beverly went over the schedule for the morning. They would assemble at the hotel at ten. Two minivans would be waiting to take them out to John Quincy Adams's place.

"What about the guest list? Has anybody seen it?" Janine Caravaggio asked.

Beverly shook her head. "I have asked Mr. Adams to fax it to me. He has replied that he doesn't have a fax machine."

"He doesn't have a *fax machine*?"

"Apparently not."

"Has anybody been out there to look around?"

"It's an old farmhouse with rusting automobiles in the front yard."

"What about security?"

"We will have two off-duty state troopers. Which we will have to pay for."

"With what?"

"Let me be frank," Beverly said. "I have opposed this fund-raiser from the beginning. I have told the senator that on more than one occasion—"

"Oh, stop being such an old lady, Beverly. We're going out there to eat pancakes and smile for the camera. I'm going to make a little speech. And we're going to raise some money. It's called politics."

There was a tense silence around the table.

"Sometimes," Rav Monsjar mused out loud, breaking the tension, "when you lie down with dogs, you get up with fleas. And sometimes you get up with five hundred thousand dollars."

"That's right," Dickie Thong said and put the campaign's maxed-out Visa card on top of the dinner check.

There was a Montpelier cop in the hallway outside the Green Mountain Suite on the ninth floor of the stately old hotel. Woody shook his hand and said, "I thought only the governor got this kind of treatment."

"I'm off-duty, Senator, and you're paying for me," the cop replied.

"Thanks just the same." Woody smiled and walked past him to the room.

The sitting room of the suite was furnished in late Early American, the TV hidden away in an oak armoire, the lamps all antique brass. Woody helped himself to a Courvoisier from the minibar, poured it into the snifter, and went into the bedroom.

Dressed in a Marks and Spencer bathrobe, Daphne was sitting up in one of the two pre-negotiated twin beds reading legal papers.

"Billing hours, are we?"

She looked at him over her half-moon reading glasses but didn't respond.

"You know, there's something very nostalgic about this scene—you in bed reading legal papers, me with my snifter of brandy. All that's missing is the whir of the fax machine spilling out pages of deposition."

"Talking to you was not part of the deal."

"Then I guess a blow job is out of the question."

Taking off her glasses, she looked at him with her I'm-not-fucking-around look and said, "Would you like me to go in the other room and work?"

"No, please. I wouldn't want to disturb you."

He went back into the sitting room, closing the door behind him. Sinking into the couch, he turned the TV on, hit the *mute* button and gazed absently at the silent ten o'clock news, trying to picture Daphne in a nurse's uniform. He wondered whether Pavlov worked if you changed the wattage of the lightbulb.

There was a graphic over footage of a woman standing near a pile of books in a bookstore. It read, DENISE MEZZOGIORNO, DR. HAAS'S RECEPTIONIST.

Grabbing the remote, he turned the sound back on.

Denise Mezzogiorno was holding up a book entitled *Ernie and Audrey: Beyond the Veil.*

The sound byte said, "It seems as if everyone is cashing in on the Audrey Haas case. Denise Mezzogiorno, Dr. Haas's receptionist for eleven years, has just come out with a book purporting to reveal heretofore-undisclosed facts surrounding Dr. Haas's death last March twenty-seventh in Schenectady, New York . . ."

Woody turned the sound up louder, as they went to a reporter outside the Schenectady County Courthouse.

"The trial of Audrey Haas for the murder of her husband is scheduled to begin here shortly. Both sides are predicting victory in this closely watched murder case that has gained worldwide attention as a test case for stronger sexual-abuse laws for women. . . ."

Woody hadn't thought about Dr. Haas since he had read the *People* magazine article about him in the Senate barbershop. The woman who wrote the book, Denise Mezzosoprano, or whatever the fuck her name was, had spoken with him on the phone. Worse, she had seen him in the doctor's office. She could identify him as James Monroe.

What if she mentions him in the book? *What if there's some sort of record of the Testoderm patches?*

He fished his Casio pocket organizer out of his attaché case, called up March 27 on his electronic calendar, and found the following references: Molly Stark Trail, Brattleboro paper, Marlboro College.

The day of the scrotum shave in Schenectady.

He went into the bathroom off the sitting room and locked the door. Running the shower, he dialed the cell.

"Hi. Call me Ishmael. Leave a message at the beep."

"Call me as soon as you pick this up," he whispered. "No matter what time it is."

He went back to the couch and turned the TV sound lower. He'd wait for Ishmael's phone call. By then, Daphne would be asleep.

He was on his third Courvoisier, nodding out over a how-to-creosote-your-fence-posts show on the local-access cable channel, when Ishmael called back.

"Senator?"

"Ishmael, I want you to go out first thing in the morning and pick up a copy of a book called *Ernie and Audrey: Beyond the Veil* and read it."

"May I ask what this is concerning?"

"I want you to check if there is any mention of James Monroe having been a patient of Dr. Haas."

"James Monroe, the President?"

"No. James Monroe, the patient."

"Senator, I have a meeting with Carl Kanush's committee staffer on the Tourette-syndrome bill and a lunch with your African Affairs aides . . ."

"The critical date is March twenty-seventh."

By five minutes past ten the following morning, Woody, Daphne, and the Vermont staff were in the minivan, buckled up and heading east on Route 2 out of Montpelier toward John Quincy Adams's place.

To look at them, you wouldn't have thought they were on the same team, or, for that matter, even knew one another. Daphne was, as usual, drop-dead fashionable in a Donna Karan East Hampton frock, with off-white Lauri Johnson shoes and a *Last Year at Marienbad* floppy summer hat. The senator was in tailored slacks, Gianni Boni loafers, and a Lacoste knitted T-shirt with a pair of Ray-Bans tucked into the neckline.

Beverly was wearing a plaid shirt, a denim skirt, and, even though the mud was long gone, a pair of rubber-soled Kmart boots. Her hair was tied back in a functional ponytail. She hadn't worn lipstick since the victory party in 1996. She made Janet Reno look like Cher.

Dickie Thong looked like the frazzled accountant he was, in a wrinkled wash-and-wear suit. Janine Caravaggio wore a pair of jeans at least a size too small for her and a pair of heels at least an inch too high for her. Brian Petrunich wore a T-shirt that said, IF YOU CAN READ THIS YOU'RE OVER-EDUCATED, in Latin. And Rav Monsjar looked like Allen Ginsberg on a bad hair day—his salt-and-pepper beard straggly, his khaki trousers high on his waist held up by a Boy Scout belt, a faded flannel shirt, and a Boston Red Sox baseball cap.

Conversation was spare. Daphne stared absently out the window. Woody studied his speech—an amalgamation of the Emerson-Thoreau and the tough-as-granite speeches. Janine Caravaggio would introduce him with the "Where's Woody? He's there" number. The usual drill. They'd done it a hundred times. Two hundred times. Deer at a salt lick.

There were maybe thirty cars lined up along the dirt road that fronted John Quincy Adams's place. Not a great showing, even for rural Vermont.

The maple-syrup kingpin had done his best to camouflage the peeling paint and rusted automobile carcasses with red, white, and blue bunting draped over the sagging front-porch railings. An American flag hung limply from a pole in the middle of the dried mud in the front yard. Beside it was a large hand-lettered sign that read COME HAVE FOURTH OF JULY BREAKFAST WITH SENATOR WHITE.

The two rented troopers waved the minivan into the yard. Woody got out and helped Daphne down, as John Quincy Adams and his fellow maple-syrup distributors came forward to greet them.

Daphne shook hands with their host, flashing her two-thousand-watt smile. The locals hadn't seen anybody like her in a while. It was reminiscent of Jackie Kennedy in Appalachia.

Woody and Daphne worked their way down the receiving line, shaking hands with the maple-syrup distributors—Elbridge Gerry, Ethan Allen, John Stark, Josiah Bartlett, Matthew Thornton, William Whipple, Stephen Hopkins, Lyman Hall, and Button Gwinnett.

They were followed by Beverly, who looked the way Eleanor Roosevelt might have had she been invited to the Adirondack Conference, and the rest of the campaign staff.

Though Beverly had told their own staff photographer to take the morning off, she was chagrined to find that there were flashbulbs popping nevertheless. The local papers had sent their stringers to get some shots of their senator during one of his rare appearances in Vermont.

After the handshakes, John Quincy Adams led them inside to see his scale-model replica of the Battle of Bennington, which was set up on a Ping-Pong table in the back parlor off the kitchen.

On a topographical map of the Bennington area, he had set out tiny toy soldiers to represent the armies that had met there between August 14 and August 16, 1777.

As the cloying smell of fresh maple syrup drifted in from the kitchen, John Quincy Adams explained to Daphne and her husband the tactics used by the Continental Army and the Green Mountain Boys to defeat the British at Bennington.

"You see, the Redcoats' strategy was to bring Burgoyne down from Canada to meet up with Howe coming up from New York and cut the colonies in two right along the Hudson Valley. 'Course, Howe was up to his ears in Philadelphia and never made it . . ."

Daphne listened attentively, her two-hundred-dollar-an-ounce Bulgari perfume wisping through the room.

"Now John Stark and Ethan Allen had scouts all along the Vermont–New York border and knew they were coming. The Green Mountain Boys were just sitting pretty to the south and the east of the town here." He indicated the toy soldiers with buckskin and blue on two sides of the model. "So when the Hessians came down from Lake Champlain"—he indicated the toy soldiers with tricornered hats and red uniforms—"they were like raccoons in a coon trap."

"How interesting," Daphne said and almost sounded as if she meant it.

"Yes, ma'am. We sliced up those little hired Krauts real good. They came back for more the next two days, and we made liverwurst out of them. 'Course, most people think Saratoga was the turning point of the war. But if the Hessians hadn't had their asses handed to them—you'll pardon my French—at Bennington, they would have been on Burgoyne's right at Saratoga, and it would have been a whole new ball game."

As Daphne nodded, a bland-looking woman with a notepad said, "I didn't know you were interested in local history, Mrs. White."

Daphne, Woody, and John Quincy Adams turned, all three of them at once, to face the woman, who said, by way of introduction, "Hermione Hingle, *Rutland Herald*."

"Bit of a drive for you, isn't it, Miss Hingle?" John Quincy Adams said.

"It's not often that we get a chance to see our senator up here in Vermont, Mr. Adams. Not to mention his lovely wife."

"Let me tell you something, Miss Hingle," John Quincy Adams said, looking as if he were about to chain her to the tractor for a spin through the cow chips. "We are fortunate to have a senator so devoted to his work that he don't get the chance to come up here as often as he'd like."

"Amen," Elbridge Gerry replied. "Anybody want some pancakes?"

"You bet," John Quincy Adams said, and they all went out to the back of the house, where long tables had been set up over the dried mud that Roland Boyden had so thoroughly rototilled back in March.

The senator and Daphne sat at the head table, John Quincy Adams on one side of them, Elbridge Gerry on the other. The campaign staff was interspersed among the maple-syrup distributors, whose wives served the pancakes and poured the coffee.

"What a lovely day, Mr. Gerry," Daphne said in a valiant effort to make conversation with the taciturn first lieutenant of the VMSDA.

"Not so as you'd know it," he replied.

"Pardon me?"

"It's a spot muggy."

"Well, compared to Washington, this is nothing."

"That so?"

"Yes."

"Well, I'll be damned."

"I beg your pardon?"

"Son of a gun."

On her right, Woody was chatting with John Quincy Adams.

"I appreciate your putting this together, Mr. Adams."

"Glad you could make it, Senator."

"The pancakes are terrific."

"You got Betsy Gwinnett and Marge Bartlett to thank for that."

"How's the maple syrup been this year?"

"Sweeter than a lamb's pussy. . . ."

Button Gwinnett told Janine Caravaggio that his mare was pregnant.

"How nice," she replied, smiling.

"'Course, we don't know just who the daddy is. Though I suspect it could be Hiram."

"You have a horse named Hiram?"

"No, ma'am. That's the name of the hired hand. Another pancake, Miss Caravaggio?"

Rav Monsjar and Stephen Hopkins were talking about compost.

"I find that donkey dung works a whole lot better than chickenshit."

"Tell you what I prefer," Stephen Hopkins said. "I prefer to sprinkle a liberal amount of cow pucky over a bed of mulch, coffee grinds, and re-gurgitated dog food."

"You must have a lot of sick dogs, Mr. Hopkins."

"No sir, I just lace the kibble with ipecac. Brings it all up in about two minutes."

But the most significant conversation that took place over pancakes that morning was one between Lyman Hall and Brian Petrunich.

"Can't tell you how much we appreciate the senator's looking out for us down there in Washington, D.C., Mr. Petruney. Specially for getting that Italian fella off Mr. Q.'s back."

"Italian fella?"

"Yes, sir—that federal attorney up in Burlington name of Ruggiero. The man was harassing the dickens out of Mr. Q. Son of a bitch was threaten-ing him with an indictment."

"Oh."

"The senator got him appointed to the Second Circuit and now he don't bother us anymore. Now, that's what I call a constituent service."

Seated on the other side of Lyman Hall, into her third pancake, was Hermione Hingle, the reporter from the *Rutland Herald*. In her knitted pocketbook was a small state-of-the-art digital recording device capable of picking up conversations twenty feet away. Its Japanese-made computer chip was designed to register sound quality so clearly that you could do a voice-print test off it that was admissible in court.

Hermione Hingle's recording device was not, however, within twenty feet of the transaction that took place on the sunporch off the kitchen that functioned as John Quincy Adams's office at home. Although it wouldn't have made much of a difference had it been there. The horse, as they say in Vermont, had already kicked in the corral gate.

After Woody's speech, Elbridge Gerry asked Dickie Thong if he would step out to the sunporch for a moment, where he handed the campaign's finance manager a case of maple syrup.

"Here's a little something for the senator, Mr. Thong."

"Thank you very much."

"Don't mention it."

"You people throw a good breakfast."

"Ayop."

"The pancakes were very tasty."

"Ayop."

They stood there for a moment, having run out of pleasantries. Until Elbridge Gerry said, "Might rain."

Dickie Thong, having been brought up in Vermont, took his maple syrup and excused himself.

In the minivan on the way back, Woody asked Dickie Thong how he thought they made out.

"We won't know until we get their check."

"When do you think that'll be?"

"It better be soon. Or else we're going to have to start paying people with maple syrup."

He pointed to the case at his feet. When he removed a bottle to show the senator, he saw the money.

On the bottom of the case, insulating the maple syrup against breakage, was a bed of $100 bills.

They were neatly stacked, held together by rubber bands. Dickie Thong did a rough count in his head and said, "I'd say it's between three and four hundred thousand dollars."

"Well, that's good news," said Woody. "We can hang on to the maple syrup."

19

WOMEN WHO RUN
WITH THE WOLVES

BEFORE THE SENATOR put his wife in the car to take her to the Burlington airport that afternoon, they had a brief exchange in their suite at the Capitol Plaza.

Daphne had changed into a traveling outfit and was sitting at the vanity table adjusting her makeup. Woody stood near the entrance to the bedroom watching her, his hands deep in the pockets of his slacks.

"You're staring at me," she said.

"Am I?"

She took out her eyeliner and expertly worked on the almost imperceptible line above her dark-green eyes. He sat down on the bed, stared at her some more.

"Do you miss Helmut?"

"Why would I miss Helmut? He was your dog."

"That's funny, Daphne. I always thought he was your dog."

"You brought him home."

"It was a present for you."

"If you had asked me, I would have told you I don't like dachshunds."

"It's the thought that counts."

"That's the problem with you, Woody. It's all gestures. And gestures don't hack it in the end."

"What does hack it, Daphne?"

She continued with her eyeliner, then touched up her lipstick.

"Where did you meet her?" he asked abruptly.

He saw her face contort. She smeared the lipstick, then started to try to fix it.

"Of course it's none of my business . . ."

"That's right, Woody—it's none of your business."

"When your marriage is being wrecked by—"

"What marriage?"

He started to say something but stopped himself. She was right. How did you wreck a wreck?

She put the lipstick in her purse and got up and faced him. When she finally spoke she had regained her equanimity.

"I lived up to my part of the deal. You better live up to yours."

"Or else?"

"You don't want to know."

And she walked past him and out the door.

That evening, after vigorous sex on a futon in the bedroom of Janine Caravaggio's house in Barre, Brian Petrunich communicated his uneasiness about the pancake breakfast to the senator's press secretary.

"Did you notice that most of the members of VMSDA were signers of the Declaration of Independence?"

Janine Caravaggio muttered something unintelligible. She was still in a post-orgasmic stupor, and, in any event, she didn't know who had signed the Declaration of Independence and who hadn't. With the exception of John Hancock, who hadn't been at the pancake breakfast.

"They must be some sort of noms de guerre," he murmured.

"Noms de *what*?"

"Aliases. Beverly said the guy sitting next to her had a gun in his pocket."

"Maybe he was just happy to see her."

"Anyway, what really made me nervous was what this Lyman Hall guy told me. He said that the senator sponsored a judgeship for the Second Circuit, a federal attorney by the name of Ruggiero who had been trying to indict John Quincy Adams."

Brian Petrunich put his hands beneath his head and stared up at the water-stained ceiling. He remembered the words of the little man in the sports shirt and suspenders. *Now, that's what I call a constituent service.*

"They'd have to prove quid pro quo," he mused out loud. "They'd need evidence that the request was made specifically by Adams to Woody and that Woody acted on that request."

"Woody's too smart to do that."

"Right . . . So do you think he and Daphne are going to make it through the campaign?"

"By the skin of their teeth. Maybe."

"Did you hear about the twin beds?"

"Yeah. I just hope that the *Rutland Herald* doesn't find out."

"Can you see the headline? SENATOR AND WIFE SLEEP IN SEPARATE BEDS."

"I think I may have a yeast infection."

In addition to the normal flow of legislative and committee work that Ishmael Leibowitz had to coordinate on behalf of the junior senator from Vermont, he was now burdened by FBI agents calling him with questions pertaining to the senator's dachshund—now missing for over two weeks and presumed no longer in the state of Virginia—by having to read a tell-all book by the former receptionist of a Schenectady, New York, urologist who had gotten his dick removed by his wife after kinky sex, and, as if that weren't enough, by Owen Lundkeim, the speech-challenged aide to Representative Carl Kanush, who had taken to heart the Tourette-syndrome legislation in Medicaid and Health Care and was deluging Ishmael with drafts of the proposed bill.

A conversation with Owen Lundkeim took at least three times as long as any other conversation he had during the course of a day. Ishmael tried to be tolerant of Owen Lundkeim's stuttering problem, but it wasn't easy. He found himself putting him on the speakerphone and attending to other business while the aide fought his way through a sentence like an asthmatic fighting for air.

Occasionally, he even had a completely different phone conversation on his private line while Owen Lundkeim was going over the research on the various pharmacological treatments for TS that needed to be funded by the bill.

On the Monday morning after the July Fourth weekend, Ishmael was talking to Kevin, who now called him every day, on the private line about Barbra Streisand and James Brolin's getting married, while Owen Lundkeim was outlining the various drug therapies now in use against the condition.

"Ha . . . Ha . . . Ha . . . loperidol has unpl . . . pl . . . easant side effects such as aka . . . ka . . . ka . . . thelsis . . . nightmares and weight ga . . . ga . . . ga . . . in . . ." Owen Lundkeim was saying as Kevin confided, "I just don't see what's in it for him. Chicken soup? Menopause? She's selling the Malibu house . . ."

Barely listening to either conversation, Ishmael was trying to coordinate the senator's calendar to accommodate Trent Lott's lawyers' deposition dates with Medicaid and Health Care hearings on Tourette syndrome when he was struck by an inspiration.

It was a brilliant inspiration—the type of inspiration that was worthy of Senator Woodrow Wilson White's chief of staff. You didn't run Woody White's life without being capable of this type of two-birds-with-one-stone resourcefulness.

He told Kevin that he had to take a call from the senator, but not before confirming that he, Barry, Jack, and Denny would be breakfasting at the Chickadee coffee shop on Eighteenth and S tomorrow morning at the usual time. Hanging up on Kevin, Ishmael took Owen Lundkeim off speaker and said, "Listen, Owen, maybe you and I ought to get together and hash this out in person."

"Gr . . . gr . . . gr . . . eat."

"There's a coffee shop on Eighteenth and S. The Chickadee. About seven-thirty, okay?"

"S . . . s . . . s . . . sure."

Sharon Rosinski sat among the skiing trophies in the knotty-pine den of her house in Shaker Heights, air-conditioning on high, her two cats—Bill and Jill—on her lap, telling Lee Schumock that she felt that her marriage to Woody White had been in another lifetime.

"It was before I had read *Women Who Run With the Wolves.* I was an appendage. I raised the kids, sent out the Christmas cards, went to the fund-raisers, ate the rubber chicken, chatted with John Glenn. And what did I get out of it? A mortgaged house, inadequate spousal support, and a hysterectomy."

The writer nodded his head sympathetically. Unlike his interviews with the mother and the children, which were halting and difficult, this one was going to be largely a question of holding back the torrent. This woman was seriously pissed off at her ex-husband.

"Did you know that I'm taking him to court for an adjustment in spousal support?"

"No I didn't."

"He expects me to live on table scraps. I've had to take him to court twice already. He keeps pleading that he's broke. Meanwhile, he's making big book deals. Am I right?"

"I really don't know what they're paying him—"

"A million-two. My lawyer found out."

"Tell me—how did you and the senator first meet?"

"He threw up on me."

"What?"

"When we were in college. I went to UVM on a scholarship. But I grew up on the west side of Cleveland. A girlfriend fixed us up when we were both home from college during spring break. He took me to hear Wayne Hays speak. Talk about an exciting date. Then we go out for a few beers and he tells me he's going to be a U.S. Senator someday. Right. I figure this guy's kind of cute, but he's no JFK. He drinks a lot of beer, twice what I could put down and I'm no slouch with the suds, and on the way back he nearly goes off the road twice. We park in front of my parents' house and he tosses his cookies right in my lap. I don't know why the hell I agreed to go out with him again."

"Why did you?"

"I had insufficient self-esteem. In fact, my self-esteem was so low that I married him."

"How were the early days?"

"Who remembers? I was comatose. I'll tell you, though, I wasn't getting much out of the marriage. Right from the beginning. He was in the state legislature and spent half his time in Columbus. He was never home, and when he was, he really wasn't there. Then, one day, in 1979, I think it was, he announces that he wants to move to Vermont."

"Why Vermont?"

"He hated Columbus. He wanted to go to Washington as a senator, and he was convinced that he was dead in the water in Ohio. Glenn had a lock on his Senate seat, and the other seat was up in '82. Woody didn't think he'd be ready by '82. So we all had to pull up stakes and move to Peru, Vermont. To this A-frame in a place that doesn't even have a bowling alley. He gets himself elected to the Vermont legislature so he's in Montpelier and never really home and I've got two teenagers and a house with a leaky roof and then he runs for the Senate in '86. Of course, by that time he was already fucking the lawyer from D.C."

"You mean Daphne?"

"You know of any other Washington lawyer he was fucking at the time?"

When Barry, Kevin, Jack, and Denny arrived at the Chickadee coffee shop on Eighteenth and S for breakfast at 7:45 in the morning, they found Ishmael Leibowitz in a corner booth engaged in a tête-à-tête with a fair-skinned young man in a tan sports jacket and a color-coordinated paisley tie.

Owen Lundkeim may have been the only male heterosexual in Washington with the taste to have chosen that tie with that jacket. He was, hands down, the best-dressed aide in the entire Minnesota congressional caucus.

Moreover, Ishmael, not wanting to leave things entirely to an interpretation of wardrobe taste, had put on exactly the same clothes, down to the socks, that he had worn yesterday, when he had lunched with the boys at La Coquette.

So it all looked pretty apparent to Kevin, Barry, Jack, and Denny.

"Hmm . . . ," Barry observed dryly.

"Hmm . . . ," Kevin replied, less dryly.

After a long, very pregnant silence, Denny said, "I'd kill for that tie."

"Did you catch the shoes?"

"Gorgeous. Gianni Rocca?"

"They're Armani. I saw them yesterday at Via Veneto."

"How much?"

"Three fifty."

At Ishmael and Owen Lundkeim's table, meanwhile, the conversation ran to new diagnostic techniques to detect Tourette syndrome.

"There's el . . . el . . . el . . . ectroencephalogram and P . . . P . . . P . . . ET scan."

"A PET scan?"

"P . . . p . . . p . . . ositr . . . tr . . . tr . . . on em . . . m . . . m . . . mission t . . . t . . . t . . . tomograph . . . ph . . . ph . . . phy."

"Uh-huh," Ishmael said. "You know, just yesterday I was reading that TS sufferers do not adequately process serotonin in the brain."

"Pr . . . pr . . . pr . . . precisely. As f . . . f . . . far as we know, it's c . . . c . . . c . . . caused by the rand . . . d . . . d . . . om misfiring of neur . . . r . . . r . . . rons in the br . . . br . . . brain."

Back at the other booth, Jack Hernden continued to stare at Owen Lundkeim's feet.

"Nice socks, huh?" he remarked.

"Fabulous socks."

There was a moment of silence as the four of them appreciated Owen Lundkeim's socks. Finally, Kevin sighed deeply and muttered, "Well, maybe he'll have a good influence on Ishmael. His socks are atrocious."

"You really think so?"

"Yes. And I thought that yesterday as well."

20

THE SMOKING GUN

WHEN DEBBIE SUE ALLENBY checked the secure fax machine on Tuesday morning, she found another anonymous fax addressed to the senator. She couldn't tell whether this one was threatening or not because it was in Italian.

Neither could Sergeant Harvey Grimes of the Capitol Police, who didn't speak Italian either. It read, in its entirety:

SENATORE,

COME STA? IO SONO BENE, GRAZIE. ANCHE HELMUT. TUTTAVIA, SI LEI VUOLE ANCORA VEDERE IL SUO CANO, ARRANGI I COSI CON IL INS SUBITO!

ARRIVEDERLA . . .

Sergeant Grimes got the fax translated by the last Italian barber in the Senate barbershop, a dapper little man who had arrived in Washington about the same time Mike Mansfield had, and looked it.

"If the senator doesn't arrange things with the INS, the sender is threatening to do harm to the senator's dog, who, nonetheless, is doing well," Salvadore Didziocomo explained to Sergeant Grimes.

Dario Farniente, who had taken the precaution of writing down the senator's office fax number for future reference the day he had faxed him from *la signora*'s bedroom, had not bothered taking the precaution of removing the transmitting-fax number from the top of this particular fax, and Sergeant Grimes had only to refer to the area-code page in the phone book to trace the transmitting machine to Houston, Texas.

Though the fax was sent to a senator within the grounds of the Capitol, which was in his jurisdiction, the death threat was actually against a dog in Houston, Texas, which was not in his jurisdiction.

Sergeant Grimes decided it was better to be safe than sorry, and he called Special Agent Sonnenfeld in the Hoover Building on Ninth and Pennsylvania.

"We've got another threat this morning against Senator White on the office fax," he explained to the domestic-terrorism specialist.

"What did it say?"

"It was in Italian."

"Italian?"

"Yeah. It looks like it's from the housekeeper who stole the dog. He tells the senator to fix things with the INS if he wants to see his dog again."

"You got a trace on the fax?"

"Houston, Texas."

"Number?"

He read him the number off the fax.

"All right, bag it for evidence. And beef up the security on the senator."

"He's in Vermont."

"Till when?"

"Tomorrow."

"All right. I'll deal with it out of Boston."

"The threat's against the dog, not against the senator."

"Grimes, you do your job. Let me do mine, all right?"

"No problem," said Sergeant Harvey Grimes, frankly just as happy not to have to deal with the Italian housekeeper and the dachshund.

He bagged the fax, sent it over to Ninth and Pennsylvania, and went to lunch.

The shit hit the fan at approximately the same time that the two plain-clothes agents made it up to Vermont from the FBI's regional office in Boston. Earlier that day in Burlington, Rebecca Gatney had called a press conference for 6 P.M. promising to reveal indisputable evidence of influence-peddling on the part of Senator Woodrow White. This sensational tease guaranteed that the press conference would be carried live on the six o'clock news.

The two federal agents arrived at Woody's campaign headquarters in Montpelier to set up security procedures just as the senator, Beverly, Brian

Petrunich, and Janine Caravaggio were settling into a booth in the bar of the Capitol Plaza Hotel to watch the news.

Agents Austin and Buchannon had just finished badging the senator when Doug DeBoeuf announced that they were going live to Burlington. Rebecca Gatney appeared at a rostrum at the Burlington Hyatt, in her prosecutorial suit, and read from a prepared statement.

"We have come into possession of an audiotape, which I shall play for you in just a moment. But first, let me give you some background . . ."

Woody sat there stony-faced over a Johnnie Walker Black and listened to his opponent spell out, in excruciatingly thorough detail, the entire scenario that, she claimed, would link Woody White with Vincent Ruggiero, the seat on the Second Circuit, John Quincy Adams and his alleged loan-sharking activities, and two sizable campaign contributions.

She finished up by playing the tape that her undercover agent, Hermione Hingle, had made of the conversation between Lyman Hall and Brian Petrunich on the Fourth of July while she was masquerading as a *Rutland Herald* reporter.

She then rewound and repeated Lyman Hall's closing sentence: "Now, that's what I call a constituent service."

The smoking gun.

The reporters were so completely blown away by the revelation that, for a moment, there were no questions.

Then the hands flew up.

"Do you intend to pursue this?"

"You betcha."

"How?"

"First of all I am demanding that Woody White explain to the people of Vermont the connection between his putting forward the Ruggiero nomination and the donation of five hundred thousand dollars to his campaign in March. Then I'm going to ask for an accounting of the funds raised at the Fourth of July pancake event at Mr. Adams's home in Montpelier."

"Are you calling for him to step down?"

"I don't think I have to bother with that. The people of Vermont will boot him out in November. That is, if the Senate Ethics Committee doesn't throw him out first. You know that campaign slogan of his—'Where's Woody'? Well, we finally found out where Woody is. He's in John Quincy Adams's pocket."

The little group in the corner of the bar at the Capitol Plaza Hotel stared silently at the TV screen. Agents Austin and Buchannon sat down in the adjoining booth and started in on the cocktail peanuts.

After a few moments of collective catatonia, Janine Caravaggio said, "Somebody call Rav."

. . .

Rav Monsjar was playing Fender bass with a country blues group in Guil-ford when the phone rang at his empty place outside Brattleboro.

"Hello. You've intruded on the privacy of Rav Monsjar. Though the chances of my returning your phone call are slim to none, you can leave your name and number at the beep. In any event, don't bother calling back."

"Jesus, Rav, where the fuck are you? We've got a red alert here," Brian Petrunich said to Rav Monsjar's machine from the phone in Woody's suite.

The next call was to Ishmael in Washington.

"Did you hear?"

"Yes."

The chief of staff had gotten the news from Vermont reporters, who had started calling the Washington office when they couldn't get through to the senator's suite in Montpelier.

"Is it on local down there?" Brian asked.

"Not yet."

"There's still . . . what, ten minutes to Lehrer?"

"I don't think he'd go with it this raw. But I bet you it's on here at eleven. What does Rav say?"

"We can't reach him."

"Do we have a statement?"

"No. We have nothing."

Ishmael closed his eyes and pictured the whole yard full of chickens coming home to roost. It all came flooding back to him—the maple syrup in the Potomac, the Vincent Ruggiero file, the phone calls to the White House . . .

"You got any ideas for a statement?" Brian asked.

"I think we need a Woodyism," Ishmael said.

"Like what?"

"How about . . . let . . . she who has clean hands toss the first cow chip?"

"That's awful."

"I know. Is he coming in tomorrow?"

"We have him on the nine o'clock out of Burlington. What do you think—Washington or Vermont?"

"I think he's better off down here at the moment. It's out of range of the cow chips. Besides, he's got committee hearings scheduled for later in the week."

"On what?"

"The Tourette-syndrome bill in Medicaid and Health Care."
"The Tourette-syndrome bill?"
"Don't ask."

Woody felt a peculiar sense of calm come over him as the phones rang off the hook and his lieutenants scurried around trying to set up a fire line. Suddenly feeling completely exhausted, he excused himself and went into the bedroom of the suite, closing the connecting door behind him. He took off his shoes, stretched out on the bed, and put his head down on the over-starched pillow.

It was all reminiscent of '95, when the staffer had accused him of sexual harassment in the back of the campaign bus. The frantic phone calls, the damage-control meisters lining up with the fire buckets, the spinning of the spin . . .

In '95, however, the charge was flimsy. The woman was a sexual preda-tor, a loose cannon who wore short skirts and wiggled her ass every time she was in his sight line. He had fallen asleep in the back of the bus and was awakened by her hand in his pants. After her book tanked, she moved to California and wound up working in out-call massage.

This one, however, wasn't going to go away that easily. He had known what he was doing when he'd agreed to put Ruggiero forth for the seat on the Second Circuit. On a moral level—and Woody White did have a moral sense, in spite of his twelve years in the Senate—he was convinced that he had merely furthered the career of a meritorious Vermonter who deserved to be on the bench whether Woody had put forth the nomination or some-one else had. That was the real constituent service. It wasn't getting John Quincy Adams out from under the guns of the U.S. Attorney's office. That was merely a fortuitous by-product.

It went with the fucking territory. How the hell did they think Lyndon got electricity across the Pedernales? And what about his great-great-uncle-in-law, Senator Marcus Alonzo Hanna? Did they think the Panama Canal got built without enriching the robber barons and industrial mag-nates who got Mark Hanna elected to the Senate?

It had become the Reign of Terror. One by one, politicians were being carted off to the guillotine by the guardians of public morality. He had got-ten hauled off there once before and had talked his way out of it.

But in '95 he was right in the middle of his six-year term, three years on either side of an election. This time he was up for reelection and he wasn't dealing with a dippy staffer in a tight skirt. He was dealing with an ex–state's attorney with a collie, four kids, a Vietnam-war-hero husband, a pew in the First Congregational Church of Burlington, and a devoted crew of fanatics who went around sneaking into his fund-raisers with tape recorders.

It was going to be a long, hard, bloody battle. But he would win. If it killed him.

Rav would call soon with the solution. Beverly, Brian, Janine, and Ishmael would implement it. They would fire back. By the end of the week, while he was sitting in the committee room listening to the plight of TS sufferers, he would be counterattacking.

As he lay there envisioning the mortar shells flying into Rebecca Gatney's camp, his thoughts drifted.

It was no doubt the crispness of the freshly laundered pillow against his cheek. As he inhaled the aroma of fresh starch, Ivan Pavlov showed up, waving his flag.

Her number was written on the inside of his reading glasses' case, along with Ishmael's cell.

He dialed it, suddenly eager to hear her voice.

21

AN INVITATION
FROM THE GESTAPO

WOODY WAS LYING in the darkened room waiting for his procedure and thinking about Ernie Haas, when he should have been thinking about the reply he was going to make to Rebecca Gatney's charges. He had flown into New York that morning, had taken a cab from La Guardia to JFK, and caught a Toronto one-stop into Dulles instead of the direct flight from Burlington into National in order to avoid any reporters who might be waiting for him at the gate.

He had called Ishmael from the airport, told him not to do or say anything until they tracked down Rav, and took a cab directly to Evelyn Brandwynne's apartment in Georgetown, where he was now lying quietly, his eyes closed, thinking about his former urologist.

There was a hint of ammonia on top of the sandalwood aromatherapy candle, just enough to evoke the examining room in Schenectady that fateful day last March when Dr. Haas's nurse, Esmeralda Perkins, had inadvertently brought Woody back to life.

Ishmael had vetted the book written by the doctor's receptionist, Denise Mezzogiorno, to be assured that there was no mention of a James Monroe's having consulted Dr. Ernest Haas only hours before the doctor had apparently gone home, put on a woman's dress, handcuffed his wife to the kitchen stove, and paid the supreme sacrifice for his exertions.

Ernie Haas had taken it in the dick for the team. It made Woody shudder just to think about it.

The shuddering, however, lasted only as long as the first whiff of the starched nurse's uniform that the lobbyist for the National Association of Health Prophylaxis Industries wore as she entered the room with her Crabtree & Evelyn shaving accessories. Evelyn Brandwynne was wearing nothing but a pair of off-white pantyhose under the uniform.

Off-white pantyhose with a section missing. In Evelyn Brandwynne's middle drawer beside her sink, just below the condom-sample drawer, were a dozen pairs of altered off-white pantyhose ordered from a nursing-supply mail-order catalog. Only Woody and her cleaning lady knew they were there. Only Woody knew what they were there for.

"And how are we doing today?" she asked in her homogenized nurse's voice.

"Fine."

"Ready for our procedure?"

"You bet."

In the steam room of the Senate Health Facility, the hot topic was Rebecca Gatney's accusation of influence-peddling on the part of their colleague Woody White.

"Woody'll land on his feet. He always does."

"What about Cranston and Packwood? They didn't land on *their* feet."

"They've got to prove quid pro quo."

"Let me ask you something, Senator. Suppose I'm on Transportation, and I get a contribution from the Teamsters. Then suppose I support a bill in committee for federal funds to improve the interstate-highway system. That quid pro quo?"

"No. That's doing your job."

"I should hope so."

"Is she calling for an indictment?"

"They won't indict on the tape."

"What if she drags him in front of Ethics?"

"How can she do that?"

"Demand an investigation."

"All she has to do is demand an investigation?"

"That's right. Someone just has to write a letter to the committee, and the next thing you know, you're in Gestapo Headquarters up on the second floor of Hart answering questions."

There was a moment of dripping silence, a silence that conveyed the consensus among the men in the steam room that they were living in parlous times.

"The hardest thing in politics is having to disprove a negative. Ladies and gentlemen of the jury, I maintain that I didn't beat my wife. Then your wife says, 'Of course he didn't beat me. Whatever gave you that idea?' Meanwhile you lose twenty to twenty-five percent of your women's vote and you're back practicing law in Tulsa with thirteen million dollars of campaign debts to pay off."

"Or worse. You have to go to work as a lobbyist."

"God forbid."

They finally got ahold of Rav Monsjar late that Wednesday night. The pundit was just walking in the door of his ramshackle house outside Brattleboro, aloft on a cloud of beer and Merle Haggard, when his phone rang for the tenth time that evening.

"What!" he barked into the phone.

"Where the fuck have you been?" Brian Petrunich barked back.

"Playing Fender bass. Where the fuck have *you* been?"

"Didn't you hear?"

"Hear what?"

"Jesus, you didn't hear? She's claiming Woody's in John Quincy Adams's pocket."

"That so?"

"She got a tape of the pancake breakfast. Some questionable stuff about constituent service. She's saying that Woody got Vincent Ruggiero appointed to the Second Circuit to get him out of the U.S. Attorney's office."

"That so?"

"Ruggiero had been going after the VMSDA on loan-sharking and money-laundering charges."

"That so?"

"They think they have quid pro quo."

"That so?"

"Can you get down to Washington first thing tomorrow?"

"No."

"No? Rav, this is a crisis."

"I've got to go over to Dummerston to get a posthole digger and some creosote."

"Can't you do that next week?"

"I don't get my vegetable garden fenced, the hedgehog's going to take what he hasn't already taken."

"Woody needs you by his side."

"He's already got my cucumbers. Now he's going after my radishes."

"Rav, we need to figure out what to say."

"We don't say anything."

"We have to say *something*. Every goddamn reporter from here to Cucamonga is calling."

"You don't start plowing while the snow's still coming from the northeast, do you?"

"Huh?"

"Stay inside. Bank the stove. Play some checkers."

"You want me to tell the senator that?"

"That's right."

"He's going to go ape shit."

"Might rain."

Rav Monsjar disconnected so abruptly that for a moment Brian Petrunich didn't realize that the phone was dead.

"Rav? Rav . . . Fuck!"

He slammed the phone down.

"What did he say?" Janine Caravaggio asked.

"Stay inside. Bank the stove. Play checkers."

Janine Caravaggio was sitting in the conference room of the Montpelier office making a list. Janine Caravaggio was a list-maker. No matter what the crisis, it always made her feel better to get out the yellow pad and make a list.

Brian Petrunich flopped down beside her on the worn leather couch, rubbed his eyes, and looked down at the yellow pad. There was a short list of short names written on it.

"What's that?"

"The seven dwarfs. I've got six of them. I can't remember the seventh. There's Dopey, Happy, Sleepy, Grumpy, Sneezy, Doc . . ."

A staffer came in from the outer office.

"Anybody want to talk to the *Free Press*?"

Brian grabbed a phone.

Janine Caravaggio looked up from the couch, knitting her eyebrows. "Thumper? Was Thumper one of the seven dwarfs?"

"Thumper was one of Santa's reindeer," the staffer said.

"We'll have something tomorrow," Brian Petrunich said to the *Vermont Free Press*. "And then again, maybe we won't."

"What about Gimpy?" the staffer said.

Brian Petrunich hung up and plopped back down on the couch and closed his eyes.

"He's worried about his radishes. The water's coming over the top, and he's worried about his fucking radishes . . ."

"What about Sleazy?"

. . .

The Fire Brigade met in Woody's Washington office on Thursday morning at nine In addition to Ishmael and Debbie Sue Allenby—with Beverly Levesque, Dickie Thong, Brian Petrunich, and Janine Caravaggio on speakerphone from Montpelier—Woody had invited Burton Armature, the top-drawer Washington lawyer who had defended him in the grope-in-the-back-of-the-campaign-bus affair and to whose office furnishings the senator had also contributed substantially.

The lawyer began by asking Woody if he had any problems with his staff being privy to their discussions.

"No," Woody replied.

"Good. In addition to getting their input, it establishes larger parameters for attorney-client privilege, should there be depositions and subpoenas. Down the road."

Woody looked at his lawyer bleakly. "You don't really think they're going to go for an indictment, do you?"

Burton Armature tilted his head slightly. It was one of the gestures in his large repertoire of noncommittal gestures that Woody recalled from the harassment case. Burton Armature was a master of the noncommittal.

"They may or they may not," he said, rubbing his pencil eraser against his perfectly shaven cheek. "In any event, there's nothing wrong with being prepared. You see, though the tape is hearsay and not admissible in court, it is admissible in front of a grand jury. Of course, a sensible grand jury would understand that there is no point in indicting if the principal piece of evidence is inadmissible. But grand juries are not always sensible. Anyway, let's not worry about a grand jury for the moment."

The lawyer turned to a fresh page on his legal pad and, with no noticeable change of inflection, said, "Let's worry about the Ethics Committee."

Woody felt the first lick of acid against the wall of his stomach. His lawyer had mentioned the two words that produced acid in the stomach of all senators.

The Senate Select Committee on Ethics, as it was referred to in Senate Resolution 338, which created it, was, in principle at least, the only non-partisan committee in Congress. Though the chairmanship went to the majority party, its membership was split right down the middle of the aisle—three Democrats and three Republicans.

In order to burn a senator at the stake, therefore, you needed at least one vote from the senator's own party. In addition to public immolation or banishment, the Ethics Committee had a variety of lesser punishments and humiliations at its disposal. It could censure you. It could reprimand you. It could rebuke you. It could strip you of your committee chairmanships.

The committee seniority they could have, as far as Woody was concerned. He was ranking Democrat on both Medicaid and Health Care and African Affairs, but unless the Democrats retook the Senate in November, there were no chairmanships in the offing.

The truth was that he was floating around the middle levels of the fraternity without much purchase on the slippery slope of real power. He had few allies and a number of enemies. The Majority Leader hadn't liked him even before he had backed into his Ford Explorer in the parking garage.

They'd throw him to the wolves. And fast. They'd take away his cubbyhole office and carve up his turf. Like Latvia. Or Angola. They'd occupy him, stick a flag in him, despoil his meager resources . . .

"The problem with Ethics, Senator . . . *Senator?*"

Woody was pulled out of his paranoid drift by the air-brushed voice of his attorney.

"I was saying that the problem with Ethics, as you know, is that there is no due process. The preliminary investigation, should there be one, is very similar to a grand-jury investigation. They have the power of subpoena. We don't get to cross-examine anyone. There's no discovery, there's no disclosure."

"It's your basic witch-hunt."

"I wouldn't say that in public, Senator."

"Well, what *do* we say?" Janine Caravaggio asked on the speakerphone.

"I would keep it short and simple. Issue a statement to the effect that the senator is not aware of having broken any campaign laws, but should it be determined that the contribution was improper, he would, of course, return the money."

"Return the money?" Dickie Thong whined.

"You'd have to."

"We've spent most of it."

"I suppose you'd have to raise some more then."

"We're already scraping the bottom of the barrel."

"Burt, if this thing goes to Ethics, they'll cut off my supply of soft money."

"Well, see that it doesn't go to Ethics."

"How do we do that?"

Burton Armature slipped the legal pad into his Gucci attaché case and went out on a limb.

"The same way you do anything in Washington," he said. "You go after the votes."

22

ICE FISHING

BURTON ARMATURE'S proactive strategy of going after the votes didn't fit well with Rav Monsjar's reactive strategy of banking the stove and getting out the checkers.

When the pundit finally checked in again by phone, having creosoted his garden fence, he told Woody that trying to line up Ethics Committee votes before a complaint was filed was like announcing before you even got to town that you were going to open the valise in the middle of the town square.

"You do that, you're saying there's something in the valise."

"All she's got to do is get someone to file a complaint."

"She can do that, all right. Anybody can do that. I can do that. You can do that. My dog can do that."

"So we don't do anything?"

Rav Monsjar blew his nose right into phone. "Sorry about that, Senator. Pollen count's high. . . . Listen, here's what you do. You do what you're supposed to be doing. Whatever the hell that is."

"Business as usual?"

"That's right. You're a legislator, aren't you? So you legislate."

"I've got hearings on a bill scheduled in Medicaid and Health Care."

"Hear the shit out of that bill, Senator."

So that Thursday afternoon, while Janine Caravaggio issued the senator's official reply to Rebecca Gatney's charges in Montpelier—"Though Senator White is not aware of having broken any campaign laws . . ."

—Woody sat in a committee room in Russell and, in the absence of the Republican chairman, who, not believing that there were enough voters with Tourette syndrome, took advantage of the hearings to slip off to Tennessee and mend some fences, presided over hearings on the ravages of the disease.

One after another, victims of TS testified to the general insensitivity on the part of American society to their condition and to the paucity of public-health facilities to deal with it.

Senator White occupied the chair with tact and compassion. He prodded gently where prodding was needed and backed off when he felt that the witness was on the brink of breaking down emotionally.

There was one young woman who nearly brought everyone in the room to tears when she recounted how her condition had been misdiagnosed, how she had been put in mental hospitals, received electroshock treatments, given medication meant for psychotics—all because of her uncontrollable spasms and outbursts.

"Is your medication covered by insurance?" Woody asked her from a list of questions prepared for him by his staff.

"No. The insurance company claimed it was preexisting and refused to cover me."

"How about disability?"

"No, because they claim it's not work-related."

"So do you feel that your government is doing enough for you, Ms. Meiskeit?"

"Hardly."

"Those of us fortunate enough to be untouched by the ravages of TS cannot even begin to imagine how you must feel, Ms. Meiskeit, suffering with this terrible condition and having to get along with little or no help from the government you pay taxes to. . . ."

The Republicans on the committee pulled their punches, even though Woody was clearly playing to the C-SPAN cameras. Later one of them remarked privately that he felt he was attending a muscular dystrophy telethon, with Woody White playing Jerry Lewis.

In any event, Woody did exactly what Rav Monsjar told him to—he heard the shit out of the bill. His fellow senators, the committee aides, and the press could only marvel at his grasp of the issues surrounding Tourette syndrome.

Everyone who witnessed it agreed it was a bravura performance. Especially a man in the rear of the room, an African who had forgone his usual colorful native dress for the occasion. He sat there and listened to every word uttered by the witnesses and by the senator.

Kodjo Kponvi identified himself to the reporter beside him as the director of NAPTOTS, the National Association for the Prevention and Treatment of Tourette Syndrome. He told the reporter that Senator White's work on behalf of victims of Tourette syndrome was simply splendid.

"VMSDA."

"Yes. Good morning. This is Everett Hodge of the *Vermont Free Press*. I'd like to speak to Mr. Adams, please."

"And what would this be regarding, Mr. Hodge?"

"I'd prefer asking him that in person, Miss . . ."

"Adams. Abigail. No relation."

"We'd like a statement from him."

"That so?"

"Yes. That's so."

"And what would that statement be regarding?"

"Look, Miss Adams, I'm the editor in chief of a major Vermont newspaper. Do you think it would be possible for me to speak directly to Mr. Adams?"

"That would depend."

"Upon what?"

"Upon whether he wants to speak to you, now wouldn't it?"

"Yes, I suppose it would. Would you mind asking him?"

There was no *hold* button on the phone at the headquarters of the Vermont Maple Syrup Distributors Association. Abigail Adams merely put the receiver down on top of her knitting and walked back to the conference room, where John Quincy Adams was playing three-handed pinochle with Elbridge Gerry and John Stark.

"Everett Hodge of the *Free Press* is on the phone, Mr. Q."

"What's he want?"

"To talk to you."

"About what?"

"Didn't say."

"Ask him."

Abigail Adams picked up the extension phone sitting on top of the Nok-Hockey board in the corner and said, "Mr. Adams wants to know what this is regarding."

"We'd like a statement from him."

"About what?"

"Is it or isn't it possible to speak to him directly?"

"Maybe. Then again maybe not. You might want to begin by replying to the question."

"I want to speak to him about Rebecca Gatney's charges."

"You do?"

"Yes, I *do*."

"Don't have to get short with me, Mr. Hodge."

Abigail Adams covered the receiver with her hand and said, "Wants to talk to you about the Rebecca Gatney charges."

"He does, does he?"

"Ayop."

He put his cards down and took the receiver from her.

"John Quincy Adams."

"Mr. Adams, this is Everett Hodge of the *Free Press*."

"That so?"

"Would you care to comment on Rebecca Gatney's accusations regarding you and Senator White?"

"Nope."

"You have no comment?"

"Ayop."

"You want me to write that John Quincy Adams has no comment with regard to accusations of corruption and bribery?"

"Mr. Hodge, I don't give a rat's ass on a rainy day what you write in your paper."

"Do you realize that these are very serious charges?"

"Might rain."

"All right, look—I'm going to press in an hour and a half. If you change your mind, call."

"Don't hold your breath."

John Quincy Adams hung up and went back to the pinochle game. Picking up his hand again, he looked at the cards and frowned.

"John, you ever do a newspaper editor?"

"Can't say that I have, Mr. Q."

"Trouble is you do one, another one comes right up in his place. Like crabgrass."

"We do anybody, we ought to do the one who snuck in here and got Lyman Hall on the tape recorder," Elbridge Gerry said.

"We do her, the finger's going to point right at us, you see what I'm saying?"

"What if we just do Gatney?"

"Where does she live?"

"Burlington. We could get what's-his-name out of Montreal."

"Monty Calmette."

"That's right. Him."

John Quincy Adams lit his pipe, rotating the match around the bowl to make sure the tobacco took evenly, and leaned back in his chair.

"Price the job out, Elbridge. Just out of curiosity."

"Ayop."

"If he comes in high, Canuck him down."

During the next few days, Ishmael coordinated the implementation of Rav Monsjar's latest variation of the valise-denial strategy. He planned and prioritized. He fed the senator edited intelligence from Barry, Kevin, Jack, and Denny about who was saying what about him.

They worked the phones, the senator and he, reassuring congressional allies and their aides that there was no substance to Rebecca Gatney's charges.

There were meetings with Teddy, with Daschle, with Gephardt, with the Minority Whip, and with the Democratic Caucus. They sat with the senators and with their chiefs of staff, sipping decaf on bone china and reducing Rebecca Gatney's charges to an orchestrated mud-slinging campaign, financed by the Republicans.

"They're throwing money at the seat," Ishmael explained to his new friend and ally Owen Lundkeim, who, along with Gephardt's aide, was working the House on Woody's behalf.

Owen Lundkeim stuttered his way through the House aides, throwing in a good word for Woody White while proselytizing for TS.

"It's R . . . R . . . R . . . Republica . . . ca . . . ca . . . can soft mo . . . mo . . . mo . . . ney," he explained before launching into an attenuated pitch for the incipient White-Kanush Bill.

At the same time as he was working to douse brushfires for Woody White, Ishmael was doing what he could to start them with Barry, Kevin, Jack, and Denny. Phase two of his strategy to remain a confidant to that particular group without having to watch *Beaches,* or worse, involved selling his relationship with Owen Lundkeim as more than a one-night stand.

So Ishmael invited Owen Lundkeim to lunch with the boys at La Coquette. The congressional aide showed up wearing a beige Bill Blass blazer and a chocolate-brown shirt that took Barry, Kevin, Jack, and Denny's collective breath away.

It took Owen Lundkeim awhile to get into the swing of things. After a glass of Chardonnay, he told the boys about the congressman from Minnesota's Seventh District who went ice fishing in his hometown of Wadena and got his nuts frozen to the stool he was sitting on.

"Th . . . th . . . th . . . ey had to g . . . g . . . g . . . get a bl . . . bl . . . bl . . . owtorch."

"Aggh!" Denny cried.

"No!" Barry screamed.

"You're putting us *on*!" Jack protested.

Owen Lundkeim just smiled, and the whole table roared. To Ishmael's surprise, Owen Lundkeim's folksy northern-Minnesota humor was a hit. He wouldn't have thought this group would have gone in for ice-fishing stories. Maybe it was the Bill Blass blazer and the perfect shirt. Who knew?

Whatever the case, Owen Lundkeim passed the test. Lunch was a success. There was only one tense moment. It was after the crème brûlée. They were dividing the check up when a tall, buxom woman walked by the table.

Owen Lundkeim looked at her and said, "Di . . . di . . . di . . . did you see the kn . . . kn . . . kn . . . knockers on her?"

Nobody at the table had, except Owen Lundkeim and Ishmael, who were hardwired in that direction.

Thinking fast, Ishmael pulled the fat out of the fire. "Forget the knockers. Did you see the scarf?"

"The scarf?"

"A *pink silk scarf* with *those* knockers?"

The spark caught. Everyone broke out laughing. Even Owen Lundkeim, who wasn't sure why.

Hank Leventhal no longer trusted the telephone, either at his office in the Chester A. Arthur Building or at his home in Silver Spring. Ever since the threatening fax to Woody White's office and the FBI investigation that followed it, the asset-forfeiture associate director had taken to contacting the junior senator from Vermont from various phone booths around the city.

Smack in the middle of his damage-control campaign, Woody got an urgent phone-booth call from Hank Leventhal wanting to see him right away.

"We can't discuss this on the phone, Hank?"

"No. There's a McDonald's on Sixteenth across from Meridian Hill Park. I'll meet you there at one."

So instead of having a working lunch with the ranking Democrat on the Ethics Committee, a hard-ass whom he wanted to soften up preemptively should he need the senator to manage things on the inside, Woody found himself in a red molded plastic seat picking at his Chicken McNuggets while Hank Leventhal wolfed down a Quarter Pounder with cheese and informed him that the deportation papers for Sonja Aura had worked their way to the last desk they had to work their way to before being sent out by registered mail to the status violator's last known address.

"Oh, Jesus, Hank . . . shit."

"What? Isn't this what you wanted?"

In the chaos brought about by Rebecca Gatney's charges and the ensuing intensive damage-control campaign, Woody had forgotten to call Hank Leventhal off in accordance with his deal with Daphne to hold the deportation order for thirty days.

"Yes. But not right now."

"What do you mean not right now?"

"The thing is that if the papers go out right now, it'll cause me problems. Can't you just hold them?"

"You don't understand, Senator. In order to get these papers issued, certain procedures had to be put in place. Files were ordered. Memos were written. There's a paper trail now."

"Look, just tell whoever it is whose desk it's on to put it in his drawer for a month."

"First of all, I'm not even supposed to be involved in deportation, as I explained to you months ago. I'm way out on a limb here."

"Hank, if you're not out on a limb in this town, you're nowhere."

"What the fuck does that mean?"

"Watch your language. We're in McDonald's."

Woody took a long pull off his chocolate shake.

"Okay, now listen to me," Woody said in his calmest voice. "Worst-case scenario, you're doing your duty, aiding a United States senator in his work to rid the taxpayers of the burden of supporting a parasite. What's wrong with that?"

"I'd be in a better comfort zone if I were in the loop here."

"Hank, trust me. You really want to be out of the loop here."

23

NON-DENIAL DENIALS

THE OFFICIAL LETTER of complaint arrived at the office of the Senate Select Committee on Ethics on the second floor of the Hart Senate Office Building a week before Congress was due to adjourn for the August holiday. It arrived on stationery with the letterhead of the Vermont Citizens for Ethical Government, with offices on North Champlain Street in Winooski.

Harold Kinder, chief counsel to the committee, read the letter to his staff. It was short and *pro forma*. The Vermont Citizens for Ethical Government respectfully requested that the committee "investigate the ethics of Senator Woodrow White with regard to his relationship with the Vermont Maple Syrup Distributors Association, specifically with a certain John Quincy Adams, a.k.a. Johnny Q., and with respect to certain campaign contributions from Mr. Adams that appear not only to violate specific campaign-finance laws, enumerated below, but to have engendered illegal and unethical services that the senator performed as quid pro quo for these services."

As far as the Ethics Committee staff was concerned, the timing of the complaint, a week before recess, couldn't have been worse. In all probability, the senators would direct them to look into the charges in August while the senators themselves would be back in their home states attending cattle fairs and writing their memoirs.

Although the Ethics Committee staff had been waiting for the other shoe to drop ever since Rebecca Gatney made her charges public, they were hoping that the complaint would come in September, after the recess, so that they, too, could get out of the steam bath of August in Washington.

"Let's just write back and tell them our caseload is so heavy that we can't get to it until September," Lydia St. Cloud, the assistant counsel, suggested.

"And then we take off August?"

"How are they going to know where we are in August?" David Forensic, the staff investigator asked.

"They'll know, believe me," Harold Kinder replied.

They sat around the conference table in the windowless room, a room that had to be cleared for bugs each time hearings were held, and tried to figure how to salvage their vacations.

Lydia St. Cloud was going to California to try to resolve once and for all a relationship she was having with a married TV producer. David Forensic had scheduled long-overdue arthroscopic knee surgery. Harold Kinder had taken a house on Cape Cod for the entire month of August.

"Look," Harold Kinder said, "maybe we can get through this by the fifteenth."

"How are we going to do that?"

"As far as I can see, our job at this time is merely to verify dates and amounts of the contributions and dates and circumstances of the senator's contact with Adams and actions, if any, he may have taken on his behalf. And to do that we have to interview two people—the senator himself and John Quincy Adams."

"What about Vincent Ruggiero?"

"He's not mentioned in the complaint."

"Yeah, but he's the guy with the goods on Adams."

Harold Kinder was a former professor of law at Georgetown and the author of a book on senatorial ethics.

"This is merely a preliminary investigation, which means that all we have to do at the moment is determine whether there is sufficient probability that an ethics violation has occurred. We do not have to launch a full-scale investigation into Mr. Adams's background. Moreover, if the alleged violation did in fact occur, it occurred irrespective of the character of John Quincy Adams."

"Sounds good to me," Lydia St. Cloud said.

"Let's run it up the flagpole," David Forensic agreed.

The chief counsel drafted a reply to VCEG and copied the six senators on the committee before calling his travel agent to see if he could delay the rental on the Cape Cod house to the fifteenth of August.

. . .

"They're filing for summary judgment," Phil Yalowitz told him on the secure line.

"What about discovery?"

"Senator, you went to law school, didn't you?"

"It was a long time ago."

"Summary judgment precludes discovery. It asks the court to resolve the litigation on its face and award the plaintiff damages based on an overwhelming preponderance of evidence in its favor."

"How much?"

"Ten thousand dollars."

"It's a used Ford Explorer."

"They're asking only fifty-five hundred for the car. The rest is their legal fees."

"They want me to pay *their* legal fees?"

"They're claiming that your lack of response to their complaint has made the action on their part necessary."

"What about a continuance? I'm up to my ears here with a goddamn ethics complaint. Not to mention my Tourette-syndrome hearings."

"Senator, let me cut through this for you. What we have here is a stationary traffic accident in which the total amount of damages, excluding legal fees, barely exceeds the limits for small-claims court. No court likes its calendar encumbered by this type of case. Not only are you looking at summary judgment against you but you also may be looking at summary judgment with prejudice against you. The court may even decide to fine you, or reprimand me for allowing the case to get this far. It's a turkey, Senator. A real gobbler. You should have settled it months ago for fifty-five hundred. Now you're looking at fifteen thousand. Out the door."

"I thought you said *ten*?"

"I haven't billed you yet for my fees."

"Jesus, Phil, you guys really got a racket going."

"As I've said on numerous occasions, Senator, if you'd like to shop around for cut-rate legal services . . ."

"All right, all right. Call them up, offer them seven-five."

"Seven thousand, five hundred dollars?"

"Out the door."

There was another long silence. Then Phil Yalowitz cleared his throat and said, "Now, in the matter of the complaint from your first wife—"

"Phil."

"What?"

"Let me get back to you on that. I've got a roll-call vote on the Floor."

There was only so much bad news he could take in one phone call. And it wasn't just Trent Lott and his first wife. They were coming at him from all sides now. That morning he had been on the phone with his other lawyer, Burton Armature, discussing how to respond to an official request on the part of the Ethics Committee for an interview.

"If it's not a subpoena, then they're treating this in a very tentative manner for the moment," Burton Armature had told him. "My guess is that they want to get out of here for recess and they're trying to stall this to September."

"So do I agree?"

"Absolutely. Make yourself available."

"Do I answer everything?"

"Yes, you do."

"Admit to the contact?"

"Uh-huh."

"And the contributions?"

"Uh-huh. Only one thing to watch out for, Senator. Are you on the secure line?"

"Yes."

"Here it is in a nutshell. The entire quid-pro-quo case rests on the supposition that you knew that John Quincy Adams would benefit from the appointment of Vincent Ruggiero to the Second Circuit. If you didn't know that, you could have run through hoops for Adams and it wouldn't mean a thing. So when they ask you, and they will, if you knew that Vincent Ruggiero was investigating John Quincy Adams, you'll know what the correct answer is."

"Got it."

"Now I can't tell you to give that answer to them if it isn't true, you understand, but I want you to know what the answer is, in case it is true."

"I appreciate your candor, Burt."

"Anytime, Senator."

"You do divorce work?"

"Afraid not."

"What about litigation?"

"Pay Trent Lott for the damage to his front end, Senator, and be done with it."

"It's fifteen thousand."

"Next month it'll be twenty."

"The meter never stops running, does it?"

"Like the day followeth the night."

They sat in Daphne Melancamp White's smartly furnished corner office, the flat early-August sunlight struggling through the half-closed Levolors, and sipped mineral water.

As he watched the flashing lights on the console of her extension phone, Lee Schumock marveled at the gracefulness with which she tucked her legs beneath her on the plush leather couch against a wall crowded with photos of her with fashionable people, horses, and yachts.

"I'm terribly sorry about Helmut," Lee Schumock said, for openers.

She nodded gravely, then issued a brave smile.

"I suppose the lesson here is to be more circumspect about whom one hires."

Lee Schumock nodded back, trying to keep his eyes averted from the area above her knees exposed by the rather short, but nonetheless businesslike, skirt that went with the Liz Claiborne power suit.

He already knew a fair amount about Daphne Melancamp White. The rumors were all over town about her marriage to the senator. He was tempted to just come right out with it. *So when was the last time you slept with your husband?* See what happened.

She would have him thrown out of the office. Worse. She had the connections to call his publisher and complain. And he'd wind up with nothing, or, worse, thrown off the book.

So he asked her the stuff he either already knew or could imagine and let her walk gingerly around the land mines, whose location she knew even better than he.

"Tell me about Woody White when you first met him. It was at a Washington dinner party, wasn't it?"

She recounted the dinner party in December of 1985, just after Woody had officially thrown his hat in the ring for the following November. Lee Schumock knew that Woody had still been married to Sharon Rosinski at the time and that Woody and Daphne had carried on an affair right up to the time the divorce papers were finalized.

"He was quite charming. Unfortunately, he was married at the time, and so we just became friends."

Lee Schumock stepped gingerly over that lie and lobbed another softball at her.

"He separated from Sharon, I believe, right after his victory in November of '86. That was when you started dating him, right?"

"Yes. He was new to Washington. He needed someone to show him the ropes."

Her tact was exquisite. She knew exactly how to phrase an answer so as to lie with the minimum amount of distance from the truth.

She spoke of the early days of the marriage, when Woody was one of the new Great White Hopes of the Democratic liberal wing in the Senate, when there was even talk of running him for Vice President in '92. They had been courted by Teddy, by Bob Byrd, by Chris Dodd, and by Tip and Gephardt over in the House. There were choice committee assignments, junkets, dinner parties.

"For a while it looked like Woody was going places," she said. "Then things sort of fell apart. Clinton went with Al Gore in '92, and then there was that canard with the staffer . . ."

Lee Schumock looked down at his notes, where he had written, *Sexual harassment charges???* He had been undecided whether to get into that with Daphne. But since she herself had brought it up, he pounced on it.

"How did you . . . feel when that was going on?"

She looked at him with the brave kidnapped-dog smile. "It happened, didn't it?"

"Well, yes. . . ."

"It's no secret that my husband is not a saint," she said, making it seem more a virtue than a character defect. "Whatever happened in the back of that campaign bus is really not very important. It's all about spin, isn't it?"

She shrugged.

He shrugged back.

"I learned a lesson from Hillary on that one. Stand by your man. One way or the other."

She left the *one way or the other* hanging in the air like a strand of confetti drifting slowly to the ground. It was his answer. The best one he was going to get.

It was what Woodward and Bernstein called a non-denial denial. The ball was squarely back in your court, and you had no idea what to do with it.

He looked back down at his notes. He had written *discotheque photo—ice-skater?* and then crossed it out.

Did he have the guts to get into *that?*

She took a sip of the mineral water, glanced at the flashing lights on the phone console, and solved the dilemma for him.

"I'm afraid we're going to have to wrap this up," she said. "There's a partners' meeting in fifteen minutes."

She got up from the couch, smoothed her skirt.

"If you have any other questions, just jot them down and send them to me. And I'll do my best to answer them."

You don't happen to be fucking a Finnish woman ice-skater, by any chance?

She extended her hand.

He shook it. It was cool and dry. She could beat a lie-detector test, he was sure of it.

24

HELMUT'S EAR

HAROLD KINDER flew to Burlington and rented a Ford Tempo from Avis. It was ninety-two and humid. Almost as hot as in Washington. But in Vermont the heat seemed so much crueler, because you looked up at the mountains and expected, if not *The Sound of Music,* at least a little relief.

The committee had dispersed, leaving the staff to initiate a preliminary investigation of Senator Woody White's alleged influence-peddling. Harold Kinder had decided to go to Vermont himself and interview John Quincy Adams, leaving Lydia St. Cloud to handle the senator.

It was all *pro forma* anyway. Unless they had complete idiots for lawyers, they would have been informed of the one question to answer in the negative. Everything else was immaterial, at least at this stage of the investigation.

David Forensic had given Harold Kinder a file on John Quincy Adams's alleged criminal activities, which the investigator had received from the acting U.S. Attorney's office in Burlington. He had read it cursorily, knowing it was irrelevant to the matter at hand, but marveling nonetheless at the diversity of illegal activities the man was reportedly involved in, from loan-sharking and extortion to hijacked liquor and maple-syrup price-fixing.

Vincent Ruggiero's temporary replacement had told Harold Kinder on the phone that John Quincy Adams accounted for 80 percent of the organized crime in Vermont.

"Who does the other twenty percent?" Harold Kinder had asked, intrigued.

"The French Canadians. Out of Montreal. They used to run the whole thing, until Adams muscled them out."

And so it was more out of simple curiosity than for anything else that Harold Kinder had appointed himself to interview John Quincy Adams. He wanted to meet the man who ran 80 percent of the rackets in Vermont.

He took 89 to Montpelier, then Route 2 east out of town, following the directions he had been given on the phone by a man named Ethan Allen. Then there was a series of smaller roads that led, eventually, to a sagging farmhouse with rusted automobile carcasses in the yard and an American flag hanging limply from a paint-chipped flagpole.

A nasty Doberman pushed open the screen door and came out growling as the car pulled into the yard. Harold Kinder stayed in the Tempo until a big man in Bermuda shorts came out and yelled, "Aaron Burr. Place."

The Doberman slinked off to the backyard, and Harold Kinder got out of the car with his briefcase.

"Mr. Kinder?"

"How do you do?"

"Sorry about Aaron Burr. He thinks everyone comes in the yard is Alexander Hamilton. Ethan Allen, pleasure to meet you. Directions okay?"

"Perfect."

Ethan Allen took him through the house and out to a screened back porch that had a couple of rocking chairs and not much more.

A short, unshaven man with big ears got up from one of the rocking chairs and said, "Howdy do."

They shook hands, and the man offered him the less ratty of the two rocking chairs.

"Care for some lemonade?"

"No thanks."

"Ethan squeezed the lemons himself."

"That's okay."

"He squeezed them till they sang, didn't you, Ethan?"

"Sure did, Mr. Q."

"Bring Mr. Kinder some lemonade, Ethan."

The man in the Bermuda shorts went off to the kitchen, as Harold Kinder took a yellow pad out of the briefcase.

"I appreciate your being cooperative in this matter, Mr. Adams."

"The least I can do, Mr. Kinder. What with you coming all the way up here from Washington, D.C. Must be hotter than the bottom of a bitch in heat down there this time of year."

"Please understand, Mr. Adams, that this is merely a preliminary inquiry brought about by a complaint filed against Senator White. We are obliged to look into all complaints that come into the office, and the fact that we are talking to you doesn't mean that we have determined that there is substance to the complaint."

"I understand. You don't know if there's any sugar in the maple till you put the tap in. You ever tap a sugar maple, Mr. Kinder?"

"No I haven't. . . . Maybe we should get started, so I don't have to take too much of your time."

"Let's do it."

"Now, can you tell me, Mr. Adams, the circumstances of your first meeting with Senator White?"

"It was in a restaurant, actually more a diner than a restaurant, in Burlington. Sometime in mid-March, I believe. I can have Ishmael get you the exact date if you need it."

"Mid-March will be fine for the moment, Senator," Lydia St. Cloud said.

She sat across from the senator in his office in the Dirksen Senate Office Building, the curtains drawn against the blinding mid-afternoon August heat. Dirksen—or the New Senate Office Building, as it was called before the construction of the Hart Senate Office Building—had some of the least charming offices in the Capitol.

Senator White had installed an artificial fireplace to give the office a modicum of hominess. The walls featured Currier and Ives snowscapes, a handwoven quilt, and some photos of birch trees, and, behind the big mahogany desk, looking straight into the eyes of the visitor, was a painted photograph of Robert Frost with the words GOOD FENCES MAKE GOOD NEIGHBORS.

The senator was voluble and charming, witty and relaxed. He had served her tea on beautiful bone china and volunteered to make the electric fireplace work, even as the air conditioner struggled to make headway against the stultifying August heat.

Eventually she managed to get out her yellow pad and ask the questions she had to ask.

His answers were forthright.

"Mr. Adams had phoned the office while I was in Vermont. My chief of staff suggested that I meet with him to thank him personally for the contribution that his organization had made to my reelection campaign. As it happened, I was due in Burlington the following day to tour a hockey-stick factory—did you know, by the way, that pretty soon they're going to be playing hockey in Africa?"

Lydia St. Cloud did not know.

"It truly is a global economy. In any event, I met Mr. Adams for lunch in this charming little diner in Burlington. I had a Spanish omelet. Best damn Spanish omelet I've ever had, as a matter of fact . . ."

"Did Mr. Adams ask you for any particular help at that lunch?"

"He didn't ask me for help. But he did suggest a candidate for the Second Circuit. A fellow Vermonter named Vincent Ruggiero. Turned out that Mr. Ruggiero had terrific credentials for the seat. I had my staff do a thorough background on him and was so impressed that I wound up recommending him to the White House."

It was time to ask *the question*. Lydia St. Cloud decided she'd just slip it in with the other questions and hope that it might catch him off-guard.

So, without changing inflection, she asked, "Were you aware at the time, Senator, that Mr. Ruggiero was investigating Mr. Adams for alleged criminal activity?"

"Nope."

"You had no knowledge of the U.S. Attorney's office's interest in Mr. Adams's activities?"

"Now, Lydia, if I had, do you think I would have recommended Mr. Ruggiero for the seat?"

She decided that the man was either a pathological liar or a terrific poker player. Of course, he could also be telling the truth.

Lately Lydia St. Cloud had been wondering if she hadn't spent too much time as counsel to the Senate Ethics Committee. She had begun to lose her faith in the essential goodness of human nature. At least with respect to senators.

On the other hand, if he was telling the truth, they could wrap this up and she could get to California by the tenth, the fifteenth at the latest.

"So your recommendation of Mr. Ruggiero was based solely on his qualifications for the seat?"

"That and the fact that he came from Vermont. Now isn't that why we're elected?"

One more shot at it and then she'd let it go.

"Can you tell me the date of Mr. Adams's second contribution to your reelection campaign?"

"After the pancake breakfast fund-raiser. We passed the hat, managed to come up with a tidy sum for the senator."

"Do you know the amount?" Harold Kinder asked.

"Somewhere north of three hundred thousand, I believe."

"May I ask you, Mr. Adams, why your organization decided to make a second substantial contribution to Senator White's campaign after having already donated five hundred thousand in March?"

"Ayop."

John Quincy Adams drained his lemonade, smacked his lips, and said nothing. After a long moment, Harold Kinder followed up.

"You were saying why your organization decided to make a second contribution?"

"Nope. I was saying you could ask me. I wasn't saying I was going to answer it."

"I see."

"The fact is, Mr. Kinder, my forebears shed blood so that we wouldn't have to answer these types of questions. What about your forebears? Where were they in 1776?"

"Silesia."

"My point exactly."

"I'm just doing my job, Mr. Adams."

"So was King George. You got a Declaration of Independence over there in Silesia?"

"Actually, it's part of Poland now . . ."

"My point exactly."

"We're almost finished here . . ."

"Might rain."

Harold Kinder looked out at the cloudless blue sky and wondered what he was missing.

"The whole point of representative democracy, Mr. Kinder, is that people like us have a voice in Washington. Woody White's our voice. We like him up here. And we intend to keep him. So if you got any more questions, ask them. Otherwise, I got to go out to the barn and toss some hay."

"I think that should do it," Harold Kinder said, quickly putting his yellow pad back into his briefcase.

"Glad to hear it. Ask Ethan to give you a gallon of maple syrup for your trouble."

"I'm not allowed to accept gifts."

"Horseshit, Mr. Kinder. The goddamn government isn't going to collapse over a gallon of maple syrup."

Harold Kinder left the gallon of maple syrup in a toilet stall in the men's room of the Burlington airport, after carefully wiping his fingerprints off it.

The intern's scream brought both Debbie Sue Allenby and Ishmael Leibowitz out to the front office, where they found Trisha Padnick, a UVM sophomore spending her summer down in Washington, standing white-faced over an open package.

As Trisha sank into her chair, Ishmael walked over to see what had caused the young woman to scream. Wrapped in tissue paper was what appeared to be a dog's ear.

There was a note in Italian accompanying it. Debbie Sue Allenby picked up Trisha's extension and dialed the Capitol Police as Ishmael tried to comfort the intern.

"It's just some sick joke, Trisha."

"I thought . . . since it had been through the metal detector . . . it'd be safe to open . . ."

Ishmael checked the package for a return address. There was none, but when Sergeant Harvey Grimes arrived, he picked up a zip-code directory from one of the intern's desks and pinpointed the postmark as Lake Jackson, Texas, a suburb of Houston.

"We'll get the ear analyzed in Bethesda," he said, already used to the drill, and called Agent Sonnenfeld at the FBI.

When Special Agent Gary Sonnenfeld of the FBI's Domestic Terrorism Division arrived, he and Sergeant Grimes went down to the Senate barbershop to find Salvadore Didziocomo for a translation. The barber read it several times before saying, "It's very sad."

"Sad?"

"It says that he is distraught by silence, that he yearns to hear the magic words of his beloved with the ear of his heart. It's from Gabriele D'Annunzio. *La Primavera della Mala Pianta*."

"Obviously from the housekeeper," Agent Sonnenfeld said. Sergeant Grimes nodded.

The FBI had traced the threatening fax that had arrived last month as far as a copy store in Houston before the trail went cold.

"It was written about Eleonora Duse," Salvadore Didziocomo said.

"Who?"

"The great Italian actress. D'Annunzio was in love with her," the barber elaborated.

"No kidding."

"Passionately."

The two lawmen stood for a while in the Senate barbershop, trying to decide how to proceed.

"Still looks like extortion to me," Agent Sonnenfeld said after a long pause.

"Looks like that to me too," Sergeant Grimes concurred.

"How do we get a match on the ear?"

"We can ask the senator to identify it. Then we ship it to Bethesda for a DNA match."

Senator White had just said good-bye to Lydia St. Cloud when Agent Sonnenfeld and Sergeant Grimes arrived in his office.

Woody had assured the Ethics Committee assistant counsel that if she had any further questions, he was at her disposal. After she had left, Ishmael entered with the two cops.

"Sorry to disturb you, Senator, but there's been another communication from your ex-housekeeper," Ishmael said, to explain the presence of the two cops in the office.

Woody looked past his chief of staff to the two men in off-the-rack suits. One of them was holding a Baggie with something unappetizing in it.

"We need you to I.D. your dog's ear, Senator," Agent Sonnenfeld said.

Sergeant Grimes nodded, as if this were a perfectly normal question to ask a United States senator.

Woody nodded absently and looked at the contents of the Baggie. He had no idea whether it was Helmut's ear. Frankly, he could barely remember what the dog looked like, let alone his ear.

He shook his head and said, "Sorry. I really can't tell."

"I don't suppose you have a DNA sample around somewhere?"

"You keep DNA samples of your dog around, Sergeant?"

"I don't have a dog, Senator."

"Obviously."

25

THE DOG DAYS

IT TOOK ONE CALL from Ishmael to Barry to put the news of the dachshund's severed ear out on the wire. By the next morning, condolence phone calls and faxes had flooded into the office.

Meanwhile, the story went out on the national news under the sound byte "Beleaguered Senator Receives Death Threat; Kidnapper Mutilates Dog and Mails Body Parts to Him. Details at Eleven." At eleven, they qualified the story to explain that the death threat wasn't directly to the senator but to his dog. Still, the story played. Big-time.

Irwin Posalski did an overnight telephone poll and called the senator with the results.

"You're up three-point-six percent across the board. And it's not just among Dog Lovers Who Have Not Heard About The Ethics Committee Complaint, but right across the dial."

"That's great."

"Maybe you can arrange for this guy to cut off a body part every month." He chuckled.

When Woody didn't respond, Irwin Posalski quickly added, "Just kidding, Senator. I know how fond you are of that dog."

Washington in August was full of hot tourists, walking around in shorts, $9.99 WASHINGTON D.C. T-shirts, and Nikes, looking for their congressional representatives and finding only summer interns sitting around answering mail.

The whole town was on vacation—fishing, hiking, touring, junketing.

Except those who were up for reelection in November. They were back home working the hustings.

Much to Beverly's chagrin, Woody stayed in town for almost an entire week after adjournment. He had pleaded exhaustion and the need to deal with the Ethics Committee complaint, but the truth was that he wasn't ready quite yet to resume the Jell-O-squares-and-American-Legion circuit.

When Ishmael had begged for a week off, to get away with Maud to Virginia Beach, Woody balked.

"You want to go on vacation in the *middle of an election*?"

"Just a week. Seven days . . ."

"Ishmael, why do you think I hired the smartest man in town to be my chief of staff?"

"I'd be in phone contact all the time . . ."

"I can't do this without you. You're indispensable."

"Everyone's out of town . . ."

"More than indispensable. Irreplaceable."

"Debbie Sue's staying in town . . ."

"All right. Fine. Go. I'll be statistically dead by September anyway."

In the end Ishmael couldn't deal with the combination of flattery and guilt or what he knew would be the 2 A.M. phone calls to Virginia Beach, and so he told Maud that he wouldn't be able to go with her.

She replied that it really made no difference because he had spent so much quality time with her lately that she really didn't need any more time with him.

Between Maud's sarcasm and the senator's guilt trip, Ishmael was looking at a lose/lose proposition. So he wound up staying in Washington and holding down the fort, virtually the only aide left in town.

Barry and Kevin, whose senators were not up in November, were off to Provincetown. And Jack and Denny, who were trying to make it work again after having broken up in May, were renting a cottage in Cherry Grove on Fire Island, where they would spend August getting tanned to a turn and making exotic salad dressings for each other's friends.

The only other congressional aide left in Washington, it seemed, was Owen Lundkeim. The first-term aide from Minnesota had decided to stay in town to use the Library of Congress facilities for his ongoing research into the ravages of Tourette syndrome.

Ishmael was so lonely and bored that he had sought out Owen Lundkeim to have dinner. It was either him or Debbie Sue Allenby, who wouldn't have permitted herself a vacation while Woody White still drew breath. Or one of the pretty little summer interns whom Woody White seemed to attract in droves. But they all looked like they were about sixteen, and even the aides were running scared in post-Packwood Washington. Getting laid these days had become legally problematic.

So, deprived of all social or sexual life, and unable to bear another evening sitting alone in some restaurant reading over Woody's speeches that were faxed down to him from the Vermont staff, Ishmael had called Owen Lundkeim and suggested dinner at La Bavette, any night that week.

"Th . . . th . . . th . . . thank you b . . . b . . . b . . . but I am up to my e . . . e . . . e . . . ears in w . . . w . . . w . . . work."

It was fairly apparent that Owen Lundkeim was avoiding him. Finally, after being turned down for the third time, Ishmael phoned Owen Lundkeim at his home and said, "Look, Owen, it's pretty clear that you're avoiding me. So if it's something I said or did, I'd like to apologize."

"It's n . . . n . . . nothing."

"We don't have to be friends. We can still work together."

There was a long silence on the other end of the line, then: "Th . . . th . . . th . . . this is very diff . . . ff . . . ff . . . icult."

"What?"

"Pl . . . pl . . . pl . . . pl . . . ease don't take th . . . th . . . th . . . this the wrong w . . . w . . . w . . . way."

Another long silence. Ishmael was on the point of hanging up.

"I'm not g . . . g . . . g . . . g . . . g . . . g . . . gay."

For a moment, Ishmael said nothing, then he started to laugh. When he was finished laughing, he said, "I'm sorry, Owen, I really am. Is that the reason you've been avoiding me?"

"Y . . . y . . . y . . . yes."

"Can I tell you something in strictest confidence?"

"It's o . . . o . . . o . . . kay. G . . . g . . . g . . . gay people are o . . . o . . . kay. I j . . . j . . . j . . . just didn't w . . . w . . . w . . . want you to g . . . g . . . g . . . get the wrong im . . . im . . . pr . . . pr . . . pression about m . . . m . . . m . . . me."

"Owen, neither am I."

"Wh . . . wh . . . wh . . . what?"

"I'm not gay either."

"Y . . . y . . . y . . . you're n . . . n . . . n . . . not?"

"It's a cover."

"For wh . . . wh . . . what?"

"Intelligence work."

"Ar . . . ar . . . are you pu . . . pu . . . pu . . . putting me on?"

"No. I swear. I can't tell you the details, but it goes all the way up to the National Security Agency."

"Je . . . je . . . je . . . sus. Are B . . . B . . . B . . . arry, K . . . K . . . K . . . evin . . ."

Ishmael cut him off. It would take minutes to get through all four names.

"Please don't ask me any more questions, all right?"

"All . . . all . . . all right."

"And don't breathe a word of this to anybody, especially Barry, Kevin, Jack, and Denny."

"I pr . . . pr . . . pr . . . promise."

"Otherwise I'll have to have you killed."

"How much?"

"A hundred."

"Did you try Canucking him down?"

"Wouldn't budge. Says she's a public figure and that's the going rate for public figures."

John Quincy Adams crumpled some more Saltines into his cream-of-tomato soup and shook his head. "What the hell ever happened to the work ethic? Used to be you could get someone done for twenty-five. Then it went to fifty. But a hundred. That's extortion."

"The way I figure," said Elbridge Gerry, "maybe we don't have to do her at all."

"How's that?"

"*Rutland Herald* says she's down a point or two. Seems this dog-ear thing is helping Woody out."

Elbridge Gerry went to the refrigerator and took out a pitcher of Ethan Allen's lemonade, poured them each a glass.

"We do anybody, we do Ruggiero."

"We don't have to do him no more. He's in Washington, Elbridge."

"We can do him retroactively."

"Now, why'd we want to do that?"

"Send out the message. Like we did with Roland Boyden. After Roland took a trip around the yard, we didn't have trouble collecting from anybody else, did we?"

"We start doing everyone retroactively who had it coming to him, we'd wind up doing half of Montpelier, now, wouldn't we?"

John Quincy Adams finished his soup, belched, blew his nose, pushed his chair back from the table, and fished his corncob pipe out of his pocket.

"You get the cable fixed yet?"

"Friday."

"Jesus, Elbridge, you know I like that program what's-its-name that's on Thursday night."

"*ER*."

"That's it. I like that program. You know who I'd like to do? The god-damn cable guy, that's who I'd like to do. I'd pay a hundred to do him, and he's no public figure."

John Quincy Adams lit his pipe, then exhaled a large puff of Red Barn tobacco smoke.

"'Course, if push came to shove, we could always wire Roland Boyden to the TV and have him stand up on the roof with tinfoil wrapped around his dick."

"Roland's dick, you couldn't even get Burlington."

The part of Vermont above St. Johnsbury, bordered by Canada on the north and New Hampshire on the east, is referred to colloquially as the "Northeast Kingdom." It is the poorest part of the state, with the lowest population density, per-capita income, and educational level.

They weren't very fond of Woody White up there. But then they weren't very fond of anybody. As far as the people in the Northeast Kingdom were concerned, Washington, D.C., might as well have been in South America—that's how remote it was from their lives.

In '86 and '92, Woody hadn't even bothered to make an appearance up there, having decided that there just weren't enough votes worth chasing. But this year, with the election so close, Beverly had determined that a swing through the Northeast Kingdom would be cost-effective.

So by August 15, Woody found himself mobilizing for a swing through the Northeast Kingdom. The message up there, he was told, was the economy, jobs, price supports for dairy farmers, Social Security entitlements. Bread and butter. They hadn't heard much about John Quincy Adams and the Ethics Committee complaint, or about the severed dachshund's ear. They generally turned in before the ten o'clock news, right after the farm report.

Woody had flown up to Burlington, where a car was waiting to drive him to St. Johnsbury. He spent the night there at the Holiday Inn, where he had gotten a call from his mother, who had tracked him down, as she always did, by calling Ishmael in Washington.

"The Jewish boy gave me your number," Adele Hanna Weit said, when the senator answered the phone in his room.

"How are you, Mother?"

"How do you think I am?"

"I don't know."

"How would you feel if you had to walk around goddamn Palm Springs as the mother of a man who cuts the ears off dogs?"

"I think you got it backward . . ."

"Don't contradict me, Woody. Tom Brokaw said so. And he generally tells the goddamn truth."

"Apart from that, Mother, how are you?"

"You owe me eighty-one hundred dollars."

"For what?"

"The goddamn air-conditioning. It doesn't work worth shit."

"I'm sorry about that, but according to your helper, it works fine."

"She's a Filipino. What the hell does she know about air-conditioning? You better send me the money, Woody, or I'll have my attorneys contact you."

His mother's attorneys could get in line behind Trent Lott's attorneys, Sharon's attorneys, Daphne's attorneys, the Ethics Committee's attorneys. They could have one big circle jerk, litigating and billing one another to their hearts' content.

Beverly had rented a large Winnebago, which would serve as a movable campaign office and command center. To save money, Beverly herself drove. A school-bus driver when she wasn't running Woody White's campaigns, Beverly drove the Winnebago, as well as everything else, with authority.

They left St. Johnsbury early in the morning, heading north, stopping at Lyndonville, Burke, Newark, and Island Pond before lunch. Woody would get out at the post office or the I.G.A. and shake whatever hands there were to shake, while the volunteers handed out literature and Beverly kept them on schedule.

It was grass-roots campaigning at its very basic, and Woody found that he still had the ability to charm even the sullen electorate of the Northeast Kingdom. Especially the old ladies in the seersucker dresses, sitting out on their rocking chairs, listening to their arteries harden.

Woody would walk up to the porch, stick out his hand, smile, and say, "Now what's a good-looking woman like you doing in a rocking chair on a beautiful day like today?"

This type of cornball charm still played up here. Let Rebecca Gatney show up with her Ethics Committee complaints and her character assassination. They wouldn't give her the time of day. Of course, whether or not the old ladies got off their rocking chairs and got to the polling place on November 3 was another matter.

They pulled into Morgan Center at twelve-thirty. Right on schedule. Woody addressed the Morgan Women's Club Luncheon at one, telling the assembled women, after a short speech on the importance of dairy farming to Vermont's economy, just why a hummingbird hummed.

He judged the mince-pie contest, and they were back on the road, heading over to Bloomfield for a cattle show at three, then back up to Newport for an Elks Club dinner.

Beverly kept them moving. Pull into town. Hi, how you doing? I'm Woody White. Glad to meet you. You know why a hummingbird hums?

Brian Petrunich and Janine Caravaggio worked the cell phones in the back of the Winnebago, making sure that whatever local media there was up here knew exactly where the senator was going to be next and when.

So there was a local TV-news crew out in the pasture in Bloomfield as Woody participated in a cow-chip-throwing contest. Throwing dried cow shit for distance was an occupational hazard for a Vermont politician, and Woody actually came in second, a foot and a half behind a large man with eyes set very close together who looked like he could throw Woody almost as far as he threw cow shit.

As they took off their gloves and shook hands for the photo op, the man leaned forward out of the range of the TV camera audio and whispered, "You want to get your cock sucked, I'll be behind the firehouse at nine o'clock."

"Beg your pardon?"

The man whispered, "You prefer, I can stick it up so far it'll come out of your nose."

Woody smiled and thanked the man for his support.

While Woody was tossing cow chips in Bloomfield, his opponent was tossing cow chips at a meeting of the Chamber of Commerce in Montpelier. Rebecca Gatney stood at the rostrum of the John Dewey Room of the Montpelier Hyatt and lit into the incumbent Senator from Peru.

"It's just one scandal after another. You can't turn on the TV set these days without hearing about someone else who's complaining about the senator, or suing him. Even his own colleagues in the Senate are investigating him. Right now, there are investigators from the Senate Ethics Committee interviewing him and his pal John Quincy Adams, a man who had been under the scrutiny of the United States Attorney's office for extortion and loan-sharking until Woody White got the federal attorney investigating him appointed to the federal judiciary and out of Mr. Adams's hair. . . ."

The crowd, about a hundred or so businesspeople, shifted restlessly in their seats, like a congregation waiting for the pastor to really lay it on. And Rebecca Gatney did not disappoint them.

"I don't know about you, but I'm wondering just what my senator is doing down there in Washington, D.C. When he's not running over to the White House to recommend judges, he's defending himself in front of the Ethics Committee."

Heads nodded.

"When he's not talking to his lawyers, he's holding hearings on Tourette syndrome. A worthy cause, no doubt, but did you send Woody White down to Washington to spend his time raising money for a disease that affects less than one half of one percent of the population of this country?"

Heads shook.

"And when he's not holding hearings on Tourette syndrome, he's sitting on the African Affairs Subcommittee trying to get Congress to spend your tax dollars to stimulate the phosphate industry in Togo. How many of you even know where Togo is?"

She had the crowd pretty worked up, shaking their heads and moaning their assent. Especially two men sitting toward the rear, wearing nearly identical plaid sports jackets, short-sleeved shirts, and cotton wash-and-wear ties.

William Whipple leaned over to Button Gwinnett and said, "Heard enough?"

"Ayop."

William Whipple rose from his seat and said right to the rostrum, "Miss, you're so full of cow pucky it'd come out of your knees if you had any."

Rebecca Gatney looked down at the little man in the plaid sports jacket and said, "It's very rude to interrupt someone, sir."

"Not when she's standing there tossing cow chips at the best senator this state ever had. You don't know jackshit about this state or about Woody White. So you want to continue spreading the compost, go ahead, but I've had just about enough."

"And so have I," said Button Gwinnett. "The worst cow pucky I've heard since Gerry Ford came up here and told us he pardoned Dick Nixon to spare the country the ordeal."

"Excuse me—I believe I have the floor here . . ."

"Yeah, you got it, all right. Now why don't you go sweep it," was William Whipple's Parthian shot as he and Button Gwinnett walked up the aisle toward the door.

On the way out, William Whipple turned to Button Gwinnett and said, "Wouldn't mind hanging her upside down in the smokehouse."

"Better the outhouse. By her feet. Right over the hole."

26

THE GARY HART
LECTURE CIRCUIT

THERE'S AN OLD SAYING in Vermont that there are only two seasons. Winter and August. It certainly felt that way to Woody White as he crisscrossed the state in his Winnebago, trawling for votes. The towns and villages began to blend into one another—the red barns and the white churches and the jagged stone walls that demarcated the pastures full of grazing, indifferent cows.

In some of the resort areas, Woody would draw crowds of what the Vermonters call disdainfully "summer folk"—people with $100 haircuts, Porsche Carrera sunglasses, and Banana Republic work shirts. They were, by and large, liberal Democrats, inclined to support Woody White, but they didn't vote in Vermont. They came out from their vacation condos and *Architectural Digest* summer homes to hear Woody for the entertainment value, tired of mosquitoes, corn on the cob, and CNN.

It was the hearts and minds of the people in the eight-dollar haircuts, without the sunglasses, wearing JCPenney work shirts and shitkickers with real cow manure on them, that Woody needed to win over. And they were a hard read. They stared at him from the back of the Elks Clubs and American Legion halls, the state fairs and the cow-chip-throwing contests, without tipping their hands.

Irwin Posalski's polls indicated that Woody was treading water. While Woody was painstakingly working the Jell-O-squares circuit, Rebecca Gatney was screaming like a banshee about him on radio and TV. Woody was beginning to question whether it was worth it—the long days in the

Winnebago, the mince pies, the rooms in the Holiday Inn off the Holidome with the Ping-Pong tables and the swimming pool full of screaming kids and their overweight parents.

By the time they got to Bennington, just before Labor Day, morale was dipping. They sat around the table at the Ramada Inn, after yet another dinner of southern fried chicken, biscuits, and iced tea, and spitballed ideas.

"We've got to start doing TV," Janine Caravaggio said.

"It's too early to do TV," Brian Petrunich countered. "We do TV in October, when it counts."

"The rates are a lot higher in October. We can get some cheap space now."

"That's because nobody's watching now."

"It'd be nice if we knew what the Ethics Committee was going to do."

"We won't hear anything till they're back."

"Still, we ought to have a contingency plan. In case Ethics goes against us."

"What're we going to say—Woody's being persecuted politically by the Republicans? It's a nonpartisan committee."

"Is there a loose Democratic vote?"

They all turned to the candidate, who was doodling on a menu. He was wearing his summer campaigning outfit—pressed jeans, a plaid shirt, and work boots. He had removed his Caterpillar hat and sunglasses, and looked, for the moment, like a tired city guy who had spent the day digging rocks out of the south forty.

Woody shrugged. "These days, every vote is loose."

It wasn't so much the remark as the defeatist manner in which it was made that discouraged the staff from pursuing the matter. After a brief silence, Brian Petrunich said, "Let's challenge her to a debate."

"We should do that in October too."

"Yeah, but by then . . ." Brian Petrunich did not finish the sentence. He immediately regretted saying it and just sat there picking his teeth with a mint toothpick.

"The field," Rav Monsjar suddenly muttered, to nobody in particular.

The staff was used to these types of non sequiturs from Rav Monsjar, and so they merely waited for elaboration.

"A field full of cow shit," he said. "Two white pine rocking chairs and a blackboard . . ."

People nodded even though they had no idea what Rav Monsjar was talking about. The pundit put the tip of the pencil end he had been chewing into his ear, scratched around, and said, "Here's how we do the debate. We put Woody and her in a field, preferably one that is still full of cow shit. To symbolize the type of campaign she's running. We have both of them in rocking chairs. Then we get someone like the president of Marlboro College to stand by the blackboard and make a mark after the candidate's name each time one of them tosses a cow chip at the other. At the end of the debate, the winner is the one with the lower bullshit quotient."

The idea was stupefyingly simple, on its face. It made Woody think of Calvin Coolidge, who had run for reelection in 1924 from his rocking chair in Plymouth, Vermont, saying that he was available to talk to anybody who wanted to come to see him on his front porch.

"What if she says no?" Janine Caravaggio asked.

"Well, then, we put Woody out there in his chair next to an empty rocking chair with a sign that says REBECCA GATNEY. And we have someone ask, 'Where's Woody?' And we reply, 'He's *here*. Where's Becky? She ain't.'"

"That's fucking brilliant, Rav," Woody said.

"Glad you like it. I'm going home now."

And he got up and walked out.

On Labor Day, after a rally in Rutland, during which Woody unveiled his debate challenge to Rebecca Gatney in front of the media, he stole away to Peru for a much-needed assignation with Evelyn Brandwynne.

The lobbyist for the National Association of Health Prophylaxis Industries came up from Washington with her nurse's uniform, medicinal alcohol, razor, and toiletries to meet the senator in the A-frame at the end of various dirt roads outside Peru, Vermont.

As remote as the A-frame was, and as blasé as the people of Peru had become over the years about the senator's residence there, a certain amount of discretion was still called for. Unless you wanted to go into the lecture-circuit business with Gary Hart, you didn't get caught committing adultery two months before an election.

As prearranged, Evelyn Brandwynne parked her car at the I.G.A. and walked as far as Joshua Karton's sugar shack a quarter of a mile out of town, where Woody met her and drove her to the house. Then he went back to the I.G.A. to get her luggage out of the trunk of the rental car.

It had been a while for both of them, and in their eagerness to get down to the procedure, they forgot about it. As soon as Evelyn and Woody were in the door, they started ripping clothing off, and, before they could even get the nurse's uniform out of the valise, they found themselves entwined on the handwoven Vermont rug in front of the defunct fireplace, going at it like high school kids in the back of the car.

Woody had put a bottle of white zinfandel on ice, fired up the Jacuzzi, and programmed the CD player for two hours of Nat King Cole, but wound up dispensing with it all as soon as he smelled the subtle trace of Je Reviens that Evelyn Brandwynne had freshened herself up with in the car in front of the I.G.A.

Afterward, as they lay together on the rug, Woody marveled at the extent to which Ivan Pavlov's delicate system of conditioned reflexes could be short-circuited. At first it had required the actual procedure in the doctor's office, then that had been transferred to the procedure at home, then to the mere smell of the medicinal alcohol, then to just the sound of the starched uniform. And now, apparently, all that was needed was a trace of the perfume that his brain already associated with the uniform, the medicinal alcohol, and the procedure to trip the chain of synapses needed to get the blood rushing back to the right place.

He got up whistling, fetched the white zinfandel and two glasses, and switched on the by-now-gratuitous Nat King Cole.

"Well," Evelyn Brandwynne reflected, "whatever it was that you've been doing up here seems to have agreed with you."

She took a sip of the wine, stretched out luxuriously, and said, "That was quite lovely, though I might actually begin to miss the nurse's uniform."

"Put it on anytime you want. It's okay with me."

"You think Pavlov needs a booster shot now and then?"

"I suppose we'll find out, won't we?"

"Will we?"

The question was not flirtatious. The bantering tone in her voice had given way to something more vulnerable and genuine. The question was not just academic.

Woody had realized that sooner or later he would be in for this conversation, but, like most men, he had been hoping to postpone it.

"Is this the where-is-this-relationship-going conversation?"

She nodded, smiling tentatively. "I'd like to say not, but I'm afraid it is. I mean, after all, my bill isn't going anywhere. So I'm beginning to wonder if I'm not going anywhere along with it."

Woody leaned back and closed his eyes. He wished he had Rav Monsjar here with him to come up with the strategy. The truth was that he had become more and more attached to Evelyn Brandwynne without really admitting it to himself.

She was a terrific woman—attractive, smart, independent, low-maintenance. Though maybe she couldn't stop traffic dead at a White House cocktail party, like Daphne could, Evelyn could certainly slow it down to a crawl. He could see the President, Al, Teddy, Gephardt, et al., inching along bumper-to-bumper through the circulating trays of domestic Chardonnay.

"I'm very . . . fond of you, Evelyn," he said, eyes still closed.

"*Very fond* isn't going to cut it, Woody."

"I didn't think so. . . . How about excessively fond?"

"Uh-uh. Feels too much like a double negative."

It definitely was *that* conversation.

"Are we talking the *c* word here?"

"A moderate commitment could work."

"Six months?"

"I was thinking more along the lines of a year."

"Six months and your bill out of committee?"

"Fuck the bill," she said.

He opened his eyes and turned toward her.

"I'm glad you said that, Evelyn."

"So am I."

"It's not just that I'm up to my ass in Ethics problems already, but—"

"Woody, that's no way to sweet-talk a woman."

She was backlit by the pale late-summer twilight seeping through the smudged glass of the A-frame. Her rich red-brown hair fell down over her shoulders, brushing her breasts.

He leaned over and kissed her softly, then whispered, "How about eight weeks, from here to the election, with an option to extend, exercisable within seven working days after the vote is counted?"

"That is so romantic."

He kissed her again, then slid his lips down and gently tongued the nipples.

"How about seven days in Tahiti as soon as the divorce papers are served on Daphne?"

"I'd need fourteen. On the inside," she replied, her voice starting to go a little liquid around the edges.

Gently, he parted her legs and let his fingers slide down the inside of her thighs, circling slowly, one hand clockwise, the other counterclockwise.

One of Woody's talents as a politician was his ability to recognize the right moment to close the deal.

So Woody closed.

The tip of his tongue found the spot that if you hit it exactly right renders most women irrational. In Evelyn Brandwynne's case, it rendered her completely gaga.

Before she went to pieces, she managed to mutter, "How about three days in a motel room in Rockville?"

. . .

Later Woody and Evelyn lolled upstairs in the lukewarm Jacuzzi watching the six o'clock news cover his debate challenge earlier that day in Rutland.

Woody had stood on the steps of the county courthouse, flanked by his staff, and challenged Rebecca Gatney to meet him in the field with the rocking chairs and the blackboard at any date and time convenient to her.

"I'll be there. Wherever and whenever you want," he said, as if he were looking at her right through the camera.

Then, in a spontaneous demonstration of support, a group of college students had shouted, "Where'll Woody be?" And then they had responded, "He'll be there."

There was, of course, no way that Rebecca Gatney was going to let any grass grow under her mouth. As soon as they were finished with coverage of Woody in Rutland, they cut to his opponent in Burlington.

"He's trying to make a travesty out of the election, and I'm not buying it. I'll meet him in a hall, in a church, in an auditorium, in any town in Vermont and debate the issues, but I'm not about to sit on a rocking chair in a field full of cow droppings and indulge in some sort of silly game show he's dreamed up."

Before she could escape, one of the reporters said, on camera, "Mrs. Gatney, the president of Marlboro College has already agreed to moderate the debate in the field . . ."

She just shook her head and pretended not to have heard him before hurrying away and getting into her Range Rover.

The Rutland anchors, Larry Levalle and Linda Lutz, turned toward each other for some filler banter.

"Well, Larry, it looks like these two candidates don't like each other, doesn't it?"

"I don't think they're on each other's Christmas list, Linda."

Then Larry Levalle turned back to the camera and read his TelePrompTer.

"With Congress recovening in Washington later this week, there is a lot at stake for Woody White. A spokesperson for the Senate Ethics Committee said that there is a meeting of the full committee scheduled for Thursday, during which the question of pursuing the complaint brought by the Vermont Citizens for Ethical Government against the incumbent senator will no doubt come up. . . . Closer to home, a terminally ill wallpaper hanger from Manchester, distraught over his medical bills, ran himself over with his own lawnmower in an apparent attempt to end his life. . . ."

Woody zapped the TV and leaned back against the tile. Tomorrow he was flying back into the war zone, after three weeks of relative safety.

He was in the home stretch. Eight more weeks. According to Irwin, he was now running neck-and-neck with Rebecca Gatney. The rocking-chairs-in-the-field gambit could jack him up a few points. Maybe he could pull this thing out after all.

He had to hope that the Ethics Committee walked away from the VCEG complaint, that John Quincy Adams kept a low profile, that the Tourette-syndrome bill didn't blow up in his face, that Daphne didn't do anything stupid, that the leadership kept him in enough soft money to stay afloat, that nobody towed Evelyn's car from in front of the I.G.A. . . .

Among other things.

27

HEGEL'S DIALECTIC

On the Wednesday morning after Labor Day, the breakfast club reconvened along with Congress. Ishmael met Barry, Kevin, Jack, and Denny at the coffee shop at Eighteenth and S for nonfat lattes and bran muffins.

After a month sitting on the beach with their reflectors and romance novels, all four of them looked tanned and rested. Unlike Ishmael, who looked like he had spent the month reading budgets under fluorescent lighting.

"You don't look very well," Kevin said.

"Some of us had to work all August."

"He didn't give you any time off at all?"

"He's up in November. Remember?"

"Still. August in Washington. That's cruel and unusual punishment."

Finally, it was Jack who asked the question that had been on everybody's mind since Ishmael had walked in alone at 7:45.

"So . . . how's Owen?"

"Fine," Ishmael said, deciding to leave it at that and let them draw their own conclusions. Which, of course, they immediately did. After a quick, almost subliminal exchange of looks among the four of them, Kevin asked, "Did something happen?"

Ishmael shrugged.

"What?"

"Nothing."

"*Ishmael . . .*"

"We're trying it apart for a while."

"Shit, we're sorry," Barry said, for all four of them.

"It's no big thing," Ishmael assured them.

Another quick, silent consultation, then Kevin asked, "Was there . . . someone else?"

"I really don't want to talk about it, okay?"

"There was, wasn't there?"

"Who?"

"That bastard."

They went on for a while, shit-listing Owen Lundkeim, until Ishmael said, "I told you—I really would rather not discuss it."

"Ishmael, the worst thing you can possibly do now is keep this bottled up inside you. It just festers that way."

Ishmael didn't want to overplay his hand. He was walking a fine line. After all, if Barry or Kevin thought he was on the rebound from Owen, they might start moving in again, and then Ishmael'd be right back where he'd started.

"I'm fine," he said. "I really am. I just need a little space right now, okay?"

"All right, but we're here for you if you need us."

"I appreciate that."

They all nodded sympathetically and went back to their nonfat lattes. After a respectful interval, Denny said, "So, did you hear who's working Tipper out?"

"*Who?*"

"He's the most inspiring man I've ever met."

"How so?"

"I don't even know where to begin," said Debbie Sue Allenby, removing her tortoiseshell glasses with one hand and running the other through her short dark hair in a gesture that struck Lee Schumock as passionate, even sexual.

If Woody White had an acolyte in Washington, it was his chief legislative assistant. She had been with him for eight of his twelve years in the Senate, coordinating his committee work, his Floor motions, working impossible hours, standing beside him on the bridge in all kinds of weather.

Thirty-seven years old, never married, not even close, she went home every night to her one-bedroom apartment in Takoma Park, fed her fish, and got into bed with the *Congressional Record*. She was a member of a one-nun order, and there was nothing Woody White had done or could do that would shake her faith in him. If he shot Trent Lott in the middle of the Senate chamber, Debbie Sue Allenby, like Sirhan Sirhan's mother, would show up every day at the prison with home-cooked meals.

In any event, to Lee Schumock it was a change from the nuanced, if not jaundiced, opinions of Woody's mother, his children, his ex- and present wives, whose feelings about the senator were complex, at best, if not downright hostile.

"When did you first go to work for him?"

"In 1990. I heard him speak at the Foreign Affairs Forum at GWU. Believe me, that place can be a viper pit, with those snotty poli-sci profs showing off for the graduate students, but the Senator just stood up there and deflected all the sarcasm and innuendo with an incredible amount of intelligence and charm. So I wrote him a letter. I mean, I tried not to sound like some dippy intern with a crush, but I said how impressed I had been, and he called and invited me to lunch. . . ."

Lee Schumock listened to Debbie Sue Allenby describe her eight years with Woody White the way some women describe an idyllic marriage.

"I think Clinton should have gone with the senator instead of Al Gore again in '96 . . ."

"Really? What about the sexual-harassment scandal in '95?"

"What scandal?"

"The woman in the back of the campaign bus."

"Please. That was just the desperate attempt of an unbalanced woman for attention. The only reason it even got to Ethics was that we lost a Democratic vote on the committee. It was strictly in retaliation for the Senator's refusal to vote up SR 986."

"What was SR 986?"

"You know where Rebecca Gatney's money comes from?"

Lee Schumock went with the pitch. "Where?"

"Her husband's family's got millions in shopping centers in New Brunswick. They bring it back in the country in Canadian dollars, avoiding IRS scrutiny, then launder it through a couple of out-of-state banks and put it into the Vermont Citizens for Ethical Government."

"I didn't realize that," Lee Schumock said, looking for a trace of irony in her misty eyes.

Did she actually believe this shit?

"That's nothing," she went on, her chapped lips curving into the tilted smile of the true conspiracy theorist. "Did you know her daughter was thrown off her high school cheerleading squad for smoking?"

The writer shook his head.

"And she's got a second mortgage on her ski condo."

. . .

The full Ethics Committee convened on Thursday afternoon in the windowless room on the second floor of Hart. The chairman, looking hale after ten days of white-water rafting, gaveled the meeting to order and greeted the other five senators, their aides, and the committee staff.

Rarely were all six senators, their various aides, and the entire staff present, but on this particular Thursday afternoon, there wasn't a spare seat in the room.

After a few words of welcome to his colleagues and an expression of gratitude to the staff for their having sacrificed half their August vacations, the chairman asked Harold Kinder to report on their preliminary investigation of the complaint against Senator White.

Harold Kinder recounted his interview with John Quincy Adams in Vermont and Lydia St. Cloud's interview with Senator White in Washington.

"They were both generally cooperative and forthright, though Mr. Adams did get a bit testy when pressed. Since I was working without a subpoena I didn't insist upon certain responses that I ordinarily would have insisted upon had this been a deposition—"

"So what's your call on this, Harold?" the vice chairman interrupted.

"Well, Senator, both Ms. St. Cloud and I feel that at this point, given the limited scope of the inquiry to date and the limitations of staff time and resources—"

"Bottom line, Harold?"

"I don't think there's enough here even to go for a subpoena."

"You agree, Lydia?"

"Yes I do, Senator. The key question—that is, did Senator White know that Mr. Ruggiero was investigating Mr. Adams?—was answered clearly in the negative by Senator White. Without that, we have no quid-pro-quo case."

There was a certain amount of nodding and murmuring of agreement in the room.

"I don't know about you, gentlemen," the senator from Virginia said, "but I think we take a pass on this."

The other senators assented, clearly relieved to be able to wash their hands of the whole matter. Everyone except the chairman, a liverish four-term Republican with high blood pressure, who was no friend of Woody White's and would have to report back to the party leadership the results of the meeting.

"I must say, it feels to me that we're being a little too cavalier here. These are serious charges. And, I might add, this is not the first time that Senator White's behavior has come before this committee."

"What are you suggesting, Mr. Chairman?"

"I think we should consider deposing them under oath."

"What do you think about that, Harold?" the senator from Oklahoma asked.

"My honest opinion is we'll get the same answers under oath that we got in the interviews."

All six senators, as well as their aides, were aware that the decision had already been made and that what was going on now was mere posturing and face-saving, the accumulation of political capital to be cashed in at a later date. It was a dance that took place in every committee room in Congress, the only difference being that this particular dance was not being televised on C-SPAN.

So the dance didn't last any longer than necessary. The chairman waited for everyone in the room to have a trip around the floor before calling the question.

"Well, it appears to me," he said, with the appropriate amount of resignation in his voice, "that the consensus of this room is clearly in favor of dropping the investigation, so, unless anyone objects, it is so moved."

The vote was recorded as 6–0, and the committee proceeded to its next order of business—evaluating the ethics of the gift of a case of Napa Valley pinot noir received by the senior senator from California and duly reported to it.

Even before it was officially announced in a hastily called news conference at five-thirty that afternoon, the news made its way downstairs to the Senate Health Facility steam room, where a half-dozen senators were schvitzing and hypothesizing about the Ethics Committee's decision.

"Looks like Woody dodged another bullet."

"There was no bullet to dodge. They didn't have the goods. You don't institute an ethics investigation two months before an election unless you got him standing over the body with the smoking gun."

"The truth is the chairman couldn't find a loose vote on the other side."

"What did he expect? You don't hand the opposition a seat at this point."

"Woody's a stretch horse. He'll win at the wire—don't you worry about it."

There was some murmured assent among the senators. Then someone threw out the Big Question.

"You think he knew?"

"Maybe he did, maybe he didn't . . ."

"Apparently, this Adams guy is dirtier than Charles Keating."

"Well, I'll tell you what I think—I think they're going to look at every goddamn dollar you raise now through a goddamn microscope. We're going to wind up on the street corner with dark glasses and a cup in our hand, begging for spare change."

"It's merely Hegel's dialectic," said a veteran senator, a classical scholar and moralist.

"Hegel's what?"

"The great sweep of history—each movement creating an excess, causing reaction to sweep back excessively, beyond the original point of departure."

"Anybody know what the hell Bob's talking about?"

"Gentlemen, for years we got our money anywhere and everywhere. We abused the system. And now we're just paying the historical price. It's strophe and antistrophe."

"I don't know about strophe and antistrophe, but I'll tell you this— Woody White's just the tip of the iceberg. They'll be coming after us all pretty soon."

This disturbing thought drifted through the steam room, as each senator reflected upon just how well he'd do under the microscope. After a long, troubled silence, another hypothesis was thrown out for discussion.

"So . . . you think Trent'll get the money for his car now?"

Woody White had been in politics too long to overreact to the news of the Ethics Committee's vote. He was relatively blasé when Burton Armature called to give him the official notification of the committee's decision not to pursue the matter.

"I suppose that's good news, Burt."

"That's good news, Senator."

"Should I make a statement?"

"Why? You got the chairman making the statement for you. You make a statement, it looks like you're trying to oversell. 'Ladies and gentlemen, see, I'm really not a crook.' You won, Senator. Take the trophy and go home."

What trophy? They didn't give you a trophy when they exonerated you. And the truth was that they hadn't even done that. The chairman didn't say that Woody White was not guilty. He had said, for the cameras, merely that there was insufficient evidence to pursue the investigation.

Woody didn't feel as if he had won. He felt as if he hadn't lost. Still, as he sat in his office in the early-evening twilight, he tried to look at the positive side of things: At the very least, there would be one fewer lawyer in his life. That alone was worth celebrating.

So he buzzed Ishmael and told him to come in for some roasted almonds and a glass of single-malt Scotch.

"Well, congratulations are in order, I suppose," Woody said, once they were settled.

Ishmael nodded and took a token sip of the Scotch.

"Now we can concentrate on the campaign. I'm telling you, Ishmael, I feel as if we've turned the corner."

Ishmael smiled and nodded, trying his best to contain his congenital Eastern European pessimism in the face of the senator's confidence. There was a little dark spot inside him that feared that there was no such thing as unmitigated good news.

A therapist had once told him that he was suffering from CHSS—the Children of Holocaust Survivors Syndrome. Ishmael's father had been shipped to Treblinka in the closing days of the war, and though he had spent less than a month there and had survived, the experience had, according to the therapist, profoundly affected the way he had brought up his late-in-life son. The father had unconsciously transmitted the fear and anxiety he had experienced to the son, so that even though Ishmael was born in New York twenty years after the war, he carried the Holocaust around inside him.

"It's your cross to bear," the doctor told him.

Ishmael had never forgotten the doctor's words. They came back to him once again as he sat sipping single-malt Scotch and listening to the senator express optimism that the worst was behind them.

For some reason, Ishmael Leibowitz felt that the worst was not behind them.

As it turned out, he was right.

28.

TOGOGATE

KODJO KPONVI sat at the gunmetal-gray desk of his Seventh Street office eating a meal of fried yams, peppers, and onions that he had just cooked on his hibachi and speaking on the phone to his brother-in-law in Lomé, Kossi Gbagba, who, besides having married Kodjo Kponvi's sister, Kumla, happened to be the Togolese Foreign Minister. For security reasons, they used Kotokoli—one of Togo's forty-four native languages and one spoken by fewer than 100,000 people in the entire world, none of whom currently worked for any United States intelligence agency.

The topic was additional military hardware for the Togolese air force. Kossi Gbagba had asked his brother-in-law in Washington about the feasibility of getting the U.S. Senate to get the Pentagon to allocate a couple of high-tech missiles for the arsenal. In reply, Kodjo Kponvi asked Kossi Gbagba what they were going to put the high-tech missiles *in,* since the Togolese air force had nothing more high-tech than a few obsolete French Mirage fighters.

Kossi Gbagba told him that it didn't really matter as long as Togo's enemies believed they could deliver the missiles.

At that point, there was a phone call on NAPTOTS's other line. Kodjo Kponvi put Kossi Gbagba on hold and said, "National Association for the Prevention and Treatment of Tourette Syndrome, how may I direct your call?"

A woman, introducing herself as a journalist from *The Wall Street Journal,* asked if she could interview the director of NAPTOTS.

"Most definitely, *madame*. When would be convenient for you?"

"Tomorrow morning at ten?"

"Splendid. Do you have the address?"

"Yes."

"Your name, *madame*?"

He jotted down the name and went back to his brother-in-law in Lomé. He told the *ministre des affaires étrangers de la république du Togo* that ordinarily he would contact his particular senator, the one responsible for the phosphate money, but that his particular senator was under attack at the moment and might have to keep a low profile.

Kossi Gbagba asked if another $400,000 would raise this particular senator's profile. His brother-in-law told him that he would step on the snake and see if it bit. They switched back to Ewe for the salutations.

"*Alafiya*, Kodjoga."

"*Alafiya*, Kossivi . . ."

He hung up and wrote down $400,000 on the pad beside the name of *The Wall Street Journal* reporter. He underlined it several times in red pen. Then he looked back at the name of the reporter and wondered how you pronounced it. *Hermione Hingle*. It sounded Greek to him.

The photo op was the elegant solution to a thorny problem. There had been a protracted discussion in Montpelier about the "dog problem." The kidnapped dog had been worth three to four points in the polls, but by now people were starting to forget about the mutilated dachshund. Woody White was now simply a candidate without a dog.

And Rav Monsjar delivered a simple political dictum: "You don't get elected in Vermont without a dog."

"Yes, but if the FBI doesn't find the dachshund soon, what do we do?" Janine Caravaggio asked.

"We get him another dog," Brian Petrunich suggested.

"Isn't it insensitive to run out and get another dog so soon after this one died? What if he's not dead?"

"Then it's a photo op. You know how much a photo of Woody and Daphne with a one-eared dachshund would be worth?"

"Five points, easy," predicted Irwin Posalski.

"What would be better—a live one-eared dachshund or a dead one-eared dachshund?" Brian Petrunich speculated.

"A dead dog isn't worth jackshit," Rav Monsjar said.

The compromise was that they would get what would appear to be a candid photo of Woody and Daphne going through the pound looking for a new dog to adopt. They'd have it run with the caption BEREFT SENATOR

AND WIFE LOOKING TO REPLACE THEIR BELOVED HELMUT, KIDNAPPED IN JUNE.

But they wouldn't actually get the dog because their visit to the pound made them so distraught that they were actually unable to choose a dog. This way they would get enough of the dog sympathy vote to counterbalance the New-Dog-Before-the-Body-of-the-Old-Dog-Is-Cold vote.

Brian Petrunich called the senator in Washington to pitch the idea.

"You think your wife will go along with it, Senator?"

The fact was he had actually been looking for something else to extort from his future ex-wife since his return to Washington. The thirty days' moratorium on the deportation of the ice-skater had expired, and it was time for her to pay the piper again.

"I'll give it a shot, Brian," he said, hanging up and dialing her number at Meagen, Forresy, Bryce.

"Ms. Melancamp's office," her secretary said.

"This is Senator White, Brandon."

"She's in court, Senator."

"Let me have her cell, please."

"She doesn't like to be interrupted in court."

"It's about the dog, Brandon."

"Did they find him?"

"Just give me the cell, will you, Brandon?"

Woody got Daphne in the corridor of the courthouse, just as she was negotiating an eleventh-hour settlement deal minutes before trial.

"I can't talk now."

"Perfect," he said. "Meet me at the pound at ten tomorrow morning."

"What?"

"I'll leave the address with Brandon."

"I can't . . ."

"Oh, yes, you can. And look good."

"I'm fine. Really."

"Has he called?"

"No."

"Not even to see how you're feeling?"

"Barry, look—it was all very civilized. We talked it out and decided that we'd just be friends."

"There's no such thing as *just being friends* with someone you've been involved with, Ishmael. Believe me."

When he had made up his cover cover story, Ishmael hadn't anticipated having to deal with Barry, Kevin, Jack, and Denny's solicitude. They were calling every day, concerned, wanting to know how he was getting along; they were sending cheerful little cards, the type you send to people who have just gotten out of the hospital.

They were like a tag-team suicide watch. To the point that Ishmael was considering getting back together with Owen Lundkeim in order to put a stop to the phone calls and cards.

One of the interns came into Ishmael's office to tell him that there was an FBI agent in the outer office.

"Gotta run, Barry. The FBI's here. Talk to you later."

Ishmael found Special Agent Gary Sonnenfeld, of the FBI's Domestic Terrorism Division, standing next to the Togolese fertility statue.

"I need to see the senator," he announced gravely. "It's urgent."

"Did you find the dog?"

"I'm not in a position to discuss that with you, Mr. Leibowitz."

"My clearance not high enough?"

"Would you please just tell me where he is?"

"On the Floor."

"Can you call him?"

"No."

"How do you contact him?"

"You go to the cloakroom and find a free Senate page to deliver a message to the senator on the Floor."

"Will they do that for me?"

"No."

"Why not?"

"Because your clearance isn't high enough."

"Look, Mr. Leibowitz, I don't have a lot of time to play games."

"Neither do I. Now, if you wait a minute, I'll go down there with you and get him."

They found the senator not on the Floor but in his cubbyhole office, grabbing a sandwich between votes. On the cluttered desk was a picture showing Daphne and him searching in vain for a new dog at the North Washington Animal Shelter. It had been on that morning's front page of the *Rutland Herald,* and his staff had faxed it down to him.

Woody looked up sadly from the photo and told Special Agent Sonnenfeld that whatever he had to tell him he could tell him in front of his chief of staff, who, he said, knew more about his life than he himself did.

"Well, Senator, the lab results are back from Bethesda. And it appears as if the ear you received in the mail is not your dog's ear."

"How do you know?"

"The ear is an ear of a ten-to-twelve-year-old animal, and, according to your veterinarian's records, Helmut is four years, seven months old."

"Well, that's—that's great. Just great."

"In fact, though this is not conclusive, it may be that the extortionist took the ear from an already-dead dachshund."

"So," Woody asked, "what's your next move?"

"At this point, we have to wait for him to act. We've established surveillance in and around Lake Jackson, with the hope of finding either Mr. Farniente or Helmut."

"You'll keep us posted, then," Woody said.

"Yes, Senator."

After Special Agent Sonnenfeld left the office, Woody asked Ishmael how he thought they should handle this latest development.

"It's good news about Helmut."

"Yes, of course. But should we put this out now? I mean, this is one hell of a picture," he said, pointing to the *Rutland Herald* photo on his desk.

"I don't know, Senator. You want to talk to Irwin?"

"Irwin is strictly an *ex post facto* guy. He just reports the news. No, we better talk to Rav."

"Rav says you need a dog."

"Apparently I still have one."

"He's just not here."

"Best damn kind of dog you can have," Woody said, as he picked up the phone to call his pundit and tell him the good news.

Rav Monsjar's pronouncement was, as usual, categorical. "Let sleeping dogs lie."

That was it, four words left on Ishmael's office phone machine at three in the morning while the chief of staff was sleeping soundly in Maud's off-white and baby-blue bedroom on Chipmunk Lane in Alexandria.

It had taken some serious self-criticism, just this side of begging, to get back in bed with Maud after she went to Virginia Beach by herself in August while Ishmael held down the fort in Washington for his senator.

Maud had returned from a vacation that she spent, she claimed, getting to know her vibrator better. She had composed a ten-page document she called her personal mission statement. Before she would allow Ishmael even a peck on the cheek, she read the entire manifesto to him.

She was tired of being discounted. She was finished being less important in Ishmael's, or any other man's, life than his work. She would no longer tolerate last-minute changes of plans, unless there was a personal medical emergency. She demanded one-on-one quality time with him at least twice a week. She demanded fulfilling, mutually gratifying sex on a regular basis . . .

It was comprehensive and nonnegotiable. If Ishmael wasn't interested in this type of relationship, let her know now. Otherwise, he had to sign on. Literally.

She had him actually put his signature next to hers on the bottom of the mission statement. After he signed it, they drank a glass of wine to seal the deal, and then she went to put her daughter to bed while he lounged on the living-room couch watching Redskin highlights.

By the time she emerged from the bedroom in a black lace teddy, he had nodded off. Already in breach of the agreement. Nevertheless, she approached the couch, and, as he lay there snoring lightly, straddled his face.

He reacted instinctively. But it wasn't until she grabbed him by his hair, in a violent paroxysm of passion, that he was completely awake. Recovering quickly, he swam with the current. He had to hold his hand over her mouth to keep her from waking her daughter up.

When it was over, fulfilling and mutually gratifying as it may have been, they had another discussion about self-esteem and commitment. It was almost one before he was permitted into the bedroom, where he fell into bed to sleep the sleep of the repentant and the exhausted.

So at 8 A.M. the next day, as Ishmael drove into the District with the morning commuter traffic listening absently to the news on the radio, he was still not completely awake. He was partly cloudy to foggy, staring through the windshield at the gray procession of cars inching toward the Potomac.

Though not for long. In a matter of minutes he was fully awake. And on the cell phone.

He got Debbie Sue Allenby, already at the office.

"Did you hear the news this morning?" he asked her.

"No. Why?"

"They're going back after him."

"On what?"

"Rebecca Gatney is claiming that NAPTOTS is a front for the Togolese government. She's saying that the whole Tourette-syndrome business is just a laundering operation for Togolese money used to buy influence in the Senate. You know what they're calling it?"

"What?"

"Togogate."

29

STALINGRAD

THIS TIME the Gatney campaign didn't go off half cocked. This time they got someone else to go off for them. And with both barrels blazing. After Hermione Hingle reported to her employers that the NAPTOTS office was in a run-down building on Seventh Street featuring an out-call massage business and a detective agency and was run by an African in native dress with one phone, a cat, and a hibachi, Rebecca Gatney did not rush off to call a press conference.

After leaking the headlines to the wire services, she picked up the phone and called a couple of gunslingers from *The Washington Post*. Mitt Hornsby and Nat Birnbaum were two hotshot investigative reporters who specialized in political-corruption stories. They were fast, they were thorough, they took no prisoners.

It didn't take them long to learn that Kodjo Kponvi was a Togolese national in the country on a diplomatic visa, that he was the brother-in-law of the Togolese Foreign Minister, that NAPTOTS was an organization that had begun life only four months prior to its large donation to Senator White's reelection campaign, that Woody White was the ranking minority member of the African Affairs Subcommittee, that the subcommittee had voted 40 million dollars to help stimulate Togo's phosphate industry, that the White-Kanush Tourette-syndrome bill now being marked up in a Senate-House conference committee postdated the receipt of the contribution.

It was all laid out, nice and neat. Quid pro quo pro quid.

The lead on the radio story was, "Less than two weeks after the Senate Ethics Committee chose not to pursue allegations of political corruption against him, Vermont Senator Woody White is back in hot water today . . ."

The story was on its way across Washington before Ishmael was across the Potomac. Instead of going to the office, Ishmael headed for the TV studio downtown where the senator was taping a TS commercial that they were planning to run in Vermont as a campaign commercial masquerading as a public-service announcement.

He arrived as the cameras were about to roll. The senator was standing in front of a blue-sky background, each arm around a kid with TS, and saying to the camera how your help can make life a whole lot better for Kim and David . . .

Ishmael decided not to interrupt the shooting. They were already in for the studio rental and film costs, in any event. Besides, he wasn't looking forward to breaking the news to the senator.

Even though they had anticipated the possibility of the phosphates-for-hockey-sticks thing unraveling, they had not anticipated the extent to which the details had been ferreted out. This wasn't just someone with a clandestine tape recording. This was *The Washington Post*. This was Hornsby and Birnbaum, two names that could strike terror into the heart of any politician.

They weren't going to be able to explain this one away simply as cannon fodder financed with Republican soft money. This one was going to require some exquisite tap-dancing. And no one knew that better at the moment than Ishmael Leibowitz, who had visited NAPTOTS and seen with his own eyes the hibachi and the cat litter, who had been instrumental in devising the strategy of the *ex post facto* White-Kanush bill to cover their tracks.

Ishmael shut off the cell and sat behind the camera watching the senator go smoothly through all six takes. When the producer said they had what they needed, Ishmael went out on the set to greet the senator.

"Meet my chief of staff," Woody said to the kids. And Ishmael shook their already-shaking hands. He was moved by the sight of the kids. Whatever the motivation, he told himself, it was a worthy cause. Let history record that, at least.

The first law of politics, as in medicine, should be: First do no harm. If the very worst result of phosphates-for-hockey-sticks was that the citizens of Vermont made a greater per-capita contribution to the eradication of Tourette syndrome than they should have, then so be it. He could live with that on his conscience.

Ishmael watched the senator personally thank the entire production crew, none of whom voted in Vermont. Then he got Woody out of there before any of the reporters from the TV station discovered his presence, and whisked him to his car, where he laid the whole thing out for him.

When Ishmael was finished, Woody leaned up against the fender of the Mercedes and laughed. It was a good laugh. A cathartic laugh. A desperate laugh.

Ishmael joined him. What else was there to do?

The two of them, senator and chief of staff, stood there beside the old 230 D and roared like hyenas.

When they were finally finished, Woody said, "Well, there goes my junket to Togo . . ."

And as he got into his car, he was still laughing.

After Hermione Hingle's visit and several long phone conversations with two aggressive, if not cheeky, *Washington Post* reporters—conversations in which some very pointed questions were asked him about his involvement with Tourette syndrome, as well as about his immigration status, Kodjo Kponvi had telephoned his contact in the Togolese Embassy and asked for an emergency meeting.

Kodjo Kponvi met Kwami Assavi, the cousin of his father's third wife's uncle and the embassy's intelligence officer, at a barbecue restaurant on Georgia Avenue and, over ribs and beer, discussed the situation. For security reasons, they spoke in Basawi, a northern Togolese dialect spoken by fewer than sixty thousand people in the world, none of whom currently were working for any United States intelligence agency.

What follows is a rough translation of their conversation.

"So, we are in deep water, are we not, Kwamiga?"

"We are coping with the situation at hand, Kodjovi."

"What has the ambassador said?"

"The ambassador is in Hawaii. Under medical supervision. His gall bladder will have to be removed. Arthroscopically."

"I am sorry to hear that. Perhaps you can send my best wishes in the diplomatic pouch."

"Of course. So we are keeping a low profile."

"*Tant mieux.*"

"You must stay at a safehouse. You may watch TV there. You may send out for delivered foods. Under a nom de guerre, of course."

"I order pizza under an assumed name?"

"Precisely. Until we extricate you from this situation. We are hoping that damage control will proceed accordingly."

"Perhaps a visit home? Dapango is lovely this time of year. The plantains are in flower."

"This is no time, Kodjovi, to contemplate flowering plantains."

"Of course."

"Do not worry. We shall emerge clean."

"How?"

"Spin."

"Spin?"

"Yes, spin. The *yovos* think that they have invented spin. They are mistaken."

"I am comforted to know that."

"The baby-back ribs are succulent."

"Splendid."

"We must leave separately."

"Of course."

"I'll leave first. You pay the check."

"By all means."

"In cash."

"I would assume so."

"*Alafiya,* Kodjovi."

"*Alafiya,* Kwamiga."

They left separately, ten minutes apart, and took separate cabs, Kwami Assavi back to the embassy on Massachusetts Avenue, and Kodjo Kponvi to the safehouse, whose address Kwami Assavi had slipped him on a napkin.

Unlike Kodjo Kponvi, Woody White did not have a safehouse to go to. The press had long ago ferreted out his *pied-à-terre* in Wesley Heights and would no doubt be covering it as well as the house in McLean, where he no longer lived.

For the moment he was taking refuge behind the closed doors of his private office in Dirksen, holed up with Ishmael and Debbie Sue, the Vermont staff on the speakerphone from Montpelier.

Rav Monsjar had been contacted, but there was no telling when he would check his machine, if he ever did. And Burton Armature's office said that the attorney was racing the thirty-six-foot sailboat that Woody had helped pay for in a regatta in the Caribbean and was not due into Antigua till Saturday, at the earliest.

So for the moment they were without the counsel of either their pundit or their lawyer.

"Well, it's still pretty controllable, I think," Janine Caravaggio said in an attempt to say something positive.

"Right," somebody in Montpelier said.

"Uh-huh," someone else said.

Brian Petrunich said, in an attempt to be proactive, "Debbie Sue, can you dig up any Tourette-syndrome legislation that the senator may have been involved in that pre-dates the contribution?"

"There isn't any," Debbie Sue Allenby replied.

"Have you checked the *Record*?"

"Yes. The White-Kanush Bill was introduced by the senator into Medicaid and Health Care on June twenty-sixth. Carl Kanush introduced it into the Health Subcommittee of Ways and Means in the House on July second. The contribution from NAPTOTS was received in this office on May eleventh."

There was silence, broken only by the sound of pumps sucking dry air, as they tried futilely to come up with fresh ideas.

"Can we move on?" Woody said finally. "Let's look at the alleged NAPTOTS-Togo connection. They need to demonstrate that we were aware of this when we accepted the donation. And we simply weren't, were we?"

The people in the room nodded. The people on the speakerphone uttered a variety of replies that were meant to signify that, no, they were not aware.

"As far as we knew, NAPTOTS was a legitimate organization concerned with raising funds for Tourette syndrome. My introduction of the bill in Medicaid and Health Care was a response to a legitimate medical need . . . right?"

"Right."

"Beverly, can you get us some Vermont TS statistics?"

"I suppose so, Senator, though Rebecca Gatney is claiming that TS affects fewer than one half of one percent of the population of this country."

"Irwin, can you come up with some better numbers?"

"I don't have the database for diseases per capita, Senator."

"Well, get the database."

"Right."

"What about support from the legitimate TS organizations? This shouldn't affect the need to raise funds, and it shouldn't affect White-Kanush. No one is pretending that the prevention and treatment of TS is not a worthy cause, right?"

"Right."

"And let's get documentation of the vote trail on the phosphates bill. It didn't get reported out of African Affairs until the chairperson switched her vote. Right?"

"Right."

"Let her testify under oath that the President called her to lobby her personally on that bill. Right?"

"Right."

"He called her from the White House. There's got to be phone logs, right?"

"Right."

"We can subpoena the President if we have to."

"Right."

"Maybe we can even get Ken Starr in on this . . ."

"Sure . . ."

"So let's get out there and counterattack. Okay?"

"Okay."

In the silence that followed Woody's attempt at a pep rally, he could sense a vacuum. The low level of enthusiasm was palpable. It had been a long time since he'd had to deliver a Gipper speech—not since the sexual-harassment business in '95, when he had gathered his staff around him and read the St. Crispin Day speech from *Henry V.*

If there was a time to go once more unto the breach, he sensed that it was now.

"People, we've all been together a long time," he began, not sure exactly where he was going. "Ishmael, Debbie Sue, Beverly, Dickie, Irwin, Janine, Brian—we've lived through a lot together. We've had buses break down on us in the middle of blizzards. We've been up all night sending out mailings, working phone banks. We've shaken hands till our bones ached. But no matter how hard it was, we've always stuck together. Through the good times and the bad times."

He stopped for a moment, in order to keep his own voice from quavering. His words may have sounded histrionic but they were also true. They *had* been together a long time. They had been on the bus together for over ten years. An eternity in politics.

"So the way I see it, we've got two choices now. We can walk out of the bunker one by one with our hands over our heads, or we can charge out of there together with our guns blazing. Now, I don't know about you, but I'm coming out with my gun blazing. And I hope you'll be right behind me. The way you've always been."

Debbie Sue Allenby stifled a gut-wrenching sob. She was already out the door of the bunker, her gun blazing. And the others, it turned out, would be right behind her.

Woody's speech had touched them. They were, in fact, very much like an army platoon that had seen a great deal of action together. And the one thing they felt to a person was that Woody White, for all his faults, was their man.

So they went charging out of the bunker together, guns blazing. In the aftermath of the Gipper speech, the staffs in both Washington and Vermont were reenergized. They mobilized for the final six weeks of the campaign with renewed fervor. They were back on the bus.

To many in Washington, Togogate looked like Dunkirk. But Woody preferred to think of it as Stalingrad.

Now all they had to do was win the goddamn war.

30.

ET TU, TEDDY?

EVEN BEFORE the Senate Select Committee on Ethics received the compendium of press clippings dealing with Togogate sent them by the VCEG, along with their official letter of complaint against Senator Woodrow White, the members met in confidential session to consider how to proceed.

And this time the votes weren't there to head off an official preliminary investigation. Though such an investigation was indeed preliminary and could only result in a recommendation to the full Senate of any action to be taken, it was, nevertheless, an official inquiry imbued with the power to depose witnesses and request subpoenas.

The vote was 6–0 to proceed, without even *pro forma* resistance from the three Democrats on the committee. The party had begun to implement what was seen on the Hill as a gradual distancing from their wounded senatorial candidate.

In a number of hastily called closed-door caucuses, the Democratic leadership weighed the advantages of trying to keep the Senate seat against a possible contagion spread by the beleaguered senator to the other Democratic candidates running that year. And they came down on the side of quarantine.

The Typhoid Mary phenomenon was just one of the ways it was referred to in the steam room.

"They're locking him out of the fort."

"They're cutting him off from the herd."

"They're throwing him to the wolves."

"He's a dead man. They're not even going to show up at his funeral."

"They're not even going to bury him. They're going to leave him out for the coyotes."

And so forth.

When Woody walked unexpectedly into the Tuesday-afternoon caucus, there was a sudden hush among his colleagues. The Minority Whip hastily segued to an education bill that was coming up for a vote that week.

There was a lot of coughing and throat-clearing and avoiding of eye contact.

They were all there—Daschle, Glenn, Inouye, Teddy, Dianne, the Barbaras, Leahy . . .

Woody looked over at his fellow Vermonter, the senior senator, and shook his head.

Et tu, Pat?

And Glenn, who'd had his brush with the Ethics Committee a few years back and wound up with a wrist slap.

Et tu, John?

And the man who had left a nice Polish girl at the bottom of the pond while he figured out the spin with his handlers. He had a dagger in his hand also.

Et tu, Teddy?

Woody White was being thrown out of the fraternity. He was on his own now. He and his zealots would be charging out of the bunker without any aerial or artillery support from headquarters.

Senator White was officially informed of the Ethics Committee's decision to conduct a preliminary investigation by Chief Counsel Harold Kinder.

In his letter dated September 29, Harold Kinder referred to SR 338, which gave the committee jurisdiction to investigate "improper conduct that reflects upon the Senate, regardless of whether such conduct violates a specific statute, and that may derogate from the integrity of the institution of the Senate as a whole."

The language, according to Burton Armature, was broad enough to drive a truck through.

From his hotel room in Antigua, the attorney told his client not to panic. He'd be back next week, after the Antigua-to-St.-Kitts leg of the regatta. He had a good shot at the cup. If his jib didn't fray.

When Rav Monsjar finally called in, he was also breezy.

"Go back to the field," he said.

"What does that mean, Rav?"

"The debate. If she wants to talk about Togo, tell her you'll talk about it in the field. Bring a map of Togo. Show everyone where it is. Use a pointer like Ross Perot."

The out-of-the-bunker-with-guns-blazing strategy was kicked off by a press conference that Friday. The staff prepped him extensively for the launching of the counterattack. They stayed up into the wee hours throwing at him every nasty question they could come up with, and by the time the slightly bleary-eyed, coffee-fortified senator faced the press at 9 A.M., he was ready for anything.

"Are you considering dropping out of the race, Senator?" An A.P. reporter whom Woody didn't like, Larry Herkhimer, asked him for openers.

"Nope."

"Isn't it true, Senator, that the profusion of scandals has severely damaged your poll numbers?"

"Nope."

"According to CNN, you're now running behind Mrs. Gatney."

"That so?"

The A.P. reporter was getting visibly frustrated by Woody's Calvin Coolidge style of monosyllabic judo.

"Is that all you have to say, Senator?"

"Oh, I have a lot to say, Mr. Herkhimer. But I'd prefer to respond to questions that are actually questions and not merely statements with a question mark thrown in at the end. The CNN poll that you refer to, Mr. Herkhimer, begins with the question, quote, in view of Senator White's investigation by the Ethics Committee, will you continue to support him in November? Unquote. Now, Mr. Herkhimer, that's not a question either. That's a statement. We say in Vermont that if you paint a cow green, it's still a cow. I think you and CNN are trying to sell us a green cow here, Mr. Herkhimer. . . . Next question?"

Woody pointed to Sam Donaldson.

"Senator, are you aware that it is illegal for foreign governments to contribute to political campaigns?"

"I sure am."

"In that case, why have you accepted a four-hundred-thousand-dollar donation from the Republic of Togo?"

"Sam, we can do a little better than that, can't we?"

"I beg your pardon?"

"Why don't you just come right out and ask me if I'm a crook?"

"Senator, I wasn't implying—"

"Yes, you were. Sam, if you're going to throw a punch, throw it."

The rest of the Washington press corps, who for years had had to sit and listen to the veteran ABC reporter's posturing, began to enjoy his discomfort.

"Sorry, Sam. But my polls are telling me that *your* numbers are slipping."

Big smile. Then: "Look, first of all, of course, I wasn't aware that NAP-TOTS is an arm of the Togolese government, if it in fact is. We don't know that yet, do we? All we know at the moment is that a political-action group funded by wealthy supporters of my opponent has written to the Ethics Committee asking them to investigate. And here I am, under attack from you and others, just because somebody made an accusation. I intend to cooperate fully with the Ethics Committee. I believe in the integrity of the process and the integrity and dignity of the Senate and I have absolutely nothing to hide from the committee. . . . Nina?"

Nina Totenberg's hand wasn't up, but Woody was ready for her nevertheless.

"Senator," she asked, "if you believe in the integrity and dignity of the Senate, as you just said you do, aren't you concerned that this is the second time in just two months that your ethics have been questioned?"

"Nina, the Ethics Committee declined to proceed on the previous allegations because there was simply no evidence. Now, in our system, the presumption of innocence is supposed to adhere. Don't you think that I, as any other American, deserve the presumption of innocence?"

Nina Totenberg found herself nodding in agreement, in spite of herself.

Round Three went to Woody.

And Round Four was going to be his, as well. A tall, attractive woman in the rear of the room, wearing a *NAHPI Quarterly Journal* press pass and carrying a pocketbook full of condom samples, was recognized by the senator.

"Madam? You in back of the room?"

Evelyn Brandwynne went into her windup and lobbed the softball right into Woody's wheelhouse.

"Senator White, why do you think these attacks are being launched against you at this particular time?"

Woody tried to avoid the saucy Clinton toss of the head or the Reagan chuckle. He looked at his watch and smiled his noblesse oblige smile.

"Let's see . . . my calendar says it's four and a half weeks to election day. Hmm . . ."

His timing was impeccable, and he got a nice laugh.

"I believe deeply in the essential fairness of the American people. I believe that they are able to look beyond this type of spurious character attack and cast their vote on the issues that concern them. And I believe they're concerned about the quality of their lives and not about the kind of petty name-calling we've been seeing in this campaign. . . ."

"Who is that woman?" Sam Donaldson whispered to Larry Herkhimer, who shook his head.

"Now let's look at what's actually happened. I propose an extremely qualified judge for a seat on the Second Circuit, and I'm accused of influence-peddling. I help get desperately needed foreign-aid funds to an impoverished West African nation so that it can build up its own industry and become self-sufficient and a market for American exports, and I am accused of corruption. I introduce a bill in committee to help fund research for the prevention and treatment of a dread disease, a disease that, in one form or another, affects eleven percent of all Americans, and I'm being investigated for impropriety. . . ."

Larry Herkhimer whispered to Sam Donaldson, "He's making a fucking campaign speech."

"So let me say in conclusion to my somewhat roundabout answer to your question, the timing of these attacks is clearly political. Fine. I've been in the kitchen long enough to handle the heat. All I ask is a level field. So, with that in mind, I'm going to provide the level field. It's in Shaftsbury, Vermont. Jim Goldstone's farm. About ten acres of newly mown hay. Saturday, October seventeenth. High noon. You're all invited. I'll be there, sitting on my rocking chair ready to talk face-to-face with my opponent. The president of Marlboro College will be there with a piece of chalk and a blackboard to make sure we stay on topic. There'll be a second rocking chair facing mine with Rebecca Gatney's name on it. So, wherever you are out there, Rebecca, and I'm sure you are out there somewhere, stop tossing cow chips and come out to the field and let's talk. Okay? I'll be waiting for you."

"I thought he was very macho. Without being too macho, you know what I mean?" Barry said.

"I loved the rocking chairs in the field. That was brilliant," said Denny.

"How were his numbers this morning?" Jack asked.

"Up two-point-six," Ishmael replied.

"See? Strong, macho, proactive, but not a bully. Eastwood in *Bridges of Madison County*," said Kevin.

"You kidding?" Jack protested. "Eastwood was doing silent and sensitive in that picture. He was doing John Wayne without the chaps."

"I thought Meryl was going to eat him up, didn't you?" said Barry.

"Frankly, I thought she looked like she was going to gag every time he kissed her," Kevin insisted.

"Well, if *she* doesn't want him . . . ," Jack said with an impish smile.

"Are you kidding? He's *ninety*," Kevin said.

"Right. You'd throw him out of bed?" Jack said.

"This cappellini is to die for," said Denny. "Here. You have to taste this."

Denny passed the cappellini around the table as Ishmael's beeper went off.

"Jesus, it's nine-thirty. You're off-duty," Barry said.

Ishmael excused himself and went to the pay phone, even though he had his cell in his pocket. When he saw Maud's number on the LED and not the senator's, he was not as relieved as he should have been.

He had been going out there almost every night since he had signed on to her mission statement, and, frankly, the regular, mutually gratifying sex was getting a little too regular, given the type of hours he was putting in at the office.

Maud had enrolled in a Tantric-yoga evening class at GWU, which had the effect of making her sexually ravenous. She was getting her daughter to bed earlier and earlier. By ten o'clock, she was already breaking out the Astroglide.

And between the long bouts of Tantric sex, keeping him up till one, two in the morning, and the long morning rush-hour drive back in at seven, he was starting to wear thin.

"What are you doing?" she asked.

"Working."

"Can you break away?"

"I really can't, Maud."

"Tell him you've got to take care of your mother."

"My mother's dead. He knows that."

"Tell him there's a woman in Alexandria who's going to go absolutely stark-raving mad if she doesn't feel you inside her in the next thirty minutes."

"Jesus, Maud . . ."

"You want to know what I'm wearing?"

"Look, I've got to get back to the table . . ."

"I'm wearing black leather boots and white gloves. And nothing else. Absolutely nothing else, Ishmael."

"Uh-huh . . ."

"I'm dripping. I'm wet and getting wetter. By the time you get here, you'll have to swim to me . . ."

"I'll call you at work in the morning."

"I'm like the Euphrates, Ishmael. You could dog-paddle inside my warm, fragrant waters for hours, days . . ."

Ishmael returned to the table and sat down, looking distracted and tired. Barry, Kevin, Jack, and Denny exchanged a concerned look.

"Problems?"

Ishmael shook his head in a halfhearted denial that meant just the opposite to Barry, Kevin, Jack, and Denny.

"Was that Owen?" Kevin asked.

If he told them about Maud and the Euphrates, they would lose their dinners. So he confirmed that it had indeed been the aide from Minnesota.

"Really?"

Another four-way look.

"So, what's going on?"

Ishmael had already decided it was probably easier to be involved with Owen Lundkeim than not to be involved with Owen Lundkeim. Their communal solicitude was tapering off and gradually moving back to interest. Kevin had invited him to see *Giselle* at the Kennedy Center last week.

"Well," he said, "we're . . . we're kind of seeing each other again."

"You *are*?"

"Yes."

"How come you didn't say anything?"

"I didn't know if it was going to work out."

"Is he making some sort of commitment this time?"

"Well, you know, we're just taking it day by day."

The tiramisu arrived with the cappuccinos. And Ishmael used this moment to flee.

"Listen, guys, I've got to go."

"Ishmael?" Barry said with his motherly look.

"What?"

"You know what you're doing?"

Ishmael nodded. He had no idea what he was doing, except that he wanted to get out of the restaurant, go home, and get some sleep. And not with either Owen Lundkeim or the Tantric nymphomaniac in Alexandria.

"Call me first thing in the morning, okay?" Barry said.

"Okay."

After Ishmael was gone, Barry said, "If that little bitch hurts him, I'll kill him. I fucking will."

Though Vermont politics was not ordinarily big news in Texas, an excerpt from Senator White's Washington news conference was picked up by a local TV station on a slow news day in Houston. Sitting on the couch of the sprawling ranch house in Lake Jackson that his cousin, Silvio, was taking care of for a retired power-company engineer, Dario Farniente watched the *senatore* answer questions from the reporters.

As he sat there, he hand-fed Helmut *zabaglione* that he had baked that afternoon. And as he did this, he absently stroked the dachshund's ear.

Like the great majority of dachshunds, Helmut had two ears. Though Dario Farniente did not want anybody to know this—certainly not the *senatore*. His cousin knew someone who worked for a veterinarian who routinely cremated dogs that had to be put down. And so Dario Farniente had placed his order for a dachshund's ear and merely waited for one to become available.

And it was that ear that the illegal right-wing Italian ex-housekeeper had mailed to Senator White. He would have cut his own ear off before taking a knife to the dachshund. He would have blown his brains out, as Vittorio Grappino did in D'Annunzio's *La Città Morta,* when cataracts strangled his eyesight.

However, real ear or no real ear, the *senatore* was doing nothing to regularize his ex-housekeeper's immigration status. Worse, he had sent men to arrest him; there was a national dragnet to capture him and send him back to Trieste, or worse, to a maximum-security prison for five years or more, where he would be rape bait for the hardened black convicts. Five years or more without a shower. Five years of eating meatloaf cooked with canned tomato sauce and thickened haphazardly with bread crumbs . . .

He decided that he could no longer wait for the *senatore* to act. Tomorrow he would have his cousin call the friend at the veterinarian's office and put in an order for another ear. Or better, a paw.

Feeling a sudden wave of anxiety, he got up and took a trip to the power-company engineer's medicine cabinet. There was a bottle of 10-mg Valium. He dropped the Valium with a glass of San Pellegrino.

The power-company engineer had a .38 in his bedside night table. Behind the Bible and the Trojans.

Dario Farniente would take his own life before surrendering. Right after taking Helmut's. Tenderly. Lovingly. Two dozen Halcion in the *zabaglione.* And as the dachshund quietly expired in his arms, he would take the power engineer's .38 to his own temple. They would be united in heaven. *Se Dio lo vuole.*

31.

EVERETT DIRKSEN TURNS OVER IN HIS GRAVE

AFTER SEVERAL UNRETURNED PHONE CALLS to NAPTOTS's office on Seventh Street, Harold Kinder forwarded the Ethics Committee's request to interview Kodjo Kponvi to the Togolese Embassy.

The embassy's deputy chief of mission, Victor Kassabi, replied that Mr. Kponvi's whereabouts were presently unknown but that they would make inquiries and contact the committee should their inquiries prove fruitful.

Recognizing a kiss-off when he read one, Harold Kinder asked the chairman to have the committee authorize contacting the State Department to find out if they could exert diplomatic pressure on the Togolese government to produce Kodjo Kponvi to testify.

The chairman brought the problem to the Republican leadership, who, mindful of the approaching election date, instructed him to bypass the committee and call the Secretary of State directly.

The Secretary of State told the chairman that he'd discuss it with the President and get back to him.

The chairman knew that the Secretary of State would not discuss it with the President, or even get back to him, for that matter, and so he instructed Harold Kinder to draft a subpoena request from the full Senate.

Harold Kinder told the chairman that a subpoena wouldn't be very useful if they couldn't find Kodjo Kponvi to serve him with it.

The chairman then phoned the Federal Bureau of Investigation and asked the director if the Bureau could try to locate the vanished director of the National Association for the Prevention and Treatment of Tourette Syndrome so that they could serve him with a congressional subpoena.

The director of the FBI said he would discuss the matter with the Attorney General. The chairman knew that the director of the FBI would not discuss the matter with the Attorney General, and so he phoned the Attorney General herself, who, though nominally a member of the opposing party, had been taking a beating in the press lately for a slavish devotion to the President and his interests. A limited action contrary to the President and the party's interests in what was essentially a fifth-page news story could be useful in deflecting those charges.

Accordingly, the Attorney General contacted the director of the FBI and asked him to devote Bureau resources to locating Kodjo Kponvi. The director of the FBI didn't see a lot of downside in assigning a few agents to track down the fugitive Togolese, and he agreed to institute a search for the director of NAPTOTS.

Meanwhile, the object of all this high-level political activity was spending his days and nights in an apartment in Cathedral Heights rented in the name of Rich Lusskin, the American husband of the embassy's visa-and-immigration officer, on a month-to-month basis, with first and last months' rent in cash.

The apartment was clean and cozy and featured a thirty-five-inch TV wired to a sixty-four-channel cable system. Kodjo Kponvi spent his days watching soft-core pornography and ordering take-out pizza under various noms de guerre.

Once a day he called in to Kwami Assavi from a phone booth on Wisconsin Avenue. Even if the FBI had tapped the Togolese Embassy's phone, they would have been at a loss to understand what was being said because the conversations were in Gwamba, a dialect of Kotokoli and spoken by fewer than twenty-five-thousand people in the world, none of whom were currently employed by any United States intelligence agency.

The junior senator from Vermont, on the other hand, was accessible to the committee and, through his attorney, agreed to testify before it, though, given the senator's campaign schedule, he requested that such testimony be deferred until after November 3.

Harold Kinder wrote back to Burton Armature that, though sensitive to the senator's time constraints, the committee felt that it was beholden to the senator's colleagues in the Senate and to the voters of Vermont to clear up this matter as expeditiously as possible.

Burton Armature wrote back to the committee that the senator, too, was eager to clear this matter up as expeditiously as possible but that he needed the time to review his records in anticipation of responding to questions that might be asked him.

So as the exchange of letters proceeded back and forth between the second floor of Hart and Burton Armature's Connecticut Avenue office, November 3 rapidly approached, making the setting of the date for the senator's testimony before the committee more and more significant.

At the moment Woody was involved more intensely in debate prep than in prep for his appearance before the Ethics Committee.

The White Campaign had effectively shamed Rebecca Gatney into saying she would appear in Shaftsbury on October 17. She reluctantly agreed to the field and the rocking chairs, but balked at the blackboard.

"It makes the whole thing look like a TV game show," her campaign director protested.

"The president of Marlboro College is going to be standing next to that blackboard," Beverly Levesque said.

"We'll show up. But no blackboard."

They compromised by agreeing to the president of Marlboro College's conducting the debate in the field without the blackboard but with the ability to interrupt when he felt that either candidate was going "off topic" when responding to questions posed by a panel of distinguished Vermont journalists.

Lee Schumock, who had returned to Washington from his series of field interviews and was once again a fly on the wall in the senator's office, was permitted to attend debate prep. He listened as Ishmael and Debbie Sue Allenby, as well as Janine Caravaggio and Brian Petrunich, who had flown in from Montpelier, bombarded the senator with questions.

"Senator, Vermont's economy is increasingly dependent upon tourism. What can you do in Washington to change this?"

"Senator, your support of NAFTA has caused industry to leave Vermont. How do you justify this?"

"Senator, what is your position on partial-birth abortion?"

Lee Schumock marveled at Woody White's ability to handle the booby-trapped questions like a demolitions expert, dismantling each bomb before it blew up in his face.

Eventually the staff threw some mud balls at him in the event that the president of Marlboro College failed to sift out any off-topic questions that the distinguished Vermont journalists decided to throw at him.

"What about the zipper problem, Senator?"

"Are you in John Quincy Adams's pocket?"

"Is it true that you backed into Trent Lott's Ford Explorer in the Senate parking garage?"

"Where is Kodjo Kponvi?"

Where *was* Kodjo Kponvi?

Woody hadn't a clue. He had never met the man, as he explained to David Forensic when the committee investigator called him for information on the Togolese's whereabouts.

"Mr. Forensic, if we had to do a background check on every PAC that sends us money, we'd be in the investigation business instead of the legislation business."

According to unnamed sources in the Justice Department, the Ethics Committee had the FBI looking for Kodjo Kponvi. *People* magazine ran a story on ethics in government, in which Togogate was featured as an example of political-fund-raising abuses run amuck. There were photos of the Seventh Street office building, the lobby board with NAPTOTS right above Atlas Out-Call, Senator White on the ski slopes of Vermont.

Hornsby and Birnbaum continued to hack away at Togogate in *The Washington Post*. They had researchers checking in Washington, Lomé, and London, where Kodjo Kponvi had served as the visa-and-immigration officer at the Togolese Embassy until, according to Hornsby and Birnbaum's sources, he had been asked to leave by the British when it was alleged that he was involved in an abortive plot to kidnap the Princess of Wales.

U.S.-Togolese relations were strained by the scandal. The Togolese ambassador, the Honorable Guillaume Tchakpame, back in Washington and convalescing from arthroscopic gall-bladder surgery, was called in to the State Department and handed a strongly worded protest.

In the Senate, meanwhile, a rider was attached to an education bill that would call in the Togo phosphate-aid credits prematurely, and Woody had to scramble to the Floor for debate. He appealed to his colleagues not to allow tabloid journalism to influence their decisions.

"If you kill this funding, we all might as well go home and let *The Washington Post* and *People* magazine run the government for us," he said for the *Record*. "We can have Kay Graham and Time/Warner calling the shots. Mr. President, I am just as eager as anyone else in this chamber to get to the bottom of this matter. If it turns out that the Togolese government attempted to influence the political process of this country, then not only will I return the money but I'll make the motion myself to impose economic sanctions against Togo. But until that happens, let's not allow the media to do the job of the Ethics Committee."

There was a smattering of applause from the visitors' gallery, but that was pretty much it in the way of support. Woody looked around in the hope that some of the other ninety-nine members of the Senate would rise in his defense. Someone. Anyone. Daschle? Teddy? Dianne? Barbara? Either Barbara?

Finally, little Barbara rose. All five feet of her.

"Mr. President," she said, "I am in full sympathy with my friend from Vermont's assertion that we should allow the Ethics Committee to do its job. But in order for that committee to do its job, it needs the full cooperation of the senator from Vermont, who, I believe, is being disingenuous when he tells us that he knows nothing of this matter except what he reads in the media. . . ."

Woody sat there, flabbergasted, and listened as his fellow Democrat warmed to her task.

"The fact is, Mr. President, this is not the first time that the senator from Vermont has been the subject of an Ethics Committee inquiry. Those of you who were here in 1995 may remember a matter that was particularly abhorrent to the women in this chamber, as well as to the women of the entire nation. . . ."

He looked around the chamber, incredulous. She was dredging up the grope in the back of the bus. And they were letting her do it. There were no protests. No points of order. She was completely off-topic, flogging her own political agenda on his back.

When she finally sat down, after trying to turn a rider to a bill to call in a foreign-aid credit into a referendum on sexual harassment, there was dead silence in the chamber. No one could look at Woody, or at anyone else, for that matter. Little Barbara had simply walked up to him and kicked him in the balls in full view of everyone.

The Minority Whip was picking his teeth with the edge of a file folder. Byrd was looking up at the ceiling. Teddy was scratching his earlobe. Big Barbara was searching through her briefcase.

And the Republicans. They were trying not to lick their chops too loudly. With enemies like this, who needed friends?

What the hell was happening to the Senate? An ad hominem attack on a member by someone in his own party?

Mansfield would have silenced her. Hubert would have delivered such an excoriation that the galleries would still be shaking. Lyndon would have taken her to the woodshed with a dull ax. Even the opposition wouldn't have permitted it. Simpson would have risen and publicly disassociated himself from the lynching.

In the awkwardness and confusion that followed the senator from California's speech, someone had the presence of mind to suggest the absence of a quorum, even though there were clearly over ninety senators present.

During the quorum call, the leadership negotiated a quick deal to table the vote on the rider until each side could regroup and figure out how to proceed.

Woody didn't stick around for the quorum call. They didn't need his vote. As soon as he saw Daschle huddling with Trent Lott, he headed up the aisle.

Ishmael, who had been in the visitors' gallery, caught up with him outside the cloakroom, and the two of them strode quickly across the rotunda and downstairs to the subway.

When they were in the subway car alone, Ishmael said, "She was just playing to the C-SPAN cameras, Senator. It was completely uncalled-for."

"Then why didn't anyone get up and say that?"

"They didn't have the guts."

"If Everett Dirksen were still alive . . ." But Woody's voice trailed off. Everett Dirksen was dead. And had been for nearly thirty years.

As they got off the subway and headed for the office, Ishmael said, "I'm sorry to have to give you some more bad news, Senator . . ."

"What?"

"Phil Yalowitz called. They turned down the seven thousand five hundred."

"They really expect me to give them ten thousand dollars for a dented fender?"

"Actually, they're up to fifteen."

Lee Schumock asked Ishmael Leibowitz the question that Senator Woodrow White's chief of staff often asked himself: Just what was it about the senator that inspired such devotion from his staff?

They were in Ishmael's office, late afternoon. The political biographer's book was now tentatively entitled *Why a Hummingbird Hums: The Life and Times of Woody White*. It was a title that his editor at Random House, May Manedle, hated.

"It sounds like the biography of an ornithologist," she protested.

"It's Vermont Zen Buddhism," Lee Schumock explained, tenaciously hanging on to his title, even though he knew that eventually his editor would prevail. She'd bring the marketing people in, and they would recite their litany of irrefutable statistics, and that would be that.

Ishmael Leibowitz liked the title. In a strange way it helped explain the phenomenon of Woody White, the carpetbagger from Cleveland who had managed to stake out a spot in Vermonters' hearts. As well as in their barns. There was an almost equally large number of Vermonters who probably thought of the senator every time they shoveled manure out of the horse stalls.

"That's the thing about the senator. It's hard to find someone who's indifferent to him. You either love him or you hate him," Ishmael said to Lee Schumock.

"Why do you think that's so?"

"He shoots from the hip."

"How so?"

"The views of most politicians have become so homogenized that it's hard to tell the difference between them. You may not like what Woody White says, but at least you know what he's saying. Of course, sometimes he's altogether too unhomogenized for his own good. Sometimes, I feel like he's Mr. Magoo. You know, he walks around blindly managing to avoid the cars trying to run him over."

"You think he's going to get run over by this Ethics Committee thing?"

Ishmael reflected for a moment. "I don't know," he said. "There are a lot of cars gunning for him out there."

And he left it at that, refusing to speculate further in spite of the writer's attempt to push him in that direction. Instead Ishmael spoke of the early days in Washington, when Woody White was a first-term senator.

"Those were pretty heady days. I came in as an intern right out of Brooklyn College. In two years I was running the legislation study group, then I was coordinating media buys, and by '92 I was press secretary. With the senator, either you move up fast or you're gone."

"Do you think he would have been Vice President today if it wasn't for the harassment charge in '95?"

Ishmael thought for a moment and shook his head.

"Why not?"

"He wouldn't have balanced the ticket. Al is a leavening agent. He brings the President back within the metabolic rate of Middle America. When he talks, you feel like you've just taken a tranquilizer. When the senator talks, you hang on to the armrests. You're in for a ride."

And as if to prove the point, Ishmael's cell phone rang.

"Excuse me." He flipped the phone open. "Senator?"

Lee Schumock watched as the senator's chief of staff listened to his boss on the other end of the line.

"When?"

Then, "How much?"

Ishmael wrote down a figure on a yellow pad.

"I'll get right on it, Senator," he said, then flipped the phone closed and said to Lee Schumock, "Sorry—we're going to have to cut this short. I have to find a bail bondsman in Miami."

"A bail bondsman in Miami?"

"Uh-huh. You happen to know one?"

"No. Why?"

"DEA agents found thirty-eight kilos of marijuana in the senator's son's boat. Possession with intent to sell. Bail was set at two hundred and fifty thousand dollars."

32.

SPAGHETTI

THOUGH BOBBY WHITE was thirty-one years old and, ostensibly, on his own in life, his being arrested with thirty-eight kilos of marijuana in his boat provided yet more ammunition for his father's growing list of enemies.

"The apple doesn't fall far from the tree," Rebecca Gatney remarked privately, but not privately enough to keep it out of the *Burlington Bugle*.

The article pointed out that Woody White had enough problems these days without having to post bail in Florida for his son. This was not the first time that the senator's son had gotten in trouble, the reporter went on to say. There were also marital problems and IRS problems.

As usual, the senator's problem quickly became Ishmael Leibowitz's problem. Finding a bail bondsman to write a $250,000 bond without any local collateral was not easy. Time he should have been spending in debate prep, in press damage control, in lobbying committee votes for White-Kanush, which was still rattling around in Medicaid and Health Care in spite of Togogate—not to mention the quality time he now had to spend in Tantric sexual contortions with Maud—was spent instead on the phone trying to convince various bail bondsmen that the word of a United States senator ought to be sufficient to guarantee the appearance of his own son in court.

Eventually Ishmael got Kyle Tibbetts, a veteran Dade County bail bondsman, to write the bond, but not without a second mortgage on the house in McLean. Ishmael had to run the paper through banks in two states and get Daphne's signature on the mortgage document, all while arranging last-minute details for Saturday's debate.

Woody asked Rav Monsjar if he ought to go to Miami for the arraignment.

"The way I see it, you're fucked both ways," his pundit told him. "You go, you'll get thirty seconds on the eleven o'clock news. Vermont senator posts bail in son's drug bust. You don't go, the radio call-in crazies'll be all over you. What kind of parent isn't at his son's side? So it boils down to a lose/lose, and when you're dealing with a lose/lose, you do what the fuck you want to do. You want to go, go. You don't want to go, don't go."

He thought about Rav's lose/lose analysis for about ten seconds and then buzzed Ishmael and told him to get him on a morning flight to Miami.

So yet one more lawyer started billing hours at Woody White's expense. Vernon Kleinmitt, a Miami lawyer who specialized in drug cases, met him at the airport and drove him to Kyle Tibbetts's office, where Woody handed him an executed second-trust deed to the house in McLean, and then they proceeded to the courthouse to liberate Bobby.

After bail was posted, Woody and his son walked down the courthouse steps together, like Teddy and his nephew during the rape trial in Palm Beach.

"I'm here to help my son," Woody told the reporters waiting for them.

Woody gave Vernon Kleinmitt a $4,000 retainer and then went out to lunch with Bobby. Their relationship had been tenuous under the best of circumstances, which this wasn't.

They sat in a nearly empty Cuban restaurant near the courthouse and tried to have a conversation.

"Look, Bobby, I'm not going to lecture you about this. You're thirty-one years old. It's about time you got your life together, don't you think?"

"I thought you weren't going to lecture me."

"Okay, let's forget about you, then. Let's talk about me. I have to come down here in the middle of a very tough campaign and post a bond for a quarter-million dollars."

"Probably cost you a shitload of votes, huh?"

"That's not the point."

"Sure it is. It's always been the point with you."

"I resent that."

"The fact is, we deserve each other."

"What the hell does that mean?"

"Look, Dad, let's not bullshit each other. We just don't connect, you and me. We never did. I'm not a very good son. I admit it. I never call you to wish you a happy birthday. I just call you when I'm in trouble. And you're not a very good father. You never had time for me when I was growing up and you don't have time for me now. So let's just call it even and forget about it so we can just get through this, okay?"

"What do you mean—get through this?"

"Lunch. Let's get through lunch."

Woody leaned back in the smooth leather booth and stared at his menu. Whatever the truth of what his son had said to him, it hurt him. Deeply.

"Bobby," he said, after a moment, "I did my best to find time to be with you—"

"Dad," Bobby interrupted him. "We're past this."

"I'm sorry, Bobby, you're still my son. And I'm still your father."

"Hey, you showed up. You bailed me out of jail. I appreciate that. Let's not drown it in a whole lot of sentiment. Let's just have lunch."

"Just have lunch . . ."

"Yeah. Try the *pollo campesino*. It's out of sight."

They ordered *pollo campesino* and two bottles of Cuban beer. They had lunch. When it was over, Bobby drove him to the airport in his IRS-liened BMW.

He dropped his father at the curb in front of the terminal.

"See you," he said.

"See you," Woody replied, got out of the BMW, and disappeared into the airport.

"It's d . . . d . . . d . . . dying."

"What do you mean it's dying?"

"We've lost thr . . . thr . . . thr . . . thr . . . thr . . . thr . . . thr . . ."

"Three?"

Ishmael usually tried to avoid finishing Owen Lundkeim's words for him, but he didn't have the patience at the moment. He had the aide to the Minnesota congressman on speaker while he tried to make some order out of the mess on his desk, which was cluttered with Irwin Posalski's polls, mortgage-application papers, body-shop estimates, vote counts.

"Th . . . th . . . three key v . . . v . . . votes on the com . . . m . . . m . . . ittee. It's this T . . . T . . . T . . . T . . . Togo thing."

"Owen, it's just a preliminary investigation."

"G . . . G . . . G . . . Gephardt s . . . s . . . s . . . says that where there's sm . . . sm . . . sm . . . sm . . . sm . . . sm . . . sm . . . sm . . . sm . . ."

"There *is* no fire. Trust me. It's just Rebecca Gatney tossing mud right before the election . . ."

Ishmael was interrupted by an intern who told him that there was an urgent call for the senator from his wife.

"Owen, I've got to go."

He hung up and picked up the senator's line.

"Mrs. White. This is Ishmael."

"Where is he? He's not answering his cell."

"He's on a plane back from Miami."

"When is he landing?"

"Six twenty-five. At National."

"Are you picking him up?"

"I'm sending a car."

"Cancel it."

"I beg your pardon?"

"I'll pick him up. Airline and flight number?"

This was a tough call. If there was one thing Woody White hated, it was being blindsided. If you gave him enough lead time, he often said, he could prepare for anything.

"Give me the airline and flight number, please."

The senator wouldn't have his cell turned back on until he got off the plane. Maybe he could catch him in the jetway, but then he'd have to know the exact time the plane landed, how long it took them to open the doors . . .

"Ishmael . . ."

"Is this some sort of emergency?"

"Just give me the goddamn airline and flight number, will you?"

He gave her the information. She hung up without saying good-bye. She hadn't said hello either.

As Woody emerged from the jetway, he squinted for the man in the black hat carrying the sign with his name on it. He was looking for HOLLINS, the prearranged code name they were using for this trip.

These days, however, it was hardly worth the effort to travel incognito. His face had been on television so often lately that it wasn't only people in Washington who recognized him. During the flight, three people had snuck up to first class and asked for an autograph.

One of the autograph-seekers was a tall woman in a jogging suit who told him that he was a scumbag after he signed her in-flight magazine.

"I hope you get testicular cancer and die," she said before vanishing back into the coach section.

So Woody was looking around not only for the man with the HOLLINS sign but also for the scumbag woman, when he saw his future ex-wife waiting for him.

She looked fabulous, of course. A dark-gray suit, beautifully cut, with a light-blue silk blouse and an orange pastel scarf.

What the hell was she doing here?

How did she know what flight he was on?

Why hadn't Ishmael warned him?

He reached in his pocket and felt the cell phone, with the *receive* switch off. Switching it back on, he walked the fifty or so feet that separated them, trying to prepare some sort of defensive posture with which to absorb whatever it was that she was about to hit him with.

"Well," he said, "what a pleasant surprise." He gave her a peck on the cheek in case there was someone with a camera around.

"We'll talk in the car."

As soon as she had let him pay for the parking and the windows were rolled back up, she unloaded.

"You fuck."

"And how are *you*, Daphne?"

"I'll kill you if she gets deported."

"Who?"

"Sonja. Her deportation order arrived today."

"What?"

"They're giving her thirty days to leave the country. We had a deal you'd lay off if I showed up at the fucking dog pound."

"There was a mistake," he said, backpedaling quickly.

"There better fucking have been a mistake. And you better fix it."

"I'll fix it."

"You don't fix this, Woody, I'm going to ruin you before I kill you. And I'm going to make sure that you don't wind up in Arlington with a flag on your grave."

Smoke was coming out of her nostrils. She almost took them both out, cutting off a taxicab that managed to swerve out of the way at the last minute.

"I go public with everything—the house, the dog, our sex life—"

"What sex life?"

"That's right. What sex life? We didn't have a sex life."

"And why was that, Daphne?"

"Because you could never keep it up long enough."

"Bullshit."

"Bullshit. In five minutes you were spaghetti."

"You know why I was spaghetti, Daphne? Because you were Parmesan cheese. You lay there like you were under anesthesia, staring at the ceiling—"

"What else was I suppose to do?"

"Lubricate, for one thing."

"Oh, I lubricate plenty . . ."

"I bet you do. Every time your Finnish ice-skater girlfriend goes down on you."

"Well, at least her tongue doesn't get soft."

"She probably sharpens her ice skates on it . . ."

It went downhill from there. By the time they were across the bridge, they were no longer talking at all. She stopped the car and ordered him to get out.

Before she pulled away, she rolled down the window and shouted, "I faked every orgasm I ever had with you."

"So did I," he retorted as the window went back up and she roared away, tires squealing.

Hank Leventhal was already gone for the day by the time Woody caught a cab to his office in Dirksen and tried the number at INS on the secure line. He had Ishmael track down the asset-forfeiture associate director's home phone number in Silver Spring and got him just as he was sitting down to dinner with his wife and daughters.

"Can I call you back? I'm about to have dinner."

"The deportation papers went out, Hank."

"Let me take this upstairs," he whispered, and Woody waited until he picked up again from his bedroom.

"I was going to call you and explain. There was a mistake," Hank Leventhal said.

"There sure was. What the hell happened?"

"The guy whose desk drawer the order was supposed to be in apparently moved it to his *in* basket in preparation for putting it in his pending-inactive file. That's where you put deportation orders that aren't ready to be issued yet. You know, like waiting for signature, or address correction, that type of thing . . ."

"Can we cut to the chase here?"

"So what happened was that the cleaning lady when she dusted off the *in* basket mistakenly put things back in the *out* basket . . ."

Woody rubbed his eyes as Hank Leventhal explained the exact route the deportation order had to take to have been received by Sonja Aura.

"You have to quash it."

"Quash it?"

"Yes. Have the guy send a superseding order to the effect that the previous order is inoperative."

"We don't do that."

"What do you mean you don't do that?"

"The normal channels involve the recipient filing an appeal, which goes to an appeals board—"

"Hank, I don't care what the normal channels are. Just write her a letter on INS stationery telling her to disregard the order. Can't you do that?"

"No."

"No?"

"I don't have appropriate stationery at my disposal. All I have is asset-forfeiture stationery, and you can't send a letter rescinding a deportation order on asset-forfeiture stationery."

"Why the fuck not?"

"Don't be abusive, Senator. My wife and daughters are downstairs."

Woody took a deep breath and tried to focus. He was exhausted, having gotten up at five-thirty in order to make a seven o'clock flight to Miami.

"Hank," he said in as calm a voice as he could manage, "what do I need to do to make this happen?"

"Nothing."

"Nothing?"

"Senator, I'm no longer discussing this matter with you. From now on, I'm not taking your calls. If you persist in trying to contact me, I'll go to *The Washington Post* and tell them everything."

"Hank, you want to go back to Burlington?"

"Not particularly. But if I go back to Burlington, you're going back to Peru. On your shield. After you serve time in whatever correctional facility that they're sending influence-peddlers and extortionists to these days."

Hank Leventhal hung up the phone.

Woody felt the accumulation of the day piling up around him. He had dealt with bail bondsmen and lawyers. His son was throwing in the towel on their relationship. He had been called a scumbag by a woman on the plane, insulted and threatened by his future ex-wife, let out of the car unceremoniously on a street in Anacostia . . . and now this.

He looked at his watch: 7:45. He was scheduled for sandwiches and debate prep, but there was no way he was up to that. He buzzed Ishmael, told him to blow off the debate prep, and called Evelyn Brandwynne at home.

"What're you doing?" he asked.

"I was about to make myself some poached salmon."

"How big's the salmon?"

The lobbyist for the National Association of Health Prophylaxis Industries met him at the door in an apron with a glass of Johnnie Walker Black.

He sat on the stool in the kitchen sipping the Scotch and watched her poach the salmon expertly while he told her about posting bail for his son in Miami that morning and being called a scumbag on the plane.

"A perfect stranger comes up to a United States senator on an airplane as he's returning from dealing with a family emergency and calls him a scumbag?"

"People are crazy."

"What if I just retired to Vermont? Learned how to ski. Smoked marijuana in the Jacuzzi . . ."

"You've just had a bad day, Woody."

"I've had a lot of bad days lately."

"Some salmon and some sex, and you'll be as good as new."

The salmon was fine. The sex, unfortunately, wasn't. For the first time in months, he flatlined.

As he lay there at 4 A.M., too exhausted to fall back to sleep, he tried to recalculate his E.Q. He had been consistently up at "moderate to high." Would one "very low or none at all" bring the average down to "moderate," or even to "moderate to low"?

One bad outing—you get roughed up at Fenway with the wind blowing out to left—and the E.R.A. shoots back up over four.

Spaghetti was not a pretty word.

Oh how he hated her. He lay awake in the slowly lightening bedroom, counting the ways.

33

THE JEW IN THE WOODPILE

IT MAY OR MAY NOT HAVE BEEN AN OMEN, but it rained on October 17. A tarpaulin was rigged about a hundred feet beyond the stone wall that separated Jim Goldstone's hay field from the dirt road off Route 7A, three miles north of Shaftsbury Center.

Woody, Rebecca Gatney, and Tom Ragle, the president of Marlboro College, sat under the tarpaulin, all three on rocking chairs. The distinguished Vermont journalists sat under umbrellas facing them in a semicircle. The ABC station in Burlington operated the main camera feed, with local stations from Bennington to White River Junction sharing the sound and picture.

There were a couple of hundred standing spectators permitted to watch from behind the stone wall, they themselves being watched carefully by thirty handpicked Vermont state troopers. Watching the Vermont state troopers were FBI agents Austin and Buchannon, who had been watching the senator off and on since the Italian death threat.

At noon that Saturday in mid-October everybody in Vermont who wasn't shoveling manure, harvesting hay, or selling apple cider to tourists was tuned in to the Debate in the Field.

Both sets of handlers were crowded into Winnebagos, one on each side of the field, to watch the proceedings. Rav Monsjar had babied his 1971 Chevy pickup in need of a ring job over the mountains from Brattleboro. He sat back on a folding chair in front of the Winnebago, smoking hand-rolled cigarettes that Janine Caravaggio could have sworn was oregano cut with marijuana and beamed like a playwright on opening night.

Tom Ragle made brief opening remarks—a quip about the weather, an introduction of the distinguished journalists, who had the fortitude to come out in the rain, an introduction of the candidates, who had the fortitude as well, and an explanation of the ground rules of the debate.

Three minutes for each question, one minute for the rebuttal. Two Marlboro College political-science professors were armed with stop-watches and red and yellow flags.

Roger Glazebrook, from the *Vermont Free Press,* led off with a softball, asking Mrs. Gatney why she had decided to challenge a popular two-term incumbent.

"This isn't about popularity. This is about serving the people of Vermont," she said in her tart Yankee prosecutor's voice. "For the past twelve years, Woody White has spent more time serving the interests of the people of Togo than the people of Vermont. . . ."

Woody sat under the dripping tarpaulin and listened to the opening barrage of gunfire. She came right over the hill with the cavalry, guns blazing. In three minutes Rebecca Gatney accused him of being lazy, corrupt, self-serving, insincere, and morally challenged.

When Tom Ragle asked him if he wished to reply, Woody said, "Well, I think I'd better get a word in here, Tom, don't you? Or else Mrs. Gatney'll have a lynch mob after me. Now, I sat here and listened to Mrs. Gatney accuse me of just about every crime in the book. She stopped just short of murder, but if she'd had another minute she probably would have thrown that one at me as well."

He got a few flickering smiles from the crowd beyond the wall but not even a creased dimple from the distinguished journalists.

"The reason we suggested this debate out here in the field was that we thought it would be harder to toss cow chips when you're already sitting among them. In fact, we suggested that there be a blackboard and that each time one of us evaded the question and resorted to cow-chip tossing, we could have Tom Ragle put a mark up. But my virtuous opponent rejected that idea. So here we are without a blackboard. All we've got is our ears. And I think I ought to have mine checked because I heard Roger Glazebrook's question to be, 'Why did *you* decide to run for this office?' I didn't hear him say, 'Would you please list all the deficiencies, real or imagined, of Senator White?' Did you?

"Well, we certainly heard a lot about me, but we didn't hear a whole lot about my virtuous opponent. I don't know about you, but I figure I'm smart enough to find out about my senator's record myself. It's in the public record. I want to hear his opponent tell me about herself. What's she done? What are her qualifications for the office? Now, that would really be interesting. The rest of this cow pucky I can read in the supermarket rags. . . ."

It was an effective counterattack, serious enough not to sound flippant, but light enough to suggest that he was unbothered by her tactics. More important, it defined the terms of the debate, forcing her into talking about herself and not about him.

She would have to wait for the distinguished journalists to go after him.

It was Whit Nichols, of Vermont Public Radio, who, twenty minutes into the debate, went after him.

"Senator, the people I'm talking to are having a hard time understanding why the two major pieces of legislation you've sponsored this term are a bill to send forty million dollars to the Republic of Togo to stimulate their phosphate industry and a bill for increased funding for Tourette syndrome. Can you tell us, Senator, how either of these bills serves the people of this state?"

"That's a very good question, Whit," be began, "and I'm going to try to answer it as well as I can. I just hope I can do it in three minutes. . . ."

As Ishmael sat beside Beverly, Janine Caravaggio, and Brian Petrunich and listened to the senator explain the phosphates-for-hockey-sticks equation, he marveled at the ease with which his boss traced the complex economic synergy between the phosphate mines of Togo and the hockey-stick factories of Burlington.

In fact, it was so neatly constructed and elegantly explained that Rebecca Gatney called out the cavalry again in her rebuttal.

"What I'd like to know is what the senator knows about the National Association for the Prevention and Treatment of Tourette Syndrome," she said. "And why this organization, which operates out of a firetrap in Washington, D.C., is run by a Togolese whose brother-in-law is the Foreign Minister of that country and who is presently missing and being sought by the FBI."

Woody rocked a few times in his chair, a technique that helped him give the impression of careful consideration of the question—a question that they had debate-prepped the shit out of.

"My campaign receives contributions from over a hundred different organizations. If we had to investigate every one of these organizations thoroughly, we'd have to hire a staff that would eat up all those contributions, and then some. Now, I suspect that if my virtuous opponent had to live up to the standards she seems to be demanding of me, she'd be spending all her time checking IRS records, auditing books instead of tossing cow chips at me.

"Take, for example, the Vermont Citizens for Ethical Government, the same organization, as it happens, that has written to the Senate Ethics Committee asking it to investigate me. Now, if she investigated them thoroughly, she'd find out that the principal contributors to this particular political-action group are major contributors not only to the Republican Party but to Rebecca Gatney's reelection campaign as well, that the VCEG is in reality a three-legged monster for funneling money into her own campaign—Republican soft money, direct contributions to her and this so-called ethical money that's being used to attack me. I don't know about you, but that sounds like a green cow to me. You take the paint off and what you have is one of those old black-and-white cows that have decorated this field out here, don't you?"

Rav Monsjar spat on the ground and muttered, "He shut the valise right in her face."

Ishmael chuckled nervously. So far, so good. But there were three more distinguished journalists to go before they were out of the woods.

"Watch out for Wechsler," Rav muttered to himself. "He's a snake in the woodpile."

Zeke Wechsler was the editor of the *Burlington Bugle,* Rebecca Gatney's hometown newspaper, which, even before this election, had never been a friend of Woody White's. They had been all over the grope in the back of the bus in '95, and, more recently, John Quincy Adams–gate.

The rain had tapered off to a fine mist by the time they got to Zeke Wechsler. He was a chubby man with thick, curly hair and a perpetual postnasal drip. A folder filled with copious notes was open in his lap. He made a final check of his notes, cleared his sinuses, and came springing out of the woodpile with venom.

"Senator, here's a black-and-white cow for you. Would you vote for a man who was not born in this state, doesn't really live here, has spent twelve years in Washington and has no committee chairmanships, has twice been investigated by the Senate Ethics Committee, whose son has just been arrested for the possession of thirty-eight kilos of marijuana, and whose two major campaign contributors are a man who has been the subject of a United States Attorney's investigation for racketeering and an organization that appears to be a front for a foreign government?"

All twelve distinguished journalists stared back at the senator like a jury that had just been asked to vote the death penalty. The spectators out beyond the stone wall were leaning forward expectantly, the scent of blood in their nostrils.

All over the state, too, people leaned a little closer to their TV sets. There was a collective blood lust in the air, the nervous excitement that people felt at public executions.

Rav Monsjar whispered, "Grab him by the head and twist. One fast motion. Less is more."

Rav Monsjar's words reached Woody telepathically. *Less is more.*

"Yes," he replied, loudly and clearly.

Then, in the silence that ensued, he sat back in his rocking chair, let the moment play, before saying, "Can you tell me why a hummingbird hums, Mr. Wechsler?"

Zeke Wechsler uttered a little nervous laugh and shook his head.

"'Cause he don't know the words."

There were some titters in the crowd, even a smile or two from the distinguished journalists.

"If he knew the words, Mr. Wechsler, we'd hear 'em. Instead, all we've heard for the past hour and a half from my opponent and her friends in the newspaper business is a lot of humming. But no words. Not one single idea. Not one single proposal. Not one single solution to Vermont's problems. So when you think about this debate, and I hope you will, think about what my virtuous opponent, and her friend and PR man, the virtuous editor of the *Burlington Bugle,* actually *said.* Did you hear anything besides a barrelful of half-truths and red herrings? Did you hear what *they* were going to do for Vermont? Did you hear any passion, any enthusiasm, any commitment? Did you hear any *words?*"

He paused for a moment to let the words sink in, before concluding.

"So when I step into the voting booth on November third, I'm going to think about what I said and what my virtuous opponent said. And I'm going to vote for Woody White because he *said* something. He knows the words."

There was a long silence after Woody concluded his answer with two minutes remaining on the stopwatch.

"Put a fork in her. She's done," Rav Monsjar said.

Indeed, Rebecca Gatney had been thrown seriously off-balance by the senator's answer to Zeke Wechsler's question. Her reply was a garbled three-minute attempt to explain her legislative agenda.

Woody waived his rebuttal. He looked right at Zeke Wechsler and said, "Your witness, Mr. Wechsler."

Watching in Montpelier on his thirteen-inch black-and-white TV with tinfoil on the antenna, John Quincy Adams said to Elbridge Gerry, "He stole my hummingbird joke."

"Well, it's not a real knee-slapper."

"You're entitled to your opinion."

"I suspect I am."

· · ·

The first overnight poll on the debate had Woody picking up 2.3 points. But the second and third polls had him giving the points back. A week later he was looking at a net loss of .3 points.

Irwin Posalski explained the reversal as a statistical version of buyer's remorse.

"You bring the car home, take it out for a spin, hit a pothole or two. Suddenly you're back in the real world. Same thing with polls. You get a flicker one way or the other, then the random sample absorbs the media coverage around the debate just like a pothole, rethinks it, and, boom, you're looking at an equal and opposite negative flicker."

In spite of the numbers, Woody's people thought that the Debate in the Field had been a modest success, or at worst a push. For one thing, it positioned him as a victim of the *Burlington Bugle* and the media in general, which would make it harder for them to attack him without creating a backlash.

Referring to Zeke Wechsler, Rav Monsjar had revised his metaphor from a snake in the woodpile to a Jew in the woodpile. Beverly Levesque had to sit on him to make sure that this politically incorrect piece of anti-Semitism didn't leak.

"How many Jews are there in Vermont?" Rav Monsjar asked.

"That's not the point."

"He gets pissy about it, just drag out the senator's voting record on Israel."

Ishmael—whom Rav Monsjar started calling the Jew in the shitpile, referring to the extensive damage-control work the chief of staff did for Woody White—went back down to Washington to wade through the shitpile while the senator stayed in Vermont for the final two weeks of campaigning.

Ishmael found two urgent e-mails waiting for him.

Barry's said, "We *have to* talk ASAP."

Owen Lundkeim's said, "Please call as soon as you get in. Very important."

Ishmael called Barry on the speakerphone as he started to wade through the shitpile.

"I have to tell you this in person," he whispered.

"Barry, I'm up to my ears—"

"Ten minutes. The bench next to the Taft Memorial."

The Robert A. Taft Memorial was a five-minute walk from the Capitol subway terminal. Ishmael found Barry waiting for him under the statue of Mr. Republican.

"I'm sorry about this, Ishmael, but you have to know. I've been debating telling you since I found out. I almost called you in Vermont. It's . . . Jesus, I don't know what to say. . . ."

He reached into the pocket of his Bill Blass casual suit for a breath mint.

"Say something, Barry."

"All right. Look, I shouldn't have done it, but I did it. I wasn't thinking. It was an act of passion—"

"What did you do, Barry?"

"You promise you won't be mad?"

"Yes, I promise."

"I threatened Owen's life."

"You did what?"

"I sent him an e-mail saying that if he was fucking around on you, I'd have him killed."

Barry looked around carefully to make sure no one could overhear them.

"I didn't mean it. I was being hyperbolic. I mean, what would I know about having someone killed?"

"Barry, why did you threaten Owen?"

"Because . . . because I saw him with someone else. Over breakfast. At La Coquette. At seven-thirty in the morning. In sweats. They were *holding hands*. I mean, you're gone for one fucking day . . . !"

Ishmael was trying to remember just who he was supposed to be at the moment and to whom. It was getting very complicated.

"Barry, that was dumb."

"I *said* it was dumb, all right?"

"Okay, look, I'll talk to Owen. I'm sure there's some explanation."

"Seven-thirty in the *morning*? In *sweats*?"

The explanation was, of course, perfectly innocuous. When he got Owen Lundkeim on the phone, the aide to Representative Carl Kanush told him what actually happened on Saturday morning.

"I w . . . w . . . w . . . went to the pr . . . pr . . . pr . . . prayer meeting and j . . . j . . . j . . . jog at th . . . on . . . of . . . the F . . . F . . . Fellowship of Chr . . . Chr . . . Chr . . . Christian Legisl . . . sl . . . sl . . . slative Aides and then I w . . . w . . . w . . . went out to br . . . br . . . breakfast with M . . . M . . . Mitchell Meevers, the l . . . l . . . legislative aide f . . . f . . . for C . . . C . . . Congressman H . . . H . . . H . . . Hermanski."

Apparently, Barry had walked in just when Owen Lundkeim and Mitchell Meevers were holding hands across the table and saying a prayer before breakfast.

"W . . . w . . . w . . . we hold h . . . h . . . hands to show our br . . . br . . . br . . . brotherhood bef . . . f . . . f . . . ore J . . . Jesus."

"Barry didn't mean what he said, Owen."

"You d . . . d . . . d . . . don't think I sh . . . sh . . . should go to the p . . . p . . . p . . . p . . . police?"

"Of course not. Barry wouldn't hurt a fly. You see, for some reason he has it in his head that you're trying to change White-Kanush to Kanush-White. That's what he meant by *fucking around*. Fucking around with the *bill*. I have no idea where he got that notion. People make up the most outrageous gossip in this town."

"H . . . h . . . he doesn't th . . . th . . . th . . . think that y . . . y . . . you and I are, you kn . . . kn . . . kn . . . know . . . ?"

"No way."

"He's n . . . n . . . n . . . not spreading the r . . . r . . . rumor that I'm, you kn . . . kn . . . kn . . . know . . . ?"

"Owen, Barry realizes that you're straight. Believe me. No one could possibly make that mistake about you."

"J . . . j . . . j . . . just because I . . . I . . . I'm well dr . . . dr . . . dr . . . dressed . . ."

So, in the midst of all the other things he had to do, Ishmael had to broker a peace agreement between Barry, Kevin, Jack, and Denny and Owen Lundkeim, who wound up accepting their group apology and agreeing to erase the threatening e-mail from his hard disk.

Ishmael dragged his ass through the door of Maud's house in Alexandria at a quarter to ten that night. She had shipped her daughter to her mother's until Monday and had spent the day doing yoga exercises to prepare her body to celebrate its oneness with his.

She gave him a protein drink, stuck him in the bathtub, then anointed his body with aromatic oils she had gotten mail-order from the Tantric Sex Center in Maplewood, New Jersey.

Around 2 A.M. Ishmael drifted off to sleep while he was still inside her. They slept as one until morning.

34.

LARRY KING LIVE

AMONG THE MESSAGES waiting for Ishmael in the office on Monday morning, two in particular intrigued him—one from a Hollywood movie producer, and the other from a booker for *Larry King Live*.

Curious, Ishmael dialed Los Angeles and was put through to a man named Charlie Berns, who asked him if the film rights to the senator's story were still available.

"What film rights?"

"Movies, series, miniseries, long-form. We could go any way with it. It's a great story."

"And just what story would you be referring to?"

"You've got some sense of humor, Mr. Leibowitz."

"Pardon me?"

"The whole story. From the Vermont gangsters to the undercover Africans. We start with a two-hour back-door pilot on the life of a beleaguered senator, and if we put the right casting together, parlay that into twenty-two on the air—"

"Twenty-two what?"

"Episodes. Play or pay. We go for, I don't know, maybe we go for Selleck—he's available, his series tanked—and maybe give him a little P.I. business on the side. You know, he could be on the Senate Floor and get beeped by his assistant to check out a homicide . . . what about Cybill Shepherd? Her series went south too, and—"

Ishmael hung up on Charlie Berns and dialed Atlanta. The booker floated an offer for the senator to appear on the program Wednesday night. He told the booker he'd get back to her and reached Woody in Bellows Falls.

"What do you think?" the senator asked him.

"It's a tough call. On the one hand, you've got people calling questions in—all sorts of loose cannons throwing stuff at you. On the other hand, you've got an hour of coast-to-coast TV, which we could never afford to buy on our own."

"At this point, I think we take our chances with the loose cannons, don't you?"

"I think you're right."

So that Wednesday night, as millions of Americans looked on, Senator Woodrow White found himself sitting across the table from the man with the suspender fetish.

Larry King started off with one of his disarming, avuncular questions, "Senator, you've been down in Washington for twelve years. You've had a pretty good run at it. And now this barrage of attacks on you. Some of it pretty nasty. Let me ask you—is it really worth it? Is another six years in the Senate that important to you?"

"Larry, if I drop out now, I'm saying to the people of Vermont that there's truth in those attacks. I'm throwing in the towel. Well, I'm not a towel thrower. As my old friend Al Simpson was fond of saying—politics is a contact sport."

Larry King adjusted his glasses and asked, "So, what do you think the Ethics Committee is going to do with this latest complaint?"

"They're going to do their job. That's what they're there for. And after they've looked at all the evidence, or lack thereof, they'll issue a statement saying that there was no improper conduct on my part and we'll all get on with our lives."

"You sound pretty confident, Senator."

"You know, Larry, the easiest thing in the world is to make an accusation. The hardest thing is to disprove it. If I put out a story saying that you, Larry King, were an ax murderer, you'd have to go around saying, 'I'm not an ax murderer.' Just having to say it makes you sound guilty. That's the downside of the First Amendment—anybody can say anything about anybody."

"You're not suggesting that we repeal the First Amendment, are you?"

"You've just proved my point with that question."

"How's that?"

"If I qualify my answer in any way, the sound byte coming out of it will be 'White Questions Value of First Amendment,' and the next thing I know, I'm back on this program defending myself against those charges."

"All right, let's take a call. Davenport, Iowa, you're on *Larry King Live.*"

A middle-aged female voice said, "I'd like to ask Senator White if he thinks Tourette syndrome is a more serious problem in this country than crime."

Davenport, Iowa, was the first of several hand grenades that Woody handled adroitly. Shreveport, Louisiana, asked him if relations with Togo were more important than relations with Saudi Arabia. And Putney, Vermont, asked him whether he thought there was any relation between his parenting and the arrest of his son for drug dealing.

Some 4.7 million Americans, according to the Nielsen ratings, sat in their living rooms and watched Senator Woody White dismantle the hand grenades. He was articulate, charming, and witty, and he had those telegenic blue eyes that could still stop a woman in her tracks.

It was those beautiful blue eyes that struck one of those 4.7 million Americans as vaguely familiar, as she sat watching *Larry King Live* in her apartment in Schenectady, New York. Esmeralda Perkins, the procedures nurse for the late urologist Ernest Haas, knew that she had seen those eyes close up.

When they went to commercial, it all suddenly came back to her. Last March. The day the doctor died. Shaving the scrotum for a testosterone patch. The involuntary tumescence. The extra surgical tape . . .

She waited until they came back to the program to make sure. It was him. She was positive.

But his name wasn't Senator Woodrow White. It was James Monroe.

The next morning, Phil Yalowitz caught Woody in the hotel room in Atlanta just before he called for the car to the airport.

"I'm afraid I've got some bad news, Senator."

"You only call me with bad news, Phil."

"Sharon Rosinski's attorneys have gotten a duces tecum order against you."

"A what?"

"An accounting of all assets, including but not limited to bank accounts, stock holdings, mutual funds, bonds, IRAs, 401(K)'s, real estate holdings, second and third mortgages, joint ventures, limited partnerships, pension plans, life insurance—both cash value and term—precious metals, collections of value, mineral rights, motor vehicles, boats, airplanes, royalties and residuals, if any."

"Phil, I don't have time for this bullshit."

"I've already filed for an extension but this judge doesn't like extensions on paperwork."

"I'm running for reelection."

"As you know, Senator, the Supreme Court has ruled that public office does not make you unanswerable to civil suits . . ."

"Yeah, yeah, yeah . . . right . . ."

There was a brief silence, a vacuum that Woody knew would soon be filled with more bad news. Phil Yalowitz never dropped only one shoe.

"Your present wife's attorney has been in contact as well . . ."

Here it was. The other shoe.

"He said that unless you performed, the deal was null and void as of October thirtieth. Now I told him I didn't know what deal he meant, and he told me, as he has in the past, that you would know what that meant."

"I know what that means."

"If you tell me, it's privileged."

"Yes, I know. I went to law school. Look, call him back and tell him I'll perform."

"I don't like engaging in blind negotiations, Senator . . ."

"Deal with it, Phil. I've got to catch a plane."

An hour later he was paged at the airport by another one of his lawyers, Burton Armature.

"Burt, what's going on?"

"You've been served with a subpoena from the Ethics Committee."

"For what?"

"Fund-raising records, bank accounts, phone logs, appointment calendars, memos, e-mail, correspondence, personal diaries, if any . . ."

"Burt, they're backing up a truck."

"There's no Court of Appeals for an Ethics Committee subpoena."

"What if they asked for my left nut?"

"You'd have to give it to them or face contempt charges."

"What about the Bill of Rights?"

"It doesn't apply to Ethics Committee proceedings, Senator."

On the cell on the way back in from National, after an hour and a half of turbulence, Ishmael dropped the third shoe. Trent Lott had gotten the judge to declare summary judgment against him in the car-damage suit: $21,000, out the door.

Later that day, as Woody worked the phones trying to line up support on the Ethics Committee, Debbie Sue Allenby came in to toss the fourth shoe at his feet.

Kodjo Kponvi had been arrested by an undercover FBI agent posing as a pizza deliveryman.

They turned the TV on to see if the story was on CNN Headline News. It played right after a 465 drop in the Dow caused by the discovery of chemical weapons in Iraq.

The senator, Ishmael, and Debbie Sue watched the African being led into a police car in front of an apartment in Cathedral Heights—used, according to the report, as "a safehouse for covert activities on the part of the Togolese government."

When Debbie Sue went out to get a cup of tea for the senator, Woody turned to Ishmael and said, "Can it get any worse?"

Ishmael Leibowitz, the child of the Holocaust, knew it could always get worse. But he didn't say so. From somewhere in the collective gene pool, the twisted dark humor of the *shtetl*, he saw a dachshund's ear.

"Well, every dachshund has two ears."

"You mean, we could get another ear in the mail?"

"You never know . . ."

And for the second time in recent weeks, the senator and Ishmael laughed. Loudly and cathartically.

So much so that when Debbie Sue Allenby came back with the tea, she thought that they had both lost it.

"What's . . . going on?" she asked.

Woody looked at her and said, "How many ears are there on a dachshund?"

And Ishmael and the senator exploded once more with laughter. The intercom buzzed and Ishmael picked it up, still chuckling. He listened for a moment, then put his hand over the mouthpiece.

"You want to talk to Nat Birnbaum, Senator?"

Woody thought for a moment and nodded. He picked up the phone and said, in anticipation of the question, "I never met the man, Nat." He sat there playing with the phone cord and smiling at Ishmael and Debbie Sue as he gave a succession of one-line responses to the reporter's other questions.

"Not to my knowledge."

"I don't recall that."

"I'm afraid not."

"Sorry, but I can't help you there."

He hung up and switched the TV to a network station to catch the early news at five.

And there, right after the Iraq story, was the footage of Kodjo Kponvi getting into the car and the explanation of the local reporter on the story, Warren Worrell.

"The man being led away by FBI agents has been identified as forty-three-year-old Kodjo Kponvi, a Togolese who has played a shadowy role in this latest Woody White fund-raising scandal that is being referred to as Togogate. NBC News has learned that Mr. Kponvi entered the country on a diplomatic passport in February and set up an organization known as NAPTOTS, or the National Association for the Prevention and Treatment of Tourette Syndrome, which donated four hundred thousand dollars to the White reelection campaign allegedly in return for key votes on the part of the senator in the African Affairs Subcommittee in the Senate. Mr. Kponvi had no comment to make to reporters outside the Cathedral Heights apartment that, according to sources, is being rented by Rich Lusskin, the American husband of the Togolese Embassy's visa-and-immigration officer . . . yet more hot water for the beleaguered Vermont senator. . . ."

Woody shut the TV off and took a sip of his tea.

"I think they're verging on overkill here," Ishmael said, after a long, heavy silence.

Woody nodded, his mind elsewhere. In the midst of everything else, he was preoccupied by the flatlining at Evelyn Brandwynne's apartment the night of his return from Florida.

It was amazing what a man could endure if he was functioning. And it was amazing what could bring him down when he wasn't.

It was this realization that made what was to follow particularly devastating. *That* story hadn't broken yet. But when it did, it would make the other stories pale in comparison.

That story was slowly wending its way from Schenectady to Washington. And when it got there, it would make everything else look like spaghetti.

But first the second ear arrived.

35

THE NINTH CIRCLE OF HELL

THE SECOND EAR was a paw. And it didn't make it as far as the senator's office. After the first ear arrived, all subsequent packages coming into the office were opened by FBI bomb specialists in the basement of the Hoover Building.

Like the first package, this one was postmarked from Houston and contained a note in Italian. This time it was from *La Divina Commedia,* the final stanza of the canto in which Dante describes the descent into the ninth circle of hell.

The FBI contacted a professor of classical studies at the University of Maryland, who said that he could see no readily apparent connection, literal or metaphoric, between the verse and a dachshund's paw, which, once again, turned out not to be Helmut's. In fact, the paw wasn't even from a dachshund, according to an animal necrologist brought in by the FBI to examine the paw.

So it turned out that the "second ear" didn't help Woody's polls at all. The needle didn't even flinch, but instead continued in its descent toward the lower forties.

The numbers were deteriorating even among Democratic Vermonters With At Least One Dog In Domicile, Irwin Posalski informed him.

"Once you dip below forty, you're not coming back. You're in a statistical free fall without a parachute."

Things were looking so bad for the White campaign that Rebecca Gatney stopped attacking him. Her handlers convinced her that attacking Woody White at this point would only result in producing sympathy votes.

So with less than two weeks to go before the election, the smart money was getting off the incumbent.

In an attempt to make up ground, Beverly had the senator booked solid all over the state. Every day until November 3 was jammed with cow chips and Jell-O squares.

Woody was due back in Burlington late Friday night to begin the long march at the crack of dawn. Ishmael dropped him off at National in time to catch the ten o'clock flight, which would get him to Burlington a little before midnight. He said good-bye to his chief of staff and entered the terminal with his overnight bag full of polls and speeches.

But he didn't catch the flight to Burlington, as he was supposed to. Instead he approached the TV monitor that displayed the flights still to depart that night. As he stood in front of the monitor and stared at the screen, he slipped his hand in his pocket and switched the cell phone off.

The last flight out to Cleveland had left ten minutes ago. There was a flight to Chicago at eleven. From there he could connect in the morning to Cleveland and rent a car.

Maddie White had already been up for an hour when the rented Oldsmobile Cutlass pulled into the yard at six-thirty in the morning. The sound of an automobile was rare in East Gethsemane. The sound of an automobile in the yard at six-thirty in the morning was even rarer.

Boaz was out in back shoeing a horse. The dog was up and barking. The children were at their after-breakfast prayers.

They all converged on the Cutlass pretty much at the same time. The door to the car opened, and Maddie White's father emerged in a wrinkled gray suit.

He looked older and more tired than she could remember, but then she remembered that she hadn't seen him in several years.

His blue eyes were creased around the edges. His skin looked pasty. His shoulders sagged, and his shoes needed polishing.

"Father," she said, "you are welcome."

And as she said these words, his face contorted and he started to cry.

She had never seen her father cry. Even now, as he stood there openly weeping, she had trouble believing that the man in the wrinkled suit was Woodrow White.

She shooed the dog and the children away, beckoned for Boaz to leave them alone, and then went to him and embraced him. He sagged in her arms and tried to stop crying several times before he was able to.

When he recovered his posture and his speech, he said, "I'm sorry."

"There is nothing to be sorry for."

"It was the way you said, 'You are welcome.' I was prepared for you to throw me out."

"Come into the house."

"Let's take a walk. It's beautiful with the leaves changing. I saw the sun rise from the car."

She went into the house to get her shawl while Woody took his light-weight Burberry from the car, and they walked out of the yard and down the dirt road.

After a few minutes of walking in silence, Maddie said, "You don't look well, Father."

He nodded. He knew he didn't look well. Why should he look well after what he had been through?

And she hadn't a clue. She had no television, no radio, not even a newspaper. She was off-line, unplugged. To her he wasn't a scandal-ridden senator being investigated by the Ethics Committee, being sued by two women and the Senate Majority Leader, and being sent dog parts in the mail by an Italian neo-Fascist.

He was just her father, a man who showed up in a rented car every four years or so.

"I've made a mess of things, Maddie."

"There is no mess that cannot be cleaned up."

"I don't know if I have the strength to do it."

They sat down on a log bench facing a pond covered with soggy colored leaves.

"Why have you come, Father?" she asked.

"I don't know. I was supposed to catch a flight back to Vermont last night, but I didn't get on the plane. I walked into the airport, looked at the flights, and decided to come here. Just like that."

"Are you in trouble?"

"Yes."

"Is it shameful?"

"I don't believe in shame."

He picked up a twig and started to break it into little pieces.

"I . . . I really think that in spite of everything, I'm a good senator."

"Who says you aren't?"

"My polls."

"I don't understand."

"I'm glad you don't understand. That's why I came here. To be with someone who doesn't understand. You never judged me, Maddie. You were always in my corner. Bobby was never in my corner. He wants me to stop trying to make things up to him. To just forget about being his father. It makes me very sad."

"Is he well?"

"No. He may go to jail for drug dealing."

"I'll pray for him."

"He won't appreciate it."

"And how is my mother?"

"She's suing me for more money."

"There is bitterness in her heart."

"Big-time."

The sun rose higher in the east, taking some of the morning chill out of the air. Woody asked her to tell him about Boaz and the children.

She told him about each one of them. She loved them fiercely in a completely unsentimental manner. It was tough love in the truest sense of the word. She didn't gush and she didn't judge.

Woody learned all about his Amish grandchildren, Amos, Ezekiel, Esther, and Hosea. Maddie knew everything there was to know about them.

They walked back to the house in silence. They had said everything that needed to be said.

Before he got back into the car, he kissed her on the forehead. She smiled and walked back toward the house. Standing in the doorway, she watched him back out of the yard.

"God bless you, Father," she whispered.

"Have you tried Peru?"

It was 8:30 A.M., and Ishmael was already on his seventh cup of coffee. The first one was at 2 A.M. after Beverly had roused him from his oneness with Maud to tell him that the senator had disappeared.

According to Beverly, he had never gotten off the 11:45 flight into Burlington last night. Since then she had been on the phone with the airlines, the State Police of four states, and the FBI.

By eight in the morning, she was in panic mode. Ishmael, who had lived through several of the senator's disappearing acts over the years, tried to calm her down.

"Sometimes he doesn't answer the phone."

"A week and a half to go and he disappears."

"He'll turn up. He always does."

"He's supposed to speak to the Burlington PTA at noon. I've got him an hour of radio time at three, the Veterans Hospital at five . . . "

"As soon as I hear from him, Beverly, I'll call you."

Ishmael hung up the phone and drained the seventh cup of coffee. Debbie Sue Allenby paced back and forth like a mother whose teenage son was out late with the car.

"They shouldn't have taken those FBI agents off him," she fretted.

"That's what happens when your polls go down. They figure no one wants to bother killing you."

"Ishmael!"

"Don't worry—he'll surface."

But even as he said it, Ishmael wondered where the senator was. Besides Peru, there was one other possible place. It was a phone call he didn't want to make, but, given the circumstances, he felt he had to make it.

He went into the senator's office, picked up the secure line, and dialed.

"Ms. Brandwynne, this is Ishmael Leibowitz, Senator White's chief of staff."

"Yes?"

"Forgive my calling you at home, but the senator has disappeared."

"Disappeared?"

"Yes. He was supposed to fly to Burlington last night, and he never got on the plane. I don't suppose he's there, is he?"

"No."

"Would you happen to know where he is?"

"I don't know why you would think I would know where he is."

"It was just a long shot."

An extended moment of silence, then she said, quickly and under her breath, even though she was alone in the apartment, "How much do you know?"

"Pretty much everything."

"Everything?"

"I mean, just from a logistical point of view. You see, I have to know where he is all the time. It's part of my job."

"I see."

"He's painfully discreet, Ms. Brandwynne. It's just, as I said, logistical."

"Logistical."

"Just where and when. That's all. Believe me."

"I don't know where he is."

"Okay, thanks."

"Is he all right?"

"Sure. He's probably in Peru not answering his phone."

"Do you think so?"

"Yes. It's his Vermont residence."

"Well, if I hear from him, I'll tell him to call you."

"I appreciate that."

After hanging up the phone, Evelyn Brandwynne walked over to the kitchen window and gazed out. It was a lovely fall day, the leaves in full color, a smoky blue sky.

She felt her heart beating a little more rapidly than it should have been. *What the hell had she gotten herself into?*

She ought to have her head examined. She had begun this relationship with a very specific goal in mind—the passage of legislation to have the government fund the purchase of condoms for poor people, a piece of legislation that was not only in the interests of her employers but was socially responsible.

She had lobbied the key vote on Medicaid and Health Care vigorously and had wound up, in spite of herself, falling in love with him. Which was not only unprofessional, but unwise.

Woody White didn't have a great deal to recommend him to a mature woman looking for a little security in her declining years. He was on his second wife, he was more or less broke, he was under a Senate Ethics Committee investigation, he was unreliable, glib, sexually erratic.

And yet . . .

As she stood there looking out the window, she felt great tenderness for this man who, if nothing else, could make her laugh. And cry.

It was preposterous. It was beautiful.

She would wait for him to get in touch. If he needed her, she would go to him. Wherever he was. With or without her nurse's uniform.

Woody got in and out of Cleveland without anyone recognizing him. The first-class section of the flight to Boston was mercifully empty, and he slept soundly until the wheels hit the runway at Logan.

When he got off the plane, he still didn't know exactly where he was going. The cell phone had been off since 9:45 the previous evening. He wandered through the airport until he found a quiet cocktail lounge where he could sit and figure out his next move. It was 11:30 in the morning, a little early for the hard stuff, but Woody ordered a Scotch and soda, and sat at the end of the bar, his back to the terminal.

He felt like a middle-aged delinquent who had run away from home instead of a United States senator on the campaign trail.

What if he got off the bus right now? Would it be any better? Would the Ethics Committee leave him alone? Would the lawyers go away? Would perfect strangers still come up to him and call him a scumbag?

He didn't know if he had the strength to walk away. Or to continue talking, smiling, explaining. Phosphates for hockey sticks, a judgeship for Vermont, it was the President who called the chairperson to get the bill out of committee, the deportation order went out by mistake, the Ford Explorer was badly parked . . .

He was tired of explaining things to people. For the first time in his political life, he felt defeated. He was down ten points in the fourth quarter, with no time-outs left and bad field position. And there was nobody to give him a Gipper speech.

As he let the Scotch slowly anesthetize him, he heard a voice.

It was a voice from some time ago. Vaguely familiar. It threaded its way through the Scotch and into his consciousness.

Very slowly, he turned his head toward the TV mounted above the bar.

There was an attractive young black woman standing in front of a gaggle of reporters and cameras. The sound was low, and Woody could barely make out what she was saying.

The graphic read: ESMERALDA PERKINS, UROLOGICAL NURSE.

Woody asked the bartender to raise the volume.

Esmeralda Perkins said, "He used an assumed name, James Monroe. I didn't realize it was actually him until I saw him on *Larry King Live* . . ."

A reporter shouted something Woody couldn't hear.

But he heard Esmeralda Perkins's answer: "I had a pretty good look at him. I was shaving his scrotum for testosterone therapy."

Woody quickly put a ten on the bar, turned his back, and left the cocktail lounge.

He went directly to the Hertz counter and rented a Crown Victoria. He paid with the campaign's Visa card and declined the insurance.

36

DOWN A QUART

TESTOSTERONEGATE THREATENED to knock all the other gates off the front page. Public interest in federal judgeships and creative campaign financing paled in comparison to a United States senator's getting his scrotum shaved under an assumed name.

The radio talk shows picked it up on the first bounce and ran with it. The airwaves were jammed with the vox populi alternately declaiming scorn or sympathy for the Vermont senator.

Esmeralda Perkins was offered $500,000 from the *National Enquirer* for her story. She declined, saying that the only reason she went public was her concern for the integrity of the profession.

"If patients use false names to obtain medical care," she said on national TV, "it defrauds the insurance companies. Not to mention the pharmacies. And what about the prescription drug database? Where would that be at?"

In Washington, meanwhile, the Ethics Committee met in the bug-proof room on the second floor of Hart to consider the latest development in their ongoing investigation of the ethics of Senator Woodrow White.

The chairman began the meeting by recounting the allegations made by the Schenectady urological nurse and suggesting the issuing of a subpoena in order to get a sworn statement from her.

"We don't even know that the story's true. For all we know, this woman could have made the whole thing up," the senator from Virginia said.

"Senator White's not denying it, is he?"

"Assuming it is true," the vice chairman argued, "I fail to see how the obtaining of medical services under an assumed name fits the language of our mandate under Senate Resolution 338, which, may I remind you, is 'improper conduct which may reflect upon the Senate.'"

"It indicates a pattern of mendacious behavior on the part of the senator from Vermont," the chairman maintained.

"C'mon, Mitch," the vice chairman said, "if you were getting testosterone therapy, would you do it publicly?"

"I don't need any, thank you, Senator, but if I did need some, I wouldn't go slinking off to some doctor in Schenectady under a false name."

"The question is—is having a prescription filled under a false name a crime in the state of New York?" the senator from Montana asked.

They all turned to Harold Kinder, as if he had knowledge of the criminal statutes of all fifty states at his fingertips.

"I'd have to look into that, Senator."

"I propose, therefore, that we table any action on this matter until such time as counsel has been able to ascertain the operative legal context."

The vice chairman made a motion to table. It was quickly seconded and passed 5–1, with only the chairman voting against it.

As usual, Rav Monsjar was categorical. Just as he had pronounced during Helmutgate that you couldn't get elected in Vermont without a dog, now he pronounced that you couldn't get elected in Vermont, or anyplace else for that matter, without an adequate level of testosterone.

"Nobody wants a senator who's down a quart," he said, from his front porch in Brattleboro to the speakerphone set up on Beverly's desk in Montpelier, around which Beverly Levesque, Janine Caravaggio, and Brian Petrunich were gathered.

"So should we deny it?" Janine Caravaggio asked.

"And fast," Rav Monsjar replied. "The longer the image of a testosterone-deficient senator floats through the electorate, the worse it's going to be. It hits people where they live. Like Eisenhower and the bowel movement."

"What?"

"When Ike had his heart attack in '55, the stock market went into the crapper. The doctors went on TV, said everything's okay. The President's fine. He's going to be all right. The Dow doesn't budge a goddamn inch. That night the news leaks from Walter Reed that the President took a dump. The next morning, the Dow goes up a hundred and forty-three points."

"Really?"

"Uh-huh. That's how you measure health in a Protestant country—bowel movements. And you know how you measure a man's ability to get things done? Testosterone."

"That's very interesting, Rav, but we can't find the senator at the moment to get his approval. And there's no way we can put out a statement without running it by him."

"Every hour that goes by with people thinking the senator's got a woodie problem is going to cost him plenty."

"I can't call up Dan Rather and tell him that the senator's . . . his . . . his . . . testosterone level is . . . whatever it is," Janine Caravaggio said.

"Might rain," Rav replied and was gone.

After they heard the line go dead, Brian Petrunich asked, "Does anybody know who the senator's regular urologist is?"

"Ishmael would know." Janine Caravaggio picked up the phone and dialed Washington.

The chief of staff put CNN on hold to take Janine Caravaggio's call.

"We just spoke with Rav," she told him, "and he thinks we have to make a statement right away."

"What kind of statement?"

"That the senator has a normal testosterone level. It's like Eisenhower's bowel movement. It's reassuring to people. Do you know who Woody's regular urologist is?"

"No."

"What if we found a Democratic urologist who just spoke generally about testosterone? You know, a sobering guy in a white coat with a pointer . . . ?"

"Forget it."

"Rav says if we don't move fast, we're dead in the water."

"Nobody says anything to anybody about the senator's medical condition. Period. End of discussion."

Ishmael hung up with Montpelier and picked back up with CNN.

"Here's the official word on this. The senator will not dignify these personal attacks on him by commenting."

"Would you happen to know who the senator's regular urologist is?" CNN asked Ishmael.

"Didn't you hear what I just said?"

"Wouldn't you like the American people to get to the bottom of this?"

"I'm hanging up."

"Does he practice in Washington?"

Ishmael slammed the phone down. The phone calls were stacked up—

more reporters, dozens of reporters, the minority leader, Phil Yalowitz, Hank Leventhal at INS, Barry, Kevin, Jack, and Denny . . .

He instructed the intern manning the switchboard to tell callers he was in a meeting and walked out of the office, past the Togolese fertility statue, downstairs to the main entrance, and out the door.

He made a right and walked south down Constitution through the dead leaves toward the reflecting pool.

For a long time he watched the water cascade into the basin. Thinking hard.

He knew that Woody was either in Peru or on his way there. And he knew that it was only a matter of time before the reporters descended upon the A-frame.

The senator would be besieged. They would camp out there until he answered their questions. Rav was right. Americans demanded to know about the testosterone levels of their politicians.

Woody would be angry, tired, vulnerable. If they wore him down, he could start to talk.

God knows what he would say.

Even Woody White had a breaking point.

It was clear to Ishmael that his first responsibility was to protect the senator from the press. At the very least he needed to buy him some time. He needed a diversionary tactic, and, as he stared into the fountain, one came to him.

It was audacious. It was brilliant. It was completely untrue. It just might work . . .

It would involve burning his bridges with the most influential newspaper in Washington. He would have to jerk them off so badly that they would never trust him again.

On his way down on the plane from the Debate in the Field a week ago, Ishmael had been absently leafing through a magazine. Something he had read had stuck in his mind. He had no idea why until now.

He took the cell out of his pocket and dialed *The Washington Post*.

When Nat Birnbaum picked up, Ishmael said, "Nat, I'm going to give you the *emmis* on the testosterone story. I'm going to give it to you exclusively because I believe you have the fairness and sensitivity to give Woody White the consideration he deserves."

"Can I quote you directly?"

"No. This is deep background. Nat, do you happen to know what one of the statistically demonstrated causes of prostate cancer is?"

"No."

"Excessive levels of testosterone. You see, the nurse was just trying to keep a lid on the cancer story. The senator was not being treated for too little testosterone, but for too *much*."

There was an agonizingly long silence on the other end of the line. His cell phone pressed to his ear, Ishmael wondered if he had sold it.

"Where is he?"

"At a small clinic in Canada. They have some sort of new laser radiation treatment there."

"Where in Canada?"

"I'm not at liberty to divulge that information."

There was another silence, and then Nat Birnbaum dredged up a modicum of decency from the very meager supply inside him.

"I'm sorry to hear about the senator's condition."

"Nat, Woody White's a fighter. If anybody can beat this, he can."

Woody White drove west through the late-fall afternoon, oblivious to the national debate going on around him concerning the ethics of obtaining medical services under a false name. The senator from Vermont was heading home to consider whether he should ignore the controversy, counterattack, drop out of the race, or kill himself.

He kept the radio tuned to country-music stations, humming along with the maudlin ballads, whose lyrics fit his mood. If there was ever time for self-pity, it was now.

It didn't get much worse than this. He didn't need Rav Monsjar to convince him of the political liability of a testosterone deficiency, real or perceived. You couldn't get elected as dog catcher of Peru if people thought you were hormonally challenged.

The irony was that he hadn't used a single one of the thirty-day supply of Testoderm patches that he'd gotten in Schenectady under the name of James Monroe. He could go on television with the original prescription and the intact thirty-day supply and prove that he had never taken the drug.

He could sit with Jim Lehrer, count out on camera the thirty Testoderm patches, and show a copy of the prescription.

"You see, Jim, it's untouched . . ."

He had decided to take Route 2 instead of the interstate, even though it was slower. He was in no hurry. And as long as he was a moving target, he was free from harassment by the press, the lawyers, the Ethics Committee, or even his own staff, who would pester him for answers to questions he had no answers to.

It was a road he knew well, a four-lane highway most of the way, with occasional narrowing through some of the old northern Massachusetts mill towns that had not yet been bypassed by the widening of the road. It was far enough south that there were still leaves clinging to the trees and a vestige of Indian summer in the air.

In order to avoid shopping at the I.G.A. in Peru and risk being spotted by his neighbors, Woody stopped outside North Adams to pick up some groceries.

He filled the cart with canned goods, then went next door to the package store and bought four six-packs of Narragansett, a fifth of Johnnie Walker Black, a fifth of Stoli, and two bottles of Perrier Jouet Brut at $37.50 a bottle, paying with the campaign's credit card.

As he was putting the booze in the car, he saw a drugstore across the road and realized that he had nothing to kill himself with, should he decide to go that route.

He wandered through the aisles of the chain drugstore trying to figure out what would do the trick. Aspirin, he had read somewhere, was unreliable. His reading glasses on his nose, he pored over labels looking for overdose warnings.

TAKE ONLY AS DIRECTED. IF OVERDOSE OCCURS, INDUCE VOMITING. CALL PHYSICIAN AT ONCE.

Woody selected a variety of sleep aids, then helped himself to an extra large bottle of Tylenol.

DO NOT EXCEED RECOMMENDED DOSAGE. IF DIZZINESS OR FAINTNESS OCCURS, CALL PHYSICIAN AT ONCE.

An hour and half later, as the sun was going down, he was two miles outside of Peru. There was another way to the house, an unpaved road that connected with a series of unpaved roads that would enable him to reach the A-frame without passing through town.

He parked the car behind the woodshed, where it would be invisible from the road, unloaded the groceries and the drugs, reached into the bird feeder for the key, and unlocked the front door.

The house was chilly and damp. He turned on the lights, stuck the groceries in the kitchen, noticed the mice droppings in the corner, and then went back outside to turn the water on.

It was already dark by the time he had the house vaguely comfortable. He lit fires in the kitchen potbellied stove and in the fireplace, poured himself a jam jar full of Johnnie Black and a Narragansett to chase it with, settled down into the moldy cushions on the couch, lined up his collection of over-the-counter sleep aids, and considered his next move.

37

VALLEY FORGE

JOHN QUINCY ADAMS was seriously pissed off. All day he had been trying unsuccessfully to get in touch with Woody White, and when the senator's Vermont office said he was in Washington and his Washington office said he was in Vermont, he knew he was getting his chain pulled.

Elbridge Gerry suggested they take a ride down to Peru and see if they could hunt the senator up.

So John Quincy Adams and Elbridge Gerry got into the backseat of the Buick Riviera with Ethan Allen at the wheel and John Stark riding shotgun, and headed south down Route 100 toward Rutland.

It was after eight when they pulled into Peru. The I.G.A. and post office were closed. There was a light on at the Amoco station. They pulled in and found Chester Dionne under the hood of a Chevy pickup, a spark-plug wrench in one hand and a calibrator in the other.

"Help yourself to the gas," Chester Dionne said, barely bothering to look up. "Be with you in a second."

"Don't need gas," John Stark said.

Chester Dionne emerged from the hood of the pickup and looked at the four men in the Buick Riviera. The two in the front were wearing car coats. The two in the back were in plaid woolen hunting jackets and hats with the earmuffs tied on top.

It was a little early for deer season. He saw the Vermont plates on the car, and figured they ought to know that.

"Where you heading?" Chester Dionne asked.

"Peru."

"Don't move a goddamn inch," Chester Dionne deadpanned.

Nobody laughed.

"We're looking for the senator," the driver said.

"Which senator would that be?"

"The one that lives here."

Chester Dionne took another look at the four men. They talked like Vermonters, all right, but there was something off about them. Four guys in a Buick Riviera, two dressed like hunters, the other two out of the JCPenney catalog.

"Tell you the truth, I don't know where the senator lives exactly."

"You got an approximate idea?"

"No, sir. Never been out to his place."

Inside the car, John Quincy Adams lit up his corncob and said, "Invite the man for a ride, John."

As John Stark got out of the Buick Riviera and approached, Chester Dionne backed up a few steps.

"Now, as I said, I really can't help you . . ."

John Stark took the .38 automatic out of his car-coat pocket and stuck it into the man's ribs.

"Maybe a little ride'll improve your memory."

After having drunk most of a jam jar of Johnnie Black and chased that with two Narragansetts, Woody decided not to kill himself. The truth was he was feeling pretty damn good at the moment. The potbellied stove had warmed the house; the fireplace was roaring with a three-alarm blaze; the Johnnie Black had wrapped him in a mellow haze that made the world seem a lot better than it had an hour ago.

He couldn't see ruining this *gemütlich* moment with the bitter taste of Seconal. Maybe in the morning.

Suddenly hungry, he padded into the kitchen and opened the cupboard. He had bought six cans of tomato soup, another six of chili. He opened a can of each, threw them both into the same pot, stuck the pot on the stove, and was on his way back to the refrigerator to grab a Narragansett when he heard a knock on the door.

Who the fuck could that be?

He considered not answering the door, but they would see the smoke coming from the chimney and call the volunteer Fire Department. In ten minutes Bob Bartlett would be there with the truck and the fire axes.

They knocked again. Louder. Woody eyed the cell phone on the couch near the fire. He could make a run for the phone, call the town constable, tell him his house wasn't burning down and he was being harassed by vandals.

Before he could decide what to do, the front door opened. Woody had forgotten to relock it behind him. Standing in his doorway were the mobsters from Montpelier, their muscle, and Chester Dionne from the Amoco station.

He stared at them. They stared at him.

"Hope we didn't disturb you, Senator," John Quincy Adams said.

"No. Come in."

"We already are in," Elbridge Gerry observed.

"I was just fixing myself some tomato soup and chili. Care for some?"

"Don't mind if we do," John Quincy Adams said.

"Have a seat. Be right with you."

Woody reentered the kitchen, opened the other five cans of tomato soup and chili and put them in the same pot, then came back into the living room.

On the table right in front of them was the Johnnie Black with a nice dent in it and the two empty Narragansetts.

"Would you fellows care for a drink?"

"Don't mind if we do," Elbridge Gerry said.

Woody fetched five more jam jars but was told that the muscle and Chester Dionne wouldn't be drinking.

"Fact," John Quincy Adams said, "Ethan, why don't you and John run Chester back to town?"

The muscle, who had been eyeing the Johnnie Black with interest, got up reluctantly. Chester Dionne, on the other hand, looked happy to get out of there. After they left, Elbridge Gerry said, "Chester was good enough to show us how to get out here."

"Ain't easy."

"That's a fact."

Woody poured some Johnnie Black for his guests. It was dead quiet in the house, except for the crackling of the logs. The little man sat there with his hunting jacket and hat on and took a corncob pipe out of his pocket.

"Senator," he said, relighting his pipe, "correct me if I'm wrong here, but it's not looking so good for you these days."

Woody nodded, shrugged, refilled his own jam jar.

"Word is you're going in the crapper November third."

"Well, you never know, I mean . . . it's just polls, you know, the numbers go up and down . . ."

"First this Togo thing. Then this limp-dick thing. Seems to me you're getting your ass kicked from one end of the state to the other."

"I wouldn't exactly put it that way . . ."

"Let's call a coon a coon, Senator. You're in deep shit."

Woody drained the jam jar. When they didn't say anything more, he sighed and said, "You fellas don't know the half of it."

What was the point of denying it? If it was obvious to two guys with earmuffs, then it must be obvious to everyone.

"You guys want to chase this with a beer?"

"Don't mind if we do."

Woody staggered off to the kitchen to get three more Narragansetts. On the way in, he stubbed his toe on the table leg, cursed, then saw that the chili was boiling. He pulled the pot off the fire, burned his hand, cursed again.

Maybe he should lie down. The euphoric buzz was turning into a serious drunk. Sitting on his living-room couch were two men who left bodies on the bottom of Lake Champlain.

Well, fuck it. They owed him a favor or two, didn't they? There were some bodies that he wouldn't mind leaving on the bottom of Lake Champlain.

Maybe it was time to ask them for a little more quo for his quid.

He opened the refrigerator, grabbed three more Narragansetts, and stumbled back into the living room.

By nine o'clock, still unable to contact the senator, Ishmael was starting to get seriously concerned. It was going on twenty-four hours that the phone was not responding.

Ishmael needed to warn the senator about the prostate-cancer story. The *Post*'s morning edition would be on the newsstand by 6 A.M., if it hadn't already leaked from the composing room.

Beverly was calling every half hour from Montpelier. She wanted to drive down to Peru herself. Ishmael had been stalling her, afraid of what she might find there.

The truth was that Ishmael had no idea what the senator was doing in Peru with the phone off. Evelyn Brandwynne was still in Washington. If there was someone else, he would know about it—wouldn't he?

One way or the other, they needed to find the senator. And soon. The polls were dropping so fast their ears were popping. Irwin said they were getting to the point on the curve that he described as a statistical coma.

"You don't pull out of this type of condition," he explained. "You might as well just pull the plug."

They had been losing a point a day on the average. By November 3, they'd be in the twenties.

At nine-thirty Beverly called again. This time she said that she was driving down to Peru whether Ishmael liked it or not.

"All right. Call me as soon as you get there," he told her. "And listen, Beverly, if you hear anything on the radio about the senator having prostate cancer, don't worry about it."

"What?"

"He doesn't have prostate cancer. It's a cover story I leaked to the *Post*."

"You told the *Post* the senator had *prostate cancer?*"

"Bottom line, it's better to have prostate cancer than too little testosterone. Beverly, it was a judgment call. The only way to get him out of the coma—"

"Coma?"

"Irwin says he's in a statistical coma. He goes down any further, he's clinically dead. You see, I read this article in *Newsweek* about the correlation between excessive levels of testosterone and prostate cancer. And then I had this brainstorm. Not only do we get the sympathy vote, but we get the subliminal image of a man who's supercharged with testosterone."

"The nurse said he was getting a patch."

"I told Nat Birnbaum she was trying to cover up the prostate-cancer story."

"Are you out of your mind?"

"We can always deny it later."

There was a long silence on the other end, then Beverly asked, "Does the senator know about this?"

"No. Have him call me as soon as you find him and I'll fill him in. And if anybody asks you where he is, he's in Canada getting radiation therapy."

By ten o'clock, as Beverly sped toward Peru and as the morning edition of *The Washington Post* was being revised, Woody White was dead drunk in his Jacuzzi with John Quincy Adams and Elbridge Gerry.

They'd had a couple of bowls of chili soup to fortify their stomachs, knocked off the Johnnie Black, and were well into the Stoli by the time they went upstairs to the Jacuzzi to sweat it all out.

John Quincy Adams and Elbridge Gerry kept their hats on and smoked their pipes, while Woody lolled in the tepid water playing an old harmonica he had found in a drawer while he was looking for a corkscrew.

They sang a few hymns and told as many jokes as they could remember. When they ran out of hymns and jokes, it was time to talk turkey.

Woody told them about Trent Lott's fender and about Sharon's duces tecum order.

"The whole shooting match?"

"That's right," Woody said. "Everything that isn't nailed down."

"Ungrateful hoyden," Elbridge Gerry observed.

"Like to take her out to the septic tank."

"Amen."

"Anyway, Sharon's nothing. It's the present one who's really killing me. Daphne. Daphne's really squeezing my nuts."

"How's that?"

"She's blackmailing me."

"You're getting leaned on by your wife?"

"Big-time."

"What's she got on you?"

"She's a dyke."

The mobsters took a few puffs from their corncobs, looking confused. "Senator, I don't see how her being a muff diver affects you. Except for the fact you probably aren't getting your ashes hauled regular."

Woody took them through the whole business—the Finnish ice-skater, the INS, the faxes, the charade at the pound, the thirty-day reprieve, the October 30 deadline.

Elbridge Gerry looked at his waterproof Timex and said, "Now that's in six days."

"That's right. I don't get the INS to withdraw the deportation order, she's going to go public with everything. And let me tell you something, it's bad enough trying to get reelected in Vermont when your testosterone's being called into question, but when you're married to a lesbian you haven't fucked in years, forget it. You're cooked."

They sat for a moment in silence, ruminating on this problem.

"Senator," John Quincy Adams said, "looks to me like you're in Valley Forge."

"Tell me about it," Woody muttered, and John Quincy Adams took him literally.

"It's the dead of winter. You're freezing your nuts off. The army is in disarray. Men are deserting every day. The Continental Congress is secretly putting out peace feelers, while Washington's trying to keep the army together. Him and Lafayette. And von Steuben. They drill the soldiers in the snow, trying to keep the morale up. And you know what happens, Senator?"

"Huh?"

"You know what happens after Valley Forge?"

"We win, right?"

"Damn right, we win. Soon as the ice melts, Washington crosses the goddamn Delaware and kicks ass, and next thing you know, we're on our way to Yorktown."

"With a little help from the Frog fleet, of course, harassing British shipping all over the goddamn Atlantic," Elbridge Gerry added.

The three of them sat there sweating out more alcohol.

"Senator, if Washington could cross the Delaware, I don't see why you can't."

"Shit, how am I going to do that?"

"Well, we start by taking out Benedict Arnold."

"Who's Benedict Arnold?"

"Your dyke wife that's leaning on you. We remove that threat, then we counterattack."

"Counterattack, right," Woody echoed.

John Quincy Adams poured them each some more Stoli and proposed a toast.

"To crossing the Delaware."

They clinked their jam jars and drank.

Beverly Levesque had never been frisked before. And it was the type of experience, thank you very much, she could do without. So when she pulled up in front of the A-frame at eleven-thirty that evening and was asked by two large men in JCPenney car coats to lean against the Buick and spread her legs, she was more than a little put out.

"Who are you?" she snapped, not recognizing them from the pancake breakfast three months ago.

"Ethan Allen—pleased to meet you. Mind turning around and leaning over the car?"

"I very much do mind. I'm head of the senator's Vermont campaign and I'm going in to see him."

"Maybe you are, and maybe you're not."

"Look, I don't know who you men are, but you are trespassing on Senator Woodrow White's property, and if you don't leave, I'm going to call the state police."

She took her cell phone out of her macramé shoulder bag as if it were a gun.

"John, why don't you show the lady to her seat while I check with Mr. Q.," Ethan Allen said.

John Stark reopened Beverly's car door and eased her back inside. Then he reached in the open window and confiscated her cell phone.

"Who should we say wants to talk to the senator?" John Stark asked.

"Beverly Levesque."

"Canuck?"

Beverly merely glared back at him. John Stark walked up the path and

entered the A-frame just as the three men were on their way back downstairs to the warmth of the kitchen. They had abandoned the Jacuzzi when
the water temperature cooled to below tepid. Woody had put on his old
woolen bathrobe, while the mobsters had put their long johns back on.

"Woman named Beverly Levesque to see the senator."

"Canuck?" John Quincy Adams asked.

"Apparently."

"You know a Beverly Levesque, Senator?"

Woody sat down on the stairs and tried to figure out what to do. He
was getting soberer by the minute.

"You don't know her, Senator, we can take her for a ride."

"I know her."

"You want to talk to her?"

"I think I better."

John Stark went back out to get Beverly, while Woody went into the
kitchen and threw some cold water on his face. John Quincy Adams came
into the kitchen and said, as Woody was drying his face, "We're going to
head on back, Senator. Thanks for dinner."

"You bet."

"And don't you worry none, Senator. We'll deal with Benedict Arnold."

"Amen," Elbridge Gerry said.

Elbridge Gerry went upstairs to get their clothes while Woody pulled
the bathrobe tightly around himself and sat down shakily at the kitchen
table.

"A glass of buttermilk before you turn in'll make you feel better in the
morning, Senator," John Quincy Adams said. Then he and Elbridge Gerry
tipped their caps to Beverly as she walked by them into the kitchen.

"Evening, ma'am."

When they were gone, Beverly approached the table and sat down opposite Woody.

"Senator, are you okay?"

"Yes. Fine. Just drunk, that's all."

"Did those men harm you?"

"No. We just had a couple of drinks."

"We've been trying to reach you since last night."

"Why didn't you call?"

"Your phone was off."

"Was it? Jesus, I'm sorry. Where the dickens is it?"

And he patted his bathrobe pockets as if he would find the cell phone in
one of them.

"You missed an entire day of campaign appearances."

"Really?"

"Yes, and things are not looking good at all. This false-prescription-in-Schenectady business is going over very badly up here."

"I'll go on Jim Lehrer, straighten the whole thing out . . ."

"Unfortunately, we may be beyond that."

"Just tell Ishmael to book me some time on Lehrer . . ."

"Senator, Ishmael decided to try a different tack. He leaked a story to *The Washington Post*."

"What story?"

"I knew nothing at all about this until about two hours ago, believe me."

"What did he tell them?"

"That you had prostate cancer."

"Ishmael told *The Washington Post* that I had prostate cancer?"

"Yes. It'll be in the morning paper."

"Why did he do that?"

"He said it was due to excess testosterone."

"No shit?"

Beverly nodded. Woody sat there for a moment without saying anything. Then he felt the chili soup rising in his throat.

"You want to excuse me for a moment, Beverly? I've got to go puke."

38

A FINGER IN THE DIKE

THE STORY ran below the fold under Nathan Birnbaum's byline with a two-column headline.

VERMONT SENATOR BATTLING
PROSTATE CANCER

A source close to Senator Woodrow White, the embattled incumbent fighting for reelection amid a flurry of conflict-of-interest and corruption charges, has revealed that the Vermont senator is suffering from cancer of the prostate. Yesterday it was revealed by a Schenectady, New York, urological nurse that White had received testosterone therapy last March under a false name.

It now appears as if the senator was not, as was first believed, seeking treatment for a testosterone deficiency but, on the contrary, an excessive testosterone level—a condition that many medical experts believe is a contributing factor in prostate cancer. The source further indicated that the senator had used the false name so as not to cause undue alarm among his supporters, citing the high cure rate in cases of this form of cancer that are detected and treated early.

A spokesman for the chairman of the Senate Ethics Committee said that, while the committee is sympathetic to the senator's medical problems, it is nonetheless pursuing its investigation into the obtaining of prescription medication under a false name, as well as into previous charges relating to the Togogate scandal.

In a related development, Kodjo Kponvi, the Togolese national who was tracked down last Thursday by the FBI after an extensive manhunt, has invoked diplomatic immunity in response to an Ethics Committee subpoena. Mr. Kponvi is the director of the National Association for the Prevention and Treatment of Tourette Syndrome, an organization that has made substantial contributions to Senator White's reelection campaign and that has been characterized by Rebecca Gatney, and others, as a front for the Togolese government . . .

The story floated through the early shift in the steam room of the Senate Health Facility that morning.

"That's why I get a PSA every six months."

"Every six months?"

"Yes, sir. At my age you can't be too careful."

"You have a high testosterone level?"

"None of your business, Senator."

"Well, it sure as hell explains why Woody White has a zipper problem. The man's a victim of his own hormones. You get too much of that stuff pumping inside you, you wind up with a starch problem. Every time a good-looking woman walks into the room, you get a woodie."

"Maybe *you* do, Senator."

"It never happened to you? You're sitting in some committee room and this legislative aide walks in with a short skirt?"

"Not since I was sixteen."

"You're a better man than I, John."

"So how do you think this is going to play in Vermont?"

"Like gangbusters. He gets both the sympathy vote and the subconscious vote."

"What the hell's the subconscious vote?"

"The people who don't even want to admit to themselves that they think about things like this."

"You really believe that when people get in that voting booth, they think about sexual potency?"

"You're damn right I do."

"How do you explain FDR's getting elected four times while he was in a wheelchair?"

"The wheelchair didn't keep him from doing Missy LeHand, did it?"

"Yes, but nobody knew that till after he died."

"That's what I mean by subconscious. It's something you sense in a man. The electorate sensed that FDR was running on high octane. And Kennedy. Shit, Kennedy was off the charts. Women took one look at him, crossed their legs, and pressed the voting lever. . . ."

"God, how dreadful," Barry said into the speakerphone. "How long have you known?"

"Just found out," Ishmael replied.

"Is he getting treatment?"

"Yes . . ."

"Mayo?"

"No, at this place in Canada . . ."

"Where in Canada?"

The cell phone rang.

"That's him, Barry. Got to run."

Ishmael switched off the speakerphone and grabbed the cell phone.

"Senator?"

"Ishmael . . . what time is it down there?"

"Same time it is in Vermont."

"Shit . . ."

"Are you all right? You sound awful."

"I'm not well."

"What's wrong?"

"Well, besides having a bad hangover, I apparently have prostate cancer."

"Can I explain, Senator?"

"That might be a good idea."

"It was a desperate measure. I couldn't reach you. Rav said that the testosterone story was killing you. Worse than John Quincy Adams, worse than Togogate. Irwin said you were in a statistical coma. If we didn't do something immediately, you'd be dead in the water by next weekend. I got this idea from a *Newsweek* article. I ran with it. It was a finger in the dike, Senator . . ."

"A finger in the dike?"

"In a manner of speaking. We were drowning, and time was of the essence. Anyway, I figured we could always deny it. Put the story out there to counteract the Schenectady nurse's story, which I said was a cover story, and then say it was a misdiagnosis. Meanwhile, her story is dead—I mean, who's going to dare to talk about a false prescription if we're dealing with a life-threatening illness?"

There was a prolonged silence on the line.

"Senator, are you there?"

"Yes. I was just taking some Tylenol . . . Ishmael, where am I supposed to be?"

"In Canada."

"What am I doing there?"

"Getting radiation therapy. At a clinic with state-of-the-art laser radiation treatment."

"That's comforting . . . all right, listen—check the airlines and find out how long it would take me to get from wherever I am in Canada to Boston."

"So we're sticking with the story?"

"I think we'd better for the moment . . . Ishmael, is there any truth in this excessive-testosterone and prostate-cancer business?"

"That's what they said in *Newsweek*."

"So you've got to figure that if you have a borderline deficient level of testosterone as opposed to an excessive level, you'd be at a very low risk for the disease, right?"

"I don't know . . ."

"It's the corollary."

"Right."

"Look into it and get back to me, will you?"

Harold Kinder reported to the Ethics Committee that obtaining prescription drugs under a false name was not a crime in the state of New York unless the drugs were obtained with intent to sell. In that case it was a Class E felony, punishable by up to ten years in prison and/or a fine of $10,000.

"Well, I suppose we can assume that Senator White was not involved in any illegal testosterone-patch traffic," the chairman said reluctantly. "Nevertheless, there is evidence of his having lied to a pharmacist."

"Mitch, the man is ill. I think we ought to cut him some slack with regard to this," the vice chairman said.

"Illness doesn't excuse unethical behavior," the chairman persisted. "Now, with regard to the nurse—what is her name again?"

"Esmeralda Perkins," Lydia St. Cloud said.

"I propose we send counsel to Schenectady to interview her."

"Mitch," the senator from Virginia said, "Senator White is not denying having gone to the urologist under a false name."

"Well, he's made no statement to this committee to that effect."

"For chrissakes, Mitch, the man has cancer!" the vice chairman exploded.

The room was suddenly silent except for the collective intake of breath.

The vice chairman's outburst was completely out of character. The senator from Nevada was a quiet, unassuming man, known for his thorough preparation and quiet demeanor.

"Senator," the chairman said, after a long, tense pause, "our mandate under Senate Resolution 338 is to investigate charges of unethical behavior, whether or not such behavior is deemed criminal according to state or federal law. And I propose we proceed with the business of the committee. Now, if there is no further discussion, I call the question."

The vote was 4–2 to depose Esmeralda Perkins, with Woody's one Democratic enemy voting with the three Republicans.

Accordingly, Lydia St. Cloud was to be dispatched to Schenectady to depose Esmeralda Perkins.

The urological nurse had turned down big money from the tabloid press. She refused to say anything further on the subject, just as she had previously refused to encourage the media feeding frenzy surrounding the death by dismemberment of her former employer, Dr. Ernest Haas, and the sensational trial of the doctor's wife, Audrey.

Esmeralda Perkins said, with respect to that trial, "No way I'm going to compound the tragedy by participating in a free-for-all of opinion spinning around all over the place about the doctor. He's dead. I don't know what happened. End of story."

With respect to Senator Woodrow White's final visit to the urologist, which occurred ironically on the same day that Ernest Haas died, she said, "My one and only concern continues to remain the integrity of the prescription drug database. I got no comment otherwise."

Lydia St. Cloud said to Harold Kinder, as she prepared to leave for Schenectady, "I'm going to talk to a hostile witness about an event that is no longer material to an investigation of someone who is looking more and more like a lame-duck senator."

"Ours is not to question why, Lydia."

"Thanks, Harold. I'll keep that in mind. Well, I ought to look at the bright side, I suppose. I get a trip to Schenectady at government expense. A flight into Albany, my favorite airport, a compact rental car, and a night in the Holiday Inn."

"You get thirty-five dollars a day for meals."

"I'll book a table at the Sizzler."

Nat Birnbaum's *Washington Post* story made it up to Vermont by that evening. A series of "according to *The Washington Post*" stories were all over the local TV news.

John Quincy Adams and Elbridge Gerry were having an early dinner in front of the TV when Doug DeBoeuf reported the prostate-cancer story.

"Jesus, Elbridge, the Big Casino."

"Amen."

"Talk about hitting a man when he's down. It's bad enough his wife is squeezing his nuts. Now he's got to worry about his plunger. You get ahold of Tom Paine yet?"

"I left a message on his machine this morning."

"It's going to cost something, that's for sure. Out of state job. Not a whole lot of lead time. I figure we're looking at fifty, at the very least."

"Didn't Monty Calmette quote us a hundred on Rebecca Gatney?"

"That's because she was a public figure. This woman's the wife of a public figure. We ought to get a decent rate."

"How high you willing to go?"

"I'll go as high as seventy-five if I have to."

"Seventy-five, all in? Including transportation and accommodations?"

"Seventy-five out the door."

39.

ADIÓS, BENEDICT ARNOLD

THE WASHINGTON POST prostate-cancer story spiked the senator's numbers by seven points, according to Irwin Posalski's overnight poll. They were now a point shy of forty, with eight days to go before the election.

"That's pretty dramatic in twenty-four hours," the pollster told Woody.

"Yeah, but we're still eleven points shy of getting reelected."

"There's an error margin of plus or minus three points. You could be at forty-two."

"I could also be at thirty-six. Listen, Irwin, what's your opinion on the timing of the denial?"

"It depends on which way the arrow moves tomorrow. If the prostate-cancer story has legs, we don't want to kill it too soon. We may get another couple of points before it dies. It's like the stock market. You can never be entirely sure when the price is going to peak and it's time to get off the roller coaster."

Beverly, who was with them in the senator's suite at the Capitol Plaza in Montpelier, cut this conversation short by informing him there was a car outside, motor running, ready to take him to Middlebury College to address the students and faculty.

"Be right there, Beverly. Just have to make one more call."

"Five minutes?"

"Scout's honor."

As soon as she left him alone, Woody dialed D.C.

When Evelyn picked up, her voice sounded both sympathetic and ac-
cusatory.

"Jesus, Woody, why didn't you tell me?"

"I'm sorry, Evelyn. It's been completely crazy."

"I have to read about it in the goddamn paper," she blurted, then, immediately regretting the outburst, she asked, "Are you still in Canada?"

Woody took a moment, wondering if he could do this in the five minutes Beverly had allotted him. He decided that if he owed anybody the
truth, it was Evelyn Brandwynne.

"I never was in Canada."

"What?"

"Evelyn, I'm going to have to make this quick. Here it is. The whole
truth and nothing but the truth. I don't have prostate cancer, never did.
My chief of staff leaked it to the *Post* to counteract the testosterone story.
We're going to issue a story that it was misdiagnosed either tomorrow or
the next day, depending on my numbers. I didn't call you because I didn't
know the story was out there. And I was depressed and thinking of quitting. I shut off my cell phone and went to see my daughter in Ohio. Then
I went to Peru and bought a lot of sleeping pills, which I didn't take. Instead I got drunk with some gangsters in the Jacuzzi. Which actually may
have saved my life. It wasn't until late Saturday night that I found out
about the prostate-cancer story. I didn't have your home number with me
or else I would have called as soon as I sobered up. I feel like shit not having told you. But I'm calling now to tell you this, and to tell you that . . ."

He skidded to a dead stop. He hadn't planned to say what he was about
to say. It had taken him completely by surprise. After what he had been
through in the past 48 hours, his emotions were on a hair trigger.

He could qualify it, cover himself if he regretted it later. Or he could just
put it out there on the table without any wiggle room.

Fuck it. It's what he felt. Why not say it?

"Evelyn, I love you."

Nothing. The silence on the line was agonizing. His other line was
blinking. It was undoubtedly Beverly, telling him that the car was in gear.

"Evelyn, you there?"

"Yes, I'm here."

"I suppose this wasn't the best time to say that. I mean, I probably
should have told you in person, sent flowers . . . the whole package . . ."

"Shut up, Woody."

A moment, then she asked, "Do you mean what you just said?"

"Yes."

"Direct quote? Or 'reliable sources report'?"

"Direct quote."

"Uh-huh."

"Uh-huh."

"I figure we have about eight strikes against us."

"At least."

"I've got to think about this, Woody."

"Okay. But don't think too much."

"I won't."

Lee Schumock had been planning on starting his book by recounting the events of the evening of November 3, then flashing back to the west side of Cleveland in the 1940s, and from there taking the senator all the way up to his victory or defeat in the election. *In medias res*. A time-honored literary technique.

His editor at Random House liked the idea so much that she had gotten an increase in the first printing to 150,000 books. They had both the Book-of-the-Month Club and the Literary Guild salivating to see the manuscript, she said.

And now this prostate-cancer business had thrown a wrench into the entire structural design of the book. There was a pall hanging over Woody White that threatened to turn an exciting, dynamic story into a depressing saga of illness and defeat.

Prostate cancer just didn't sell books, May Manedle explained to Lee Schumock. It made men very uncomfortable. A hold was put on the press release announcing the book for late fall, and the writer was told to find out the extent of the problem.

Ishmael was in the process of downloading information on prostate cancer and testosterone levels from Nexus when Lee Schumock approached him.

"Listen, can I talk to you?" the writer asked.

"As long as it's quick. I'm up to my ears."

Lee Schumock sat down on the edge of Ishmael's desk, hesitated for a moment, then began, "You see, I'm trying to deliver this book right after the election so Random House can crash it through and pub it by the end of the year. Which would be great for the senator. Both financially and otherwise. The problem is that after the book comes out there could be some dramatic developments in his life that would overshadow the book entirely. The book would be outdated before it even got out there. So . . . I was wondering if you could tell me what the senator's chances are."

"Chances of what?"

"Of, you know, not being around six months from now."

"You mean, losing the election?"

"No. I mean . . . dying."

"Dying?"

"Uh-huh. Of prostate cancer."

"Oh *that,*" Ishmael said, as he hit the printer switch to generate a hard copy of the Nexus data.

"So what's the prognosis?" Lee Schumock persisted.

"No problem. Barring the senator's getting hit by a bus, he'll be around."

"I thought that the disease could be fatal if not caught in time."

Ishmael got up and started to collect the pages as they rolled out of the Hewlett-Packard LaserJet.

"Depends on the overnights," he said. "If the senator peaks at forty and starts to drop, his medical condition will be markedly improved by the end of the day."

"I don't get it," the writer said.

"It's real simple. The senator's medical prognosis is inversely proportional to his poll numbers."

"Inversely proportional?"

"Remember from algebra? When one goes down, the other goes up. And vice-versa. Listen, would you excuse me? I've got to run this stuff down to the printing office."

When Ishmael was gone, Lee Schumock picked up the phone, called May Manedle, and recounted his conversation with Senator White's chief of staff.

"You think it has something to do with his morale?" she asked.

"If it did, it would be directly proportional to his numbers, not inversely proportional, wouldn't it?"

"You'd think so. Listen, I think the only solution is to have alternate pages ready to go. In one version you start at the doctor's office with an upbeat prognosis. In the other you start at the funeral."

"You know something," Lee Schumock said, after a moment's reflection. "The funeral's not bad. It's a great way to introduce the people in his life. It gathers all the characters together in one place at the same time. It's like beginning the history of World War One at the funeral of Edward VII. Everyone was there, even the Kaiser."

"Well, let's hope he doesn't pull through, then."

They closed at sixty-five, including expenses. Which was just as well. You didn't want to have to invoice your expenses when you were doing a job. Especially one like this, which had to be done very quickly.

John Quincy Adams had told him that he had to get the job done before the thirtieth. He didn't like working under this type of time constraint, but he was taking a beating in the bond market lately and, frankly, he needed the money.

Tom Paine drove down from Philly in his BMW 740i. He had too much equipment to carry on the Metroliner, and then he probably would have had to rent a car in any case. The fainter the paper trail, the cleaner it was.

He had a picture of the target, her name, and the name of her law firm. Usually he allowed at least a week of tailing the target to settle on the best place and time for the hit. In this case, however, he had two, maybe three, days to establish the routine and decide when and where to do her.

He drove south on 95, keeping to the speed limit, his trunk chock full of state-of-the-art equipment. He had both day and night vision scopes, which could put an insect in the crosshairs at two hundred yards. All his weapons had silencers and delivered fragmentation shells, which were not only lethal but untraceable.

When he passed Baltimore, he turned the car radio on, looking for a weather report. Rain never helped. People moved quickly in the rain. You wanted people to move slowly, strolling leisurely through their last few seconds on this earth. It gave you a better squeeze of the trigger, as well as the thought that you were sending them to oblivion with a smile on their face.

He found an all-news station and, waiting for the weather report, listened to the business report. The Dow was up 112 points, which would help offset his bonds. Tom Paine had a few hundred grand in the market, the rest in CDs and bonds. If he wanted to retire in a few years, he needed the market to hang in there.

The lead item in the national news was the FBI's capture and arrest in Houston of an Italian terrorist who had been trying to extort a United States senator by sending parts of the senator's kidnapped dog to him in the mail.

Jesus, Tom Paine thought, what next?

"I told you to eat more fiber. Now look at the mess you're in."

"Mom, I'm okay."

"If you don't plan on living too long," Adele Hanna Weit told her son on the phone from Palm Springs. "Kirby Drench crapped out after only six months. And he left his wife without a penny."

"It's just a story . . ."

"And what's to become of me? What about the eighty-one hundred dollars you owe me for the air-conditioning? I suppose I'm going to have to wait for probate."

"Mom, I don't have cancer . . ."

"I'm going to have to line up behind the lawyers and the ex-wives."

"Mom, will you please listen . . . I don't have cancer."

"You expect me to believe that? Ted Koppel said you had cancer. If Ted Koppel says you have cancer, then you have cancer."

"It was a story we leaked to the press."

"Just because I'm ninety-seven, Woody, it doesn't mean I'm an idiot. I don't have Alzheimer's. I have a lot of other things wrong—you don't want to know the half of it."

"I'm only going to say this once more, and then I'm going to hang up."

"Go ahead, threaten me."

"I don't have prostate cancer. I'm not planning on dying in the near future, whatever Ted Koppel said. And I don't owe you eighty-one hundred dollars. I have never owed you eighty-one hundred dollars. That was the price of the central air that I had installed in your condo five years ago and paid for myself. And you're not ninety-seven. You're eighty-nine."

"You sound just like your father now. He would lie through his teeth and expect me to believe him. And he didn't make a living either. I had to go through probate with him, too, not that there was anything worth waiting for . . ."

Woody put the phone down gently and lay back on the bed of his room in the Rutland Ramada Inn. On the table lay a barely touched room-service dinner—a shrimp salad that tasted like it had been shipped from Louisiana in formaldehyde. Beside it were notes for three speeches that he had to give tomorrow. Beside the notes was a pile of phone messages, mostly from reporters.

There were two calls from Special Agent Sonnenfeld in Washington, reporting, no doubt, that his dog had been recovered in Houston. Woody already knew that. Janine Caravaggio had gotten the news off the wire earlier that day and told him as he was getting back on the bus for the drive to Rutland.

"Good news, Senator. Helmut's alive and well."

"Uh-huh."

"Apparently, your former housekeeper was sending parts from dogs that were already dead. The FBI staked out the vet and got him this morning."

"That's great."

"We ought to get him up here right away. I think it would be a definite plus to have you out there with Helmut."

"Good thinking, Janine."

Woody decided not to call back Special Agent Sonnenfeld. There would be charges to be filed against Dario, papers to be signed, statements to be made. He didn't have the time for that right now.

There was one more phone call he would have to return before he could go to sleep. It was a Montpelier exchange. He lifted the phone back up and dialed the number.

"Ayop," the increasingly familiar voice said on the other end of the line.

"Mr. Adams. It's Senator White."

"Little late at night for a phone call, isn't it, Senator? Elbridge and me were just turning in."

"I'm returning your call."

"Ten hours after I made it."

"Sorry. I've been campaigning all day . . . Did you call earlier for a . . . special reason?"

"Other than shooting the shit, I thought you'd want to know that we've taken care of your problem."

"What problem is that?"

"The problem you described to us the other night in the hot tub."

"We discussed a problem in the hot tub?"

"Sure did. And it's being dealt with."

Woody tried to remember what he had said to John Quincy Adams in the Jacuzzi. They were all wrecked. All he could remember was Valley Forge.

"Valley Forge?"

"Ayop. It's colder than a witch's tit. But you're drilling the troops in the snow."

"I'm crossing the Delaware, right?"

"You sure as hell are. Sleep tight, Senator. You got nothing to worry about. *Adiós,* Benedict Arnold."

"Huh?"

"We're putting her out of commission."

"Right," Woody said absently, yawning, exhaustion already beginning to overtake him.

Woody hung up, crawled between the sheets, and closed his eyes.

In less than a minute he was wallowing in a deep, dreamless sleep.

Two and a half minutes later, he woke up suddenly. John Quincy Adams's words had penetrated the ether and dragged him back to the surface.

We're putting her out of commission. The operative word was *her.*

Benedict Arnold was a man.

He must have misunderstood. It was late, he was exhausted . . .

Jesus. Was it possible that the guys in the earmuffs thought he wanted

Daphne killed? Of course he wanted her killed. But not by a professional assassin.

He was being ridiculous. He had merely misheard the pronoun. It was that Yankee accent. You could barely understand every third word.

He'd call in the morning and clarify things.

40.

FAIL/SAFE

WOODY WAS AWAKENED at eight with the good news. They were up two points to forty-five in the overnight poll.

"You're only five points away, Senator. Plus or minus three points, that is," Irwin Posalski told him.

"So . . . we hold the misdiagnosis story?"

"No. You're skewed out on the cancer."

"But you said we were up three points."

"That was on the dog."

"Uh-huh. So . . . you think I ought to get the dog up here?"

"I don't know, Senator. Better run that by Rav."

Rav, of course, didn't answer his phone.

"Hello. You've intruded on the privacy of Rav Monsjar . . ."

He hung up, ordered breakfast, then, remembering his Benedict Arnold conversation with John Quincy Adams, he dialed the house outside Montpelier. Just to be on the safe side.

When nobody answered, he called information and got the number for the Vermont Maple Syrup Distributors Association on Prescott Street in Montpelier.

"VMSDA," Abigail Adams answered.

"Good morning. May I speak to Mr. Adams?"

"Maybe. And maybe not."

"This is Senator White."

"Oh, Senator, it's you. Why didn't you say so? Mr. Q.'s seeing a man about a horse."

Woody had lived in Vermont long enough to know what this meant. "Should I hold?"

"Might rain."

"Could you have him call me as soon as he buys the horse?"

"Okey doke."

"I'm at the Rutland Ramada Inn until nine. Then he can reach me on my cell."

He gave her the numbers and hung up just as his breakfast arrived with a copy of the *Rutland Herald*. The story was on page one, below the fold.

SENATOR WHITE'S DOG FOUND UNHARMED IN HOUSTON

Acting on a tip from a veterinarian's assistant, FBI agents surrounded a home early yesterday morning in Lake Jackson, Texas, a suburb of Houston. After approximately two hours of negotiation by telephone, Dario Farniente, 47, an illegal Italian immigrant and Senator White's former housekeeper, surrendered to authorities.

Mr. Farniente had kidnapped the dog in June from the senator's McLean, Virginia, home. Since then he has been sending faxes threatening to harm the four-and-a-half-year-old brown dachshund unless Senator White interceded with the INS on his behalf to resolve his immigration status. In addition to the faxes, the illegal immigrant and neo-Fascist sympathizer had been sending parts of dogs that he claimed belonged to the senator's dachshund, Helmut, but that turned out to be body parts from euthanized dogs taken from the Lake Jackson Animal Hospital.

Special Agent Gary Sonnenfeld of the FBI's Domestic Terrorism Division said that the dog appeared to be not only unharmed but well fed.

A spokeswoman for Senator White said that the senator and his wife were immensely relieved that Helmut had not been harmed and were looking forward to being reunited with him.

Janine could have milked it a little more. "Immensely relieved" sounded, frankly, a bit dry.

He needed to call Daphne and find out what she wanted to do about Helmut. It would surprise him greatly if she wanted the dog. After the kidnapping she had barely mentioned him. It was perfectly possible, though, that she would want the dog only because she thought he wanted him.

He decided to wait to hear back from John Quincy Adams before calling his future ex-wife. While discussing the dog with her, he could suggest, *en passant*, that she have someone start her car for her in the morning.

Looking for a quote from the senator's wife on the return of Helmut, the press had tried unsuccessfully to reach her in McLean, where she almost never was. Apart from a weekly drive there for a change of wardrobe and a check of the mail, Daphne had abandoned the house for the place on the quiet street near the National Cathedral.

She had gone to great pains to keep this apartment secret, this apartment she slipped away to every night to be with her lover. She parked her car in an underground lot on Wisconsin and walked the three blocks to the quiet side street where Sonja was waiting for her in paisley bathrobe and fluffy slippers.

Soon the secret would be out. Unless Woody performed. And it was looking more and more like her future ex-husband wasn't going to get the deportation order rescinded before the deadline.

Well, she had put the gun on the table and now she had to be prepared to fire it. She'd call Nat Birnbaum at the *Post*. He would run with it.

After a difficult night with Sonja, who was getting more and more petulant as the days rolled by and the deportation order was still in force, Daphne woke groggy and out of sorts. She was premenstrual and crampy. It was barely eight o'clock when she slipped out of bed, careful not to disturb the sleeping ice-skater, dressed hurriedly, and left the apartment.

It was a damp, drizzly day. She put the collar of her Burberry up and walked down the quiet street toward Wisconsin Avenue to get her car.

As she walked, she was, unbeknownst to her, being perfectly framed in the sights of Marine Ranger binoculars held by a man slumped down in the front seat of a BMW parked across the street from the apartment. Last night he had followed her here from her office.

Tom Paine liked the street. It was almost always deserted, even during the day. And at night, except for the occasional passing car or the person walking a dog, it was dark and quiet, with only one streetlight, which he would take out before he took her out.

Either tonight or tomorrow night, Tom Paine decided. There was no point pushing it to the thirtieth. The thirtieth was his fail/safe. He hoped the drizzle would stop by tonight, but he could work around it if he had to.

He waited until she rounded the corner, then started the engine. He'd grab some breakfast at a place near her office. Buy *The Wall Street Journal* and see how his bonds were doing.

. . .

John Quincy Adams returned Woody's phone call ten minutes before the senator was to face reporters at the Rutland Press Club. Woody had ducked into the men's room for a last-minute touch-up when the cell rang in his pocket.

"Hello," he said, trying to hold the phone with one hand and comb his hair with the other.

"Howdy do, Senator."

"Mr. Adams, listen, I'm about to give a press conference, but there's something I wanted to talk to you about. Can I call you in an hour?"

"You can, but I won't be here. I'm taking Elbridge to the podiatrist in Montpelier."

"When will you be available?"

"Depends on how long it takes him to get his corns scraped."

Woody looked around quickly, making sure he was alone in the men's room. He ran the water and lowered his voice.

"All right, look. I know this sounds silly but . . . you were kidding, weren't you, about that Benedict Arnold business?"

"What business would that be?"

"That you were . . . were taking care of him. I mean her."

"Senator, I don't kid about business."

"You don't mean that you're actually going to . . . to have my wife . . . assassinated?"

"Fact is, it's costing me an arm and a leg. I had to go to sixty-five . . ."

The door to the men's room opened, and Brian Petrunich said, "They're ready for you, Senator."

"Be right there," he said, waving.

Woody waited for the door to close again, then whispered into the phone, "I wasn't serious when I said that in the Jacuzzi. I was drunk."

"Should've told me that before I went to all this trouble."

"Can't you stop it?"

"Maybe. And maybe not."

"What do you mean? Call the . . . guy. Tell him it's a mistake."

"Don't got his number."

"You don't have his phone number?"

Woody was no longer whispering.

"Got his phone number in Philly. But he's not in Philly at the moment. He's in Washington."

"How does this guy know . . . where to find her?"

"Oh, he'll find her, all right. Don't you worry about that. Now, if you'll excuse me, Senator, Ethan's got the Buick running out in the yard."

The phone went dead. Woody shoved it in his pocket and splashed water on his face. His heart was bouncing around in his chest.

Instead of thinking about what he was going to say to the assembled reporters about his medical condition, he was constructing a defense against the charge of conspiracy to commit murder. It would all hinge on the jury's interpretation of the exchange in the Jacuzzi.

If he tried to warn Daphne, it might establish some sort of mitigation. He could say he tried to stop it as soon as he realized. But then he'd still be liable for conspiracy . . .

Brian Petrunich opened the door again. "Senator, they're getting a little restless out there."

"Vamp for a few more minutes, Brian. I've got to make one more phone call."

When Brandon picked up, Woody said, "I need to talk to her right away."

"Senator?"

"Yes, Brandon. It's an emergency."

"That's what you always say."

"For chrissakes, will you just put her on the goddamn phone?"

"I'm sorry. She's in with the partners. And her standing instructions are never to interrupt her again when you call."

"Brandon, it's a matter of . . ."

He stopped himself just in time. That's all he needed—another witness they could haul in front of a grand jury to testify against him.

"All right, Brandon," he said, struggling to be calm. "When she emerges, ask her to *please* call me on my cell phone. As soon as possible."

He gave the cell number to him, clicked the phone off, and looked at himself in the mirror. His face was drained of color. His hands were shaking. It could be the demeanor of a man who had narrowly escaped cancer. Or of a man who had unwittingly ordered the assassination of his wife.

Woody opened the press conference by reading a statement, prepared by Ishmael, relating the basic medical facts. He had gotten a positive PSA at a routine checkup. They had ordered further tests. The results had been inconclusive. It was determined, therefore, that he should go to a small clinic in Canada for a more definitive diagnosis. And it was only this morning that he'd found out that the biopsy was negative.

"Therefore, I am pleased to announce that I have been given a clean bill of health, and I am looking forward to serving in the United States Senate for another six years," he concluded.

A dozen hands shot up. Woody recognized the AP man, who had driven down from Montpelier for the press conference. "Rudy."

"Senator, we are, of course, all very relieved that your health is improved. But, nevertheless, can you account for the fact that the misdiagnosis of your condition has caused a seven-point rise in your polls?"

"Rudy, I think it simply reflects the sensitivity and compassion of the people of this state. And, let me tell you, and them, how very grateful I am for their concern and their support . . . Marcy."

"Senator, can you tell us the name of the Canadian clinic where you were treated?"

"Marcy, as I'm sure you will appreciate, the last thing a small, discreet medical clinic wants is media attention. So I am respecting their wishes and keeping their name out of the press. Bill?"

The *Vermont Free Press* political-affairs editor, Bill Muller, had endorsed him in '86 and '92. In this race he hadn't come out one way or the other.

"Senator, Esmeralda Perkins, the procedures nurse for the late Dr. Ernest Haas, whom you consulted in Schenectady, is being questioned by the Senate Ethics Committee. If this is a private medical matter, why is the Ethics Committee interested in Ms. Perkins's testimony?"

"I suppose you'll have to ask them, Bill." He smiled. Then, realizing he hadn't sold it, he went on, "The Ethics Committee is supposed to be a nonpartisan, politically disinterested committee. Unfortunately, my opponent doesn't see it that way. Her political-action group has been deluging the committee with accusations against me, which, as a sitting senator, I have to respond to. She has transformed the Ethics Committee into a political weapon and is using public money to sling mud at me. Anyway, let me just say this, in the way of response—I have already been cleared of wrongdoing once by the committee. I am confident that I will be cleared again."

As he said this, his cell phone went off in his pocket. He shut it off, and said, "Ladies and gentlemen, I'm afraid I'm going to have to wrap this up. My press secretary, Ms. Caravaggio, will remain to answer whatever further questions she can for you."

As he started to leave, the Jew in the woodpile sprung. "Running away again, Senator?"

Woody turned around abruptly and stared right at Zeke Wechsler, the blood rising within him.

"Mr. Wechsler, I have never run away from anybody or anything. But I have a wife, a son, and a daughter, whom I haven't had a chance to explain this fully to. Now, if you'll excuse me, I'm going to talk to my family right now."

And he walked off the podium and out the door, leaving Zeke Wechsler nailed to the floor.

Brandon put him right through this time.

"This better be good news, Woody," she said.

"I wish it were, Daphne, but it isn't."

"All right. You asked for it. I gave you till the thirtieth. That's the day after tomorrow."

"Daphne, this is more important than that."

"Maybe to you it is . . . where the hell are you, anyway? I can barely hear you."

He was standing outside the Rutland Press Club, across the street from Beverly and the van.

"I can't go into details, but I have reason to believe that your life may be in danger."

"Jesus, Woody, you are really pathetic. Coming up with a cheap trick like this at the eleventh hour."

"It's not a trick. Someone's trying to kill you."

"The only person who might want to kill me right now is you. Because if those papers don't arrive by the close of business Friday, you're going to wish I *was* dead."

"Vary your routine and don't go out alone."

"What?"

"Don't go to McLean. And don't go to her apartment. Have someone accompany you to a hotel, check in under a false name, and don't answer the door."

"You must think I'm a real idiot."

"I'm just trying to save your life. Though God knows why."

"Woody, you can't tap-dance your way out of this one with a cocka-mamie story. I'm a lot smarter than the voters of Vermont. Here's the bottom line—if those deportation papers are not rescinded by the close of business on the thirtieth, I'm calling Nat Birnbaum and telling him everything. Chapter and verse. You, me, and the dog pound."

"Daphne . . ."

"So long, Woody. The next time you call me, it better be with good news."

And she hung up.

Woody stood alone on the street holding his cell phone. Beverly called to him from across the street.

"You okay, Senator?"

He nodded, putting the phone in his pocket.

He had done what he could. Okay. If they killed her now, at least his conscience was clear. And as he crossed the street, he began to entertain the notion, not without a certain amount of pleasure, that John Quincy Adams couldn't reach the guy from Philly in time.

It would solve a lot of problems.

Tom Paine picked her up coming out of the parking garage of her office building, as he had done the previous night. He would follow her to the underground garage on Wisconsin and leave her there while he drove the three blocks to take up his position. Then he would wait for her to walk down the street to the apartment, pop the streetlight, and sight her with the nightscope.

The weapon was loaded and ready. The dummy plate was on the car. It wasn't raining. Fish in the barrel.

He glanced at his watch: 7:45. They ought to be at Wisconsin a little after 8:00, at her apartment around 8:20.

Traffic was heavy through Dupont Circle and up Massachusetts Avenue. Still, he kept four car lengths behind her. He didn't want to take any chances at this point—though he had a feeling that this woman wouldn't have noticed a fire engine with the sirens blasting on her tail.

She drove erratically, running lights, rarely looking in the rearview mirror. She was a perfect target. Distracted, unobservant, preoccupied. If he had to, he probably could get out of the car, walk right up to her, and put one between her ears.

At ten after eight, she turned north onto Wisconsin. The traffic had thinned out somewhat as they approached the National Cathedral. A few old women were coming down the steps of the church with kerchiefs on their heads.

Tom Paine hoped someone had prayed for Daphne Melancamp White's soul.

As she swung the car into the garage on the east side of the street, he hooked a right and drove the three blocks to her apartment.

It was still early enough so that there were parking spaces available. He had checked that out as well. An ounce of preparation was worth a pound of cure.

Swinging the car around to face the west end of the street, he parked across from her apartment building, killed the engine, and doused the headlights. Then he took out the Marine Ranger glasses and scoped the street. Not even a stray cat.

They were go for liftoff.

41

CROSSING THE DELAWARE

C. PAYNE LUCAS, the parking attendant in the underground garage and the last person to see Daphne Melancamp White alive, said that she seemed unusually distracted.

Most nights, he told police, she waved to him or said good evening. This night, however, she had her head down and walked right to the elevator without waving.

It happened so quickly that nobody on the bus could remember seeing her before they heard the brakes squeal and the soft *thump*.

The bus driver, Jasmine Jefferson, a fourteen-year veteran of the D.C. transit line, said she was doing the speed limit, thirty-five miles an hour, when suddenly the woman just appeared in her path, as if out of nowhere. Skid-mark analysis would later corroborate her story.

In his report, Officer Tyme Winters said that the victim appeared to have emerged from the door of the parking garage that led directly to the street and, without looking, started to cross Wisconsin Avenue just as the bus was accelerating around the curve from the traffic light.

According to the forensic officer on the scene, it was a one-in-a-hundred chance. The bus had to be going at least thirty-five miles per hour; it had to be exactly at the blind spot where the street curved and in the process of accelerating; and the victim had to step out exactly when and where she did.

The body was pronounced DOA at Georgetown University Hospital.

Police identified the victim from her driver's license and credit cards in the I. Magnin pocketbook that had been crushed under the bus wheels.

At nine-thirty that evening, Officer Winters telephoned the house in McLean and got a message machine. The message was in Italian. Thinking he had dialed the wrong number, he verified it and redialed. Then he called the station house and had someone check the reverse directory for McLean.

It was only at this point, nearly ten o'clock on the night of October 28, that anyone knew that the victim of the freak bus accident on Wisconsin Avenue was the wife of Senator Woodrow Wilson White.

A police cruiser with two District officers was sent out to the house in McLean to inform next of kin. But the house was empty. Not knowing where else to call, the police tried the senator's office number in Dirksen, thinking there might be an emergency number.

When the emergency number rang at 11:07 that evening, Ishmael was locked carnally with Maud behind the hot-water heater in the basement of her house in Alexandria.

The cell was in his suit jacket, which was hanging on the handle of the furnace. Ten feet away.

"You're not going to answer that, are you?" Maud said in the over-aspirated voice she used when aroused.

"I have to," he gasped. "I'm on call tonight. Debbie Sue's in Vermont."

Managing somehow to keep himself inside her, he waddled over to the furnace and fished the cell phone out of his pocket.

"Senator?"

"This is Officer Winters of the District police. I'm trying to get in touch with Senator White."

"He's in Vermont," Ishmael muttered. "What's the problem?"

"Do you have a number for him there, sir?"

"Is there something wrong, Officer?"

"I'm afraid I need to speak directly to the senator."

"I'm Ishmael Leibowitz, his chief of staff."

Ishmael covered his free ear with his other hand to drown out Maud's heavy breathing.

"Maintain the energy bridge," she whispered, trying to breathe through his covered ear.

"I'm sorry, Mr. Leibowitz, but regulations call for informing next of kin directly."

"Next of kin?"

"Yes."

Ishmael told Officer Winters to call the Ramada Inn in Rutland, Vermont, and clicked the phone dead. He hit the *call* button and dialed the Ramada Inn, whose number he had called at least ten times that day and knew by heart.

He wasn't about to let the senator be blindsided again.

Woody was on the phone with Evelyn Brandwynne, discussing their relationship, when Beverly knocked on his hotel-room door.

"Hang on, Evelyn, it's Beverly."

Putting the phone down on the night table, he went to the door and found his Vermont campaign chairwoman in a woolen bathrobe over her pajamas.

"I'm sorry to bother you, Senator, but your line's busy. The switchboard put Ishmael through to my room. He says he has to talk to you right away. And that you shouldn't talk to the police until you speak to him."

"The police?"

"That's what he said."

As they were standing there in the doorway, the elevator opened and the night manager emerged.

"Senator," he said, "the Washington police are trying to reach you."

"What's going on?"

"They didn't say."

"All right, would you keep them on hold? I'll take the phone call in just a minute."

Beverly followed him into the room. Woody picked up the receiver on the night table and said, "Evelyn, the Washington police are trying to reach me. And so is Ishmael. I'll call you back as soon as I know what's going on."

He hung up and called Ishmael.

When the cell phone rang, the chief of staff was still down in the basement but, unable to maintain the energy bridge, he had let Maud slide slowly down to the floor, where she was now lying, hyperventilating.

"Ishmael, what's the matter?"

"I don't know, Senator. The police must have gotten my cell number off the emergency referral at the office. They wouldn't tell me anything except that they had to notify next of kin."

"Next of kin?"

"That's what they said."

Woody sank down onto the bed and took a deep breath. *Next of kin.*

Either some drug dealer took out Bobby, a lightning bolt hit East Gethsemane, Ohio, or . . . John Quincy Adams couldn't get through to the guy
from Philly in time.

"Senator, you there?"

"I'd better take the call, don't you think, Ishmael?"

"Yes. I just wanted to prepare you."

"Thank you."

He hung up, buzzed the front desk, and told the manager to put the
Washington police through.

There was a brief moment of air before a voice he didn't know said,
"Senator White?"

"Yes."

"This is Officer Winters of the District police. I'm afraid I have some
bad news for you. At approximately nine-thirteen this evening, your wife,
Daphne Melancamp White, was pronounced dead on arrival at Georgetown University Hospital."

"Huh?"

"Your wife was killed this evening, Senator."

"I see," he muttered, his mind turning cartwheels.

They must have had the guy from Philly in custody and were trying to
entrap him into confessing the conspiracy before he spoke with a lawyer.
It wouldn't be admissible, in any case, but . . .

"Senator?"

"Yes."

"We'll need you to identify the remains as soon as possible and deal
with the disposition of the body."

"Right." Then he blurted out, "What happened to her?"

"She was run over by a bus on Wisconsin Avenue at approximately
eight-fifteen this evening. Witnesses say she ran directly into the path of
the vehicle."

"A bus? She was run over *by a bus*?"

"Apparently, Senator."

"It was an accident?"

"That's the preliminary indication."

"Uh-huh."

"My condolences, Senator."

"Thank you."

It took Woody a moment to realize that Officer Winters had hung up.
He sat there catatonically holding the dead phone until Beverly gently
asked him, "What happened?"

"Daphne was run over by a bus."

"Oh, my God . . ."

"She apparently walked right into traffic on Wisconsin Avenue."

"Senator, I am *so* sorry."

She went over to him, wanting to hug him, but wound up shaking his hand instead. It was a peculiar gesture at a moment like this, but it was the best that Beverly Levesque was capable of.

"Beverly, I think I'd like to be alone for a while."

"Call me if you need anything."

"Thank you."

After Beverly closed the door behind her, Woody got up and walked over to the minibar.

He stared long and hard at the split of Champagne before settling for the Courvoisier.

42.

POST COITUM OMNI ANIMAL TRISTE EST

IT MADE THE GRAVEYARD EDITION of the *Post* and the morning news programs. Even before the senator himself knew what had happened, the police station and hospital stringers had phoned in the story.

By eleven that night, the local twenty-four-hour news stations were already leading with it, filling the night with the scant, staccato details of the accident. Wife of a senator. Hit by a city bus. Freak accident. Et cetera.

The *Post* story that would appear the following morning was almost as sketchy.

WIFE OF SENATOR KILLED IN BUS ACCIDENT

At approximately 8:15 P.M. last night, Daphne Melancamp White, the wife of Vermont Senator Woodrow W. White, was run over and killed by a bus on Wisconsin Avenue near the National Cathedral. In what appears to be a freak accident, Ms. Melancamp, 47, a partner in the Washington law firm of Meagen, Forresy, Bryce, reportedly stepped off the curb in front of her parking garage just as the bus was rounding the corner.

Officer Tyme Winters, of the District police, told reporters that even though a preliminary investigation indicated that the bus was not exceeding the speed limit, the bus driver, Jasmine Jefferson, 37, was administered drug and alcohol tests before being questioned and released by police . . .

Senator White, who is in Vermont winding up his campaign for re-election, was unavailable for comment as this edition went to press. . . .

There is no telling what comment Woody would have made if a reporter had managed to get him on the phone at midnight while he was in his room at the Ramada Inn in Rutland quietly depleting the minibar's allocation of Courvoisier.

As it was, he was spared that ordeal by Beverly, who fielded incoming calls from reporters with the reply that the senator was "alone with his grief at the moment and would have a comment in the morning."

Meanwhile, Woody sat in his room getting quietly blotto and wondering if it were possible for a Vermont maple-syrup kingpin to have managed to place a hired assassin at the wheel of a Washington, D.C., bus.

According to the radio news flashes, the bus driver was a woman who had worked for the city for fourteen years. Could the mobster have placed her there in deep cover fourteen years ago, waiting for the occasion to arise when he needed to knock off someone in Washington?

He was just a little guy with earmuffs. Not God Almighty.

But as Woody drifted off into the cognac, he decided that the Lord indeed worked in strange ways. He might never know who sent that bus. And, in the end, it really didn't matter, did it? The important thing was that he was on his way across the Delaware.

Adiós, Benedict Arnold.

As Rav Monsjar was fond of saying—you didn't look a gift horse in the ass.

Exhausted, he tried to fall asleep, but he tossed and turned for hours before finally conking out just as it started getting light again.

He was up again at six. He took a shower, dressed, and buzzed Beverly's room. She was up waiting for his call.

"Beverly, can you get me to Washington as soon as possible?"

"I've already made arrangements, Senator. There's a car on call to take you to Burlington. There's a one-thirty flight into National."

"Thank you."

"Is there any statement you want Janine to release to the press?"

"Something short and dignified. . . . Beverly, I'd like to have the funeral up here."

"In Vermont?"

"Yes. In Peru. Daphne loved Peru. Something small and dignified. A service at the local church, burial ceremony in the churchyard."

"Do you have a plot?"

"No. See if you can get one for Monday."

"This Monday?"

"Yes. And we'll need a pastor."

"Is there any denomination?"

"Denomination?"

"I mean, was she . . . are you . . . Congregationalist, Lutheran, Episco-palian?"

"What do you think?"

"Me? I don't know . . ."

"How about Lutheran? They have hymns, don't they? Daphne liked hymns . . . Listen, there's one more thing. I need to get in touch with my daughter, Maddie. She lives in Ohio under the name of Ruth and has no phone. Can you get a telegram delivered to her? Ishmael has the address."

"Of course. What should I say?"

"Tell her . . . she won't know that Daphne's dead. Just tell her that I need to talk to her and give her my cell-phone number."

"Ruth what?"

"Just Ruth. She lives with Boaz the blacksmith."

When Ishmael arrived at Dirksen in the morning, the interns were already fielding phone calls. He gave them a list of reporters he would talk to and then disappeared into his office, where he found Lee Schumock waiting for him.

"Unfortunate timing," the writer said.

Ishmael nodded and began to wade through the senator's phone log.

"So, when's the funeral?"

"Monday."

"Where?"

"In Vermont. Listen, Lee, I've got a hundred things I have to do right now, so if you'll excuse me . . ."

"Hey, no problem. You'll let me know where and what time, okay?"

Barry got through at nine-thirty, between two reporters.

"Boy, never a dull moment, huh?"

"You don't know the half of it, Barry."

"This was a marriage of convenience, right? So is this convenient or not?"

"Five days before an election?"

"Hey, it can't hurt. Sympathy vote. Bereaved widower."

"Barry, this is not a good time . . ."

"Well, we never see you anymore. It's like you dropped off the face of the earth."

"It's the campaign."

"So how's Owen?"

"Fine."

"Is he going to the funeral?"

"Barry, it wasn't my wife that died."

"Well, there's no danger of that, is there?"

It may have been the fact that Ishmael's nerves were raw. Or that he had been so sexually depleted by Maud that he was running on fumes. Or that at three o'clock that afternoon he would have to pick the senator up and drive him to the morgue to identify the remains of his wife.

Or it may have simply been that, after all this time, he was fed up with the whole charade.

In any case, at nine-thirty on the morning of October 29, Ishmael Leibowitz blew three years of painstaking undercover intelligence work with one sentence.

"Barry, I'm straight."

There was a moment of silence, then Barry started to laugh.

"Right . . ."

"You don't believe me? Let me tell you where I was last night. I was in Alexandria fucking the brains out of a woman from the Agriculture Department in her basement behind her hot-water heater."

"Sure you were."

"We did it for hours—tantrically connected by an energy bridge."

"So you're bi. Big deal . . ."

"I'm not bi, Barry. I'm hetero."

Barry stopped laughing. There was a moment of pained silence, then, "Does Owen know you were with her?"

"Owen is straight too."

Now it was Barry who was starting to get mad. "You want to be hurtful, go ahead. Dump on me . . . dump on Owen . . ."

"Barry, I'm not dumping on anybody. I'm just telling the truth."

But Barry went plowing on, oblivious to what Ishmael was telling him.

"You're distraught, Ishmael. You don't know what you're saying. It's perfectly normal to get emotionally confused in times of crisis."

"This is one thing I'm not confused about."

"I don't believe a word you're saying."

"Fine. Don't believe it."

"I won't."

For several moments, neither of them spoke. Then Ishmael said, "Look, I have to talk to the senator."

"I suppose you're going to tell me that *he's* straight too . . ."

. . .

John Quincy Adams did not get *The Washington Post*. And the story didn't break in time to make the morning *Rutland Herald*. So when Tom Paine called at nine o'clock on the morning of October 29 the maple-syrup kingpin didn't know yet what had happened to Daphne Melancamp White.

"Mr. Q., I don't like being set up," the contract killer told him, drinking Postum in his Early American kitchen in Philadelphia. "If you're going to back me up, you let me know going in."

"Beg your pardon?"

"The guy you got to cut the brake cable on the bus. I don't know he's there. He probably doesn't know I'm there. Meanwhile, I'm sitting there with my Kalashnikov waiting to pop her and she never shows up."

"What the hell you talking about, Tom?"

"Maybe you got enough money for a redundant contract, but I don't like working for someone who doesn't have the confidence that I can do the job."

"Look, Tom, you're not making a lot of sense here, but it's a good thing you called. We got a problem. It seems as if the buyer wants to cancel the order."

"That so?"

"Ayop. I didn't have a number for you down there, else I would've called you."

"Well, you tell the buyer that you can't cancel a job when it's already done."

"The job's done?"

"That's right. And not only is the buyer paying the brake-cable cutter, but he's paying me. A hundred cents on the dollar. I went down there, prepped the job for two days, and was ready to pop her. You can't pop someone who's already popped."

There was a staticky silence on the line. Then John Quincy Adams said, "You telling me she's popped?"

"That's right, Mr. Q."

"Who popped her?"

"Okay, I'm terminating this conversation because I don't see it going anywhere. But I want my other fifty percent, as agreed."

"She's really dead, Tom?"

"Deader than Nathan Hale."

After Tom Paine hung up, John Quincy Adams looked at Elbridge Gerry, who was at the sink stirring the oatmeal, and said, "Elbridge, looks like someone else don't like the senator's wife."

"Really? She get popped by someone else?"

"Apparently."

"Well, I'll be damned."

"Don't burn the oatmeal."

The best he could do for the trip down to Washington was a charcoal-gray sports jacket, black pants, and black loafers. The photographers at the gate at National kept a reasonably respectful distance as he came off the plane.

Woody nodded gravely and walked past the flashbulbs with Ishmael—like Rainier with Albert walking past the paparazzi to go to identify Grace's body.

On the drive in, Ishmael told him that condolence calls had been flooding the office since early in the morning.

"The President called at ten-thirty. He said he was with you in your moment of trial."

"I don't suppose Trent Lott called?"

"No. But the Republican leadership sent flowers. And the FBI wants to know when you want to take delivery of Helmut."

"Maybe for the trip back to Vermont. He ought to be at the funeral, don't you think?"

"Was . . . Daphne . . . your wife . . . very attached to him?"

"She was crazy about him. I was thinking about Lutheran. What do you think?"

"Think about what, Senator?"

"For the funeral service. Lutheran. They have hymns, don't they?"

"To be honest with you, I don't know."

"Of course. Why would you know? Ishmael, maybe it would be nice to have a rabbi say a few words. Sort of ecumenical. Do you know a rabbi?"

"Well, not in Vermont . . ."

"There are rabbis in Vermont."

"I'm sure there are . . ."

"You think the President will send Al?"

"I wouldn't think so, Senator. Usually it's only for heads of state that they send the Vice President."

There were more photographers and a few minicams waiting in front of the morgue.

Woody got out of the car and stepped into the sea of TV cameras.

"Senator," he was asked, "are you going to drop out of the race?"

"No, I'm not. Death is a part of life. My wife, Daphne, understood that. She was a very brave woman, and I know that she would want me to continue my work for the people of Vermont. Now, if you'll excuse me . . ."

Simple and dignified.

The next few minutes were neither. In spite of everything, he was unable to look at his wife's body without emotion. They'd had a couple of good years in the beginning. He tried to remember a moment or two from those happier times. Their wedding day at her father's home in Virginia. The honeymoon in Florence. The victories in '86 and '92. But all of that dissolved in the face of the threats and the blackmail.

I want everything, Woody . . .

Well, she got everything.

What the bus had done to Daphne was not a very pretty sight. It was the only time he could remember seeing her when she didn't look elegant. Even when she was pointing a gun at his head, she had looked elegant.

He was able to give it ten seconds before turning to the morgue attendant and nodding. Woody was then led out and down the hallway to an office, where he dealt with the formalities.

I'm sorry for your trouble, Senator.

When they were through, he asked Ishmael to take him to Dirksen so that he could deal with some pressing business.

The interns rose as one when, twenty minutes later, he entered the flower-infested office with Ishmael. But nobody knew what to say. So Woody said it for them.

"I'm grateful for your expressions of condolence during this difficult time. Thank you."

He disappeared alone into his private office, sat down, and picked up the secure phone.

A strange voice picked up the line.

"Excuse me—I'm trying to reach Hank Leventhal."

"He doesn't work here anymore," he was told.

Woody dialed the number in Silver Spring and got the former asset-forfeiture associate director on the line.

"Jesus, Hank, what happened?"

"I got downsized, Senator, that's what happened. Look, I'm sorry about your wife, but I told you not to call me anymore."

"I'm calling to tell you everything's okay now. The order can go through. There's no problem anymore. We're all set."

"I'm glad to hear that, but I don't know what you're talking about."

"I'm on a secure line, Hank . . ."

"You have the wrong number. Good-bye." Hank Leventhal hung up on him.

Rummaging through his desk, Woody found his private phone book and dialed Miami.

"Bobby, it's your father."

"Dad. Bummer . . ."

"Thank you for your sentiments. The funeral's going to be in Peru on Monday. I want you to be there."

"Peru. I mean, that's like . . . far."

"Take a plane to Boston and rent a car."

"I'm not supposed to leave the state. I could forfeit bail."

"It's my bail you'd be forfeiting. And that's only if you don't make your next court date."

"Man, I don't know . . ."

"Bobby, if you do only one thing for me for the rest of your life, make it this."

And he hung up before his son could say no. He made one more phone call before leaving the office. When she picked up, he said, "I really hope you don't have plans tonight."

There was an agonizing silence on the other end of the line.

"Or for the rest of your life, for that matter," he added, to put it over the top.

Her reply was, as usual, precise, "My place. Linguine with clam sauce and Sancerre. Eight o'clock?"

"I'll be there."

After the linguine and clam sauce. After the Sancerre and fresh strawberries. After the Chopin polonaises and Sarah Vaughan singing "You Go to My Head." After the rustle of the starched white uniform and the sheer white stockings. After the overture and the intermezzo. After the poco adagio and the allegro ma non troppo. After the forte and the diminuendo . . . he lay in her arms listening to a fine rain powder the rooftop and his breath grow even.

He felt at peace and incredibly sad. *Post coitum omni animal triste est.*

He lay watching the home fires flicker on the side of the cave. It was a wonder that men ever got up from this to go back out and slay more dragons.

But he would. Soon. But not right away.

"You know," he said, breaking the silence, "we all have a bus with our name on it somewhere. Her bus just happened to be a bus."

"She was not a nice woman, Woody."

"I know. I wanted her dead. I ordered a tank. But they sent a bus."

"You had nothing to do with it."

"Maybe. And maybe not."

"Wishing someone were dead doesn't kill them."

He nodded, leaving it at that. Someday he would tell Evelyn every-thing—the extortion, the deal, the Benedict Arnold conversation in the Jacuzzi . . . but for the moment, he would be quiet and let her love him.

In the morning he would strap his sword back on and leave the cave in search of dragons. And on Tuesday, he'd go into the booth at the post of-fice in Peru and push the lever opposite his name, smile for the TV cam-eras, then drive up to Montpelier for the wait and the speech.

"Do you want me to be there?" she asked, just before they both drifted off to sleep.

"Only in spirit."

She kissed him and whispered, "Watch out for the buses."

He closed his eyes and slept dreamlessly till morning.

43

AMID THE ALIEN CORN

THE MORNING OF NOVEMBER 2 broke cold and gray, with ground fog rising slowly through the nearly leafless trees. One more good rainstorm and the leaves would be gone till April. Good funeral weather.

With her usual excessive competence, Beverly had taken care of everything. She had delivered the church, the cemetery plot, the minister, the extra generator for the press-pool cameras. She had even dug up a rabbi—a bearded young man from a Reform synagogue in Rutland—for the ecumenical look.

Small and dignified. But not shoddy. The church was decorated with flowers. There was a sound system that would broadcast the service to those who couldn't get inside the 100-seat Lutheran Church in the middle of town, opposite the post office.

The President didn't send Al. But Gephardt, already trawling for national votes, showed up. And so did Teddy, who was in Boston for the weekend and made the drive across Route 2 and over the Vermont line.

There were expressions of sympathy from some of Woody's congressional colleagues. Carl Kanush sent a large wreath made of Minnesota fir. Jesse sent him an inscribed Bible. The Minority Leader sent him a book of inspirational Iowa poetry.

John Quincy Adams sent a sampler with the words THE LORD GIVETH AND THE LORD TAKETH AWAY woven in black needlework.

And, in spite of the recent fund-raising scandal, the Republic of Togo sent a hand-carved burial figurine.

Woody stood tall and grave in the first pew, his two children at his side, as the Reverend Halsey Hicks conducted the service from the Lutheran prayer book. His sermon was from the Book of Ruth. Daphne, like Ruth, he said, would be buried in her husband's land, "amid the alien corn."

But it was the scene in the graveyard that was particularly wrenching. As Reverend Hicks read the Twenty-third Psalm, the senator stood beside the open grave, flanked by Maddie and Bobby, with Helmut in his arms.

"The dachshund could put him over the top," Rav Monsjar theorized to Irwin Posalski as they stood among the guests sipping coffee in the A-frame after the burial service.

"We'll see tomorrow," the pollster replied.

A few feet away John Quincy Adams was chatting with Dick Gephardt.

"I like your chances in 2000, Congressman."

"Well, Mr. Adams, this is hardly the occasion to discuss that."

"Why not? How often do you get to Vermont?"

"Not as often as I'd like to."

"You don't want to look those three electoral votes in the mouth. They could come back and bite you in the ass."

Maddie and Bobby sat beside the old wood stove and reminisced.

"Never thought I'd be back in this place," Bobby said.

"God has brought us both back, brother."

"C'mon, Maddie, you're not going to start with that God shit, are you?"

"Whether you recognize it or not, Bobby, you have God inside you. Otherwise you wouldn't be here."

"The fact is I'm in violation of my bail being here. You want to excuse me a second?" he said, and he went outside in back of the woodshed, the place where he used to smoke joints when he was in high school, and lit up.

Lee Schumock stood in a corner trying to remember exactly who was there for the opening chapter of his book. And as he stood there, absorbing the ambient conversations around him, the first sentence of the book sprung to mind.

On this gray, cold November day, as his wife's body was laid to rest amid the alien Vermont corn, Senator Woodrow Wilson White, a man at a crossroads in his life . . .

As Debbie Sue, Janine Caravaggio, Dickie Thong, and Brian Petrunich worked the room, Ishmael stood by the door, greeting people and wondering why he had come. The senator was being very well taken care of by his Vermont people.

The postelection party at the Capitol Plaza in Montpelier tomorrow night would be slow torture. They'd watch the returns come in—first from

Burlington, Rutland, and Montpelier, then from the south and the Connecticut River Valley, and finally from the Northeast Kingdom. And as they watched the numbers dance, the mathematical probabilities would wax and wane before their eyes.

Though the last-minute polls had Woody gaining ground on Rebecca Gatney, Ishmael remained skeptical. As far as he was concerned, there was just so much ground you could make up beside your dead wife's grave with a dachshund in your arms.

Teddy made a fast trip around the room and headed for the door, where he stopped to shake Ishmael's hand.

"Leahy didn't show up, did he?" the senator from Massachusetts remarked.

"No, he didn't, Senator."

"If my father were still alive, he'd have reamed him out."

"Thank you for coming."

"Woody's been through some rough sledding. I know how he feels. When that business with my nephew in Florida went down, it cost me fifteen points off the top. Had to fight my way back with a machete. Good luck tomorrow."

When all the mourners had gone, and the reporters had packed up their minicams and left, Woody was alone with his staff and his two children. Beverly had brought in a small, dignified supper of fried chicken and potato salad.

They sat around the old oak table that Sharon had bought at an antique sale and ate. The conversation was desultory. Woody expressed his appreciation to both his children for making the trip—one violating his bail agreement, the other violating her religious convictions by riding in machine-driven vehicles.

After the pumpkin pie and coffee, people started getting ready to leave. They would spend tomorrow together counting the votes. It was time to go home.

But as the staff was getting up from the table, Debbie Sue Allenby, the acolyte, banged her spoon against a glass until there was silence.

She rose from her seat, holding a mug of coffee like a Champagne glass, and, in a resonant voice, she asked, "Where's Woody?"

There was just a moment's hesitation. And in that moment everybody at the table knew why they were there.

They rose as one with their coffee cups held high and responded, loud and clear, "He's there."

Janine Caravaggio and Beverly cried. Even Ishmael Leibowitz felt his eyes moisten.

Rav Monsjar cut the treacle before it got downright maudlin.

"Where else you want him to be?"

Woody kissed Maddie on the forehead as she got into Bobby's rental car.

"Thank you for coming, Maddie. You have no idea what it meant to me."

"Yes, I do. God bless you, Father."

When he hugged his son, he could smell the marijuana on him.

"Are you okay to drive?" he asked, a reflexive paternal concern resurfacing from the distant past.

"Never been better."

Woody stood in front of his A-frame and watched his children drive away. When the last sound of the last car motor dissolved in the damp cold of the November night, he turned and went back into the house.

Beverly had left everything spotless. It was dead quiet except for the ticking of the grandfather clock.

Helmut was lying on the couch, rolled up snugly on the handwoven Shaker quilt. Woody sat down beside him and stared absently into the dying fire.

After a moment, his hand reached out unconsciously and began to stroke the dachshund.

"Where's Woody?" he muttered.

The dog shivered with pleasure but didn't reply.

44

OVER THE TOP

IN THE END, Daphne's death and the reunion with Helmut did, in fact, put Woody over the top, just as Rav Monsjar had predicted. At 1 A.M. on November 4, with 88 percent of the precincts reporting, WBRL in Burlington projected Woody White the winner in the closest senatorial race in Vermont history.

Woody walked away with 49.4 percent of the vote versus 49.1 percent for Rebecca Gatney. He carried the south, Montpelier, St. Johnsbury, White River Junction, and, for the first time, the Northeast Kingdom.

Rebecca Gatney did not concede the election until 3 A.M. And in her concession speech, she reserved her prerogative to demand a recount after she had examined the vote more closely.

If the vote held up, she said, it was a very dark day in Vermont history.

Senator White was more gracious. In his victory speech, delivered at 1:10 A.M. in the Champlain Room of the Capitol Plaza Hotel in Montpelier, he referred to his intrepid opponent as a good pace horse, who by running so fast had made him run faster. He hoped that she would join him in working together for Vermont.

The postelection analysts attributed Senator White's victory to his continued appeal to women and to younger voters and to his better-than-expected showing in the Northeast Kingdom.

But, according to Rav Monsjar, it was the dachshund beside the open grave that had put it away for him.

You could turn away from a reunited master and his dog, he explained.

You could turn away from a dead woman's stepchildren. You could turn away from a widower and prostate-cancer survivor standing with his dead wife's stepchildren beside the open grave of his dead wife, taken before her time. But you couldn't turn away from a widower and prostate-cancer survivor standing beside the open grave of his dead wife, taken before her time, her stepchildren next to him, with a recently reunited dog in his arms.

That combination was a winner.

So in January, Woodrow Wilson White began a third consecutive term representing Vermont in the United States Senate.

In February Esmeralda Perkins invoked her First Amendment privilege against self-incrimination in response to a Senate subpoena to testify to "prescription-drug irregularities" on the part of Senator White.

In March the senator's attorney, Burton Armature, received the following letter from the Senate Select Committee on Ethics.

Dear Mr. Armature,

This will inform you that the Senate Select Committee on Ethics has closed its investigation of your client, Woodrow W. White, and has declined to recommend to the full Senate that any action be taken against him.

Sincerely,
Harold Kinder
Chief Counsel

In April a federal grand jury indicted Dario Farniente on extortion charges, but, thanks to the intercession of the third-term Vermont senator, the illegal immigrant from Trieste was deported instead of being put in prison.

The neo-Fascist housekeeper protested his deportation, saying that he preferred to be jailed in the United States than to be a free man in leftist Italy. But his lawyers were unable to get him into jail, and in June he was put on a plane for Rome with a one-way coach ticket.

Sonja Aura had better luck resisting deportation. She was admitted into the Virginia Institute of Cosmetology and was able to retain her student visa. Shortly after Daphne Melancamp White's death, the Finnish ice-skater retained an attorney to contest her lover's will.

Kodjo Kponvi, for his part, was able to return to Togo without being either prosecuted or deported. His claim of diplomatic immunity went high up into the State Department before floating back down in a series of memos that became academic when the Togolese national simply boarded an Air France flight to Paris, from where he connected to the twice-weekly Air Afrique flight to Lomé.

The White-Kanush Bill died in committee, after Carl Kanush succumbed to Republican pressure to abandon his alliance with the Democratic Senator from Vermont. Owen Lundkeim, disillusioned with Washington politics, left the congressman's service, returning to Minnesota to work with speech-challenged victims of Tourette syndrome.

Barry, Kevin, Jack, and Denny saw less of one another after Ishmael dropped out of the group. Barry's senator would not be seeking a sixth term, and Barry decided to leave his service and to go into public relations. He is presently working for the National Association of Health Prophylaxis Industries, running a public condom-use-awareness program in Dupont Circle.

Hank Leventhal returned with his family to Burlington, where he managed to land a job with the Vermont Department of Fish and Wildlife. He examines dead fish pulled from Lake Champlain for signs of pollution poisoning.

Bobby White pleaded no contest to possession of illegal drugs with intent to sell and received a two-year suspended sentence, a $15,000 fine, and 120 days of community service. He runs a weekly senior-citizen pain-medication-addiction workshop in Miami Beach.

Maddie White is presumably alive and well in East Gethsemane, Ohio.

In May John Quincy Adams was indicted on RICO charges by Vincent Ruggiero's successor in the United States Attorney's office in Burlington. John Hancock, the attorney for the director of the Vermont Maple Syrup Distributors Association, claims that the government's case is "full of cheese" and predicts that his client will be fully exonerated.

Adele Hanna Weit, after recovering from a motorized wheelchair accident, is suing her son, Woodrow White, for $8,100 for nonpayment of air-conditioning.

Lee Schumock's book *Amid the Alien Corn: The Woody White Odyssey* was reviewed by *The New York Times* as a "hyperbolic, overwrought romp through the roller-coaster career of one of America's most improbable politicians."

Maud Summers took disability leave from the Department of Agriculture after an accident in her Alexandria, Virginia, home. According to her insurance claim, Ms. Summers fell off the storage rack in her garage while searching for work-related papers. The insurance company is disputing the claim, which is now in litigation. Ishmael Leibowitz, also injured in the accident, has been deposed by both Ms. Summers's and the insurance company's lawyers.

After the election, Ishmael Leibowitz took a much-deserved vacation to Europe. The senator's chief of staff visited his family's village outside Kraków, Poland, where he shed tears and began to understand the source of his pessimism.

Wondering if politics was really the best career for him, he communicated this revelation to his boss on his return. Senator White told him point-blank that if he quit he'd have him run over by a bus.

Woody White and Evelyn Brandwynne have decided to wait six months before announcing their engagement. In lieu of a prenuptial agreement, the senator is exploring various legal insurance plans that would cover him in the event of a third trip through the tulips.

His E.Q. is holding steady in the "moderate to high" range.

He has settled with Trent Lott for $25,000, out the door, thereby sparing the Senate Majority Leader the trouble of having to put a lien on his colleague's salary.

The July issue of *Vermont Life* features photos of the third-term senator rototilling his vegetable garden in Peru and spreading compost over the tomatoes, and a full-page picture of him placing flowers on his dead wife's grave.

Beside him, looking mournful, is the family dachshund, Helmut.

ABOUT THE AUTHOR

Peter Lefcourt is the author of four previous novels—*The Deal, The Drey-fus Affair, Di and I,* and *Abbreviating Ernie,* each notorious in its own way. His day job is writing for film and television. He lives in the Hollywood Hills and is no relation to any character in this book, real or imagined.